OLD BONES

OLD BONES

The Loves and Losses of Cecily Neville

Rachel Di Placito

The manufacturer's authorised representative in the EU for
product safety is Authorised Rep Compliance Ltd,
71 Lower Baggot Street, Dublin D02 P593 Ireland (www.arccompliance.com)

Troubador Publishing Ltd
Unit E2 Airfield Business Park,
Harrison Road, Market Harborough,
Leicestershire. LE16 7UL
Tel: 0116 2792299
Email: books@troubador.co.uk
Web: www.troubador.co.uk

Cover Artwork: Katherine Crimes

ISBN 978 1836283 256

British Library Cataloguing in Publication Data.
A catalogue record for this book is available from the British Library.

Printed and bound by CPI Group (UK) Ltd, Croydon, CR0 4YY
Typeset in 10pt Minion Pro by Troubador Publishing Ltd, Leicester, UK

This book is dedicated to

Owen and Kitty, for making me a proud mama
Paul, sorry about the Welsh references

And to

Teresa, for touching all those walls with me

In beloved memory of Mum and Dad

House of Neville

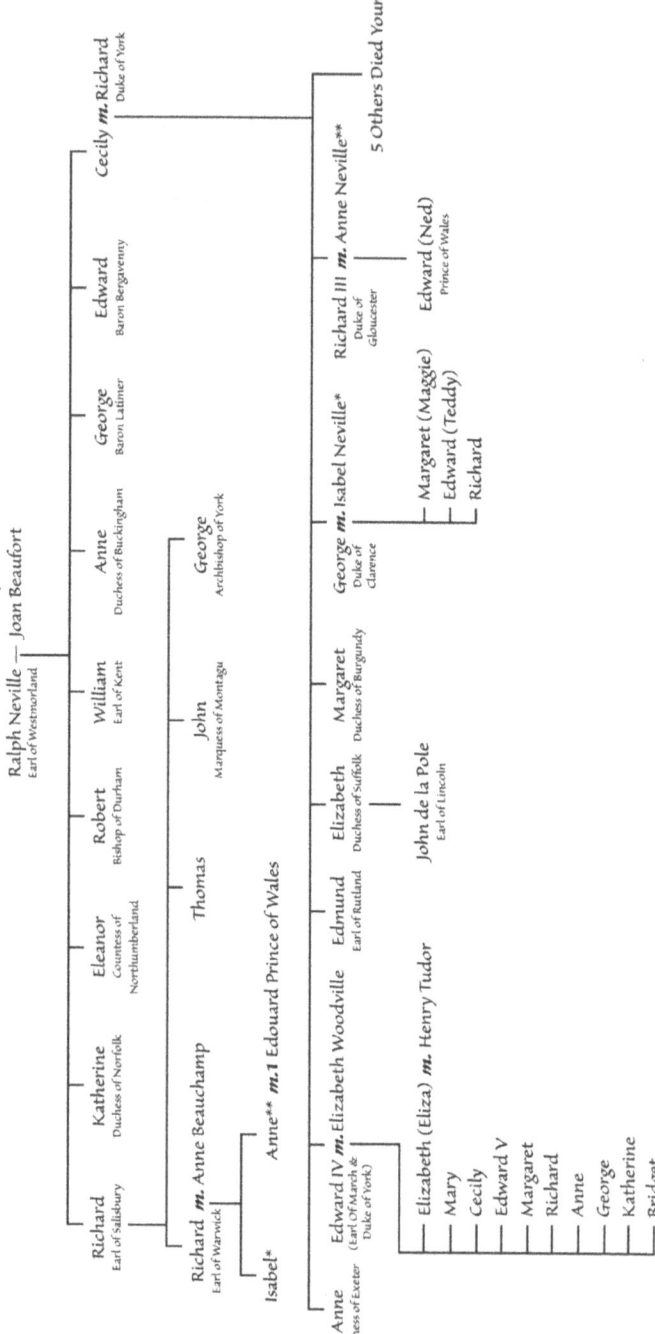

Royal Lines of England

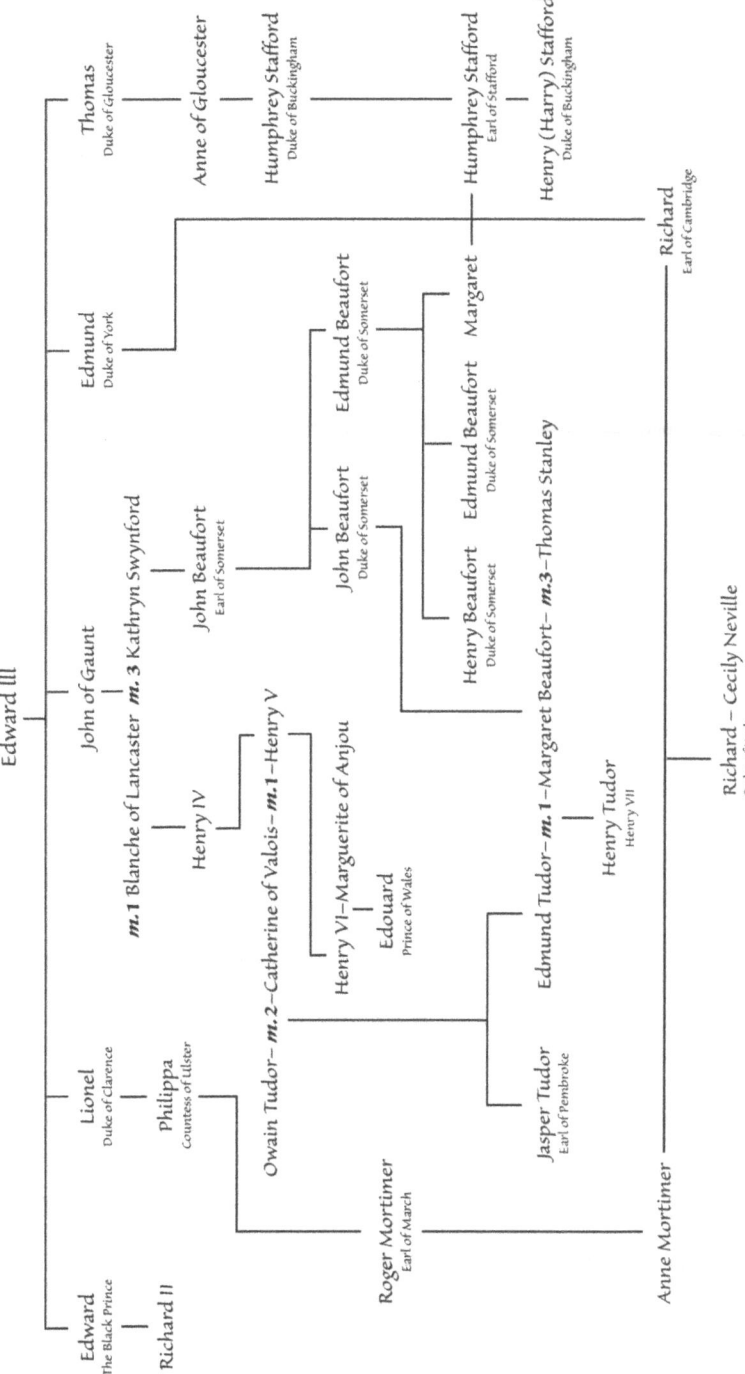

PROLOGUE

Requiem aeternam dona eis Domine:
et lux perpetua luceat eis.
Eternal rest give unto them O Lord:
and let perpetual light shine unto them.

Berkhamsted Castle, Hertfordshire, 29ᵗʰ August 1485

As she opened her holy Book of Hours, Duchess Cecily could hear the voice of her father calling down the years. "Make old bones, my dear, pray God we make old bones." Ralph Neville's words were hollow, Cecily thought. She could see him clearly in her mind, sitting by the fire in his wife's solar in Raby Castle, feet up on the fender, goblet of wine near his hand. The warm and cosy room of her mother Joan was one of Cecily's favourites as a child. It was where she felt safe, content within the heart of her family, listening to her parents talk and smelling the smoke of the logs. She knew what her father had meant by those oft repeated words; she knew he was hoping for a peaceful future after the turmoil of the past where he had fought against the Scots, supported Henry IV, he they called Bolingbroke, and served the regency of that king's grandson, Henry VI. He prayed his children would live to a great age in a safe realm under the boy king and would live to see their own offspring continue his legacy of begetting children, building castles and founding dynasties. Cecily had been beautiful when she was young; now here she sat, Dowager Duchess of York, an old lady wearing mourning blue, grey hair hidden under her wimple, wrinkles and tears on her face.

These were not the times and trials her father had wanted. Ralph, Earl of Westmorland, wanted peace and longevity for his family. His marriage to his second wife Joan Beaufort, daughter of John of Gaunt, son of King Edward III himself, brought him wealth and honour. When he arranged the marriage of his youngest child Cecily, his Rose of Raby, to young Richard Plantagenet Duke of York, he thought it would be the start of another new great family, furthering the prestige of his line, not the beginning of a challenge to the monarchy. But there was a lot that Ralph couldn't see back in 1424.

King Henry VI, son and grandson of warriors of the House of Lancaster, was weak. Coming to the throne as a babe, his regency was led by his two uncles; Humphrey of Gloucester in England and John of Bedford in France. As Henry had been crowned king of both realms, the Duke of Bedford fought on French soil to protect the lands and interests of his nephew. When he died, his role as Lieutenant-General of France was given to Richard Duke of York, now a great magnate of England who, with his royal blood, was as close to the throne as none other. York secured Normandy for his king, but at his own expense. However King Henry was more interested in spiritual rather than military matters. Coming of age, his kingdom was at war and factions divided his country; Henry was persuaded to agree to a peace treaty with France, secured by a marriage between himself and Marguerite, daughter of Rene Duke of Anjou. Under the terms of this agreement, England would cede the counties of Anjou and Maine to France, which was foolhardy both in military and financial terms.

With the death of Humphrey of Gloucester, in disgrace, Edmund Beaufort, second Duke of Somerset and of the Lancaster line, became a huge influence on the king, and a favourite with his wife Queen Marguerite, even if he was descended from the illegitimate line of John of Gaunt and Katherine Swynford. Somerset was sent to Normandy to command the area, but failed miserably and the region was surrendered. The powerful barons of England, including Richard of York, blamed Somerset for this failure and rivalries between the great houses of Lancaster, the Red Rose, and York, the White Rose, were ignited.

Displaced English troops and families from France returned to England in poverty, to find a country that was poorly ruled, filled with corruption, heavy taxation, with unpopular lords surrounding the feeble king. A 1450 rebellion against the malfeasance of the rule of the king led by Kent man Jack Cade achieved little, except to express the dissatisfaction of the people and highlight Henry's incompetent governance. Henry's advisors took the opportunity to use this rebellion to stoke the flames of fire with Richard Plantagenet, as Jack Cade had called himself Mortimer, the heir to the throne of King Richard II, and one of the lines from which the Duke of York had royal descent.

Richard of York, returning from his post in Ireland as Lieutenant where the royal advisors had sent him to decrease his influence within England, inflamed the rage of Edmund

Beaufort when York demanded that the king dismiss his corrupt advisors, repay the money he was owed from his command of Normandy and make him heir presumptive. Richard may have been son of an executed father, but he could trace his descendancy from the second and fourth sons of the great Edward III. Henry VI was from the line of the third son, and in Richard's view was a poor but anointed king surrounded by base advisors. Richard was now an enemy to Somerset and, perhaps more significantly, Queen Marguerite of Anjou, who had taken Beaufort as her chief advisor. Beaufort relished stoking the Queen's fears by maintaining a whispering campaign against the Duke of York.

Two years later, with no reform led by the king, the Duke of York marched to confront him. At Dartford, King Henry agreed to the arrest of Somerset, so Richard conceded to the peace terms of the royal army which had gathered against him and disbanded his troops. But he was fooled and forced to swear an oath of allegiance to the king, and was allowed no further part to play in the governance of the realm.

King Henry's mental health, always fragile, finally broke in 1453. He was in a sleep-like trance and could not speak to, or hear, those around him. He was unaware of the birth of his son Edouard of Westminster, although gossip mongers in the land named the Duke of Somerset as the infant prince's true sire. Those same scandal-spreaders already believed he had had an illicit affair with Dowager Queen Catherine of Valois, who later married her serving man Owain Tudor. Queen Marguerite attempted to make herself Regent during the king's illness and during the minority of her son, but the lords of the realm gravitated towards the Duke of York, who had the support of the Earls of Salisbury and Warwick, and the following year

Richard was made Protector of the Realm and Somerset was finally imprisoned.

Richard of York was dismissed from his post in 1455 when the king returned to a degree of health. York and his affinity feared the Duke of Somerset would take revenge on them for his earlier imprisonment and criticism, and armies of York and Lancaster marched towards the Hertfordshire town of St Albans. Attempts to parlay were made and failed, although York declared his loyalty to the king but not to his advisors, specifically Somerset. A short, mean battle ensued, ending with the wounding of the king and the death of York's enemy, Edmund Beaufort Duke of Somerset. It was a victory for York but alongside Somerset, other magnates were killed; Henry Percy Earl of Northumberland and Thomas Clifford of the powerful and vengeful Skipton family. These men had sons, strong sons who would not forgive the death of their kin. The Duke of York, alongside Salisbury and Warwick, knelt before the king and reiterated their allegiance. They accompanied Henry back to London, and York was made, until Henry revoked the titles a few months later, Constable of England and Protector of the Realm.

Several years of uneasy peace followed, with York, his brother-by-law Salisbury and his powerful nephew Warwick, and the Neville affinity on one side for the Yorkists, and Queen Marguerite, the new Duke of Somerset Henry Beaufort, the Percy family, the new Lord Clifford and the Tudor boys who were half-brothers to King Henry on the other for the Lancastrians. King Henry, in an attempt to impose peace on his ungoverned land, forced the warring factions to walk hand in hand through London to a service St Paul's in a parody of a 'Love Day', showing that the Red and White Roses were united.

The following year, 1459, Marguerite of Anjou attempted to raise troops herself to fight the York affinity and protect the rights of her son, but overstepped her role as Queen Consort. While Richard Neville, Earl of Warwick came from his base at Calais with troops and the considerable support of Sir Andrew Trollope, his father the Earl of Salisbury at Middleham rallied his men to support York, and all forces headed to Ludlow on the Welsh marches. Salisbury's men were intercepted by Queen Marguerite's army wearing her insignia of the silver swan at Blore Heath in Staffordshire and a bloody battle was won by York's brother-by-law. Marguerite watched the battle from a spire of the nearby church in Mucklestone. As she saw her forces defeated, she commanded the local blacksmith to reverse the shoes on her horse for fear of being followed and apprehended. A few days later, troops under the King faced the combined Yorkist forces at Ludford Bridge near Ludlow. The Yorkist intention was to force Henry to listen to their grievances and take Duke Richard as his principal advisor, but to face the Royal army, marching under the banner of the King was to dice with death and treason. This cousins' war was set to continue at first light.

Ralph Neville, beloved father to Cecily and counsellor to the old king, had seen battle throughout his lifetime. He was well married, father to over 20 children by his two wives and a defender of England's borders. His political skill and diplomacy did not enable him to see the husband of his cherished child bringing the country to war against a weak king and a militant queen. He could never have envisaged his son-by-law, Richard Plantagenet, coming so close to the throne and making his daughter queen.

Ralph could not see these things, and he passed to his reward before they came about; an old man dying in his bed, just as it should be.

Now, sitting in her private chamber, a lonely widow with no sons, Duchess Cecily turned the pages in her precious book, and scanned the names she had written in her own hand next to the words of the Office of the Dead, the *Officium Defunctorum*, when she learned of their deaths. Some names were harder to read than others, blotted and smudged, but she could remember how she felt when she had written them. The names were her most dearly beloved, the family she had known, nurtured and loved and never expected to outlive. They were her kin, they were who she had lived for, and they were those she had shed bitter tears over.

> *Richard, Duke of York, beloved husband*
> *Edmund, Earl of Rutland, second son*
> *Richard, Earl of Salisbury, brother*
> *Richard, Earl of Warwick, nephew*
> *Anne, Duchess of Exeter, eldest daughter*
> *George, Duke of Clarence, third son*
> *Edward IV, King of England, first son*

And the most recent entry, the most painful, the one she hoped she would never write:

> *Richard III, King of England, fourth son*

Fidélium ánimæ per misericórdiam
Dei requiéscant in pace.
May the souls of the faithful departed,
through the mercy of God, rest in peace.

CHAPTER 1

De profundis clamavi ad te Domine:
Domine exaudi vocem meam.
From the depths I have cried to thee O Lord:
Lord hear my voice.

Ludlow Castle, Welsh Marches, October 12th 1459

'Back to Ludlow! Captains, we ride for the castle! Now!'
The Duke of York shouted over his shoulder as he kicked his
destrier, the huge grey warhorse, and whirled him around,
away from the array of tents and campfires. As he galloped
over the bridge with his men and his guards, a mantra
sang through his head; 'That bastard Trollope, that bastard
Trollope'. On and on they pounded, covering the few miles
back to his strong fortification on the banks of the River Teme.
As the plum-coloured walls came into view, he glanced behind
him, pleased to see his captains pulling up their coursers as
they entered through the outer gatehouse of the castle, the
stars and a faint moonlight helping the grooms' torches light
the way.

'Trollope! God curse him!' The duke turned to Warwick.
'You've known him since Calais, did you have any idea?'
Gathered in the great hall amid the tables and benches, family,

1

servants and soldiers clustered around, but quite silent in their fear and turmoil.

'That he was a turncoat? No, of course not.' Richard Earl of Warwick spoke quietly. He bowed his curly head and looked down at his boots, aware that his aunt Cecily and the children were nearby. He raised his head and looked his uncle in the eye. 'When I got word, when I heard what he'd done, I came straight to you. We need a plan my Lord uncle,' he said softly. His father, Richard of Salisbury, looking like a relic of the past, kept his eyes on his sister Cecily.

'First, I want to hear everything. Bring me the messenger!' The duke called loudly to his squire.

The red-faced man in the livery of the Duke of York's colours of murrey and blue came before him, shown in by his faithful man Deveraux. The man's head was bowed, his breath still coming fast. The smoke from the central hearth lent an acrid air to the room, already poisoned by treachery.

'Tell me what you know.' The duke pulled on his neat black beard.

'My Lord, I know no more than the words I told my Lord of Warwick,' he breathed. 'Sir Andrew Trollope received a private herald from Queen Marguerite in his tent. We were all set to meet Lancaster in the field on the morrow, I don't know whether to battle or parley, but Sir Andrew has fled and gone. He's gone over to the Lancastrian army, my Lord. Trollope is a traitor to York. Our troops are gone. The Queen has issued a pardon to the common men if they betray you, begging your pardon my Lord.' The man stepped back, hoping the wrath of the duke would not fall upon him.

The anger and rage left the Duke of York, as he looked over towards his wife and youngest children. Not yet fifty years, he stroked his black beard which he had grown with such pride. His two fine blonde strapping sons, Edward Earl of March and Edmund Earl of Rutland, were armoured at his shoulder, but his two little boys George and Richard and his blossoming daughter Margaret stood with their mother, fear and confusion writ plain on their faces.

'A plan Warwick?' He spoke quietly to his nephew. 'We have but one option.'

'Beloved, all will be well.' He looked for reassurance in Cecily's eyes, and unsurprisingly found it.

'It is not what I would have wished, not what I planned, but this is our best chance.' He took her hands in his. 'I did not intend to give battle against the king, only for him to listen to our grievances and bring peace to this land. I feared, when we Yorks and Nevilles were not summoned to the last Parliament, an accusation of treason would soon follow. I did not set out to fight the royal troops, but we have been forced into this position. Queen Marguerite and the Duke of Somerset are against me, and the king will not listen. We cannot face Henry in the field; indeed we want no battle with one such anointed, but with our forces gone over to Lancaster we must scatter, divide, and return in strength when we are able. I *will* get those poisonous advisors dismissed, and the king will know me for his most loyal man.'

'Of course Richard,' his wife answered. Her voice was calm and modulated, to hide the pounding in her chest. They stood in the doorway of the Great Hall, the torches casting shadows on the tapestried walls and the servants shuffling away behind them. She turned to her three youngest children behind her; Margaret and young Richard were clasping hands, George was kneeling to fuss the duke's hound.

3

'Your father and brother Edmund will leave for Kildare in Ireland, and your brother Edward will go to the English fortress at Calais with your cousin Warwick and my brother Salisbury. Your father rightly decides that the heirs will not stay together, for safety. We will stay here, at Ludlow, to protect our servants and treat with the king. On his charity, we will be safe and your father can regroup with his men and devise a new strategy to bring good governance to the realm.' She turned back to her husband. 'Time to say our farewells my dear.'

Duke Richard drew his beautiful wife to his shoulder and embraced her. 'Keep safe,' he whispered into her golden hair. 'Presume on your past friendship with the queen to protect yourself and the children. You were her lady once, you escorted her to England for her marriage. She won't forget that, and with God's grace she will look kindly on you.' He dropped to one knee, asking for her blessing. Cecily rested her hand on his black hair, and none but him could hear her whispered words.

He rose and turned to Margaret, his pretty thirteen-year-old daughter. 'Be of use to your Lady mother, follow her direction and care for the little ones my dear.'

Margaret bravely nodded her head, and curtsied. 'Yes, my Lord father. And I will pray for your safe return.' She looked so much like the duke, and she showed all his strength. She gestured to young George and Richard. 'Boys, bid our father safe travels.'

The young boys, one fair like his mother and the other dark like his father, stepped forward.

'Behave yourself George, and be sure to look after Merry.' George made a formal bow, grasped the dog's collar and turned away to make way for young Richard. The dark-haired lad grasped his father around his waist.

'Bless you, Richard.' The boy smiled up at his father,

4

hugged him briefly and turned away. The duke followed them out of the Great Hall in the direction of the inner bailey, where his family were preparing to be split apart. Duke Richard ran lightly down the steps, starting to issue his orders. He took several steps towards the keep but suddenly stopped. He turned to his left to the chapel. The round nave, so unusual and yet so familiar to him, towered up toward the rising sun. He knelt on the cobbles and clasped his hands in a brief prayer. He rose and approached his men. 'To horse!' At his cry, the company mounted and gathered their reins. The York men turned in their saddles to catch Cecily's eye. As one, they raised their right fists in their gauntlets and held them over their hearts in salute. Only then, Duke Richard, followed by his captains, straightened his shoulders and trotted out into the cold dawn and uncertainty.

On the road to Ireland, 13th October 1459

'I thought I was doing right.' The duke sat at the rough wooden table, Edmund silent at his side. 'My intention was never to challenge or harm the king, but he must see that those who surround him ride with devils.' He could hear the voices of the locals in the tavern, a low hum from behind him. 'I swore that oath before God stating I was his liegeman, but he is ill advised by the fools who surround him. The country is going to wrack and ruin under this poor king.'

'And that she-devil bitch of a wife,' Edmund murmured into his tankard. Duke Richard turned to look at his sixteen-year-old son, a reprimand forming on his lips.

'It's true father. It is not the place of a queen consort to command her husband, rally troops or make policy.'

The duke turned back to the bread and cold meats the inn keeper had set before them. He could feel the warmth of the central fire against the side of his face. 'You speak truth Edmund, but your choice of words for a lady, and a queen, could be rethought,' he said with a small smile.

'When I marry, my wife will be my helpmeet and my companion, not my ruler.' Edmund warmed to the subject. 'I will choose a woman like my Lady mother; devout, knowledgeable in the ways of the world without overruling her lord, able to run a castle and plan excellent meals for her children.'

'What about beauty, elegance and fertility? They are all excellent qualities in a wife, and your mother has them all in abundance;' the duke looked fondly on his handsome blonde boy who was a constant reminder to him of the wife he loved so much. 'And do you have anyone in mind, young sir, for the position of Countess of Rutland? Or shall you leave such matters to your parents?'

'I will trust your wise judgement, father, of course. However, I should want to love the lady as well as marry her.' Edmund wondered if he had said too much, but his father seemed far away now, and did not appear to hear the inn keeper addressing him.

'My Lord of York, my Lord of Rutland, the grooms have your horses prepared. Your men are assembled and your party is ready to leave.'

'Come father.' Edmund touched him lightly on the arm. 'We must continue our journey.'

'Ireland.' Duke Richard spoke to Robert Aspall, priest and tutor to Edmund. 'Of course, my son is Lord Chancellor of the damned place, but for certain knows little of the land or the politics, even though I am still Lord Lieutenant.'

Master Aspall nervously drew his horse closer to that of the duke. He wasn't an accomplished rider, for all that he seemed to spend much time in the saddle. The big bay cob seemed to sway from side to side with every step, and he felt he had to cling on over the uneven ground. The trees either side of the rough road joined overhead, making the path darker than he would have wished, but he could see that they were becoming more sparse as they approached the water's edge.

'My Lord Duke, he knows his responsibilities to the country, although his duties were carried out by older and wiser deputies. My Lord of Rutland is a wise young man, perhaps wiser than he is given credit for. He feels oft compared to his brother Edward, and of course, no son can compare to such a warrior-boy as he.'

The horses jibbed at their bridles as they crossed the narrow bridge. The port, and ship to Ireland, lay ahead, and the sun was unseasonably warm.

'Indeed, Edward is my pride and my heir, but Edmund is a more prudent soul. He has not the rashness and hot head of his brother.' The duke glanced back along the column to his second son, who was discussing saddlery with his Master of Horse. 'Perhaps his temperance and sense will come to my aid when I prevail upon my Lord of Kildare for assistance. He was my ally and deputy once, and I pray that he remains so.'

Ludlow Castle, Welsh Marches, 13th October 1459
Duchess Cecily held herself erect as the last of her lord's troop cantered through the gatehouse. She had watched her husband and two eldest boys disappear as the sun rose, but she would not flag or fail, not when many relied on her.

'Come children. We must prepare.' She gestured to Margaret and George to follow her and took the hand of seven-year-old Richard to draw him to her side. 'But first we shall eat.'

The small group crossed over the dry moat and made towards the Solar tower to their left, the flag of the White Rose fluttering above them. They climbed the stairs silently, until they were seated and served by the yeoman usher.

The children spooned their mortrew pottage, but Cecily could not force food past her constricted throat, although she knew she would need her strength later. Her chief lady-in-waiting, the brown-haired Kat, kept a watchful eye on her mistress, but stayed out of the way in a window seat.

'Very well. We will all need our wits about us today so I require that you listen and obey, as we are unsure what we will encounter.' The duchess turned to her page. 'Please ask the Chamberlain and the Marshall to attend me immediately.' While they waited Richard and George whispered between them but it seemed to contain none of the usual arguments, so Cecily ignored them. Margaret looked at their nurse, Ann, with wary eyes, but was her habitual model of deportment and good manners and remained quiet. Nurse Ann, tall and bony, was such a comfort to both the duchess and her young children. Cecily gripped the paternoster beads around her waist and whispered a silent prayer for all her children; those before her now, the powerful boys she had recently bidden farewell to, her married daughters Anne and Elizabeth and the little ones who had scarcely drawn breath before they were given back to God. They were her life. With her Lord and husband, they were the reason she drew breath in the morning and knelt by her bed at night.

The silence was broken by the entrance of Master Parry the Chamberlain and Gryffudd the castle Marshall. Gryffudd outdid Parry in height and width, but their dark hair and neat beards were the same.

'Your Grace.' Master Parry did the talking as the Marshall was unused to being in the presence of the duchess. They bowed and stood with hands clasped behind their backs, awaiting their instructions.

'Master Chamberlain, Master Marshall, the situation is grave. You are aware the royal army is mere miles away and they will come here. I fear their intentions. You must make safe the castle and servants but offer no battle to the troops. They serve the king and we will not raise arms against them. I require that you do your utmost to ensure our home is not despoiled.' Cecily glanced at the nurse and Kat, sitting close to the children. 'Do you understand me, Masters? Your task is to see nothing, nothing at all, is despoiled or abused by the king's men.'

Master Parry's mouth was slightly open and his eyes were widening in shock as the duchess spoke, but Gryffud, glancing at the serving maids clearing the table, understood.

'Children, we will go the chapel. We will wait and pray. Nurse Ann, please keep George by your side. He is not to run away, and he is most assuredly not to fetch his sword.' Duchess Cecily led the way down to the inner bailey and into the round chapel. She sat with the children on the curved bench and took up her beads. She tried to pray, she tried to focus her thoughts, but the sounds of the castle servants running and shouting to each other distracted her. She glanced at the children; Margaret and young Richard sat with their heads bowed and their eyes closed, but George was looking up at the windows, turning his head to peek through the door. His mother had refused to let him bring the hound into the chapel but he still had a look of excitement on his face, the same look he got when he followed the hunt and watched the deer being brought down. Cecily reached across and pinched the back of his hand.

'My son, turn your attention to the cross! Ask Our Blessed Lord to keep us safe this day, and to watch over us and our people!'

George bowed his head briefly, but quickly turned back to face her. 'Lady mother, are the soldiers coming? Will there be a battle?' His voice was filled with anticipation. Before Cecily could reply, the door of the chapel banged open, and the figure of Master Gryffud briefly blocked out the light.

'Your Grace, the king's army are without! Some damned, beg pardon Your Grace, some fool opened the gate, they are coming through the gatehouse!'

'What of the town, Master Gryffud? What of the people?'

'Looting and rioting, Your Grace. The townsfolk are bearing the brunt of the soldiers' rampaging.' The castle Marshall stopped, panting, waiting for his mistress, knowing what her decision would be.

Duchess Cecily looked up at the crucified Christ above the altar. She drew her breath and tested her resolve.

'Come children. If the king's army are here, the king is surely close behind. We will go out and greet him.'

With her head held high, Cecily led the group out through the gatehouse keep towards Shoemaker's Row. 'Keep looking forward children, keep your eyes in front. We must show the townspeople we are brave and not afraid.' She heard Nurse Ann coax the children not to stare at the soldiers and the mayhem they could see on the streets. But wherever they looked they could not block out the screams and the smell of smoke as the soldiers broke into ale houses and homes. They were taking whatever they wanted; women, goods and money. Fires were breaking out as the soldiers set torches to the houses and ash flittered across the marketplace with shouts and cries. The looming presence of St Laurence's Church cast a shadow over the street, and Cecily could see the holy men of the Austin Friary scuttling away from the devastation.

'Children, remember you are of the House of York. You are your father's children. Be brave.'

'Nursey Ann, what is happening?' George had lost the look of excitement from his face and was clinging to her hand, scared and stumbling in his fear. Her white wimple was covered in ash from the fires and was turning grey. Young Richard had said not a word but held fast to Margaret's skirts, looking down at his boots; two dark haired children floundering along.

'I thought the king's soldiers would be mounted on fine horses with banners and singing of glory! This is a rabble, like when the stable lads stole the mead on Twelfth Night.' George looked for reassurance from the woman who was like a second mother to him. Nurse Ann had no reply for him, except to pull him closer to her and turn his face away from the carnage around them.

Suddenly Duchess Cecily stopped still. She looked all around her and saw there was nowhere to go, no refuge to be had, no comfort to give. The rampaging soldiers seemed to give them a wide berth where they stood by the market cross, perhaps even in their drunken blood lust knowing that these nobles were too great a prize for them.

'The king must come soon.' Cecily straightened up and gathered the children around her. 'We will wait here that he may see what lawlessness royal troops commit in his name.'

The king, however, did not come. What came was violence

and the sacking of the town. Cecily stood, spirits flagging, until a captain of the royal guard cantered along the street riding toward Dinham Bridge, the badges of the Red Rose and the queen's swan on his breast. He saw the little group gathered in a huddle and drew up his horse.

'My Lady, for the love of Christ, get back to the castle! What do you mean by standing here?'

'I am awaiting my king,' Cecily called up to the rider. 'I am waiting for his justice to be brought to his men.' She looked down for a moment. 'And to me.'

'King Henry is not coming to Ludlow! He has left for Coventry with the queen! Don't expect him to ride this way!' The captain gathered his reins and kicked his horse. He turned his head to call over his shoulder. 'These men are getting their rewards, their just rewards. They'll face no punishment for this, Ludlow is their gift from the Queen. Get back to the castle if you know what's good for you.'

County Kildare, Ireland, 19th October 1459

'Welcome to Maynooth Castle, my dear friend.' Thomas FitzGerald, Earl of Kildare, greeted Duke Richard and his party in the courtyard of the square, solid castle. 'My Lord Duke, my Lord of Rutland, you are most welcome.' The middle-aged earl, with his short stature and red hair, spoke kind words but the warmth did not yet reach his eyes. 'Pray, allow me to present my family.' The party followed the earl into a large chamber lit with sconces on the wall, and heavy furniture gathered around the fire.

'My wife Joan, my son Gerald, and my daughter Eleanor.' He introduced his robust wife, strapping son and a pretty young woman with the same flame coloured hair as her father. 'I trust your journey back to our green shores was smooth.'

'A very fair crossing, Thomas. And it is good to be back in Ireland and to see my old friends again.' Duke Richard gave his son a slight nudge forward. 'You remember my second boy, Edmund, I'm sure.'

'Lord Chancellor, of course.' Kildare noticed his daughter was blushing when Edmund kissed her hand. His wife noticed too, and shooed Eleanor from the room, bidding her have the groom of the ewery fetch wine.

'I received your herald, my Lord Duke,' Kildare put his arm around the duke and lead him towards a group of chairs. 'I know what position you are in back in England, and I know Ireland holds you in great esteem from your time here as Lieutenant. I also have heard what a sorry state England is in now, with a mad king and a poisonous French woman as queen. I assume you are here to ask for help?'

'Indeed Thomas,' Duke Richard replied. 'You have long been my friend and I have great need of you now. Your help will not be forgotten by my House. We have much to discuss, and much to plan.' The earl settled back against the brocade cushions of his tall oak chair and relaxed his tense face. 'You have had my loyalty for many years, Richard. You have it still. Let's talk.'

'And where are your lady wife and younger children? Safe in your castle at Fotheringhay I presume.' Countess Joan leant forward in her chair and fixed the duke with her direct gaze. The earl and his family had listened to Richard's description of the poor rule in England and his persecution by Somerset and the Queen and the madness of the king. Neither had been surprised, but seeing their old Lieutenant again, they felt trouble could soon be at their door. 'The king's army on the doorstep at Ludlow, your forces scattered and your oath of allegiance ignored; I assume your family is safe, my Lord?' Joan spoke directly to York and did not look at her husband.

Duke Richard looked at the earl, then his son, and turned his gaze back to the countess. 'Safe? Of course they are safe. Why would they not be? Henry may not have all his wits about him, but he is a king and surely honours my Cecily. Whatever Henry may be, he is principled, and he is kindly.'

The countess sat back in her seat and took a sharp breath.

'I am sure it is as you say, my Lord. The king is venerable and pious. What, however, of his army?'

Ludlow Castle, Welsh Marches, 20th October 1459

The soldiers armed with pikes stood smartly to attention and raised their crossed weapons as Humphrey Stafford Duke of Buckingham approached. At his nod, one of the king's guard reached out and turned the handle of the door to the apartment in the Mortimer Tower where the remaining Yorkists at Ludlow had been crammed. Duchess Cecily and Kat were seated by the window, overlooking the outer bailey and the curtain wall of their castle; the bodies of the castle servants had been removed after the fires of the town had been put out by the rain. Their dresses were grubby and stained after their imprisonment and neither wore a headdress. George was pushing a wooden horse across the table and Margaret was sitting with Nurse Ann and Richard, dividing apples and bread for their next meal. The room stank, and its untidiness seemed to give Cecily a permanent pain in her chest, but she was not sure if this was fear or a lack of fresh air.

'Your Grace.' Buckingham doffed his feathered cap and briefly bowed his head. He was a tall, well-built but gentle man, and husband to Cecily's elder sister Anne. Humphrey Stafford took pride in serving Lancaster and the king, but had been fair to Cecily when he arrived after the looting; if it was because they were related or that was his nature, Cecily had not decided.

'Humphrey.' Cecily's voice was flat as she turned from the window to look at him. 'To what do I owe this pleasure? We have been locked up here since your king's men violated the town, without clean linen for me or my women, and with no fresh air for the children. How may I serve you now?' She spat the last words with acid.

'Cecily. You must have known what would happen. Your Lord husband was prepared to meet the king in the field! He fled, leaving you alone. Did you think the King and Queen Marguerite would simply ride on by and let you go back to collecting your rents?'

'What I thought, Humphrey Stafford, is that my women and children would not have to pay the price for my husband's decisions!'

'Madam, I am here to tell you that you *are* being released.' Stafford held up his hand to ward off her next question. 'But you are being taken to the king's presence at Coventry. I am afraid you will have to answer for York.' The Duke of Buckingham had no joy in his voice, but his tone was steady.

Cecily rose from her seat, and smoothed down her dirty skirts. 'Well, let us away then Humphrey. This meeting will not improve with delays.'

'What's a traitor?' Young Richard whispered to his brother George as they approached the cathedral city of Coventry. They

15

had been travelling for nearly a week in a slow and cumbersome litter, but the young lad had said hardly a word. Now that George thought about it, he had hardly heard Richard's voice since the sacking of Ludlow; the seven-year-old boy had been near silent since they had stood by the market cross and seen the devastation of the town.

'It's a man who betrays you.' George answered without turning his head towards him, so it was their sister Margaret who took Richard's hand.

'It means that someone did something they promised not to do. Someone who has broken trust placed in them. Are you thinking of Sir Andrew Trollope? That night at Ludlow?' Richard nodded, and Margaret pulled him close and put her arm around his thin shoulders. 'Father trusted Sir Andrew, but he broke his promise. He let father down by doing something he was promised not to do. He was supposed to be loyal, but he broke the trust.'

'We Yorks are loyal!' George finally looked at his siblings, determination written across his face. 'We keep our word. Any man can trust a York, we are not traitors. We do not break promises.'

The boy Richard looked at his brother with admiration and smiled. His shoulders seemed to drop with relief, and he settled into the comforting embrace of his sister.

Maynooth Castle, Ireland, 19th November 1459

'By God Richard. What a mess.' Thomas Earl of Kildare turned his gaze away from his friend and looked out over the fields. His horse threw his head up in the air, jibbing at the bridle, eager to canter across the lush fields and meadows. Edmund, with Kildare's daughter Eleanor, had cantered away towards the river, closely followed by a groom. The young couple had been smitten with each other from the first day York set foot in Ireland. By the earl's side, the Duke of York looked down at his gloved hands, resting on the pommel of the saddle. They had set out just after sunrise to clear their heads and take in the beautiful autumn morning, but the ride had so far been soured by talk of battle, betrayal and blood.

'You proved yourself as Lord Protector when the king was ill. The White Rose was triumphant. Even here we heard how you dealt even-handed with the Lords and Commons alike. Surely Henry knows you for his loyal cousin! It'll be that bastard Somerset who is poisoning his ear. They're all the same, those Beauforts; think they're royal but forget they're the baseborn offspring of John of Gaunt.'

'You're right Thomas, but I fear now that matters will never improve. The king will die one day, whether from madness or illness or just not waking up from his long sleep, and Marguerite and Somerset will rule through the son. When that day comes, the House of York will be wiped out.' Richard lifted his head up to the sky and closed his eyes against the sunlight. He took a deep breath and looked at his friend. 'So?'

'So, they fear you, Richard. They fear the power you wield and the blood that runs in your veins. The queen and her tame duke cannot touch you for noble birth, and they know you have a better right to the throne than mad old Henry.'

'Don't say it!' The duke swung his horse around to face Kildare, but his voice was full of despair rather than anger. 'Don't say it, Thomas. Don't say that. I swore allegiance to King Henry and I am his loyal servant.'

Thomas FitzGerald looked down at the grass beneath his

horse's hooves. 'I have to say it. You have to hear it, my Lord. We can do no more here in Kildare, we must head for Dublin. It is time to claim your own.'

Coventry, 21ˢᵗ November 1459

As the litter crossed the River Sherbourne, Cecily could see the towering Priory of St Mary's ahead. It had been raining almost every day since their arrival in Coventry, but this was the first time she had been allowed to leave her lodgings near St Michael's Church, and both she and Kat welcomed the fresh air the pounding rain brought.

'I do believe my hands are trembling!' Duchess Cecily tried to make light of her nervousness. 'It must be the cold weather!'

'Yes Madam.' Kat knew her mistress so well, they had been together for twenty of Cecily's forty-four years. 'I'm sure it's the cold wind. Nothing to do with us being about to see the king and queen.'

Cecily supressed a smile as they turned into the gatehouse of the Benedictine Priory where King Henry was holding his Parliament. Buckingham had told her on their journey from Ludlow that the purpose of the Parliament was to call to account all those who had been disloyal to the king at Ludford Bridge. She knew that her presence was not necessary for the king to carry out his business, just as she knew that it was Queen Marguerite of Anjou who had wanted Cecily to be present to hear the sentences passed against her family. It seemed that her past service to the queen was long forgotten by the French woman, and Cecily could claim no friendship or assistance now. She was on her own.

'Come forth, Duchess Cecily of York!' The voice of Speaker Tresham reverberated throughout the vaulting room. 'Come forth and hear our judgement!'

Cecily stood in the doorway of the Chapter House and raised her chin. She was wearing a new gown of grey velvet that she had begged the Duke of Buckingham to bring from her sister Anne. For all his authority over her, Humphrey had looked after them well on the long journey to Coventry and had seen that she and the children had had all they needed while they awaited the king's pleasure. Her hennin was covered in grey lace, and for a brief moment, Cecily wondered if she had dressed too finely for the occasion. However, she could do nothing about that now, and she walked with measured steps to the centre of the room and stood before the king and queen.

Sir Thomas Tresham opened his scroll and began to read. 'By the Grace of God, our Sovereign Lord King Henry and his Parliament have this day agreed that Acts of Attainder are brought against the following persons for high treason against our most Christian King: Richard Plantagenet Duke of York, Edward Plantagenet Earl of March, Edmund Plantagenet Earl of Rutland, Richard Neville Earl of Salisbury and Richard Neville Earl of Warwick. By these Acts, the King and his Parliament declare their lives to be forfeit, their lands and possessions will revert to the Crown, and no children of their unions will inherit. Signed this day, Henry Sextus, King of England and France.'

Cecily swallowed, but found her nerves were steady and her head was still high. It was her pride that was sustaining her through this ordeal; she would not crumble before this weak king and his spiteful queen.

'On his most gracious honour,' Tresham continued,

19

'Our Sovereign King has agreed that no harm shall come to you, but you will be housed at his pleasure. It is decided that you shall reside at Maxstoke Castle under the protection and guardianship of His Grace the Duke of Buckingham. That is all.' Speaker Tresham let the scroll roll back together with a flourish and sat down. Cecily saw Queen Marguerite smirking, sitting comfortably in her chair next to the king. The sun suddenly broke through the rain clouds and the light poured in through the coloured glass of the Chapter House, illuminating the king, making him look almost angelic. He looked at her expectantly, foolishly, almost as if he was waiting for her to thank him. Cecily smiled at the king as she dropped a curtsey, turned her back and walked from the chamber.

Maxstoke Castle, Warwickshire, 1ˢᵗ December 1459

The portcullis clanged down behind them with a finality Cecily found daunting. Maxstoke was surrounded on all sides by a large moat, and she thought it would take a flight of angels to rescue her from the large and forbidding castle. But when they had alighted from the litter, the children with Kat and Nurse Ann stretching their cramped muscles, Cecily began to see it was a rather pleasant and comfortable looking place. Of course, her sister Anne would have persuaded her husband Buckingham to spend well on her amenities, and suddenly she was looking forward to a soft bed and a hot meal.

The castle Chamberlain ushered Cecily and the others into the large receiving chamber, but stumbled over her introduction, not knowing whether he could address her as Duchess of York any longer.

'Oh never mind Brooke, just ask for wine to be brought.' Anne, Duchess of Buckingham, stepped regally forward but quickly broke into a smile. 'Sister, I am glad to see you! And the children, looking so well!' Young Margaret, George and Richard gave obeisance to their aunt, with near perfect bows and a pretty curtsey. Nursey Ann smiled proudly from behind them, pleased that the children had not forgotten her instructions. Duchess Anne swiftly returned to her previous formal bearing, and turned to Kat and the nurse; 'My Chamberlain will show you to your rooms. I will see you at dinner. Sister, shall we sit?'

Cecily waited for Anne to be seated at one side of the polished table, then took a chair opposite.

'I believe the king has put me and mine into your care, Anne. I do hope that we will not inconvenience you too long.'

'I suppose you will stay here until something else can be arranged for you. My husband Humphrey tells me that Parliament has passed attainders on all your menfolk, and your goods and properties given to the crown.'

'Parliament? That nest of devils you mean!' Cecily snapped, but bowed her head. Her pride would not let her show how devastated she had been since that day. 'I do not see what else can be arranged for me, Anne. But I suppose it is better for us to be here than in the Tower.'

'Indeed, sister. Maxstoke is my home, but I fear it is to be a prison to you. How else can this possibly end, except with the execution of your husband for treason? Then what is to become of you all?'

'Anne, you know Richard speaks no treason. He believes, the *country* believes, that King Henry can barely stay awake and is badly advised. With the exception of your noble husband Humphrey, obviously! England is poorly managed, the roads are not safe to travel, corruption is everywhere, and he has lost most of France! All Richard asks is that the king rid himself of his bad Council and takes guidance from York!' Cecily restrained herself from banging her fists on the table to make her point, but her pride would not let her hear her husband being called traitor.

'Well, my husband Buckingham is loyal to the king. You know that. He may love you as my sister, but he has his orders from the Council. You are to stay here, under his protection. You are not to leave the castle, you are to write no letters, you are to receive no visitors.'

Cecily rose from her chair and dropped a tiny bob to her sister. 'Thank you Anne. I would like to see my room now, if you please. Or should I say my cell?'

Maxstoke Castle, Warwickshire, 26th December 1459
Cecily and Anne sat in the window seat and watched the children play in the courtyard. They had reached a sort of understanding in their forced time together. They found that if they did not mention York and Lancaster and their troubles, they got on well. They talked about old times and their childhoods at Raby Castle; harmless and comforting discussions. Duchess Anne was strict about following her husband's rules for Cecily's incarceration, but they both treated Cecily, her women and the children, well.

It was warm for St Stephen's Day, and the children were playing with a ball and sticks with Nurse Ann watching nearby. George along with Anne's grandson, four-year-old Harry Stafford, were shrieking with laughter and chasing Merry the dog while young Richard was attempting to enforce the rules of the game.

'Harry makes up his own rules, I'm afraid,' Duchess Anne chuckled. 'His nurse and tutors have been rather lax in their discipline with him.'

'Poor child.' Cecily peered down to where the boys were running in circles. 'He never knew his father, did he?'

'No.' Anne turned curt. 'My son, his father, died after the battle in St Albans. Another Lancaster lost thanks to York.'

'Anne, I am sorry. You know we women follow where our men lead. This loss of life is terrible to all; cousins, families, England. I pray one day it will end.' Cecily reached out and covered her sister's hand with her own.

'I know another young boy who will never know a father's love thanks to these wars. Little Henry Tudor lost his father before he drew his first breath. Captured and died in filth in Carmarthen, thanks to that Yorkist William Herbert, poor Edmund. Little Henry's mother Margaret Beaufort is barely a woman herself, and now a widow.' Anne's voice was rising and become shrill in her distress. Cecily sat back, looked at the chamber's painted ceiling and tried to think how to change the subject.

'I must thank you again for allowing me the comfort of the letter from my daughter Anne. We named her for you, you know.' This was not quite true; Cecily's oldest child had been named for Richard's mother, but Cecily felt sure the priest would forgive this one small lie. 'I fear she is not content with…' Cecily broke off, realising she was bringing the subject back to these wars between cousins. Her daughter was married to the Duke of Exeter, who was also a staunch Lancastrian.

'Not content with her husband? Yes, I imagine being married to Henry Holland does come with its hardships.' The sisters looked at each other and burst into laughter.

Dublin Castle, Ireland, 12ᵗʰ February 1460

The candles were guttering low and the feast was coming to an end. The food had been cleared from the boards, but the wine was still flowing. The Duke of York and the Earl of Kildare had drunk more than was possibly good for them, Master Aspall felt, but he did not begrudge them some relief from the hard debating and heated discussions that had been going on since their arrival here. He knew what they had been discussing, although he was not sure his master would have approved of him listening from behind the brocade curtains of the Council Chamber. Nevertheless, he knew his duty, and his duty was to protect the body and soul of Edmund, the boy he favoured most of all the York children. He had heard the young man's confession early this morning, before Mass was said in the castle chapel, and had to cover a smile when Edmund spoke of his love for an earl's daughter. As if the whole castle did not know already! Edmund thought he had been discreet and private, but even the girl who kept the castle geese knew.

Master Aspall, back slightly bowed from his years, crossed the hall to the high table. He stood behind Edmund and bowed. He heard him whisper into Eleanor's ear of the story of Saint Valentine curing a girl's blindness, and saw him gently touch his lips to her brows.

'Ahem. My Lord of Rutland, I believe the Countess wishes to speak to her daughter. My Lady?' The old tutor gently pulled back Eleanor's chair, and bowed as she flitted away. 'My Lord, I believe it is time to hear your confession again.'

Edmund smiled and clasped his oldest friend on the shoulder, and they walked away to find more fine Irish wine.

Dublin Castle, Ireland, 20th March 1460

The silence hung over the men like a black cloud. Kildare was seated to the Duke of York's left, on his right sat Warwick, newly arrived from Calais.

'So, nephew.' York turned to the younger man. 'Tell us the state of England, it has been near half a year since I left. News of the Attainders passed on us all reached our ears; the malice of the Lancastrians knows no bounds. What intelligence do you have?' From the chamber window where the great lords were meeting, Duke Richard could see two of the four corner towers of the castle, a place he had sat in many times over the years, with Dublin Castle being the seat of English rule in Ireland. He looked back to his curly-haired nephew and lifted an eyebrow.

'Much news, my Lord uncle.' Warwick glanced around the faces gathered at the long table, relishing the fact all eyes were on him. 'Much news and many plans in the making!'

As the sun passed from window to window, Warwick told his tales. The Duke of Bedford's widow, Jacquetta of Luxembourg, along with her second husband Richard Woodville and their flamboyant eldest son Anthony, had been captured by Warwick whilst they were assembling a fleet to invade Calais, Warwick's stronghold. Warwick was too quick for them, and apprehended Woodville and his family and took them under guard back to Calais where they were rebuked by York's son, Edward of March, and held against their will.

'We released the Lady Jacquetta and sent her packing back to England, back to her vast brood of children!' Warwick snickered. 'But we will be keeping an eye on Woodville and Anthony a while longer. They are safer locked up with us. Left in England, they will continue to recruit for Henry and Marguerite. The Lancastrians expect us to invade England any day now!' Warwick smiled at the duke. 'They expect us to come through Sandwich in Kent.'

'The men of Kent are loyal to you and to our cause,' Duke Richard replied.

Warwick nodded his curly head. 'They are indeed loyal, and you can rest assured uncle, that Edward and I will not allow Calais to be taken; it is ours!'

Duke Richard turned his head to look Warwick in the eye. 'Calais belongs to the Crown and to England. It is not your personal fiefdom lad, and I would hope that your governance there has not gone to your head.' The Earl of Warwick's jaw dropped open and he began to stutter a reply, his face flushing a mottled red. Duke Richard did not wish to further anger the proud and powerful younger man, but he thought it wise to curb his ambition somewhat.

'Warwick, nephew, I am sure you command Calais well, and I appreciate all you have taught my Edward, who I hear is flourishing under your protection. But my time in Ireland is over, I need to return to England, and to my family. Let us talk strategy.'

'Ahem.' The Earl of Kildare interrupted quietly, but got the attention he craved. 'Before we plan your return to England, my Lord Duke, we need to know what your intentions are when you arrive there.'

Prompted by his old friend, Duke Richard looked solemnly around the table.

'I have thought long and hard on this and have prayed for guidance. I am aware we have all been attainted, and all our lands and titles are forfeit to the crown. They have tried to destroy York. My wife and three youngest are all but prisoners in the home of her sister, wife to Buckingham who is a good Lancastrian loyal to the king. The time for petitioning Henry for a return to good governance is past.' Duke Richard looked at his son Edmund who was seated across from him. He held his eyes but spoke to the whole room.

'My intention, when we return to England, is to finally end the poor management of England, and the denigration of the House of York, once and for all. It is time to claim the throne, mine by right and by birth.'

Dublin Castle, Ireland, 21st March 1460

'Young Edmund! How well you look!' Warwick put his arm around the younger man as they walked through the castle keep to the stables. 'Ireland must suit you.'

'Thank you cousin, I find Ireland suits me well indeed.' A small flush of pink rose towards the blonde hair.

'Ah, so I see! Are the fair maidens of Dublin to your liking?'

Edmund looked at Warwick, the dark curly head not too far above his own. 'Nothing like that cousin. But I do wish to talk with you of my Lord father's plans.'

Warwick suddenly dropped his attempt at bonhomie and his jovial stance. He stopped his forceful march toward the stable yard and turned to the boy.

'Your father is an ambitious man, Edmund. York has great support and much of the will of England is against Henry and Marguerite, and their son is truly a devil. However…'

Edmund met Warwick's eyes. 'I have given this much thought, cousin. My father revealed his plans to me before we met with you and the other lords. I believe there is no other way to reunite England.'

'Edmund, you're just a boy, you don't understand!' Warwick exploded, but quickly regained control. 'You perhaps do not realise the consequences of the duke's plans.'

'I may be not yet seventeen, but I do understand. My father is twice royal! His blood is from Lionel of Clarence and Edmund of Langley, both sons of Edward III. He descends from the second and fourth sons of that great king! King Henry is of the third son and is not in his right mind! Surely my father, and the York line, is a better option for England?'

Warwick turned his shoulder and carried on walking, leaving Edmund behind. 'Yes, but with York as king, what good does that do me?' he muttered under his breath.

Maxstoke Castle, Warwickshire, 29ᵗʰ March 1460

'I have applied a poultice, Your Grace, and hopefully he will feel improved on the morrow. I expect the pain is due to the playing with wooden swords with the other young gentlemen.' Nurse Ann wrung her hands together in front of her thin expanse of chest, worry writ plain on her face. 'The young master Richard does not usually complain of any discomfort, as you know Madam, so this soreness in his back must truly be hurting him.'

'Thank you Nurse.' Cecily smiled at the woman who had

been with her for seventeen years, since her baby Edward was born in Rouen. She trusted her implicitly, and knew that whatever aches and agues the children suffered, she was the best person to deal with them.

'I should tell Harry and George to find more suitable games if young Richard is indisposed.' Duchess Anne turned her sewing towards the light. 'They can be rough with delicate things!'

Cecily smiled into her book. Relations with her sister were much improved recently. Their tacit understanding not to mention the troubles worked to keep the peace between them, and they generally spoke only of domestic things. However, Cecily felt their peace would be shattered if her sister knew of the secret letter she had received from her nephew Warwick. It had come to her last week, hidden in a bolt of silk she had been given permission to order from Calais. Warwick told her how proud he was of the powerful Edward, her son in his charge, and how much the men of Calais loved him. Cecily had sniffed at that, noticing he had not mentioned what the women of Calais thought of the handsome Earl of March. Warwick also wrote that her husband Duke Richard and Edmund were well, having just seen them both in Dublin. Cecily now knew of their health, and how much her second son had grown, but not what their plans were. She supposed Warwick could not risk the letter falling into Lancastrian hands and understood that, but swore, if she ever saw him again, she would sorely berate her husband for not writing himself.

Dublin Castle, Ireland, 8th April 1460

'So, my Lord of Warwick has returned to Calais already?' Eleanor Fitzgerald lay back on the soft grass, her hair spread around her face and her blue dress reflecting the sky. Edmund, propped on an elbow next to her, looked down on the pretty face.

'Yes, and his garrison was attacked by that devil Somerset while he was here, but Edward and the troops at Calais sent them packing! I think he has taught my brother well, although it seems he does have him under his thumb.'

'I wish I could meet the rest of your family.' Eleanor turned her face into the crook of her arm. 'You speak so highly of them all; d'you think they would like me?' Her soft voice was muted, but Edmund could hear her clearly.

'How could they help liking you, my dearest Eleanor?' Edmund realised the blue of her dress exactly matched the sky. 'George would worship you, Margaret would lend you lace, and young Richard would likely not speak a word from shyness. But brother Edward has never been able to resist a pretty face.'

Eleanor stood up and pulled Edmund to his feet. 'I will just have to make do with you for now then,' she whispered as she kissed him on the lips.

Dublin Castle, Ireland, 1ˢᵗ May 1460

'My Lord Edmund, pray attend to these papers. I fear you lack diligence today.'

'I am sorry, Master Aspall; I am indeed distracted. I have many thoughts in my head that I cannot order.'

The old tutor turned his face away with a smile. 'Does one of your thoughts wear a sapphire dress?' he asked smilingly.

'No! Well, not today at least.' Edmund swung round in his chair and became suddenly solemn. 'It is my father's plans that concern me. Or rather, what my cousin of Warwick makes of my father's plans.'

'The earl?' Master Aspall gathered up the neglected papers that Edmund had not read and shuffled them into a neat pile. 'Surely he is Duke Richard's right hand in this, along with *his* father Salisbury and your brother Edward? I know my Lord of Salisbury seems a relic of a bygone age, but I believe in his loyalty and courage. Master Devereaux, your father's man, told me of the invasion plans of England from Calais, although I did have wind of them before, and how Warwick is going to prepare the ground, starting in Kent, by issuing proclamations in the duke's favour, laying out his case against the king. Then, I believe, he is to persuade the lords in Westminster of your father's cause and gain their support. Indeed, without it, the case for York is lost!'

'Yes, yes I know the plans.' Edmund sat back in his seat and tipped his head up to the vaulted ceiling of his chamber. 'What concerns me, Master Aspall, is…well, can he be relied upon?'

Robert Aspall moved to stand gravely in front of his pupil, the young man he loved like his own.

'My Lord, do you know of any reason, or have any information, that my Lord of Warwick cannot be trusted? His task is to prepare the Lords and Commons of England for your father's claim for kingship. His task is essential to your father's success. Pray, speak now of your doubts!'

'No, I have nothing proven sir. But Warwick likes to *command*. He commands Calais and my brother, but never my father, he will never have influence over my father. Think Master Aspall!' Edmund stood up and towered over his tutor. 'What will Warwick gain if my father takes the throne?'

They were sorting the linen and clothes, the women of York held in captivity while their men did only God knew what. Margaret and Kat were shaking out dresses belonging to Duchess Cecily, while Nurse Ann took an inventory of the tears and rips in the boys' clothes.

'Meg, I swear you will soon be grown enough to fit in this gown!' The fourteen-year-old beauty smiled at her mother, not realising that the duchess had been this age when she had married. Margaret did not feel that she had missed out on anything really. She worshipped her parents, and loved playing mother to George and Richard. This confinement was not much of a hardship to her; she felt safe in the castle, knowing battles would not come to their door, but she would have slept much better had her father been under the same roof. She picked up the pale green gown, slim cut with draping sleeves, and held it against her slender frame.

'Thank you Lady mother. A new gown would be such a delight. I don't know what we can do about the boys' hose and shirts though. Unless cousin Harry has some spare things?'

Duchess Cecily and Kat smiled at each other, both pleased at the maternal instincts of Meg. She would make a wonderful mother herself one day. Cecily began inspecting George's boots, wondering if she would be allowed money to buy new ones, when they heard screaming from the Great Hall.

'Meg, wait here with Nursey! Kat, come with me.' Cecily grabbed her lady's arm and rushed to the door. They flew down the corridor until they reached the great chamber where huge chairs were set on the dais. They saw a man in tattered clothes with the arms of Buckingham sewn over his right breast. He was kneeling before Duchess Anne, but looked up gladly when

Cecily and Kat hurried towards the keening woman. Battles were enough for him; screaming women he could do without.

'Anne! Sister! What is it? What has happened?' Cecily took Anne's hands but could not make out any words over her sobs and cries. Tears and snot dripped down her face, and Kat thankfully passed her a scrap of lace to wipe it clean. Cecily looked at the kneeling man, now noticing the blood on his ear and muck on his boots, and realised what bad news he had brought.

Cecily sat between her two young boys tucked up in bed, their faces scrubbed clean and their eyes wide. 'So when you see young Harry tomorrow, you must be very kind to him. He has lost his father, and now his grandfather Humphrey is dead, poor child. He will likely not want to play for a while, but when he does, you must address him as Your Grace. He is Duke of Buckingham now.'

'Yes Lady mother.' George and Richard nodded, and Cecily rose. 'Mother, did the Duke of Buckingham die in a battle?' Cecily pretended not to see the hound sleeping under George's bed and turned back to her youngest son.

'Yes my dear, he did. There was a battle in Northampton, and the duke was fighting for the king, as he thought that right for his House.'

'Was there a traitor?' Richard whispered into the dark, not sure if he wanted to hear the answer.

'No Richard. Well, Lord Grey did change sides, I hear, but I believe York would have won in any case, as we had far more men than Lancaster. And now cousin Warwick is looking after King Henry for us, back in London.'

'What about the queen? Won't she be angry?' Cecily could have smiled at Richard's question, but she took it seriously, and answered accordingly.

'Well, she won't be happy, I think, but she may just return to France now. We have the king held safe under York, the queen is gone, and we can go home to London now. Let us pray your father will join us soon.'

'Was cousin Warwick at Northampton?' George yawned, but had been listening intently.

'Yes, he was there. As was your brother Edward. And that I have to explain to your aunt.'

'Have you packed your gear? Don't forget those books I am lending you, and the herbs for Richard's pain. You can take that statue of the Virgin Mary you so admired too. I am sure it is no good to me now.'

'My beloved sister, please don't.' Cecily reached out and dried Duchess Anne's tears for what seemed like the thousandth time. 'I cannot tell you the pain I feel that your Humphrey is dead, I am sorry beyond words. I cannot imagine what it is like, losing a husband. But this war is between men. It cannot come between the love of sisters.' Cecily knew that she did not really believe these words; she was committed to the House of York through marriage and love; the wars would affect everyone, men and women alike. She knew she must add this to the list of things to confess, but she was so anxious to return to London that she would wait to be shriven some other time.

'Go then. Take your children and return to Warwick and Edward. Smile and drink and toast with them, the butchers who killed my husband. I pray you'll never know my pain, Cecily. I've lost a son and a husband thanks to York. I pray you'll never walk in my shoes.' Anne turned her face away.

Duchess Cecily dropped a perfect curtsey to the cold shoulder and bowed her head. 'I know I am York, and you are Lancaster,

34

dear sister. And I know fortunes turn and turnabout. But I will pray for God to take away your pain. And never deliver it to me.'

Dublin Castle, Ireland, 29th August 1460

The young couple clung to each other amidst the trunks and packing crates and chests that filled the room.

'My love, my Eleanor,' Edmund whispered into the flame-red hair. He could feel her trembling shoulders under his hands, and he held her more tightly.

It was Eleanor who finally drew away and took Edmund's hands into her own. She looked up at him, forcing herself to smile.

'You'll soon be back with your family, I doubt you will even remember me next week! You'll just remember a girl in a blue dress who helped pass the time for you in Ireland.'

'No doubt you are right.' Edmund grinned, 'What is your name again, fair lady?'

Eleanor thumped the boy on his shoulder, and the laughter and tears came together.

'My love, when this has all settled, I swear I will speak to my father. I will tell him that I have found my Countess of Rutland, I have found my princess; your father and mine will be happy to seal their friendship with our marriage.'

Eleanor slipped a gold band from her middle finger, and pressed it into Edmund's hand. He stared at the ring with a bright blue stone in the centre and slid it onto his thumb. 'This is my reminder to you Edmund. When you look at the ring, you will be looking at me. And know that I will be waiting for you.'

'It is beautiful, and I will wear it always. But I need no ring to remind me; you are scored on my heart Eleanor, and always will be.'

Port of Dublin, Ireland, 3rd September 1460

Richard Duke of York stood on the quayside with his son Edmund and Deveraux at his side. They watched a cog unload its cargo of wine, destined for the inns and tables of Dublin, and animal hides were stacked in the warehouse entrance, waiting to be loaded and carried on their way to England and France. Seagulls screamed overhead following the fishermen out to sea. Richard's luggage was already loaded on to the carrack, its six sails ready to be hauled up when they were clear of the harbour. The rest of their party, the household and the men-at-arms, were to follow in whatever ships they could muster.

'We are ready father, the captain has given his signal.' Edmund walked to the bottom of the gangplank, never turning his head to look back. He was eager to be gone and hurried aboard while Duke Richard knelt on the stone to say a last prayer. They walked up together, their feet slipping a little on the stepped boards and the wind whipping their capes.

'I hear Edward was a credit to our House at Northampton, father. His first battle.' They stood shoulder to shoulder, watching as the dock slipped away and they headed out to sea.

'News of my heir in a battle does not fill me with joy, son, but it pleases me that Edward has the makings of a fine soldier. But now, more than ever before, my way is clear. Warwick took King Henry from the battlefield and has returned with him to

London. He will give him honour, but not his crown back. He is housed properly, but he is housed securely. What heartbreak I feel now is knowing that many more men have died because they maintained their loyalty to that broken king.'

'My cousin of Warwick will enjoy having control over King Henry, I am sure. But at least my Lady mother, Margaret, Richard and George are released now.' Edmund squinted up at the overhead sun. 'My good aunt's husband, the Duke of Buckingham lost his life on the field. Mother is no longer a prisoner in his house.'

'Yes, I rejoice that they are all free. They have returned to Baynard's in London, and your brother Edward will protect them there, with Warwick's help. The months those two spent together seem to have been good for him! I would rest more easily if Marguerite and her son Edouard were brought into our keeping though. They have gone to Harlech with that savage half-blood Jasper Tudor. No doubt they'll be skipping away on a ship soon.' They walked across the deck towards their cabins, vacated by the ship's Master and Bo'sun, closely watched by Devereaux who was ready to grab his master's arm should the rocking ship prove too strong for the duke.

'Master Aspall, are you quite well?' Duke Richard watched the older man sway and stumble as he navigated the small room. The two men were quite alone, but the rush of the waves and the creaking of the ship's wood gave them the feeling they were in a crowd.

'I fear I am a good a sailor as I am a horseman, my Lord.' The shorter man looked quite grey, and suddenly dropped into a seat. 'My natural home is behind a desk, I believe.'

'Well, that can be arranged as soon as we get to London.

Edmund will have to resume his studies as I don't believe he applied himself particularly to his books these last few months.'

'My Lord Duke, I do not believe Edmund will have much need of this old tutor soon. He is almost equal to me in his learning; he does not need a schoolmaster, he needs a knight's training.'

Duke Richard glanced at the man who had his head almost between his knees. He poured himself a goblet of wine, but thought better of offering Aspall any.

'You speak true sir. Edmund has book learning aplenty; now he needs to learn to be the son of a duke.'

The tutor shakily stood up and headed for the door. 'With respect, my Lord, what is required is the training of a prince.'

Hereford Castle, 20ᵗʰ September 1460

Cecily thought her heartbeat could be heard above the thundering of the horses' hooves and the wheels of the litter rumbling along. The imposing brown stone of the castle rose above the grassy hill and as the drawbridge drew nearer, she could see two standards flying on poles high above the castle keep. She stared at them intently until they crossed the drawbridge. The wind whipped her skirts and the veil of her hennin as she stepped down from the litter in the courtyard. Cecily, Duchess of York, held her head high as she had pretended to do, all those long months locked up at Maxstoke. Waiting for her at the top of the long shallow castle steps were the two men she had longed to see for nearly a year. Richard and Edmund, husband and son, coming towards her, Edmund taking the steps lightly and swiftly, Richard following more slowly. Her son reached her first, grasped her hands and kissed them as he knelt for her blessing. She held his hands, noticing a new ring with a blue stone on his thumb, then pulled him up and into her arms noticing how taller and broader he was since she last saw him.

'My son, my precious son,' she murmured into his shoulder. She held onto him a moment longer, just to wipe away her tears on the soft cloth of his red surcoat. She took a step back and looked up into his bright face. 'It does my heart glad to see you so hale, my boy. I have missed your wit and wisdom, and I could certainly have done with your help looking after your brother George all these months!'

Edmund laughed and started chattering away, trying to tell her of their travels and asking after his siblings, but he noticed her eyes were straying away from him, towards his father who stood silently behind him.

'If you will excuse me, Lady mother, I must see to the horses and have your gear brought inside.' Edmund turned away, realising she had neither eyes nor ears for him now.

Duke Richard waited until Edmund was no longer in earshot, then knelt on the stones in front of his wife. He looked down and could see the hem of Cecily's green damask dress and her shoes peeking out from underneath. He raised his eyes to her and his voice came out in a choked whisper. 'Forgive me.'

The boards were cleared, the servants gone. Edmund muttered something about letters that needed writing and had slipped away; only Deveraux stood outside their chamber door in case his master needed him. Richard and Cecily sat facing each other across the table and he reached for her hands.

'And how is my hound, Cecily? I love hearing about everything at home. It pleases my heart to hear how the children are well, and that Edward is keeping watch over them still. It pleases my heart even more to see *you*, my dear.'

'Then why the tears Richard? Since I apparently please you so much?' Cecily tried to be light-hearted, but she knew that to have any peace, Richard must be allowed to say what he needed.

'I never imagined it would be so terrible for you; Ludlow, Coventry, Maxstoke...I truly never believed that Henry and Marguerite would treat you so badly. And the Attainder! Well, in honesty, that did not surprise me but as for the rest, I...'

'Richard, stop. When we parted we knew what chances we were taking, we knew the worst that might happen. In truth, some uncharitable thoughts about you did cross my mind, but I took them to the priest and have been shriven! And your dog is well, and eating more meat than the cooks can provide!' Duke Richard smiled at her words and gripped her fingers more tightly.

'Well, if I am forgiven, then all is well. I cannot take another step without you my dear. I missed your counsel in Ireland, and now I must tell you of my plans. You are the better half of me, Cecily, you are my ...'

'I am your queen, Richard.' Cecily interrupted her husband, and looked directly at him. 'My eyesight did not fail, being locked up with my good sister, although I feel I may have lost some of my wits. I saw the standards, husband, flying over this castle; did you think I would not? The standard of York and the royal arms of England.'

'And?' Duke Richard stood up and put the palms of his hands on the table.

Cecily stood up also, lifted her arms to her sides, and dropped into a perfect curtsey. 'My King.'

The sounds and smells of the Thames almost brought tears to Duke Richard's eyes but he did not know if it was because of the river itself, or his pleasure at being back in the capital. As their boat drew up to the river steps of the enormous palace that was their London home, Cecily heard Richard take a deep breath. She wasn't sure if it was to steady his nerves before the ordeals that would surely face them in the days to come, or because he could see six of his children awaiting them at the top. Their two eldest, Anne and Elizabeth, had come from their own homes to greet their father. Edward, his son and heir, was trying to keep his arms around the little ones to stop them slipping down the stone stairs. As the oarsmen threw the rope and tied up their boat, the Duke of York stepped out and helped Cecily with her heavy skirts as she set foot on dry land. Edmund leapt out after his mother, then dashed up the steps to his siblings.

'Edward! All of you! I am so pleased to see you! We have such tales to tell and such news to bring you!'

'Edmund, peace.' Richard of York came behind his son as they all turned to enter the great doors to the castle.

'There is no peace here father, this is London! And there is for certain no peace when George is around!' Edmund was trying to hug everyone at once, and the babble of talk and commotion echoed around the halls as the whole family made their way to their private chambers.

'I am so pleased to see all my children here. All of you, in one place. But please, for love of the Virgin and for the sake of my ears, hush now.' Duchess Cecily settled herself in her chair, and the children came one by one, oldest first, to kiss her cheek and greet their father.

The duke had hugged them all and was trying to seat himself next to Cecily, but young Richard would not let go of his father's coat and was being dragged off by Edward, towering over the slight boy.

'My son, you are like a limpet from a ship's keel! Sit here, by my feet, and let me look at you all.'

Cecily could see the pleasure Richard took from being back in the heart of his family, but she knew that they could not discuss his plans yet. First the family would dine and enjoy being in each other's company; it had been a long time since they were all together. When the children and the girls had gone, then they would talk.

'So, Margaret, I hear you have been a great help to your Lady mother. George, have you been well behaved, have you been looking after my dog? I'll be sure to ask Nursey Ann, mind, so tell me the truth! Richard, my dear boy, how goes your studies? Anne, Elizabeth, are your husbands both well?' The duke picked up his goblet and looked around the table, eager to start their reunion.

Salisbury made sure the door was firmly shut and two guards stood outside. The ever-present Deveraux sat with Cecily's lady Kat in the window seat in the corridor, where he could see anyone approaching. York kept four hundred men at Baynard's Castle, and he hoped that every one of them was alert tonight. They wanted no intruders or spies in their midst tonight; they were all still under Attainder. In the small chamber, the duke and duchess sat nearest the fire, with Edward and Edmund on smaller stools nearby. The Earl of Salisbury and his son were the only other two present.

'So. We are agreed.' Salisbury sat next to his sister Cecily and opposite his son Warwick. He spoke from the side of his mouth as was his habit, and it was hard to tell if he was pleased. 'Your path is clear, is it my Lord?'

'We need to ask your son if he has cleared the path, I think. Warwick, have you fulfilled our plans? Are the Commons and Lords with us?' York turned to his nephew, who was, as usual, dressed much more fashionably than his father.

'I spread the word from Kent to London, uncle. The good men of the towns I passed through favour you over King Henry. They know the witless king is ruled by his French wife when he manages to stay awake, and they are ready to support you. They are surely sick of the high taxes, corruption and brigands they face each day. The people of England fear the French, and they hate his foreign wife.'

'Thank you, it is good to know that they are behind us. And what of the Lords of this realm? Did it take long to persuade them to back our cause?'

Warwick bent in his chair to scratch the head of the York's pup, the beautiful brindle Merry, and none but Edmund could see the flicker in his eyes. 'My Lord uncle, without the support of the Lords, your bid for kingship cannot happen. I am sure the Lords are even now arguing amongst themselves for the positions they hope you will bestow upon them when you have the throne.'

York and Salisbury chuckled, and Edward poured wine for them all. Cecily looked at her oldest son fondly, hardly believing that such a giant, handsome boy was hers. Edmund was a smaller version of his brother but always seemed to melt into the background when his exuberant sibling was present. Edward's high spirits were clear to read tonight; he knew that once his father had claimed the throne, it would come to him in years to come. When Edward was in the room no one had eyes

for Edmund, and so it was this night; none could see his worry
or his trouble at Warwick's evasiveness.

Westminster Palace, London, 10th October 1460

As the palace loomed before them, the morning sunlight was
warming them already. Richard Duke of York was at the head
of the column. Close behind rode Salisbury and Warwick, with
Edward and Edmund leading the York household guard, smart
in their murrey and blue livery.

'Father seemed nervous when we broke our fast this
morning. It is no small thing to make a claim for the throne!'
Edward turned to his younger brother to see if he shared his
high spirits.

'Indeed, nothing can be bigger, brother. At this very
minute, we are all attainted and our lives are forfeit. We can
inherit nothing, should we even live. But by noon, we may be
princes of England, our father the king.'

'Does that not please you Edmund? Shall we be like old
Henry of Bolingbroke? He was named traitor but turned his
luck and his fortune when he claimed the throne.'

'It does please me, Edward, but I fear much may go wrong.
The support of the Lords will be the success or the ruin of our
father's claim. Let us pray that Warwick has them in his deep
pocket already.'

Edward looked shrewdly at the younger man, then sat
straighter in the saddle as the crowds surged closer; he knew he
looked good on horseback and the maidens of London seemed
to agree with him.

As the clocks struck ten, the chimes reverberated around the outer chamber of the throne room of Westminster. Mad King Henry was locked in the royal apartments; everyone doubted he had the wit to look out of his window to see what the commotion was. The Duke of York was ready; the black and gold of his velvet coat gave him a dignified air, and the sword he held in front of his chest was shining bright. Four of his household guard held the cloth of estate above his head: It was time.

Salisbury and Warwick opened the double doors and stepped back to allow the duke to enter, with his sons close behind him. The assembled Lords, debating in the chamber, turned their heads as they entered and fell silent as the duke approached the empty throne.

Duke Richard and his company marched down the centre of the room, walked up the narrow steps and faced them. He reached out his right hand and laid it on the empty marble throne.

'My Lords! In the name of God and England, I claim this throne by right of ancestry. Before you is my authority, the coat of arms of my ancestor, Lionel of Antwerp, First Duke of Clarence, second son of King Edward The Third.' Edward already held aloft the richly embroidered standard of the arms of England, the red, blue and gold thread shining bright. Then Edmund stepped forward bearing the standard of his forebear, the lions and fleurs-de-lys echoing those in England's flag.

'Under this standard, as the living heir to the throne, I am come here to assert my case by affirmation and by birthright!' His voice was loud and firm and did not waver as he held his head high and looked towards the lords.

The room was silent. The assembled men in their fine clothes and black robes were stunned and uttered not one word. The sun streamed in the window behind the throne and slightly

45

warmed the stone under York's hand and for a moment, in the silence, he believed he could hear his skin crackle.

Into the silence came the shuffling of feet. It was old Thomas Bourchier, Archbishop of Canterbury. He walked slowly towards the vacant throne, the fur trim of his white robe fluttering in the draft he created. Salisbury, watching from the door, realised his mouth was open and snapped it shut. He glanced at his son, but Warwick seemed to be examining the ceiling of the chamber and did not meet his eye.

'My Lord Duke…' Bourchier didn't seem to be able to finish. 'My Lord Duke, did you…do you want to see His Grace the King?' Richard of York managed to look at all the men in the room without seeming to move his head. He looked to the back of the room, searching out his nephew Warwick, but had no luck. He shortened his focus to the archbishop and realised he was on his own.

'Archbishop, in this realm men should wait on me, not I on them. Did you not hear me make claim to the throne?'

'I did hear, my Lord, but I know not what…' Bourchier hesitated and glanced back at the assembled lords. 'In light of your claim, perhaps we should…' The archbishop broke off, not having any words, not knowing what to say. He looked over his shoulder at the movement he sensed behind him. The Lords of the realm were leaving the chamber, turning their backs on York, turning their backs on the throne.

Baynard's Castle, London, 16th October 1460

'Well, I thank God that is over.' Richard of York settled himself in front of the fire with only Cecily at his side.

'Parliament at least seemed to listen this time, but I could not swear that they looked kindly upon me.'

'And what was the outcome of this illustrious meeting?' Cecily reached for her wine and watched Merry circling the mat until he settled near to his master's feet.

'I presented them the scrolls of genealogy, showed them my descent, showed them my right to claim the throne. I would have shown them my heart if it would have made a difference.'

'Your heart belongs to me, my dear; to me and the children. You are head of the House of York and head of the family. And that head may wear the crown in days to come!'

'Speaking of family, I want the boys here. Deveraux! Deveraux!' Richard called, and his faithful man stepped into the chamber and bowed. 'Fetch the Earls of March and Rutland, would you?' Deveraux nodded and closed the door softly behind him. It was not long before Edward and Edmund came in, knelt for their mother's blessing, and drew up stools by the fire.

'Boys, after the meeting in Parliament today I set you a task. Did you have any luck?'

'No father, we did not. We could not find our cousin Warwick in his chambers, and his father Salisbury had no knowledge of his whereabouts.'

'And how is my brother? Do you think he sides with Warwick?' Cecily looked at her sons inquiringly.

'Well, we don't know that Warwick *isn't* on our side,' Edward replied. 'We know he raised support for father among the people, but when the Lords didn't support father's claim, we don't know if that was Warwick's doing. Warwick hates the Lancastrians, particularly Queen Marguerite; he would never want old Harry to remain as king.' Edward's loyalty to his cousin was apparent in his words.

'I believe that Warwick is opposed to King Henry, as are most of the Neville family,' Edmund interjected in his quiet voice. 'But it does not follow that he supports father as king.' Edward looked at his younger brother in surprise. Edmund brushed his hair out of his eyes, and a flash of blue from his ring caught the light. 'What I mean is, what power does it give him if York is on the throne? Cousin Warwick wants to control; he wants to be indispensable. He can never control *you*, father. He wants to be the power behind the throne, to have leverage. He is no man's lackey.'

His parents and brother stared at Edmund in astonishment. The only sound was the snuffling of the hound in his sleep, and the crackle of the fire. 'Well,' Richard of York started, 'it seems you have been paying more attention than I gave you credit for, my son. You may be right, of course, but until we can find him, we will not know. My dear,' Richard turned Cecily. 'I suggest you speak to your brother as a matter of urgency, and have young Warwick pay us a visit.'

The following noon, the chamber door clanged shut and the Houses of York and Neville faced each other. Richard and Cecily stood in front of their two eldest boys, their faces stern and Richard Neville, Earl of Warwick, knelt before them. His father Salisbury stood behind him, drawn up to his full height in his old-fashioned clothes and with a face like thunder.

'Your Grace, my uncle of York, I offer my fealty to your House and to your cause. I swear to you, on the lives of my two daughters, I will be faithful and true to your claim, and I will serve you however you see fit to use me.' Warwick offered up his praying hands in an age-old gesture and felt them clasped between the duke's palms. He let out his breath in a rush and stood up. He bowed his head to them all, locked eyes with

Edward for a moment and turned on his heel and left the room.

'Well brother, how did you manage that?' Cecily looked at Salisbury with a smile. Salisbury, father to four sons, did not return the smile but said from the side of his mouth, 'I promised him he would feel the toe of my boot or the devil's poker up his arse before the day was out if he did not declare himself openly. I cannot abide muddy waters; he is either in one camp or the other, none of this double dealing.' He turned to the Duke of York. 'Neville is with you Richard. To the very end.'

Baynard's Castle, London, 31st October 1460

'Deveraux? Where the devil is the man? Deveraux! Fetch wine! Fetch the children! Quick man, quick!' Richard Duke of York grabbed Cecily in a hug, lifting her off her feet. 'It's done, it's over my dear! It's all settled!' His excitement was infectious, and Cecily found herself laughing and clasping her hands as Richard finally slumped into a chair, frightening the hound who slunk away from the unaccustomed noise. The door clanged open and Edward and Edmund burst in, followed by Margaret and George. Young Richard brought up the rear, clutching a book and looking wide eyed at the commotion.

'My dear, settle down and tell us what has happened. You are turning the house upside down with the furore. Children, find a stool and sit. Your father clearly has good news.' Cecily turned to her husband; 'Now please Richard. What happened?'

'It's all over! It's all settled! Parliament has come through for us, Warwick has come through for us! It has all been agreed.' Duke Richard took a calming breath and continued. 'As you know, Parliament has agreed the Act of Accord, the Attainders against us all have been revoked, and there is more! The Act names me and my boys as successors to King Henry, they have made me Lord Protector of England and have bestowed on me the lands and income of the Prince of Wales! Old Henry has even agreed. Don't you see? This must mean they truly believe the Act will hold fast. If they meant to renege on the promises or to revoke it, they would never have made me Lord Protector or granted me the incomes. I believe it is the true intent of Parliament and none can break it. To raise arms against York is now forbidden by the Act. I believe we are safe.'

Warwick and his father entered the chamber, and even old Salisbury looked cheerful. 'I congratulate you Richard, and you too, my son. I believe today is a turning point in England's history. The House of York will be the ruling house when old Harry dies, but now you will be king in all but name. York and Neville, standing side by side.'

'I thank you, and thanks to you, Warwick, for your support. I doubt those old women in Parliament would have had the courage to take such steps without your influence. Your pardon, my dear!' The duke looked at his wife with a grin and flopped back against the cushions.

'Will I be a king, father?' George's voice piped up from nearest the fire. 'Will I be King George?'

'It is not likely my dear, no.' Duke Richard looked at his handsome blonde son. 'When King Henry dies, I will be king, then it will go to your brother Edward, then the crown will pass to his sons. What is important though, for both you boys, is to be loyal to Edward. He will need to be able to look to you all and know you for his most loyal subjects and brothers. That's more important than being king.' The duke whispered the last

50

part to George and young Richard and was rewarded with smiles and nods.

The younger children had been ushered away by Nurse Ann with promises of sweetmeats and stories, and left the others to talk.

'What about Queen Marguerite though?' Edmund looked around the table at his family. 'We hear she fled to Scotland, but she's not going to take the news well. We are disinheriting her son Edouard. She's not going to go back to Anjou and start lacemaking.'

'Indeed not. Her mother and grandmother were both militant rulers and she most certainly has their blood.' Cecily dropped her shoulders and, for the briefest moment, looked dejected.

'My dear, as we so often say, all will be well. Marguerite may well have made a deal with the devil, she has given to Scotland our town of Berwick in return for their help, but we have Henry safe here in London. She has no power without him at her side, and we will most assuredly keep him here. She will not be pleased but what can she do? Henry has agreed to all this. She must accept that it is over for Lancaster. The White Rose triumphs.'

'We must show the country that King Henry agrees to all this! We will demonstrate that York is now the successor to the throne, and we are as one.' Warwick's voice carried authority and wisdom, and all turned to him.

'How?' Edward sat closest to his cousin, as he had sat close to him for many months in Calais. 'How can we show that mad Henry knows his mind on this?'

'We will copy Henry's own idea. Remember the Love Day, when we all had to walk the streets of London, feigning our friendship with the Lancastrians? We will do that tomorrow;

Henry and his successor, our Lord of York, will process together to St Paul's for a service of dedication and thanksgiving and we will all follow behind. We will show England, and Marguerite, that King Henry willingly acknowledges York will succeed him.' Warwick looked pleased with his idea, and with how everyone was deferring to him. 'And with God's good grace, the she-wolf will book passage back to France.'

Westminster Palace, London, 9th December 1460

The grey mist swirled around the armoured men as they moved in the dawn light. The knights were mounted and the wagons of supplies and armaments from the Tower of London were loaded and covered in sack cloth. Five thousand men were assembled nearby, armed as best as they could be: York was on the move.

'We are as ready as we will ever be, more ready than we were when we left Ludlow!' The Duke of York tried to be cheerful in front of his duchess as he stood while his squire strapped the shining pauldron to his shoulder. 'Marguerite's forces are assembled in Scotland and will start their march south. We must move now to stop them. She's got the support of Scotland behind her now and she is breaking the Act of Accord. They cannot get close to London or we may be lost.'

'I know my dear. She is undoubtedly intending to release Henry and continue this never-ending bloodshed. I feared the news of your ascendency, and the disinheriting of her son, would be too much for her.'

'Too much for her, and too much for Somerset, God damn him.' York picked up his helm and put it under his arm. 'Thank you, John. Please tell the sergeant I am on my way.'

As the squire left the chamber, Richard knelt before Cecily. 'Your blessing please, my dear.' She placed her right hand on his now-greying hair and whispered a prayer only God could hear. She raised him up and kissed his cheek. 'My beloved husband, my love. You take my blessing with you today and always. You take my precious boy with you also. May the saints watch over you both until your safe return. I will pray so every night.'

As the cavalcade prepared to advance, Cecily stood straight in the morning light; her courage and pride would give heart to the men who rode to support her husband and her House. Mounted next to Richard was Edmund, her clever and thoughtful son of whom she was so proud but often forgot to tell him so. Her warrior son Edward had been dispatched to the Welsh Marches already, charged with raising troops and bringing them to the aid of his father who was headed north. Warwick was commanded to stay and protect London, both from the Red Rose marching south and the French raiding the coast. Her brother Salisbury was behind her husband, eager to return to his strongholds in Yorkshire, riding beside his second son Sir Thomas Neville and Edmund's tutor Master Aspall. The younger children of York had bidden farewell to their father the previous night; Cecily did not want them frightened, seeing this great host departing London to meet Lancaster, with a battle on the horizon.

Her husband and son ensured Cecily could see their salute to her as they departed, their mailed fists held over their hearts. Her heart swelled with love for them, and she impulsively kissed her hand to them all as the procession started away. She kept her eyes on the flag of York and the standard of England, held side by side at the head of the troop, until she could see them no more.

Sandal Castle, Wakefield, Yorkshire, 21ˢᵗ December 1460

The men were finally billeted around the castle grounds and the cannon from the Tower were in place. The blustering wind twisted around the small castle high on the hill, overlooking the town of Wakefield.

'Well, we're ready I suppose,' the Earl of Salisbury muttered out of the side of his mouth. 'We lost a fair few men of our vanguard in the attack at Nottingham last week to that bastard Trollope, but we have about six thousand digging in now. Thank God we made it here at last.'

'Henry Beaufort and his lords are approaching and will be drawing their forces up; maybe they will try to starve us out. They will be taking up positions right in front of the castle. We are not best provisioned here, but with luck and God's good grace, Edward will be on his way with troops from the west soon. Do you think he is up to the task?' The Duke of York paced before the fire, while Thomas Neville and Edmund stared out the narrow window of the barbican tower.

'He is named Earl of March, Richard. The Welsh Marches will gladly give him men enough to fight Lancaster. He will be here, never fear. And many men joined us on our march north, men who are true to York and fearful of the raids the queen's troops are making on their lands.' Salisbury tried a small smile, which seemed to help.

'And John Neville, your half-nephew, he too should be arriving with a force.' The duke grinned at Salisbury, then settled into a chair. 'Beaufort's men may outnumber us now, but I will rest easier when our lads arrive. Remember, Beaufort

54

of Somerset and his lords Clifford and Percy lost their fathers at St Albans; they have scores to settle.'

'Somerset and the cursed Lancastrians do not have cannon, father. We have the advantage there.' Edmund tried to put his father at ease, but he knew as well as anyone that the biting winds and swirling snowflakes would dampen the men's spirits faster than a lack of food would.

'My Lord Duke, a messenger from the Duke of Somerset is without!' Deveraux burst into the chamber, letting the freezing air in behind him.

'Shut the damn door and let us hear it then. What does Henry Beaufort have to say this merry season?' Richard of York seized the parchment and held it near the fire to see it more clearly. 'I'll be damned! The spirit of Yuletide must have entered his bones, he is offering us a truce until the Feast of the Epiphany!'

'Praise God!' Edmund jumped up to read the letter over his father's shoulder. 'I believe this is a miracle father! Edward should be here soon with his men; we won't be starved out of the castle, and we will have enough troops to stop Lancaster marching to London to release Henry and break the Act of Accord! God be praised!'

At the back of the room, unnoticed by all the soldiers of York, Master Aspall bowed his head and whispered 'Amen.'

Sandal Castle, Wakefield, Yorkshire, 30th December 1460
Edmund sprinkled sand on the wet ink of his letter and moved it gently until it dried. He folded the pages, then sealed them with red wax and the pressing in of his ring with the York coat

of arms. He held the parchment in front of his face and kissed the name, but looked over his shoulder quickly to ensure no-one had seen him. He need not have worried; his father and uncle were poring over the inventory of supplies that the castle Chamberlain was showing them and were paying no attention to him. He had no idea how his letters were to reach Ireland; he had never been on campaign before and it seemed to him they were trapped in Sandal Castle until Edward, or John Neville, relieved them. He knew, though, that Eleanor would be looking for a letter from him every day, so he continued to write to her even though they could not yet be sent. He waited until his father had turned to talk to Salisbury, then slipped the letter into Chamberlain Randulf's hand as the old castle guardian left the room. The old man sighed at the young Earl's ardour, then tucked it into his pocket as he shuffled away towards his own chambers, where he added it to the growing pile of messages for an unknown lass from Kildare.

The sparse meal had scarce been cleared from the table and the men were huddling around the meagre fire trying to keep their spirits up and their backsides warm. Christmas had been a miserable affair; freezing cold, poor food and no cheer. The men had not lost heart even so; despite the snow and the hunger they were eager for battle to make the blood flow in their veins.

'My Lord of York, a herald from John Neville approaches!' The castle Marshal was ushered into the room by Deveraux, both breathing heavily from the steep climb up the barbican steps.

'Are you sure man? Sure it's Neville? My nephew?' The Earl of Salisbury pushed past Edmund to reach the marshal. 'Did you see his banner?'

'Yes, my Lord. It's the Neville banner alright, the saltire

argent with the blue fleur-de-lis. The herald called up that his troop is under attack! Their rear guard is facing Lancaster now my lord. They call for York's help!'

'Then York will answer! Deveraux? Sound the horn, I'll take a force out now. Salisbury, you remain here, hold the castle 'til my return. Edmund, you're with me!' The Duke of York grabbed his helmet and started for the door with his son close behind, and the tutor Aspall scurrying to keep up with them both.

The drawbridge clanged down and the duke's troop cantered over, their sight not helped by the flakes of snow whirling around them. The duke was at the head of his men, but scouts galloped past him to find John Neville, led by the herald that had brought the call to arms. The main force left the castle grounds and headed down the winding hill towards the town of Wakefield, peering through the trees while their horses slipped and skidded in the snow. From the left, the Neville Herald suddenly appeared through the hedgerow and the York forces swung their horses towards him, ready to come to his aid. The Duke of York raised his right hand in greeting, then froze as he saw the quartered shield of Somerset, waving high above the heavily armoured knights charging out of the snow to surround his troops.

'Traitors! Traitors! Deveraux! Get back to castle! Tell Salisbury we've been betrayed, tell him we're under attack. Edmund, head north, get away from here, try to make it to Middleham. Raise the alarm. York needs you now, son!' The duke shouted commands over his shoulder as he drew his sword and called for a formation to confront the Somerset troops. He saw his son and his man gallop away as he had ordered, then lifted his sword in his right arm as he faced his enemy. 'York, for York!' He screamed as he led the charge forward.

Salisbury and the castle troops streamed out of the castle and down the hill where he had seen the duke head. The snow was easing now but his horse stumbled on a hidden rock, then he felt a massive blow to his shoulder and saw the lance glance off his armour. The force of it threw him backwards and his helm came clean off as he hit the ground, lying winded on his back. The earl rolled to his right, then tried to get one knee and draw his sword, but looked up to see the mocking face of Henry Percy, Earl of Northumberland, his long-time enemy. 'Look men!' Percy called to the soldiers around him, 'we have a matched pair! York and Salisbury, captured like a brace of coneys!' All around him, he could hear the clang of metal on metal where the forces of Lancaster outnumbered and slaughtered his men. Salisbury felt his sword knocked from his hand, then a strong arm came around his neck and pushed him through a copse of trees to where more men were gathered around something he could not see. The crowd parted as Salisbury was pushed forward, and he saw the Duke of York on his knees staring defiantly up into the face of Henry Beaufort, Duke of Somerset.

'Salisbury, glad you could make it!' Somerset's voice was filled with laughter. 'You bastards must answer for St Albans. We lost our fathers to you York scum, time to pay for that now.' Somerset drew his sword and raised it high in the air, a few snowflakes settling onto the steel. 'Any last words, King of York? Any last words before I send you to hell?' The Duke of York smiled up at his enemy, and his voice rang out clearly.

'Do you think this is over now, Beaufort? Do you think by killing me these troubles will end? We have sons, you know. Like *your* fathers, we have sons that will never forget, and never forgive.'

'Your sons are just pups, they can never face the might of Lancaster. Know this, my Lord Duke. York is finished now; it ends with your death.' Somerset looked to Salisbury, 'Both of your deaths. King Henry and his son will reign, while your House is reduced to dust along with your bones. Any last words?'

'Wait!' The Earl of Salisbury started forward, breaking free from the arm around his neck. 'Wait, you can grant quarter, we can pay a ransom, we can ...'

'No, my old friend.' The Duke of York turned and looked at his brother-by-law. 'It is time for our sons to step forward. They will carry the banner for York.' He bowed his head and the soldiers closest to him heard him pray, 'Lord, forgive my trespasses and take me to Your glory.' He raised his head to the grey sky above, and saw the glinting steel of Somerset's sword flash through the air.

Richard Plantagenet lay dead on the ground, his blood soaking into the soil of Yorkshire.

Edmund and his tutor Robert Aspall skirted the edge of the main forces fighting in the snow, ducking behind trees and fences, their boots already soaking. They had left the horses, thinking to go unnoticed on foot. They were headed away from Sandal Castle, heading north towards the Salisbury base of Middleham Castle. Master Aspall knew it was a three-day journey on horseback, but God knew how long it would take walking. His first concern though was to get as far away from the battle as he could. He knew, as he had known for years, that Edmund was in his care; this young man he loved like his own. They both darted from behind an upturned wagon on the road to Wakefield and could see a church looming near and Master Aspall grabbed

Edmund's sleeve. 'Quick, my Lord, head for the chapel. Perhaps we can take sanctuary there 'til it is safe to go on.'

'I should not be running, I should be standing with my father!' Edmund hissed at the old man, not sure why he was trying to keep his voice down over the shouts and cries of the men and horses facing slaughter behind him.

'It was your father who sent you to get reinforcements. We must carry out his wishes, we have to fetch help. It is your duty to obey your father, and right now, it is our duty to get out of here alive. God alone knows where Marguerite is, she could be round the next corner. York was betrayed; we must raise the alarm and send word to your brother.' The Chapel of St Mary the Virgin stood firmly on the bridge over the River Calder, its solid presence looking serene despite the bloodshed going on nearby. 'Follow me, keep close and head for the chapel's side door.'

Aspall was two steps ahead of his young charge as they approached the bridge towards their temporary safety, but when two massive chestnut horses rode up behind them closely followed by a dozen men-at-arms, it was Edmund who stepped to the front.

'York? Are you York?' A young, angry man shouted down from his destrier, his horse's legs splattered with the blood and mud of battle. 'You must be York if you are headed away north!' Aspall recognised the blue and yellow chequered arms of the Lancastrian John Clifford, held high by the squire behind his master, and pulled at Edmund's surcoat. 'We are just castle servants, my lord, trying to keep ourselves safe.'

'And since when do castle servants wear armour?' Lord Clifford looked down at Edmund, who had put his hand onto his sword hilt. 'Disarm him!' Clifford shouted to his troop who had them surrounded. 'Who are you?' Lord Clifford snarled his question.

Edmund felt his sword arm dragged behind him and jerked up towards his shoulder blades.

'I am Edmund, Earl of Rutland, son of Richard Duke of York!' Edmund spoke proudly, raising his chin in defiance of the man and the pain.

'Son of the *late* Duke of York,' Clifford smiled as he dismounted his horse. 'Your noble father is dead, beheaded, and now here we have his son! God is truly smiling on Lancaster this day.'

'My Lord Clifford, I beg you. For the love of Christ, do not hurt this boy. He is the son of a great man, and his family will pay a handsome reward for him.' Master Aspall clasped his hands together, and tried to get in front of the seventeen-year-old-boy. 'I beseech you, my Lord. Pray do not harm him.' The tears were running down the old man's face, but Clifford brushed him aside.

'We give no quarter, take no ransoms. His father killed mine at St Albans, and now, as honour demands, I will take his son.' Clifford drew his dagger, as the tutor cried out.

'Honour? This is not honourable! He is just a boy! Please, my Lord! Edmund!' Master Aspall started to kneel and beg but was dragged aside and had a short sword thrust between his ribs from behind. Edmund tried to pull away from the strong grasp holding him as he watched his old tutor fall in the shadow of the church dedicated to the mother of Christ, but felt his hair being pulled and his head tipped backwards, exposing his neck to Clifford's blade. He did not feel the slice across his throat at first, but as he was released and started to crumble to the stone ground, he brought his hands up to the wound. Edmund fell to his knees, and as he looked at his bloody hands before his face, the winter sun glinted off the blue stone on his thumb.

Baynard's Castle, London, 5th January 1461

Kat was making notes at Duchess Cecily's direction. 'So, we'll end the banquet with the custard tart and the ginger pears. Make sure Cook knows not to use the saffron this time. The price of it is quite ridiculous these days, and I'm not sure that it adds much to the dish anyway. The Epiphany Feast is about celebrating Jesus' revelation to the Magi, not to eat the most expensive spice the merchants have to offer.' Cecily sat back with a smile, while the faithful Kat gathered her papers together. 'Really, I must tell George to make less noise, he is bellowing like a bereft cow.' She rose and went to the window which looked towards St Paul's, and saw George in the courtyard below, greeting the Earl of Warwick. Her nephew threw his reins to a waiting groom, brushed the boy aside and made for the door to the private chambers.

'Kat, stay with me.' The duchess did not believe in premonitions, her faith was too strong, but she could not say why she was dreading this unexpected visit.

The Earl of Warwick knelt before Cecily. 'Beloved aunt, I ask for your blessing. I also ask for your forgiveness for what news I bring you.'

Cecily could not find her voice to answer, but drew him up to his feet. 'My Lady, the news is most grave. I have heard from the north.'

'From Richard? '

'From Chamberlain Randulf. The Duke of York, your

62

husband, is dead. Killed in battle at Sandal. My father Salisbury is also dead, taken from the field and executed at Pontefract.' Tears gathered in the corner of Warwick's eyes, but he continued to look straight at Cecily.

'Edmund.' Cecily's voice was flat and without emotion. 'Edmund lives?'

'No. Edmund is dead. The duke is dead.' Warwick drew a deep breath and continued. 'It is worse than you know, my Lady aunt. They were both beheaded and their heads mounted on spikes at Micklegate Bar in York. My father and brother Thomas too.'

Cecily felt her elbow grasped by Kat, and she was lowered into her padded chair by the fire. She grasped the beads at her girdle, lowered her head and began to pray. Warwick and Kat looked at each other over Cecily's head, both waiting for the tears to come. They listened to the sounds of everyday life continuing in the castle, the sounds of people going about their business, not knowing that their world was collapsing around them.

Finally Duchess Cecily lifted her head, but her beautiful face was dry. 'Warwick, send men to inform my son Edward. He must take his father's seat. Kat, send for the Steward, he is to commandeer a ship straight away. Tell Nurse to pack George and Richard's gear; sons of York are precious now. Go now, and do my bidding.' Cecily stood up from her chair and faced them both. 'My heart is broken, but not my spirit. Tell our people that York fights on.' Kat bobbed a curtsey and hurried away, but Warwick was slower to leave. He knelt again before her.

'I swear on the souls of my brother and father that I will see Lancaster brought down. I swear that I will guide and support your son Edward to the very throne of England. I swear all this in the name of Neville and York.' He stood, gave a deep bow to the duchess and headed for the door.

Alone now, a widow, Cecily felt the tears streaming down her face and blurring her vision. She gazed at the crucifix mounted on the wall until her eyes could see again. The only words she whispered were, 'My love, my boy, my love, my boy.' She went to her table, sat down, and drew her Book of Hours towards her.

County Kildare, Ireland, 1461

The girl in the blue dress knelt on wet grass, the letter still trailing from her hand. She looked up at the grey sky and the raindrops mingled with the tears on her face. She watched the sun try to break out from behind the clouds, and as she watched, she cried. As she cried, she sang, '*Ar dheis Dé go raibh a anam, Ar dheis Dé go raibh a anam.* May his soul be at God's right hand.'

CHAPTER 2

Exultabunt Domino ossa humiliata.
To our Lord shall rejoice the humbled bones.

Greenwich Docks, London, 6ᵗʰ January 1461

George and Richard Plantagenet stood by the rail of the small boat and watched as their mother raised her hand in farewell. They looked small and lost to Cecily as the tide took them further away from her. Both boys were in shock from the news of their father and brother Edmund, then their mother had bundled them into warm clothes and almost dragged them to the docks under the cover of darkness. Cecily knew they must feel unwanted and unloved, but she also knew she had no choice; Edward was beyond her control now, God and the Red Rose of Lancaster would decide his fate, but she would do everything in her power to keep her youngest boys safe. The House of York had lost its leader and one son; she was determined some would be saved.

A messenger had been sent ahead to Philip Duke of Burgundy, begging for safety and shelter for George and young Richard. She had sent William Colyngbourne, her most able man, and Duchess Cecily hoped their arrival in Utrecht in the Low Countries would be expected. Nurse Ann had packed their belongings in a panic and she, along with the boys' manservant Thomas Parr, accompanied them.

As the boat disappeared from view along the Thames and headed for the sea, the widow Cecily knelt on the slimy pier and prayed she would see them again in this lifetime.

Hereford Castle, 7th January 1461

Edward watched as the skin of wine dripped on to the stone floor. He made no move to right it or to stop the flow as the puddle below grew larger. The broken chairs and smashed dresser table served as a reminder of the violence he was capable of, and of the powerful grief and rage he had felt when he read the message containing news of the death of his father and the slaughter of his brother. His fury and anguish were no longer visible to his nervous squire Nate; his initial anguish was suppressed as he watched the wine seep away and he mustered his temper and his thoughts. His closest friend, Sir William Hastings, stood with his back to the door; William was a good height but not as tall as Edward, and had a black beard just like the late Duke of York which Edward found comforting but he knew he could never voice that thought out loud. The two men watched the new eighteen-year-old Duke of York while both seemed to look elsewhere.

'Will,' Edward passed Hastings the letter. 'What else does my cousin of Warwick say?' He stretched out his arm with the parchment without looking at his friend. If there had been tears on his face they had dried now, but his voice was flat and expressionless.

'After he tells of the news from Wakefield, Your Grace, the earl has news that Marguerite's army are marching south from

Scotland. Your Uncle Fauconberg has joined him in London where they expect the Lancastrians to march on the capital to retake it and free King Henry. He, umm, commands you to muster your troops and march to London to meet him and join his defences.' Hastings handed the letter to Nate, who rolled it and replaced it in the leather case.

Edward stood to his great height and lifted the wine skin and replaced it carefully on the table. 'The *Earl* of Warwick commands the *Duke* of York? What do you think of that boys?' The squire smiled and looked at his boots, while Hastings met his friend's eye.

'I think the Earl means *please* join him in London, Your Grace. Shall I send out the commissions of array?'

'Yes Will. Summon my army and we will crush these bastards.'

The Narrow Sea, 9th January 1461

George and Richard were lying in their bunks, the swaying of the ship soothing their fraught souls. If young Richard was quiet after the sacking of Ludlow, he had been almost mute since their mother had told them of father and Edmund. His world had been shattered that day, and it did not look to be improving. George had insisted on bringing his father's hound with them, and that piece of home was a small comfort to them. Tommy and Nursey Ann were on pallet beds near the boys where they both lay awake listening to their breathing. Neither had any words of comfort for the lads but were both determined to do everything in their power to protect and comfort them in the days ahead. Nurse Ann's heart was gripped with fear, not knowing how long the arm of Lancaster could reach; would it stretch out across the water and snatch her little boys away as poor Edmund had been taken? She knew she would lay down her life to safeguard her charges, but what could she do in reality if Queen Marguerite reached her claws out this far?

The weak dawn sun was breaking through the clouds when the tramp of feet was heard approaching the cabin door. Tommy Parr jumped from his straw matting clutching a slim dagger in his hand, but Nurse Ann was up before him, calm in the knowledge that at this moment at least they were safe from enemies. She opened the door to see the Shipmaster's lad, filthy in rags but wearing decent boots.

'Cap'n says to tell you that land's in sight. We're to put in at Rotterdam mistress. We'll dock by nightfall.'

Nurse Ann reached out to pat the boy on the head. He flinched from her touch, being more used to a clip round the ear than affection, but seemed pleased when she replied, 'You have done a fine job of getting us here safely sir. You are a good sailor and we have been well preserved in your care.' She turned to the boys in their beds.

'Master Richard, time to get up and find your boots. Remember to put on your warm coat.' She made an effort to sound lively and brisk. 'Master George, go with Tommy and take Merry up on deck. We'll have no mess in here thank you. Come on, we've plenty to do and not much time.' For a few moments, the nurse's hustling manner was reminiscent of being at home and the boys were content to follow her commands.

Baynard's Castle, London, 10*th* January 1461

As he rode past St Paul's, Warwick felt his mood lifting. The defeat at Wakefield, the death of his father and brother, had left him breathless with shock but he had had to pull himself together. He was a commander, he was a leader. Leaders could not feel weakness or have doubts and he was sure of his next moves. He must stop the Lancastrians at all costs; that she-wolf Marguerite, that bitch who had executed his father must be stopped. Men were looking to him now, and he must not fail. He glanced behind him to ensure his men were in good formation, smart and riding in line; the London crowds must have faith in him as their protector and he needed to look powerful in their eyes.

'Well nephew, now I have no sons. Edmund butchered at seventeen, not even a man, Edward is off in the west and I sent my little ones away. My husband is dead and I am no longer sure why God put me on this earth.' Duchess Cecily was very low in her spirits, and had given way to self-pity. Warwick was shocked at the decline in her since he had given her the news from Sandal Castle. She had looked determined then but now she was haggard and drawn; her dark blue mourning gown with the furred hem seem to hang off her and the skin was stretched across her cheeks.

'My beloved aunt, you cannot despair. York needs you now!'

'No-one needs me, except perhaps Margaret. I don't even have that dog for company, and I am not sure I was ever fond of him anyway.'

'You are the Duchess of York! You must hold the White Rose high in London!'

'I am the Dowager Duchess. My beloved Richard is dead and his head hangs on York's gate wearing a paper crown. I feel the White Rose has been trampled into the ground.'

'Not so!' Warwick took Cecily's hands in his and squeezed them tight. 'I know things look bleak but all is not lost. The little boys are safe and out of harm's way. Edward is strong and men flock to him; he is gathering troops from the Welsh Marches to form under our banner. More men gather in our ranks here every day; the Council has granted us more money so we can raise the defences in London and we are strong!'

Duchess Cecily smiled weakly at her nephew and patted his hand. She sat down in her husband's chair and nodded her head. 'You are right, of course, I know you are. It is just that without my husband to follow, I am lost.'

'You must be strong, aunt, you must rally. You *are* strong, and in London, you are the figurehead of the House of York. All will look to you; if you despair, London will fall.' Warwick sat beside Cecily and rested his hand on her Book of Hours, which she always now kept near her. 'I swore fealty to your husband and to that I hold. You have children who need you, and people who depend on you. You cannot fail now.'

The duchess took a deep breath, and rested her hand on top of Warwick's, on top of her holy book where the names of her dead were written. She must rally, or she may be forced to write more names.

'Very well.' She raised her head and looked at him with a glimmer of her old spirit. 'I hear Queen Marguerite is headed south from Scotland now and has promised her savage troops they can plunder and profit from every village they pass through. What are our plans?'

Bloemendaal, The Low Countries, 15th January 1461
The small coaching inn was comfortable and warm but the taverner's wife was not much of a cook. George and Richard

had laid down their spoons and crept out of the door to the yard when the old lady had been rattling the pots in the smoky kitchen. Tommy watched them from the doorway while Nurse Ann stayed at table, pretending to enjoy the questionable mutton stew, happy that the boys were taking an interest in their surroundings. They had docked at Rotterdam and the fishy smell permeating the air there had turned all their stomachs and they had been glad to get away. The carriage they rented was not well sprung, but they all felt better to get away from the screaming gulls and shouting trawlermen and start their journey across the Low Countries. George seemed more pleased the further they got from England, as though he felt safer the further he was away from the land that killed his father. Young Richard was the opposite, Nurse thought; his heart got heavier with each mile between him and his homeland.

The boys were collecting acorns and throwing them to the fat pigs in the rough garden of the inn while Tommy drew in the dust with a stick.

'What's to become of us do you think, George?' Richard turned to his eleven-year-old brother. 'Does our Lady mother not want us at home anymore?'

'She sent us away to keep us safe. The supporters of King Henry killed father and Edmund, she is frightened they will kill us too.' George sounded matter of fact with this statement, but his heart fluttered with fear at the thought of the slaughter at Sandal.

'But when will we go home? I don't want to live anywhere but England, I want to live with mother and Margaret and I don't know where we are going.' Richard's voice was getting plaintive and Tommy quickly stepped in.

'Don't upset yourself Master Richard. Your Lady mother knows this is the right thing to do. She knows it will be hard for you for a while, but we have to keep you safe. The Duke of Burgundy has promised you'll be safe under his protection. Think of that lad! A duke! Promising to look after you!'

'Father was a duke. He couldn't keep us safe. Anyway, we won't be living in a palace or a castle with him, we'll just be living in one of his houses.' George scuffed his boots on the dusty ground and cleared his throat. At that moment he was trying to be the man of the situation, the older brother to whom Richard could look up. If Edward were to die soon, George himself would be Duke of York, then he would be head of the family he thought. 'I'll protect you, Richard. I'll kill all the damned Lancastrians then we can go back to mother and Margaret and be happy again. We just have to wait a while 'til it's safe to go home.'

Hereford Castle, 1ˢᵗ February 1461

The new Duke of York was ready. He had men assembled from eight counties, about five thousand in all. He had good captains; alongside his dependable Hastings were the Herbert brothers from Raglan and old Lord Audley. He had an exceptionable troop of experienced archers armed with their deadly yew bows the size of a man. All he lacked was experience in battle, but he made up for this with determination, pride and the rage of a man who had lost father and brother.

Hastings and Edward were poring over a map, planning their route to London. Warwick and Fauconberg were awaiting their arrival, desperate to secure the capital from Queen Marguerite's troops who were sure to set siege to it to rescue her husband and secure the inheritance for her son. They heard a commotion in the inner bailey and the tramp of metal sabatons on the stone floor. They raised their heads as the squire Nate burst open the door.

'Your pardon, Your Grace, but the scouts are here.' Two men, fully armoured and wearing a surcoat of murrey and blue, crowded in behind the lad and bowed their heads.

'My Lord York, an army has been spotted formed up to our north. Lancastrians, led by The Tudors from Pembroke and their mercenaries. About four thousand men sire. Headed this way.' The breathless scout finished in a rush, not sure what other information he had to impart.

'To our north?' Edward looked at Hastings, his initial shock fading quickly. 'Will, we cannot head east to London with the bloody Welsh up our arses!' His excitement at impending battle lit up his eyes. 'We have to change our plans, we have to go up and cut them off. Send word to the captains and the men. North it is!'

Hastings gave a curt bow to the taller man thirteen years his junior. 'Warwick will have to wait.'

Market Square, Hereford, 3rd February 1461

The coppery smell of blood filled the air as the local people, come to see a spectacle, turned and headed for their homes. Edward and Hastings stood at the foot of the market cross, careful not to tread in the sticky blood.

'Do you think he really thought we would spare him?' Edward looked on as Owain Tudor's headless body was wrapped in sack cloth and bundled into a cart by the executioner's boys. 'Did he believe we would let him go so he could run off to France with his son Jasper? Can a man be that deceived?'

'Well, he certainly believed his head would be back in Queen Katherine's lap when he saw the axe. He didn't know you, Edward. He didn't know what a man you have become.'

Edward looked at his friend, sure there was not a rebuke in those words, but a compliment instead, which he was happy to accept.

As they turned to retrieve their horses, an old woman approached the square from a side street. She walked passed Edward and Hastings as though she couldn't see them and walked through the bloody mess as though it didn't trouble her. She bent down and reached under the makeshift scaffold that had been hastily built, and dragged out the head of Owain Tudor. She held it up to the sky and smiled into the waxen face and cradled it under her arm for a moment, before setting it down carefully on the steps of the market cross. She neatened the straggling, matted hair on the decapitated head and reached into her sleeve for a candle which she set down carefully in the filth.

The two soldiers, now blooded from their first battle, watched in amazement as she knelt in front of the head and began to pray.

'Jesus,' Edward breathed.

'Indeed.' Hastings clasped his hand on the Duke's shoulder and led him away. 'Funny folk, the Welsh.'

Utrecht, *The Low Countries, 9th February 1461*
The grey stone town house, three stories tall, was set near the marketplace which Nurse Ann thought convenient for them all. It gave her a reason to take the boys on a daily walk to keep them busy, and they could sample the fresh fruit and strange shaped

bread that they had come to love. She had been pleased with the house that had generously been assigned to them by the Duke of Burgundy; it was large and spacious but she was not sure if it was imposing enough for the sons of the House of York, but perhaps better not to advertise their presence here too much. It had a large orchard garden, where George spent hours throwing sticks for his hound. The nurse had tried to make the living arrangements comfortable and comforting for her charges, and with the help of William Colyngbourne, sent ahead by Duchess Cecily, she had been able to buy extra tapestries and warm furs to keep them cosy during the bitter evenings. Young Richard had not mentioned the pain in his back for quite a while, so Nurse was sure her ministrations were working. William had warmly welcomed them to Utrecht, but made no mention of them meeting the duke or any of his people, but instead had tried his best to be of use to the displaced little family and was kind to George and Richard. He was good looking, tall and smartly dressed in his dark red velvet short houppelande, and attracted many admiring glances when he took the lads on trips around the town and on slow boats along the canal. Nurse Ann, however, was immune to the charms of all men; she was utterly devoted only to her young charges.

Tommy found the nurse sitting in the small rear parlour she had commandeered as her own. She was sewing, attempting the white-on-white embroidery that seemed popular in the town. She had seen it on the cuffs and collars of some smartly dressed citizens, and was trying it on one of George's shirts; she gave a small smile, knowing that the good-looking young boy was taking an interest in his appearance now.

'My Lady, a letter from England, from Duchess Cecily!'

He handed her the grubby paper with a grin; 'The boys will be pleased to hear from their mother.'

'Only if it is good news, and don't call me my Lady, call me Nurse please.' She broke the seal and opened the long-awaited letter.

'Yes, my Lady. Is it good news?'

'Good news for York! Master Edward, I mean the new Duke of York, has won his first battle! Goodness me, he is very young to be in a battle, let alone commanding one! The Duchess must be sick with worry for him, I do hope he is looking after himself and eating well. You do hear such terrible things about soldiers in the field; dirty tents, poor food and no water. I hope his squire is making sure he has clean linen and sturdy boots.'

'My Lady! What of the battle? What does the Duchess say?' Tommy was breathless with anticipation and hopping from foot to foot with excitement.

'It was in the western Marches, at a place called Mortimer's Cross. What a lovely name!' Nurse Ann scanned the letter and passed it back to Tommy. 'Yes, our dear Edward has won a battle for York. Old Owain Tudor, him who was married to Queen Katherine of Valois is dead now though. What a shame for poor young Henry Tudor, lost his father now his grandfather. Shouldn't have supported the Lancastrians though, should he?'

Tommy snatched the letter and dropped into the window seat and read it avidly, savouring every detail.

'And just before the battle was to start, your brother Edward saw the most marvellous thing in the sky!' George and Richard were hanging on Tommy's every word, their eyes wide with an excitement that had not shown on their faces in months.

'It was early on Candlemas Day, and all the soldiers were formed up and ready to fight. Each side had three battles facing each other with the archers in good position. Just as they were ready to charge, the most wondrous thing happened! Three suns appeared in the sky! Three suns, just think!'

'Three suns? How is that possible, what did it mean?' Richard's sat forward in his chair, clasping his hands together. 'Were the soldiers frightened?'

'Edward told them it was a sign from God himself! He told the men the suns were for the Holy Trinity; God the Father, God the Son, and God the Holy Ghost! He said the three suns in the sky were also for the three sons of York, you, George and Edward, who will be reunited! With God sending such a sign, the men knelt and prayed, then won the battle for Edward and for York!'

'Three sons! Does that mean we can go home now? Does Edward send for us to come back to England?' George pushed Richard's shoulder so he could get closer to Tommy. 'Does mother say we can go home?'

'No.' The exuberant mood flattened. 'No, you have not been sent for yet. The Duchess says we're to stay here for now. She says it is a victory, and we must thank God for that, but it is not enough. It is not safe in England for you yet.'

L'Erber, Earl of Warwick's London Home, 11th February 1461
Warwick tried to read the letter carefully, usually pleased to hear from his wife, but found difficulty concentrating on domestic matters when he had so much to plan here in London. His Countess, Anne, wrote frequent and brisk letters to her husband,

whether she was at their castle in Warwick or Middleham in Yorkshire. She knew he missed so much of their home affairs and the progress of their daughters Isabel and Anne, that she thought he appreciated her detailed accounts of rents collected, servant disputes and the fact the growing girls regularly required new gowns. Today, however, Warwick could not have recalled one single piece of information from the Countess's letter the minute after he laid it aside.

Instead, he tightened the fur collar at his neck against the cold and moved closer to the fire. He pulled towards him the long list of armoury he had ordered to be assembled. Tomorrow he would head north to intercept and halt the ravaging progress of Queen Marguerite's army as it headed toward London, and he wanted to check again that everything was prepared. He knew the army he would face was fearsome; they were burning, looting and raping a path south and had strong Lancastrian soldiers as their captains. Warwick had about ten thousand men and he feared the Red Rose would outnumber him, but he had more than men; he had handgunners from Burgundy, good English archers, the iron ground spikes called caltrops that would stop both soldiers and horses, rolls of barbed wire, and he had his brother. John Neville was Warwick's trusted captain, a good solider and utterly loyal to their House. He felt confident, perhaps invincible, that the Neville brothers would come together to avenge their father and their lost sibling Thomas.

All this Warwick had ordered assembled and ready to leave at dawn. But he planned a further weapon to bring to St Albans; he was bringing King Henry. Warwick knew he would be facing the army of the Queen, so by bringing old mad Harry, he would be fighting under the royal standard of England without fear of accusations of treason. Of course, King Henry would not be armoured on horseback; he had ordered two good men to find a safe place to stow the feeble king and keep him safe, but the very fact that the king was in his possession made Warwick secure in the knowledge that right was on his side.

After the Red Rose had been wiped out, there was nothing in the way of Edward being proclaimed heir to the throne of England, as was his right under the Act of Accord. Warwick was certain, and Warwick was never wrong.

Baynard's Castle, London, 17th February 1461

Duchess Cecily woke from a deep slumber to Kat, her most trusted lady, shaking her shoulder. Her bed was cold, the only warm spot was the side facing the banked fire. Young Margaret had not wanted to sleep alone since the boys had been sent away and had begged to share her mother's bed, but Cecily refused, knowing she was surviving on her nerves now; sleep was vital to keep her strength up.

'Your Grace, you must wake. There is a man without, sent by the Earl of Warwick. He says he brings most important news.'

'I am awake Kat. Fetch my warmest robe, and my wimple. I'll not see a man half naked, no matter how urgent the message.'

Duchess Cecily was seated in her retiring chamber when the man was shown in. She could glimpse the moonlight though the shutters at the window, and the pale gleam helped lighten the room. The man wore a leather jupon with the emblem of the Bear and the Ragged Staff on his breast; Warwick's badge. He walked stiffly, having ridden the forty miles south at breakneck speed, his horse half-dead beneath him. His face was long and thin, his hair straggling around his collar, and he groaned quietly as he knelt before her.

'Your Grace of York, I am sent by the Earl of Warwick at St Albans. The news is not good, my Lady.'

'I am used to bad news sirrah. I am an expert in it. Pray tell your message.' Cecily took a deep breath and waited.

So the man told his tale of defeat. He told of how Warwick had tried to block Queen Marguerite's army from reaching London, coming down Watling Street, how he had set up good defences, strong defences in the town facing north, but was fooled. They were hit hard by Henry Beaufort Duke of Somerset, Lord Clifford and Sir Andrew Trollope, but they hit from Warwick's rear, and all his fine weapons were useless. They had been outmanoeuvred, attacked from the southeast, thanks to the treachery of Sir Henry Lovelace, who had agreed to betray the Yorkists as the price for his freedom after being captured at Wakefield. The rain added to the awful scene and the battle was lost amid confusion, blood and slaughter. York lost around two thousand men; the Lancastrian dead were half that number, with the only notable loss being Sir John Grey of Groby, who left his widow Elizabeth and two young sons. Worse still, King Henry, who had been taken in Warwick's train to St Albans, had been left behind in the retreat. He had been guarded by two York veterans, Sir Thomas Kyriell and Lord Bonville, who took the king to Queen Marguerite to hand him over at the defeat; he had been singing and praying in his madness under a tree during the battle. Instead of ransoming or releasing the guards, seven-year-old Lancastrian Prince Edouard of Westminster demanded they be beheaded in the field. Warwick finished his message by informing the Duchess that he would lead his remaining army toward the Cotswolds where he hoped to meet up with the Duke of York.

Duchess Cecily regarded the man kneeling before her, her cold eyes piercing in her beautiful face. 'So the king and queen are reunited, thousands more are dead, the battle lost and the army is retreating. How well Warwick does serve York.'

Utrecht, The Low Countries, 19th February 1461

'Master Colyngbourne, I do insist.' Nurse Ann was as tall as the man in front of her, but her indignation gave the illusion of greater height. 'The young masters must be told and I *will* see it happen. Duchess Cecily herself tells me so.'

'Madam, I would not countermand the duchess, but must they be told *now*? Would it not be better to wait and see what the Duke of York and Earl Warwick will do next?'

'The duchess's letter states "Tell George and Richard the news, but tell them not to give up hope. Tell them to pray to God and to their father in Heaven. Tell them York fights on." So I will tell them, and you will stand beside me when I do!' The nurse turned her head as the front door opened and the two lads came tumbling into the house. They had been with Tommy to St Martin's Cathedral to climb the Dom Tower, which from their front windows seemed to stretch right up into the clouds. The hound, left behind that morning, went romping up to the boys, and on his hind legs tried to lick their faces.

'Get down Merry, you stink! Good day Master Colyngbourne. Nursey, can we have some bread and meat?

We're so hungry we can't wait until dinner.' George took the lead in bowing to their visitor, and Tommy wrestled the dog towards the kitchens. Richard, however, was looking at the grave faces of the adults and stood as still as one of statues in the church.

'We have heard today from your Lady mother, boys.' William took a step forward; his duty clear to him now. 'Your cousin of Warwick, in trying to stop Queen Marguerite's forces, met them in battle.' George looked up hopeful for a moment, then saw the solemnity in the Colyngbourne's eyes then dropped his head.

'The battle was lost,' William continued, 'and King Henry has been reunited with his Queen and his son. But not all hope is lost; the earl has joined forces with your brother the duke and the fight goes on. So, say a prayer for the men lost, and a Hail Mary for the future.'

Richard took a step forward. 'Was there a traitor?'

Guildhall, London, 20th February 1461

The Lord Mayor of London had never been in the presence of one duchess before, let alone two. Sir Hugh Wyche was unsure of how he should address them; was it 'Your Grace, Your Grace' or 'Your Graces'? He was a good man at heart who had sworn to protect and serve the people of London, but was more comfortable dealing with merchants like himself rather than the nobility. However, times such as these called for every man to do their duty, so he slicked back his silver hair and straightened his chain of office.

'Her Grace the Duchess of Buckingham and Her Grace the Duchess of Bedford.' His page announced the two loyal

Lancastrian women and bowed them into his receiving chamber. Sir Hugh stood up and gave a deep bow.

'Your Ladyships.' That seemed sensible and safe to him. 'Please be seated.'

Anne, Duchess of Buckingham and sister to Cecily, widow of Humphrey Stafford, sat first. Her face was severe and she clasped her hands in her lap. Jacquetta Woodville, Dowager Duchess of Bedford, smiled at the nervous mayor. At forty-five, she was still beautiful, and had a fine pedigree. She was the widow of John Duke of Bedford, brother of Henry V, and daughter of the Count of St-Pol of Luxembourg. She had rather spoiled her fine heritage by marrying her late husband's squire, Richard Woodville, but she was still a great personage in the eyes of the Lord Mayor. She was also mother to Elizabeth Grey, she who had been widowed at St Albans.

'Sir Hugh, we have been conversing with Her Grace Queen Marguerite since her victory over the Yorkists at St Albans,' Jacquetta began in her soft voice, 'and have come with directives from her. As you refused her food and supplies...'

'Your Ladyship, I did not refuse her, they were stolen by the people when they heard of the robbery and pillaging of her army and of the news that the Earl of Warwick and Duke of York are near to London.' He stood and began to pace. 'I agreed to open the city gates to her if she gave such promises that would protect the people of London from these crimes.' Sir Hugh was breathless with distress, but determined that he was seen as fair and just when dealing with an anointed queen.

'Queen Marguerite has heard reports that the citizens of her capital city refuse to allow you to open the gates!' the Duchess of Buckingham barked at the man. 'Are you so weak you have no control over this rabble?'

At this, Sir Hugh seemed to swell with indignation. He stood and walked to the door.

'Your Ladyships, please relay this message to Queen Marguerite. London will allow her no access. London will not be savaged like the rest of the country. We know her soldiers are deserting and we know she has not the power to lay siege to the capital. We also know that the forces of York will be here shortly. London suggests she return whence she came.'

The two duchesses swept from the room without a word of farewell. As the door slammed behind them, the Lord Mayor collapsed into his chair, astonished at himself.

One week later, Sir Hugh stood outside the Guildhall in his finest robes, cheering along with his citizens. The new Duke of York, resplendent in shining armour, trotted his black destrier alongside the Earl of Warwick's grey warhorse, leading ten thousand victorious men of York. The loyal people cheered as the cavalcade processed through the streets of London, awed at the sight and thankful the Lancastrian threat was over. The Lord Mayor joined in with the cries for 'The Rose of Rouen' being shouted for Edward, who acknowledged the acclaim with joy and regal waves. Next to him, the Earl of Warwick smiled thinly.

Baynard's Castle, London, 4ᵗʰ March 1461

Duchess Cecily graciously inclined her head as the deputation were ushered from the great hall. The men, representing the Lords and Commons of England, bowed from the waist, replaced their fine chaperons on their heads and departed.

As the door closed behind them she fell back into her seat to the consternation of Kat and Margaret. They rushed forward as the duchess leant her head down to her knees, thinking she was faint but she came up smiling; smiling and crying.

Edward, at her side, had remained upright, still staring at the door. He looked down at his mother, and his handsome face broke out into joy.

'Edward, oh Edward! King! King at last!' Words were failing Cecily, and she stood up and grasped his hands. 'They have offered you the throne of England!'

'It is my right, or my father's right. Lady Mother, I would rather be a pauper and see father on the throne, as was promised, but as it cannot be…well, it is just and lawful that it should come to me.'

'Of course it is, my son. Your father knew you would make a good king for England, to bring an end to all these troubles.' Duchess Cecily sunk into a deep curtsey in front of her eldest son. 'My Liege.'

Utrecht, The Low Countries, 10ᵗʰ March 1461

George and Richard sat on the bench in the largest chamber in their borrowed house, their mouths open.

'King?' Master Colyngbourne nodded at George.

'Edward is king?' Nurse Ann, at the side of the children, seemed to sway from side to side. 'The baby I've looked after since his birth is King of England?'

'Yes. He was offered the crown six days ago in Westminster Abbey. He was given the sceptre and crown of Edward the Confessor and is king but refuses to have a formal coronation until the armies of Henry and Marguerite are crushed once and for all. But he is King of England.'

'Until their armies are crushed? That means another battle I suppose.' The nurse looked at Richard, and was quick to reassure him. 'Then I am sure you will be sent for, I am sure you will be able to go home.' Richard nodded, still smiling at the news. His back was aching, but for a while he could forget his pain in the joy of the moment.

Tommy tumbled through the door towards the kitchen, bidding the cook to bring wine and pastries to celebrate. The others looked at each other, grins forming on their faces. All except George. George rose, bowed to the adults present, and went outside to the orchard. Merry followed, not comfortable with the unfamiliar silence in this normally boisterous house. George lay down on the damp grass and stared at the sky. He thoughts were racing faster than a jousting horse; if Edward were to die now, in this next battle, then he would be king!

Towton, Yorkshire, 29th March 1461

Squire Nate felt sure everything was ready. When they left Pontefract Castle at dawn his master, the new King of England, was resplendent in his burnished armour; his warhorse wore a steel chanfron to protect its face and purple trappings as finery. Edward had heard a Mass said for those who had died at Ferrybridge the night before where the York forces were sent to capture the bridge, and he had given thanks that his cousin, the Earl of Warwick, had received but a minor wound to his leg during the Lancastrian ambush. Edward did not say so explicitly, but Nate was sure that he had given silent thanks that Butcher

Clifford, the murderer of his brother Edmund at Sandal, had been killed in the action. Now the whole York army, all twenty-five thousand of them, marched toward the village of Towton to finally face the army of the Red Rose. Henry and Marguerite were in York with their young son, but Edward led his army as mad Harry could not. Edward would live and die with his men, and Nate knew they loved him for it. With snow swirling around them, in their ranks they processed behind the priests who were intoning prayers on this Palm Sunday morn.

Nate's heart burst with pride for his king, this fine man of eighteen years, and the York captains had fully put their trust in him. Lord Fauconberg led the vast array of English archers, those men who could make or break a battle without wielding a sword. The Lancastrians had a better position on the ridge at Towton, but the squire was convinced God and right were on their side. As Edward finished issuing final instructions to his captains and prepared to go to the head of his men to lead the battle for England, he turned to Nate:

'Stay at the back, lad. Stay and prepare my horse should the need arise for us to give chase to these bastards. I will have need of you when this battle is over!'

'But sire! I will fight at your side! Only the women and priests stay at the back!' Nate was almost indignant, but fought to keep his voice under control.

'Stay here son. I have men enough to fight for York, but only one who can shine my armour like you!' Edward clasped his hand on the boy's shoulder, smiled at him, then turned on his heel.

'Nock, draw, loose!' Lord Fauconberg's archers were firing through the drifting snow into the faces of the Lancastrians. The wind was in their favour, and the army under the command of York's foe the Duke of Somerset were falling in rows, their own arrows falling short of Edward's army. The enemy had more men but the weather, and perhaps God, was turning against them. The battle raged on, the men-at-arms clashing violently with each other. The green fields, covered in snow, became a charnel house of blood, mud and guts. The dead were piling up, and soldiers had to fling them out of their way to get at their enemy. Nobody here could remember a worse or bloodier battle, fought in freezing weather and thousands of corpses littering the ground already. The Duke of Somerset and the Earl of Northumberland were relentless in their charges against the forces of York, and for a time it seemed as though the White Rose would get crushed along with the bodies of its men. But Edward had no thought of defeat; he ensured his lines held and repulsed the advances of the Lancastrians and was rewarded with the deaths of Henry Percy of Northumberland and Sir Andrew Trollope. Somerset continued the gruelling battle, neither side prepared to surrender.

Nate pulled his visor down and joined the next rank of the men-at-arms who were starting their advance. He was near the rear of the formation and he could barely see two rows in front, but the screams and yells were travelling back towards him. He knew Edward would forgive him for disobeying his orders, just as he knew he could not stay back as he had been commanded. He was Edward's man; he would fight alongside these men for the glory of York. His borrowed armour was not a good fit, but Nate had thought to tuck his green velvet scarf into his breastplate; it had been a gift from his mother when he had left his home to serve Edward at Ludlow, and now he thought of it as blessed and lucky. Nate fought through the ranks of men, determined to do his duty, but he stumbled, and looked down to see a man with his entrails hanging out and being crushed into the slush and mud. He could feel the vomit in the back of his throat but was heartened by the cries of 'For York, for York and King Edward!' that his comrades were shouting. Suddenly, a figure charged out of the snow towards him and he swung his mace into the belly of a boy, not much older than himself, and was astonished when the lad went down with a grunt. He stopped for a moment, not sure if he should say a prayer, and did not see as an old man with a long brown beard swung his axe towards him. Nate's head left his body in one swift stroke and the rest of him fell forwards onto the bodies desecrating the meadow.

For hours the battle raged on. All were frozen, exhausted and death began to seem the better option, just to escape this hell on earth. The smell of shit and blood filled the air. Edward was everywhere, his shining armour now stained red. He rallied his men with shouts of encouragement and led from the front; York knew who was at their head and who they were fighting for. When it seemed their cause may truly be lost, salvation came in the form of the Yorkist Jack Howard, bringing his fresh troops to smash the Lancastrian left flank. These beleaguered men gave up the fight and threw down their weapons and armour and fled towards the stream and the rout began.

Edward, a king without a crown, sat in his small tent and accepted the fealty of the defeated Lancastrians who had not been killed or had run. They said the beck was running with blood as red as the Rose of Lancaster, and the vanquished begged Edward for his forgiveness. Among them was Richard Woodville, husband to Jacquetta, and his son Anthony. They hung their heads as they acknowledged their new liege lord, held out their swords to him and muttered, 'God save the king.'

As darkness descended on the fields of Towton, Edward and Will Hastings walked among the dead. Neither had ever seen death on this scale; their feelings were a mixture of horror, revulsion and pride; pride in the men who had laid down their lives for York.

'Will we ever be forgiven, do you think?' Edward turned to his friend. 'Can God forgive as many deaths as this?'

'We should bury the dead and build chantries in their names,' Hastings replied comfortingly.

'But we do not know their names! Look at this lad here,' Edward bent down and touched the arm of a headless corpse. 'How can we honour him when we do not know who he was? He is known only unto God.'

'They are men of York, Edward. We will bury them in the name of York. What else can we do?'

Both men gazed out over the sea of dead, stunned by the carnage around them. Neither noticed the green velvet scarf crushed into the ground beneath Edward's boot.

Baynard's Castle, London, 4th April 1461

Kat was waiting outside the private chapel for her mistress to finish her prayers. Duchess Cecily and her daughter Margaret had been on their knees, giving thanks for the victory at Towton and hearing a Mass for the dead officiated by Bishop Stillington since the news had reached them that morning. The lady-in-waiting was reluctant to interrupt the solemn moment, despite the insistence of the new visitor.

'Ah, here she comes now, Your Eminence. Madam,' Kat dropped a curtsey to the Duchess, 'the Lord Chancellor is here.'

'George!' Cecily held out her hand to the Bishop of Exeter and Lord Chancellor George Neville, another of Warwick's brothers. 'How very kind of you to pay me a visit, but I have already had word from York Herald in the north. We have been giving thanks for Edward's victory, and Margaret is keen to start preparations to welcome her brother back to the capital!.' The duchess smiled at her youngest daughter who was wreathed in smiles.

'Indeed, Your Grace. However I bring further news from my brother.'

'From Warwick? How is his wound, healing well I hope?'

'Yes Madam, he is recovering well and has joined King Edward in the city of York. It is about York I bring news.' He paused, then knelt in front of the duchess. 'Your Grace, I am commanded to tell you that when your noble son entered the city after the battle, his first action was to remove the heads of your beloved husband and son, and also those of my father and brother, from the spikes at Micklegate and have them ordered buried at Pontefract.' He reached for her hand and kissed it. 'Our loved ones can now be at peace, Your Grace.'

The tears came to Cecily's eyes instantly, but she could not have said if they were of joy or sorrow. She turned to her faithful lady. 'Kat, tell Bishop Stillington to prepare his vestments once more. Come Margaret, we need to give thanks again to God.'

Ducal Palace, Bruges, 10ᵗʰ April 1461

'And may I present my wife the Duchess Isabella and my son Charles.' Duke Philip of Burgundy was expansive in his welcome to the boys; the Houses of Plantagenet and Valois were finally coming together. George and Richard were overwhelmed at the extravagance of their new surroundings. They had been whisked from their cosy house in Utrecht by the Duke's household guards and summoned to his court and were now surrounded by elegantly dressed nobility, glittering paintings and opulent furniture. Their new clothes, hastily bought by Nurse Ann, were sumptuous and rich, as befitted the heirs in line to the English throne. They were ushered to the top table and had goblets of wine thrust into their fists. The flautists began playing as the first of the many courses of the banquet were brought into the Great Hall, held high on the shoulders of the servers.

'Well, this is wonderful. I am truly amazed.' Master Colyngbourne dithered between choosing slices wild boar or the swan, but decided to help himself to both.

'Hmph.' Nurse Ann, seated next to him at the back of the hall, refused to touch so much as a morsel of bread.

'Mistress Ann, are you not happy for the boys? Finally brought to court and honoured by Burgundy! I heartily believed this is what you would have wished for them.'

'I wish, Master Colyngbourne, that they had been so honoured when first we arrived in the Low Countries and not being made to wait until it was clear their brother Edward had taken the throne! Fancy treating boys of the House of York like that, it's shameful!'

'Well, I imagine the Duke of Burgundy weighed up who it was more politic to offend; the old King of England and his French wife and thus the French King Charles, or the new King of England.'

'York has had the right to the throne since the Act of

Accord! Burgundy should have honoured York the moment my young masters' ship docked!'

Master Colyngbourne looked at the nurse and smiled. 'Let us not argue anymore. Tomorrow I will find a ship to return us all home. Shall you try the venison pie, milady?'

Baynard's Castle, London, 5th May 1461

George and Richard knelt before the new king, their brother Edward, and bowed their heads. George looked up and smiled, beyond proud that he was the king's brother and next in line to the throne of England. Richard rose, went closer to Edward and knelt again.

'I promise I will never break your trust. I promise I will never be a traitor and I will always be faithful to you.' Edward smiled at the young lad who looked so like their father.

'Thank you Richard. I know you for a most loyal brother.' Edward raised the boy from the floor, hugged him and kissed his forehead. 'Now go greet our mother.'

Richard could not seem to let go of Duchess Cecily. He wrapped his arms around her and was difficult to pry away. She was aware he was crying so she let him stay in her embrace until he was ready to step back.

'Oh mother. I have longed for this above all things.'

'Welcome home Richard.' The duchess stroked his face with her hand, then kissed his cheek. 'Welcome home son.'

Pontefract, Yorkshire, 3rd February 1462

Cecily was not sure that she could do it. She turned to Kat with a nervous laugh. 'Well, I have come all this way, I suppose I should. I don't want to waste all those miles!'

She entered the friars' chapel and made her way to the side apse where she had been directed by the priest. Clasping the paternoster beads she always wore at her waist, she approached the unassuming tombs that held the remains of her beloved husband Richard and her son Edmund. Kat remained at the door of the chapel where she could see her mistress kneel on the stone floor and lower her head. Kat knelt too, and whispered prayers asking for strength for Cecily to bear this burden, and perhaps also to finally bring the duchess some comfort knowing that the bodies of her loved ones were now in consecrated ground. She was too far away to hear that Cecily was not praying, but simply repeating the words, 'My love, my boy, my love, my boy.'

'Well, it has been a good year hasn't it?' Duchess Cecily strolled around the inner walls of Pontefract Castle, pleased that the Yorkshire sun had finally burst through the grey clouds.

'Yes Lady mother.' Nine-year-old Richard was at her side, fingering the dagger given to him by Edward as a parting gift.

'Your brother crowned King of England, George is Duke of Clarence and you off to start your knights' training as the Duke of Gloucester! Gracious me, how blessed we are.'

'Yes Lady mother. When do we go on to Middleham?'

'You shall leave at dawn Richard. But I will return now to London. You are a duke now, my son. You shall have Tommy and Rob in your train, you do not need your mother or Nursey Ann fussing over you any longer.'

'I am looking forward to seeing my cousin Warwick again, but…'

'But what Richard?' Cecily turned to her slight, dark-haired boy who had the dark eyes of his father.

'But what if I can't do it? What if I can't learn to be a great solider, what if can't wield a sword?'

'You will practise hard and learn those skills, my son. In time, you will be as great a warrior as Edward.'

'Lady mother, there is no solider as great as my brother, my brother the king.'

The small cavalcade rode up the winding hills in the Wensleydale countryside headed to Middleham, now Warwick's base in the north. It was here Richard would live and learn the skills of a knight, skills that would include mastery of sword and arrow, leadership and courtly behaviour. Tommy Parr rode just behind Richard, next to Rob Percy who they had met at Pontefract. Both lads were to serve Richard, as a duke should be served, and both would learn alongside him.

'Just remember,' Tommy hissed at Rob out of the side of his mouth, 'just remember that I am His Grace's first squire. You are to be second squire, if you survive at all.'

Easy going Rob, distant kin to the Percy family of Northumberland, smiled back. 'Then I guess we will just have to see who is better at it!'

Middleham Castle, Yorkshire, 5ᵗʰ February 1462
The Master of Henchmen was conferring with the Earl of Warwick in the outer bailey of the castle that was his northern stronghold.

'He is not to be shown any favourable treatment Master Grinton. He may be a duke, and the brother of the king, but he is here to learn as are all the boys in our care.' The earl's curly head towered above that of the man who was responsible for the knights' training of the lads but he wasn't fooled. He knew the old Yorkshireman with the grey stubble covering head and face could knock him down with his little finger.

'Yes my Lord. Due to his rank I have had rooms prepared for him in the South Courtyard but I mean to work him as I work all the lads, never worry sir.'

'Thank you Master Grinton. Have the henchmen lined up when he arrives; we will greet him well, for his sake and for the sake of the king.'

As the portcullis of the castle came into view Richard sat up straighter in the saddle and took a deep breath. He was pleased he was being treated as a man now, ready to start his training, but some fears at being away from his family and his ability to make his brother proud fluttered in his stomach. He reined in his horse, another gift from Edward, and looked over his shoulder.

'Well, we are here. Shall we dismount to enter do you think?'

'No Your Grace.' Rob Percy pulled his horse alongside Richard's, pushing Tommy out of the way. 'You outrank the Earl of Warwick sir. For that reason, you may enter his castle mounted.'

Richard looked startled, then pleased at Rob's words and tapped his heels against his horse's flanks into a trot over the drawbridge. Tommy glared at Rob, then hurried to catch up with his young master.

Richard had been introduced to the Countess Anne and her elder daughter Isabel and had respectfully bowed to the Master of Henchmen, whom he knew he would have to impress in the coming years. The countess showed him to his rooms which were hung with fine tapestries and had a warm fire glowing in the corner. He had a chest for his clothes, good candles and a writing desk with quill and ink. Tommy and Rob were unpacking his gear, arguing in undertones as to where to put the shorter houppelandes for everyday wear and the finer robes for feast days, when a girl of about six burst into the room. Her flaming auburn hair had escaped from its filet, she had mud on her skirts and laughter in her eyes.

'Good day Your Grace. I am Anne, Anne Neville. Welcome to Middleham.'

Middleham Castle, Yorkshire, 5th January 1464

The Twelfth Night Feast had ended, and the strict rules by which the castle was run had been all but forgotten. Maids and henchmen were missing from the Great Hall, the wine was flowing and the music loud enough to be heard over the laughter and chatter in the public rooms. Martyn the Fool and Master Pudsey, the Keeper of the Park, were drinking ale from their pointed shoes and the young men were placing wagers to see who would pass out first. The Master of Henchmen, old Grinton, was asleep in the corner, an empty flagon by his side.

All at Middleham felt they had cause to celebrate this year. Uprisings in the north had been put down, and Marguerite and old Henry were journeying between Scotland and France, still trying to raise troops to rebellion, but generally peace had descended on England. Edward had proved to be a good king; he had restored law and order to the country, increased the revenue of the crown without taxing the people, supported the powerful merchants of the country along with his Lords, and reduced piracy off England's coasts. He was a warrior king, but did not seek war with France as had his predecessors. He was ably supported by his cousin of Warwick, who enjoyed great influence and power, both here and abroad. Perhaps there were a few who said Warwick's influence was too great over this young king, but Edward loved and trusted him and had rewarded him accordingly. The only repeated criticism of Edward was that he was overly fond of ladies, married or unmarried, and his bedroom conquests now outnumbered his military ones. But he was a young king in his prime, and for the sake of peace in England, those misdemeanours could be overlooked.

Richard was enjoying his time at Middleham, despite some obstacles in his path. The pain in his back had worsened over the years and he had finally turned to the countess for help. Physicians were called and consulted, and a misalignment of his bones was diagnosed, which had caused his right shoulder to rise higher than the left. Countess Anne had entrusted her seamstress, Kate, to make padded doublets and shirts for Richard that would disguise this difference in height, and had ensured Richard made regular payments to Kate out of his own accounts to reimburse her for her skill and discretion. The Master of Horse, Master Franke, commissioned the experts in leather to create a saddle with a higher cantle at the back that would support Richard when on horseback, and these measures went some way to helping him. He was at times in severe pain, but he found that building muscle from hours of swordsmanship and training ensured he was as good as the other lads on the practice ground.

Tommy and Rob were fierce in their loyalty to Richard and had at first resented any who had tried to get close to their young master. However they could not keep Richard away from another henchman who had joined them in training. Francis Lovell, a young baron from Oxfordshire, accompanied Richard and his squires in all their adventures and was soon admitted to his inner circle of friends. There was another who tried to follow the boys around and join them whenever she could; young Anne Neville, Warwick's daughter. She was lively and full of joy, and the lads saw her as a little sister whom they by turns protected and teased. These were happy years in the Yorkshire countryside, and Richard felt confident all would be well for the future.

Westminster Palace, London 27th April 1464

Duchess Cecily, now also addressed as 'King's Mother', was shown into the presence chamber with her man Colyngbourne at her side. She dropped a curtsey before her son the king, and he in turn knelt to her for her blessing. She rested her hand on his fair head, then he rose to his great height before her.

'Is it true my son? My man tells me John Neville was ambushed!'

'Well, some of that is true Lady mother. I sent him to escort the Scots to our Parliament in the north to discuss peace, and that basta…that devil Somerset and Ralph Percy met him at Hedgeley Moor just north of Alnwick and, well, we lost some men.'

'But my brother John, or Baron Montagu as he insists we call him now, did beat them, my Lady aunt. Somerset ran away but Percy was killed.' Warwick, at the king's side as usual, stepped forward.

'They say his dead body made a great leap after he was killed! Trying to escape I suppose, but I doubt that story is really true.' Edward sat back on his throne and gestured to his squire for wine to be served. 'Please sit, Lady mother. You too Colyngbourne.'

'Well, I did hope that battles were in the past now. I know we must look to the future and secure your throne for generations to come Edward.' Cecily arranged her dark skirts around her, and settled comfortably in her chair. 'What news have you on that score, nephew?'

Warwick took a sip of the wine and nodded.

'Yes, I am away for France tomorrow, Lady aunt. Their new king, Louis, has agreed to see me, and I do hear that the Duke of Savoy has a daughter! A pretty little thing, well she is unmarried anyway, and Louis' sister-by-law! Very neat, very tidy I think!'

Cecily nodded and smiled at Warwick, but could not help noticing Edward's glum face.

Middleham Castle, Yorkshire, 19th September 1464
Countess Anne of Warwick sat back in her chair, astonished. She had thought all was well in the kingdom and that peace at last had come. After another York victory in Hexham which had seen the execution of the Duke of Somerset and the promotion of John Neville from baron to Earl of Northumberland, as well as the recapture of old mad Henry back into York's hands, she

thought the future was secure and that her husband would remain as the king's most trusted advisor and counsellor. Now all that had changed, and she was furious. In her anger, she sent her page to fetch the young Duke Richard off the training ground and brought to her.

'Your Ladyship.' Richard bowed to the countess, who should have curtsied to him as befitted his rank. When she remained seated, Richard knew that she was furious, and he wondered if he and her maid-in-waiting Jayne had been seen kissing up on the battlements again.

'Richard. I have heard today from my husband Warwick. Edward, your brother…' She broke off in her rage.

'My brother the *king.*' Richard was on his dignity at once, not liking the countess's tone but not wishing to be overtly rude to her. 'Yes my Lady? What of the king?'

'He is married! *Married*! What do you say to that?'

Richard sat down on a stool without being invited, such was his surprise. 'Married? To whom? When? I do not understand, my Lady. I thought he was to marry the Duke of Savoy's daughter.'

'Yes that was the plan! That was Warwick's plan, he was to marry Bona of Savoy, that was what my husband had arranged! But it seems Edward is already married. He informed the Council five days ago that he was married in secret this past May Day to Dame Elizabeth Grey!'

'Who is Dame Elizabeth Grey?' Richard was confused and wondered if the countess was having an apoplexy.

'Exactly! Who is *Dame Elizabeth Grey*? That is the very question the Council asked your brother the king! Who is she?' Countess Anne took a few deep breaths and started to calm down. 'I will assume you had no knowledge of this Richard, I imagine the king did not take you into his confidence.'

'You are correct, my Lady. I have never heard of this lady, nor did I know Edward had married her. Who is she?'

'She is the widow of Sir John Grey, a Lancastrian killed at St Albans, and by whom she has two sons. She is the daughter of the widowed Duchess of Bedford, now Jacquetta Woodville, and her second husband. This King of York has married a Lancastrian widow, this Elizabeth Woodville. And she is so much older than him. This cannot be allowed!'

Richard stood and bowed, hiding his anger at Edward but knew he was sworn to defend him. 'It would appear my brother the king has made his decision, Countess. Good day.' He left the room, closing the door softly behind him.

'Your brother the *king* has made my husband look a fool,' she muttered to the oak panels.

Westminster Palace, London, 26th May 1465

'I will not do it.' Duchess Cecily folded her lips tightly together and crossed her arms. 'I will not!'

'Yes you will, Lady mother. You will curtsey to the Queen of England at her coronation feast, and you will smile and welcome her to this family.' Edward towered over his mother, equally obstinate.

'This is folly Edward! You married a commoner widow woman! Elizabeth Grey indeed! Not since the Conquest has a king taken a commoner for a wife! And an old Lancastrian commoner at that!'

'You know perfectly well that the Woodville family are now

committed to our cause, have been since Towton. I am aware you have not forgiven me for our secret wedding but it was a year ago and you have yet to meet her. She is beautiful, Lady mother, beautiful! And more importantly, she is my queen.'

'I care not if she is Aphrodite! She is a commoner, much older than you, a widow with two children from a turncoat family with about two dozen siblings! Her mother married her dead husband's servant, who then went on to attack you in Calais! I know mad King Henry enobled her father; he can change his name from Woodville to Baron Rivers but it matters not when you scratch at the surface. Not to mention how you have made Warwick appear! He recaptured old Henry for you, he negotiated the French marriage for you, this is the man who helped you to the throne! What were you thinking?' Duchess Cecily's voice was rising and she fought to bring it back under her control.

'Your pride seems to be the issue here, mother. I am King and Elizabeth Woodville is my Queen. The deed has been done, now I suggest you reconcile yourself to matters you cannot change.'

As Cecily was conducted to the dais of the Great Hall after the Coronation Feast had ended, she eyed the new queen as she approached. She was seated on her throne, only slightly lower than her husband, and was flanked by her two sons, ten-year-old Thomas Grey and his younger brother Richard. Edward's badge of the Sunne in Splendour was mounted behind her in defiance. Cecily could acknowledge that the woman was beautiful with her silver blonde hair plucked high on her forehead, piercing eyes and wearing a dress of silver taffeta, but that meant nothing to her. Cecily would have been happy if the woman looked like a gargoyle from a cathedral drainpipe if she had been of noble Yorkist birth.

Warwick had finally told her the tale of how the King of

England had met this unknown widow and taken her to wife. She had approached William Hastings to act for her in reclaiming her lost dower lands after her Lancastrian husband was killed. Knowing his master's liking for a pretty face, he had brought Dame Grey to see him when he was on progress. Warwick, almost spitting in his anger, told Cecily that the king was so enamoured with her beauty but she held out against his charms; Edward could not resist her and married her with only her family present as witnesses. So here she was, this nobody who was better than a French princess, this beauty that could capture a king.

As she reached the newly crowned queen, Cecily nodded her head.

'You must forgive me, Queen Elizabeth. I am unable to curtsey due to an ailment in my back.' Her voice was cold and as she spoke she looked somewhere past the Queen's shoulder. She thought her high hennin covered in lace gave her extra stature to face this woman.

'I do understand Duchess. Old age and infirmity comes to us all, I suppose.' Cecily thought she heard Edward snort with suppressed laughter at his wife's reply and ignored him. She gave her sweetest smile:

'I have brought Your Grace a coronation gift, if you would be so kind to look out of the window. It was too large to have it brought inside.' Queen Elizabeth's face lit up with pleasure and she rose and hurried to the window. There below in the courtyard was a large white dappled horse.

'It is my gift to you, Queen Elizabeth. It is a Grey Mare.'

Duchess Cecily, King's Mother, was ushered from the Queen's presence chamber through to the more elaborate privy chamber. Here she found close members of her family, including the king and his chief advisor, the Earl of Warwick, all watching and waiting. None were permitted entry to the confinement chamber where the queen was labouring over her first child by Edward. Only the midwives, her mother Jacquetta and her trusted ladies-in-waiting were with her now, and even Cecily herself was the first to admit she and Elizabeth Woodville were far from close.

Baron Rivers, the queen's father, nodded to her politely before resuming a whispered conversation with his sons Edward and Anthony. By the way he was chewing his nails, Cecily thought, he was more anxious than the king himself. Warwick strolled over to the duchess, kissed her hand and drew her into a window seat.

'How is Edward coping with the waiting, nephew?'

'Like a typical anxious father, Lady aunt. He has paced the floor 'til I am sure he has left a mark, he's shouted at three pageboys and even refuses a glass of wine!' Warwick smiled fondly towards the king, who was now viciously poking the fire.

'Ah well, I am sure Elizabeth will be quick, it's not as if it's her first baby.' Cecily made the snide remark and was rewarded with her nephew's laughter.

'The king promises to make you and I godparents to the child. I cannot tell you how much he is hoping for a boy, Duchess. He knows that a prince in the cradle will secure his throne as much as twenty battles!' Warwick stretched his neck to see around the room. 'Indeed, all the Woodvilles, and God knows how many of them there are, have kept the priests busy paying for Masses to get their wish.'

'My son George is probably the one only hoping the queen has a girl.' Cecily felt she could confide in Warwick. 'A prince would disinherit him, and he does so love being heir to Edward's throne.'

'Perhaps we should get him married, take his mind off that and give him a purpose in life.' He looked sideways at her and lowered his voice. 'My daughter Isabel is only three years younger than him.'

Before Cecily could think of a reply, the door was swung open and Jacquetta Woodville bustled in and went straight to Edward. She curtseyed before leaning up and whispering in his ear. Those assembled, now on their feet in anticipation, saw the king sag slightly and his shoulders droop. Then he straightened up, like the warrior he was, and made his announcement.

'The queen is safely delivered of a baby girl. She will be named Elizabeth after her mother.' He bowed briefly to them all, and followed Jacquetta from the room to go and visit his wife. There was a brief stillness in the room before they all burst into forced applause. Perhaps only Cecily saw the smirk that crossed Warwick's face as he went after his master.

Windsor Castle, 20th April 1466

Richard Woodville, Baron Rivers, made his way to the front of the Great Hall looking as nervous as a groom on his wedding day. As well he might, Cecily thought. Once a servant to the Duke of Bedford, here he was, in the presence of the nobles of England, to join their ranks as an earl. The queen, his daughter, was seated on her throne wearing ermine and more jewels than Cecily thought possible for one person to carry. Her face was wreathed in smiles, matching those of all the Woodvilles crammed into the huge chamber. Flanking his proud wife Jacquetta were the children that, thanks to Elizabeth's marriage to the king, had been found husbands and wives that would have been unreachable to them as offspring of mere Richard Woodville. Thomas Grey, the lad born to Elizabeth Woodville's first marriage, was to wed the wealthy Ann Holland, daughter of the Duchess of Exeter and granddaughter of Cecily. The queen's sisters Mary, Margaret and Jacquetta the younger were to be countesses by marriage, but little Katherine outranked them all as the new Duchess of Buckingham. She had been married to Harry Stafford of Maxstoke, the grandson of Cecily's sister, and both were reported to be unhappy and spoilt children. So small were they on their wedding day they had to be carried, it was rumoured, but as Cecily refused to attend the ceremony, she could neither confirm nor deny it. But perhaps the most distasteful union the grasping Woodville queen had made was between her nineteen-year-old brother John and the sixty-five-old Dowager Duchess of Norfolk. She was Duchess Cecily's sister, and she had been so outraged on her behalf that the row she had with Edward regarding it caused her to nearly slap his face.

But here they were today, celebrating a further advancement for this avaricious family, watching as King Edward tied a sword belt around Richard Woodville's waist to show that his rights as Earl Rivers came from the king himself, and none should argue with that.

'Jesus Christ.' Warwick sidled up to Cecily as they watched the newly enobled earl stroll around the feasting crowd. 'Look at him, all blonde good looks and not much between the ears.' He sat next to her and leaned in.

'Enough between the ears to marry the widow of a duke.' Cecily pushed her plate away and covered her mouth with her hand, not wishing to be overheard. 'The sun does not rise as fast as that family.'

'Indeed. Have you heard that Rivers is to be made Edward's Treasurer of England?' Warwick had lowered his voice to match his aunt's. 'There really is no end to their greed.'

They both watched as the new earl stopped by the Buckingham table and kissed his little daughter Katherine.

'I think that was the worst of all, marrying the Duke of Buckingham to that girl who is no better than a serving maid.'

'Worse than marrying John to my sister Katherine?' Cecily frowned. 'Nearly fifty years older than him! I really can't talk about it without getting violent!'

Warwick smiled in sympathy at her. 'Perhaps you are right, that truly was a diabolical marriage. My poor Lady aunt, how hard it has been for you.'

'Hard for you too, nephew. I have heard little praise for the peace treaty you made with Louis of France.' She scrutinised his face. 'I believe you arranged that Louis, the old spider, would not offer any assistance to Marguerite of Anjou in return for my son Edward not helping Burgundy against the French. Two years of peace you agreed, but hardly anyone speaks of it.'

Warwick's face darkened in anger. 'Edward has no intention of keeping to the agreement. He loves Burgundy, probably because Jacquetta is from there, and I am sure he only agreed to the treaty to keep me quiet!' He broke off and took a swig of his wine. 'He has made me look a fool, Duchess. Two years of peace, thrown away just to placate the Woodvilles!' He rose abruptly and pushed away his cup. He bowed curtly to Cecily and turned on his heel.

'Dear God, Edward,' she whispered to herself. 'You should pay more mind to matters of state and less to trying to make that damned woman happy.'

Windsor Castle, 11ᵗʰ August 1467

The same people, just crowded into a different room. Duchess Cecily looked around the familiar faces; they were all here, the queen's father, all her brothers and sisters and the king of course. All here waiting, just as they waited before. Elizabeth was in the private chambers giving birth to Edward's second child, and this time he was more nervous than before. Nobody dared to go near him, not even Warwick, such was his anxiety. They lined the walls, waiting, waiting, waiting.

The room held it's breath, again. Jacquetta opened the door and made eye contact with no one but the king. She was less exuberant than last time they were all waiting for her news, and from this all guessed what the tidings would be. This time, the king made no announcement after hearing Jacquetta's whisper. He simply nodded to her and made for the door to the castle grounds, calling for his horse as he did so.

'It's a girl then.' Cecily did not realise she had spoken aloud until she saw all heads turn to look at her. She shrugged her shoulders. 'The queen has had another princess.' She avoided looking at Warwick, not wanting to see his smug face. 'We must all give thanks for a healthy child,' she looked back at them all then dropped her voice, 'and pray for a boy next time.'

Margate, Kent, 23rd June 1468

The glorious procession wound it ways through the narrow streets towards the harbour. The weather was kind that day; a bright sun and a brisk breeze that would aid the ships on their journey. The parade was led by the King of England himself, his wife riding next to him and both wearing matching suits of red velvet with gold embroidery. Pennants fluttered in the wind; the arms of England, the colours of the House of York and the Sunne in Splendour for Edward himself. Margaret, Edward's twenty-two-year-old sister, rode directly behind the king and queen, with her mother Duchess Cecily at her side. She smiled and waved at the cheering crowds and made a good show of hiding her nervousness. She had the dark good looks of her late father, Cecily thought, more like Richard than Edward, and looked radiant in her silver taffeta cloak.

As they approached the quay the grooms rushed forward to help the nobles dismount. Cecily settled onto the ground with a grunt. She was fifty-three, getting too old for horseback riding, but arriving in a litter would have ruined the look of the cortege, not to mention making her appear like an old woman. Kat came to her side and helped her straighten her hat and adjust her skirts, while the luggage wagons came forward and began loading onto the ships. Margaret, her beloved daughter, kept close to Cecily's side and took every opportunity to hold her arm.

'Well, my dear, here we are on the next step of your journey into marriage. How pleased I am for you.' Cecily was trying to appear brisk and forthright, to hold back the tears that threatened them both.

'Yes, Lady mother.' Margaret straightened her shoulders. 'I will be pleased to be finally wed, I feared being an old maid all my life!' Her attempt to inject some humour into the situation helped. 'I do wish that I did not have to go so far to find a husband though, I should have liked to live my life here and not abroad.'

'You are a Princess of York, sister.' Edward heard her last comment as he made his way over to them. 'It is your duty to make a dynastic marriage to benefit our family.'

'You didn't.' Cecily smiled at Margaret's snapped comment, but held her tongue.

'Well, that is not the point.' Edward cast a look over his shoulder at his wife. 'You will marry the Duke of Burgundy and be our good friend over the water.' He dropped his pompous tone. 'Come now, Meg, it is a good position for you. Think of how you can help England with trade rights and defending us from France!' He winked at her. 'And I do hear that Charles is handsome and virile, he already has a daughter. You will be most happy.' He kissed her forehead and walked off to speak to the captains about how they thought the wind would hold.

'He is right, my dear.' Duchess Cecily took her daughter's arm as they watched the bustle at the water's edge. 'You will be Duchess of Burgundy, and we will know that England can call on you for help and you will answer.' She reached over and kissed her cheek. 'It breaks my heart to see you leave these shores, but you are your father's daughter, you are brave and strong. He would be proud of the woman you have become.'

As the ships pulled out of the harbour, waves lapping the oak beams, the court began to make their way back to the horses and start their return to London. Cecily stayed at the water's edge, praying for a safe journey and a happy marriage for Margaret. It had not been an easy journey to this point. King Louis of France had opposed the union between England and Burgundy and had made a nuisance of himself throwing obstacles in their way. He did not want to see friendship between the two countries, and all suspected that Warwick fanned the flames of his discontent as he was known to favour a French alliance for England. Louis had tried to get the Pope to prevent the marriage, had slandered Margaret's honour and even tried to encourage an invasion of Wales by the Lancastrians. When all this failed, he tried to bribe Edward with favourable trading rights which was unsuccessful. Few had doubts that Warwick was supporting the French king in these endeavours, so keen was he to keep the alliance he had worked so hard to make. But Edward had borne no heed; he wanted a Burgundian alliance and did not care that Louis, and perhaps more importantly Warwick, would take this as an insult too far.

So here Cecily stood, alone now on the quay, watching the ships become a speck on the horizon. She thought that the distance between her and Margaret was a wide as the distance between Edward and Warwick, and she could think of no way of reuniting them.

L'Erber, London, 20th March 1469

'Quick lad, pour more wine!' The Earl of Warwick hurried the pageboy and the wine sloshed over the cups and onto the rushes. The boy rubbed them with his foot and hoped his mistake had not been noticed, but it seemed nothing could upset the earl this day. 'Off you go now, and tell the Chamberlain I said he should open a cask of ale for all below stairs.' Warwick nodded and shooed the lad out of the door. 'It is a day of celebration!'

As the door closed on his back, George Duke of Clarence and his cousin of Warwick laughed.

'A celebration indeed! No better news is there?' George raised his cup and clinked it with Warwick's.

'Indeed not.' Warwick sat back into a chair and raised his arm in a toast. 'To the Queen of England, who this day, by the grace of God, has given us another girl!'

George matched his cousin's salute and fell back onto a window seat and drank deeply. 'The bloody woman! Useless. Married to my brother the king for five years and all she can produce is three princesses!' He took another swig. 'Did Edward not want you at Westminster with him this day? Did he not want you by his side as the babe was being born?'

'No.' Warwick turned his head to look at Clarence. 'No, he did not. It seems our king wants me anywhere *but* at his side. He sends me off on fool missions and ignores all my advice. He only listens to the goddamn Woodvilles these days.'

'He forgets how much he owes you, cousin.'

'Yes! Exactly! If it weren't for me, his arse would have been trodden into the mud at Mortimer's Cross, not sat on that throne.' He took a thoughtful sip. 'It has never been in my nature to hang back, George. My place, my rightful place, is at the right hand of the king.' He lowered his voice, and George did not hear the whispered words. 'Whoever that may be.'

'I can't imagine my brother's anger when the Woodvilles had to tell him that he got another girl on that bitch!' Clarence laughed. 'Good for me though!'

'Of course.' Warwick straightened up. 'You are still Edward's heir. Should anything happen to our king, God forbid, you, my dear George, will be king.'

Clarence looked momentarily sombre. 'She may have a boy though. Then it's all over for me.'

Warwick rose and stood in front of the handsome George. 'Not necessarily, lad. Not necessarily.' He crossed to the door and turned the latch. 'My wife and daughters are waiting to greet you, my Lord Duke.'

The Narrow Sea, 4ᵗʰ July 1469

Perhaps deep in his heart, Warwick regretted what he had been forced to do. He could remember back to when Edward was crowned King of England and he had been his most trusted advisor. He remembered how the future had seemed so golden then; the House of York was on the throne, being advised by the House of Neville. Warwick knew now that things could never be the same, the rifts were too deep to heal. He blamed everything on the hellion Queen of England, and he was aware enough to be amused by that thought; for years, he had thought of Marguerite of Anjou as the bitch Queen of England, but now her place had been taken by Elizabeth Woodville. Warwick knew Edward had married her because it was the only way to get between her legs. Perhaps if her family were not so grasping and greedy, things may have worked out after Edward's unwise marriage. Her family were given places and positions all throughout England, until there was nothing left for any noble who wasn't called Woodville, and no eligible lords and ladies left untaken. And that lustful fool Edward had agreed to everything. Well, everything except the things which would placate the Earl of Warwick! The Woodville woman obviously feared Warwick's power and influence and turned the king against him. The king could only have been encouraged by his wife to dismiss Warwick's brother George from the position of Lord Chancellor, to renege on the agreement Warwick negotiated with France in order to favour Jacquetta's Burgundian family and to marry his sister Margaret to Burgundy. The Woodville queen had not even rewarded Edward with a son. The final straw was Edward, no doubt emboldened by Elizabeth, refusing to allow his brothers George and Richard to marry Warwick's daughters Isabel and Anne.

It was the lack of a son in the cradle for England that gave Warwick purpose now. Jasper Tudor, half-brother to old King Henry who was safe in The Tower of London cared for by priests and body servants, had been driven out of England and Marguerite and her son Edouard of Westminster were in alliance with him to restore her to the throne. Warwick needed to control, to lead, and found a willing bedfellow in George Duke of Clarence. With Clarence's ambitions, it turned out to be an easy matter to lead him by the nose with the promise of a throne. With little persuasion, he exhorted George to spread a scurrilous rumour that the noble and proud Cecily, Duchess of York, had betrayed her beloved husband and that Edward was in fact the son of an English bowman called John Blaybourne, therefore not entitled to his crown. With George in his pocket, all Warwick had to do now was to marry the fool to his daughter Isabel; Warwick would be father-by-law to the King of England, and in his rightful place once more.

Berkhamsted Castle, Hertfordshire, 14th August 1469
Duchess Cecily was hurriedly issuing orders to Kat and Colyngbourne, urging them to quicken their preparations so they might leave for London straight away.

'I am too old for this,' she muttered as she stuffed her Book of Hours and the miniature of her husband into a velvet travel bag. 'I am too old to be hurrying, especially to comfort that woman.'

The duchess and her household were to travel to London, to the Tower, where Queen Elizabeth had secreted herself at this latest disaster. Cecily could admit to herself that the queen had faced her fears admirably these past few months, even if she had brought her troubles upon herself. After Clarence's shocking marriage to Isabel Neville last month in Calais, against Edward's command, Warwick had set himself against the king by issuing a proclamation condemning the Woodville family and he and George led a party of rebels towards Banbury where a force led by a mysterious man who went by the name Robin of Redesdale had been leading revolts. At Danes Moor, forces loyal to King Edward lead by William Herbert Earl of Pembroke, met with those of the enigmatic Robin, who many thought to be John Conyers, Warwick's steward at Middleham. A confusing and bloody battle saw the death of Redesdale, then Warwick executed Herbert and, audaciously, beheaded Queen Elizabeth's father Earl Rivers and brother John. Edward had been caught completely off guard, and had allowed himself to be captured by Warwick at Olney in Buckinghamshire and was now his prisoner. The King of England, a prisoner! The earl now held Edward in captivity, first at his castle at Warwick then moved him north to Middleham for greater security. Having seized the king, executed the queen's father and brother, Warwick delivered his final blow and had the queen's mother Jacquetta arrested on a charge of witchcraft. Warwick held all the aces in this game of cards, obviously intending to put the fool Clarence on the throne, and now the Yorks were running around the country putting out his fires.

Cecily was leaving the comfortable castle where she was temporarily residing to distance herself from the Woodville court in London. She was astonished that she was choosing to return to the bear pit in order to sympathise with that woman!

'Queen Elizabeth, you have my deepest sympathies.' Duchess Cecily had managed to force herself to drop a small curtsey to the queen, who no longer looked proud and arrogant, but was instead curled up in her chair with her beautiful hair ruffled and her face streaked. Cecily looked at the younger woman and spoke in a cracking voice. 'I have known the murder of family. I know your pain, and I pray that God will take it from you soon.'

'I do not want my pain taken away.' Queen Elizabeth raised her head and snapped, 'It is *your* son George who has brought this pain to us. *Your* son and *your* nephew killed my father and brother and arrested my mother. I welcome this pain and I will use it to curse Clarence and Warwick, and I will never forgive or forget.'

Cecily retreated to Baynard's Castle in sorrow and anger. Her heart was breaking for the queen's losses but she was furious that she had been blamed for it. She could not settle to sewing or reading, or even praying, but strode around the room in short jerky movements until the page opened the door.

'Your Grace, the Duke of Gloucester is here.' Cecily's heart lifted to hear that Richard had arrived. No longer in training at Middleham, she had not seen him for months but he had been good in sending her information about Edward whenever he could.

'My dear boy, how my heart lifts to see you.' Richard knelt for her blessing, and she laid her hand on his dark shiny hair for longer than was necessary. He was sixteen years old, still unmarried, but regarded as dependable and trustworthy by all who knew him.

'Lady mother, you look terrible. Forgive me, I mean to say you look troubled.'

'I look both terrible and troubled Richard. The queen blames me, as George's mother, for the death of Earl Rivers and John Woodville, but I suppose I cannot censure her for that.'

'You know my feelings about the queen's family, but I was truly shocked at the murders of the earl and his son. There was not even a trial, just a hasty beheading!'

Mother and son sat in the window seat together and Richard took her hands, trying to rub some warmth and comfort into them.

'I do have some good news, Lady mother. Jacquetta Woodville has been released from the charge of witchcraft and is making her way to London now. She is safe, for which the queen will undoubtedly give thanks.'

'That is one comfort, I suppose. To execute both her parents would have been beyond the pale. But I am furious at both Warwick and Clarence. To imprison Edward! Not to mention the things they said about me! I cannot comprehend what disasters they have brought us.'

'One wants to be king and the other wants to control the king.' Richard was thoughtful. 'Warwick has Edward imprisoned in Middleham Castle but things are not going his way. I am told that Edward treats the castle like his own, insisting on fine meals and musicians and emptying Warwick's wine cellars! I doubt Warwick can keep him much longer. It would have been better for him if he had killed Edward instead of capturing him.'

'Richard!' Cecily went pale with shock.

'Lady mother, you know I don't mean I *wish* he had killed

Edward. I am the king's man through and through, you know that. I mean that Warwick's plan has failed and I am sure Edward will be released soon.'

'And what then? Will Edward accuse George and Warwick of treason and have them sent to Tower Hill?'

Richard looked up at the ceiling. 'You know, I loved Warwick once. When I lived in his care at Middleham, I thought he was everything; brave, wise and kind. I loved Clarence too, we shared so much as children. But mother,' he looked directly towards her. 'You know, I cannot abide a traitor. They are a curse on this kingdom and should be punished.'

Cecily turned her head as the tears began to flow.

'Mother, even though I feel this, I will beg Edward for their lives. I will ask him to forgive them, but I suspect he has a mind to do that already. He cannot put to death his own brother and cousin.'

'Thank you Richard. You are right, Edward knows his duty.'

'Edward also needs to put a son in the belly of the Woodville woman. Until he has an heir, I feel these troubles will continue.' He had a small smile for Cecily now, and they shared a gleam at their mutual dislike of the queen.

'Speaking of sons, Richard, how is your boy?' Cecily looked at him innocently and raised her eyebrows.

'Ah, I see not much escapes you. John is well and living with his mother in Yorkshire. He is soon to be joined in the nursery by a new sibling.'

'God in heaven.' Cecily reached for the jug of wine and poured herself a cup. 'Two illegitimate children! I am too old for this.'

The Tower of London, 7th October 1469

The Queen of England and the King's Mother stood at the entrance to the White Tower, almost deafened by the shouts and cheers of the people. Edward of York, glorious on his huge black horse and wearing cloth of gold, waved and smiled as he trotted past his loyal supporters and citizens. A king restored to his throne, he looked every inch the monarch with his vast height and noble bearing. It was impossible to see the taint of captivity upon him; he looked healthy, well-fed and happy, as if he has been on progress around his country rather than a prisoner hidden away in the north. His nobles followed behind him, with Gloucester and Hastings riding directly behind their liege lord. Of Warwick and Clarence, there was no sign.

As the meal ended, Edward sat back and patted his stomach. The celebrations at his return had finished, and he had requested to eat with just his family.

'I ate well at Middleham, I cannot deny, but to share a meal with my wife, brother and mother is a pleasure I have not had in months.' He smiled expansively at them, then glanced at the table to see if there was a dish that he had missed. 'I am glad Warwick found he had no choice but to release me, as I have missed you all.'

Queen Elizabeth, who had just picked at her food, put her knife down with a clatter. 'So, when may we expect the executions to be carried out?' Her voice was hard and bitter, and Richard and Edward shared a look.

'Are you referring to my son and my nephew?' Cecily interjected before her son could reply. 'Do you mean when can you watch them die?' There was no love, or humour, in her voice now.

'There will be no executions, wife.' Edward stood up and

strode to the side table where the wine was kept. 'Warwick and Clarence will not be punished.'

'Not punished?' The queen's voice rose to scream. 'Not punished? They killed my father and brother and tried to have my mother strangled by the blacksmith for witchery! Why are they to go free?'

'Because I must have peace in my kingdom.' Edward poured himself a glass of wine, swallowed it, then poured another. 'I will forgive them, because it is only through reconciliation that I can bring unity to this country. I will strive to never give a man reason to turn traitor against me, I must be a fair and just king.' He nodded to Richard and Cecily. 'We will welcome my cousin and my brother back into the fold, and you, wife, will have to swallow your hatred.'

Westminster Palace, London, 25th December 1469
The feast was yet to begin and the smell of the roasting meats trickled through the corridors and wafted under doors. The servers clattered the silver trays in preparation for the procession of the courses and the grooms of the ewer stood by with the silver topped decanters. A sprinkling of snow that morning had been melted away by the cold winter sun but the air carried a promise of more snow in the night.

The great Painted Chamber was full, but silent. Noble lords with their wives and families sat at their tables, knives out ready for the food, but watching as the King of England raised both arms. On the dais, kneeling before him, the Earl of Warwick and the Duke of Clarence raised their heads as the king gave his blessing over them.

'In the name of God Almighty, I welcome my cousin and my brother to my Christmas court and, before you all, I give them my forgiveness and my love.' Edward smiled around the room. 'The House of York is strong when we are united, and at this time of Christ's birth, I promise unity and harmony in this season of peace.' He held out his hand for the forgiven to kiss his ring, then raised them to their feet to embrace them both. 'Cousin, brother, merry Christmas!'

The room exploded in a relief of applause and cheers and Warwick and Clarence bowed. The former's face was hard and the sinews of his jaw stood out where he clenched his teeth. George merely smiled thinly as they both returned to their seats at the top table. Queen Elizabeth would look at none but her brother Anthony, and her beautiful, slanted eyes were as cold as the diamonds in her hair. She radiated hatred for Warwick, Clarence and even the king.

'Before the feast begins, I would crave your attention for one moment longer.' Edward reached over and clasped his brother Richard by his shoulder and forced him to stand. 'I want to honour my brother of Gloucester before you all. Not yet eighteen years and I sent him to recapture our Welsh castles back from Lancastrian rebels, and he has proven himself a fine commander, a leader of men, and a most able soldier. I thank you, Richard.' Edward raised his cup. 'I give you the Duke of Gloucester, my beloved Richard.'

It seemed the storm of shouts and acclaim flew to the rafters, and Richard retook his seat with his cheeks burning red. Duchess Cecily raised her cup in reply and looked around happily. It was the best outcome, she thought. The treachery of her nephew and son was forgiven, and here she sat, celebrating the birth of Jesus with the three sons of York reunited.

Honfleur, Normandy, 2ⁿᵈ May 1470

Thirteen-year-old Anne Neville sat at end of Isabel's bed trying to read from a book of French poems. She kept glancing at her older sister to see if she was listening but Isabel could only stare at the bed hangings, as she had been doing since their arrival. Anne was at a loss as to how to comfort her. She was out of her depth in so many ways, and she felt she had not known the peace and security of her girlhood for years now. Her father, once King Edward's greatest ally, had turned against him again. Warwick had led rebellions and even battles against the king and her world had been turned upside down. She would admit that at first she had not understood what was happening in the kingdom; her father went from being influential at the king's side to being diminished and marginalised. When he had hauled the family to Calais for Isabel to marry George of Clarence, she thought they would be closer than ever to the throne and would live at Westminster with the royal family. But what happened instead was arguments and tension and uncertainty.

Her father had taken King Edward as prisoner but had had to eventually release him as the lords would not follow his commands or orders, and Anne was breathless with relief when she found out that Warwick and Clarence had been forgiven last Christmas. But her father was not restored to his place next to the throne, his protests at the queen's family ambitions were not resolved and discontent and bitterness had grown inside him ever since. The humiliation she knew he felt at having knelt before the king and been publicly pardoned for his crimes was all for nothing, he said, and he could not take back his rightful place so he had thought again to depose Edward and put Clarence on the throne, and to make Isabel queen!

But it had all gone wrong for her father. He misled Edward, proclaiming a false loyalty to him, and encouraged Sir Robert Welles to meet the king in battle. His forces were unsuccessful and Sir Robert finally confessed that her father and George were behind the uprising, which had failed so badly the rebels threw off their coats displaying the Warwick and Clarence badges as they fled the battlefield at Rutland. Her father had been left with no choice, he said, but to leave England to raise support from his base at Calais. Her sister was heavily pregnant with her first child when they set sail and she was delivered of the babe onboard ship, but her tiny son died in blood and gunfire as the Calais Garrison, now loyal to King Edward, turned their cannons upon them and refused them permission to enter the harbour. Forced to continue their nightmare journey, they sailed on to Normandy until they disembarked, dirty and careworn, at Honfleur.

'Shall I read some more Izzy?' Anne laid her hand over her sister's and gave it a gentle squeeze. She had been lying in bed in their lodgings at St Catherine's Church since their arrival, and Anne did not want to upset her further by mentioning the stale smell that came from her.

'No. I don't want you to read. I don't want to talk. I don't want to sleep. I just want to die!' Isabel started crying again, devastated by the loss of her baby and the destruction of her hopes.

'Shall I fetch George for you? Shall I fetch mother?'

'No Annie. Mother will just give me another talk about how many babies she has lost, and I think Clarence will never touch me again!' The tears came faster and her chest began to heave with the sobbing.

'I am so terribly sorry about the baby Izzy. But I am sure you and George will have many more.' Anne felt a little helpless with these adult conversations, but it was only Anne who spent any time with Isabel here, and she knew she had to be strong for her sister.

'I see now that Clarence only married me so father would help him become king. Now that plan is failing, I am sure he will turn against me; indeed why should he stay?'

'I am sure father and Clarence love you very much Izzy, and it must be nice to be married. I think I should rather like it myself.'

Isabel smiled through her tears at her little sister; they had been so close all through their childhood, Anne was the one constant in her life.

'You mean, you should like to have been married to Richard of Gloucester! You always did moon over him at Middleham. Indeed, it is a shame that the king would not allow you to wed. It would have been nice, us both being royal duchesses together.'

Anne blushed and looked down at her book. 'I would indeed have liked to marry Richard. I believe him to be a good man, and is he not Constable of England now? He was always so kind to me. But I am sure Clarence is kind to you Izzy, and who knows, perhaps father will prevail and you may still become queen?'

Isabel looked out of the window towards the harbour and did not reply.

Château d'Angers, Loire Valley, 22nd July 1470

Warwick bowed his head a final time and backed from the

chamber, the furious Countess Anne beside him. His wife wasted no time in berating him when they were out of earshot.

'That bitch! That she-wolf! To make you kneel for so long before she would even speak to you! And King Louis, just standing there and smiling! I am beyond humiliated by the encounter, and I am surprised you could even look Marguerite in the eye, let alone bow to her.'

'Be silent wife. I have more worries on my mind than how long she made me kneel. Indeed, I have never had so many concerns in my entire life.'

Countess Anne could see that Warwick was deep in thought and contemplation and sought to moderate her voice.

'Well, then let us discuss together what you have already agreed to, husband.'

'You heard it as well as I, you agreed to it too.' Warwick entered the privacy of the garden and spread his cape on a mossy stone bench for his wife to sit. 'King Louis arranged this meeting with Marguerite of Anjou so we can enter into an alliance. I am to sail for England with a force provided by Louis to lead the invasion, depose Edward and return Henry to the throne. Jasper Tudor will enlist Wales to rise again for the Red Rose. We are Lancaster now, my dear.'

Countess Anne gave a little snigger. 'I am surprised Marguerite was willing to meet you at all. She looked as if she would claw your face rather than speak to you.'

'Marguerite knows I am her only chance of regaining the throne of England for her husband and her son after him. She also knows this is *my* only chance of returning to England with some sort of position and power. And don't think King Louis is doing this out of a sense of rightfulness, he is doing it to have French support in England and to crush the Burgundian alliance.'

'What of Clarence? You promised to put him on the throne of England. He will not be pleased to learn that this second treason against his brother Edward was in vain and now he must bow the knee to Henry and his son who comes after him.' The countess scrutinised her husband's face for any sign of regret.

'I care not for George's feelings one bit. What is important is that we return to England with an army and take back our rightful places.' Warwick looked determined and hard; there was certainly no remorse about Clarence, but what he really felt about allying himself with the murderers of his father and brother, his wife could not tell.

'And our daughter Anne? She is to be used to seal this new alliance with Marguerite?'

'Yes, Anne will marry Prince Edouard of Westminster and will become Queen of England when old Henry dies. We are back in power, my dear.'

The countess sat back comfortably. 'This pleases me well. Back in power is where we belong.'

Bishop's Lynn, Norfolk, 2ⁿᵈ October 1470

'Tell the Master to cast off Richard, we have no time to lose.' The two ships drifted away on the Purfleet towards the North Sea, and Edward felt he could finally breathe again. He looked back towards the long warehouses of the Hanseatic merchants that lined the docks, and wondered if he would ever see his England again.

'Come brother, you need to speak to the men. They are looking to you.' Gloucester clasped Edward on the shoulder and turned him towards the lords and soldiers, about three hundred of them, who gathered on the decks around him. Edward knew he had to reward their faithfulness but with his spirits so low, wondered if he was up to the task.

'You are loyal to the House of York, and for that I thank you.' Edward stood before the men and raised his voice. 'I will admit to you all that this is not what I had planned, I could not even pay the captain for these ships, but you have stayed with me during these difficult days, and I swear that one day I will reward you all.' He looked at Richard, who nodded encouragement. The sight of his faithful brother heartened Edward and he continued in a stronger voice:

'I further swear by Almighty God I will return to England!' The men began to cheer. 'I promise before Jesus Christ that I will put down those traitors who turned against me and forced me from my own country. I will take back my throne and my crown and I will remember those who did not forsake me. Before God, I thank you all.'

Edward bowed to his men, and felt Gloucester's arm come around his shoulder as he whispered to his king; 'Well done Edward. I almost believed you myself!' The brothers laughed and turned towards the covered cabin.

Once on their own in the cabin, Edward felt his mood turn sour again and he reached for a flagon of ale. In truth, it was humiliation that was fuelling his thirst and he tried to wash the sour taste away with this awful brew that almost made him gag. Warwick and Clarence had left England in defeat, he thought, but the king had been in the north when he heard that they had landed on English soil in French ships and with Lancastrian soldiers were marching to meet him in battle. Christ, he could not believe it! He had forgiven those bastards their treachery once before, and this was how they repaid him! Warwick and Clarence had joined with Marguerite of Anjou to overthrow him, and he had had the messenger repeat this several times before he could believe it. Queen Elizabeth, pregnant again, on hearing of Edward's flight had taken sanctuary in Westminster Abbey with the princesses and even Bishop Stillington was hiding with her. Warwick had made his own brother George Neville the new Chancellor and his intention was clear; kill Edward, free old Henry from his confinement and put the Red Rose back on the throne with the House of Neville back in power. Warwick and Clarence had the support of Sir Thomas Stanley, Jasper Tudor and thirty-thousand men. The other Warwick brother, John of Montagu, had turned traitor to Edward and gone back to his brother leaving Edward outnumbered and outflanked. Unprepared, Edward had found himself in Doncaster, almost defeated without even drawing his sword. Warwick's army was marching straight towards him and Edward could neither fight nor defend himself. With his few soldiers, he fled east to Norfolk and the coast with his brother of Gloucester, his great friend Hastings and his wife's brother Anthony Woodville. He was leaving England, taking ship and headed to his sister Margaret Duchess of Burgundy, praying that she would help him. He running from battle and running for his life, and the indignity was as hard to swallow as the foul ale.

Angers Cathedral, Anjou, 13ᵗʰ December 1470

'Princess. Princess!' The maid was calling to her mistress but could not seem to attract her attention. 'Princess Anne!' Anne Neville turned away from the window in the retiring chamber with a start. 'Princess, you are expected at the feast. I have been sent to fetch you.'

'Thank you Tess. I will come in a moment.' The maid left and Anne looked at her sister who had arranged her fine skirts on a padded settle.

'My God Izzy. My God.' She sounded flat and defeated. 'I am married to Edouard of Westminster, the boy who has been our enemy all our lives. Now I am Princess, one day to be Queen!' Anne's face matched the white gown she wore, with the delicate Venetian lace trailing from her tall conical hat past her shoulders.

'Are you not happy sister? You will be Queen of England one day and me the forgotten wife of a traitor.' Isabel was sour and did not mind that it showed.

'Happy? I am so very far from joy Izzy, I wish I were dead.'

'Annie, all our father's dreams are coming true. He has restored King Henry to the throne of England, he is Protector of the Realm and he has banished and attainted the House of York. King Edward and Richard of Gloucester are hiding in Burgundy and you have made it all possible for him.'

'Father sold me, he sold me to Marguerite and her devil son so he can have the support of France to put himself back in power in England. He sold me like a bushel of wheat. I hate him, I hate mother for letting him do it, and most of all I hate my husband!' Anne dissolved into floods of tears and collapsed onto the settle next to her sister.

'Well, you are returning to England soon. Perhaps you will hate it less when you've got your arse on the throne,' Isabel was scathing. 'I imagine being Queen of England will make up for a frightening mother-by-law and an abominable husband.'

Berkhamsted Castle, Hertfordshire, 24ᵗʰ March 1471

Duchess Cecily received the York Herald in her private chamber, a robe thrown hastily over her nightgown. She had abandoned all pretence at decorum in her haste to hear the news. For months she had written letter after letter to anyone who she thought might have information or might be able to help Edward, forced into exile in Burgundy. Withdrawing from London the day Warwick had marched in, Cecily had hoped to keep herself out of the way and, in truth, could not bear to see mad King Henry, taken from his comfortable confinement rooms and paraded around the capital by her puppet-master nephew. Henry had been propped up enough by Warwick to hold court at Westminster and had nodded and smiled at young Henry Tudor, son of his half-brother, when brought forth by Margaret Beaufort. This determined mother had apparently petitioned for the return of her son's title as Earl of Richmond, but this honour was in the custody of Clarence, so only God knew what payment he would want in return for it.

Cecily had worn her quill down firing off missives begging for aid, and had even written a gushing and affectionate letter to Queen Elizabeth, residing comfortably in sanctuary in the Abbot's lodgings at Westminster Abbey, when she had given birth to a baby boy, Edward's first son. If Edward could return safely to these shores, his position was more secure with a son to follow him. It was the best day's work Elizabeth Woodville had ever done, she thought.

'Well, sirrah, what news? What news of the king?' The York Herald looked confused for a moment at the duchess' question and she felt forced to clarify; 'What news of King *Edward*?'

'As you know, Your Grace, your daughter Margaret finally persuaded her husband Duke Charles of Burgundy to support our cause and the king's fleet provided by the good Charles landed at Ravenspur on the northeast coast, but met resistance there from the Lord of Barmston.'

'Martin de la See? Well he is cousin to the Clifford family, no wonder that he did not want Edward back in England.'

'Indeed, but the king prevailed and we blessed the ship *Anthony* for returning our sovereign lord to his own country. Your son is safe back in England, milady.' He took a breath. 'The king, his brother of Gloucester and my Lords Hastings and Woodville and their men entered the city of York. The king told the mayor he was come only to claim his rights as the Duke of York and was made right welcome.' Cecily smiled at this; she knew from Gloucester's letters that he had been thinking of Henry of Bolingbroke's return to England and guessed that this was his idea.

'Go on,' she urged the wearied man.

'They were welcomed and provisioned in York, then they did go to Sandal Castle, and prayed for the souls of your husband and son who met their end there. They are now headed towards Coventry, where Warwick and his forces are stationed. King Edward fears they will have to fight when their forces meet. He knows you wrote to Duchess Margaret your daughter begging for help, but your son the king asks you to write one more letter, Your Grace, one more letter that he believes can stop a death you will find hard to bear.' The herald looked down for a moment to avoid Cecily's eyes. 'The king begs that you write to your son of Clarence, the king's own brother, and persuade him to return to Edward's side and reunite as the three sons of York.'

'George will be forgiven?' Cecily breathed a silent prayer of thanks. 'Edward will forgive George his treason again?'

'Yes Your Grace. Both the king and Gloucester wish you to assure Clarence that if he reconciles himself to the King's Grace, he will be made welcome. He is of no use to Warwick now, and they feel that he is certain to agree.'

'You can be certain I will write as many letters to George as it takes to achieve this. What of Warwick though, what of my nephew? We all loved him once; can Edward forgive him also?'

'My Lady, the king still loves his cousin of Warwick. However, he feels that battle in inevitable now; he says this must end either in the death of your son or your nephew.'

Cerne Abbey, Dorset, 15*th* April 1471

Abbot Vanne tightened the leather belt he wore around his black robe before he brought the tray of wine into the lodgings he had given over to Marguerite and her party on their landing in England. He could see she was in need of some restoration after the news had arrived. Edmund Beaufort, the new Duke of Somerset, was kneeling before her chair and handed her a goblet of the wine which she sipped gratefully.

'All is not lost, Your Grace. We will raise more men as we head west and meet up with Jasper Tudor in Wales. He can raise thousands, then our fight continues.'

'No, we should return to France. We must protect the prince, his life is precious; we can return when we muster more men with the help of King Louis.' Marguerite was recovering from her shock and was rallying her thoughts. 'My husband, the true king, is imprisoned in the Tower again.'

'As your commander, and as your friend, I must disagree with Your Grace. Our best chance is to join up with Tudor and

133

finish this *now*.' Somerset was presuming on his family's long support of Lancaster to take her hand. 'This is our best chance, we should seize it now. Edward of York and his army will be headed this way and we must get to Wales first, before he catches us.'

'He is right, *maman*.' Edouard puffed out his chest. 'I need no protecting. I need to command my first battle. We will gather more troops as we go and we will meet York in the field once more and do what Warwick could not.'

Marguerite patted Somerset's hand and sat up straighter. 'I trust you as I trusted your father and brother; your family have always served us well. Of course you are right; our fight goes on. Send for the Princess so I may tell her our plans.'

'So there it is. Your father Warwick is dead; he lost us the battle at Barnet, lost our soldiers and lost his life for his failure.' She glared at Anne Neville who was stood before her. 'Some may tell you that the morning mist helped our enemies and sheltered the turncoat Clarence and his brothers. Some may tell you that Gloucester's command of the right wing was what brought about our defeat. Some may also say that men confused Edward's Sunne in Splendour badge with Oxford's Star with Rays and this is why the battle was lost, but I say no! I say this defeat was the fault of your father and his brother Montagu and they both paid the price of their failure with death.' She sat back and took a breath. 'Warwick should never have let Edward get past him at Coventry; he should have stopped him in his tracks there and removed his Yorkist head from his shoulders, but no, he let Edward and his army march straight past him, as if he were blind! Warwick had to turn tail and lead his troops down to Barnet and face York there, after Edward had already been welcomed back to London and gathered more support. Your father's failure cost him his life and the Bear and Ragged Staff is trodden into the mud. Do not think that Edward of York has beaten *me* though; we head to Wales where we will muster more men and we will fight on.' Marguerite was unmoved by Anne's tears, and Edouard smiled wickedly at his distraught wife.

'Tell her of her mother, *maman*. Tell her of Countess Anne when she heard the news,' Edouard goaded Anne. 'Tell her who will save her now.'

'Your mother showed her colours.' Marguerite stood up from the Abbot's comfortable chair and towered over the girl who had collapsed to her knees. 'Your mother has left you here. When she heard that her husband Warwick was killed in battle, she ran away to Beaulieu Abbey and has taken sanctuary there. She gave no thought to you, only for her own skin. Only Lancaster can protect you now, *Princess.*'

Tredington, Near Tewkesbury, Gloucestershire, 3rd May 1471
Squire Ralph handed around a skin of water to the lords sitting beside the brazier. The water was as cold as the night air and tasted of the dirt and dust that coated all their skin and hair. The tent flaps shuddered in the breeze and no one could see the moon's light through the clouds. King Edward and his brother Richard sat opposite each other on small stools and Anthony Woodville was cross-legged on the floor. Sir William Hastings was laid out on a makeshift bed but was the most alert of them all. The forced march west to catch Queen Marguerite had been punishing, and all the men, from the king to the lowly camp cooks, were exhausted.

'Your Grace,' the makeshift tent door was lifted as George of Clarence came in, stomping his feet to shake off the mud. 'The men have had what rations that were left and have bedded down for the night. I've sent out more scouts and set the watch.' He smiled at his brother, as he had smiled continually since Edward and Richard had accepted his apology and his renewed fealty after his support of Warwick. The humiliation still stung, but George was exultant that he had changed his coat before Barnet and the death of his father-by-law. Now he felt he had returned to the fold and his future was bright. Had he not fought alongside both his brothers at Barnet?

'Thank you George. Go and tell the grooms to drop the horses' bits but do not remove their bridles, we will have need of them shortly.' Edward did not look up to see George's glower at being sent on another errand and did not speak again until he knew he and his trusted lords were alone. 'So, we are ready?'

'Battle will be met tomorrow without doubt, brother.' Richard raised his head and brushed his dark hair out of his eyes. 'They are only three miles away, all six thousand of them, and the Duke of Somerset at their head.'

'Not Prince Edouard? I thought he would have been given command.' Anthony Woodville looked around for confirmation.

'What the hell does that devil know about battle?' Edward sniggered, 'although having that she-wolf as a mother must have taught him cruelty.'

Hastings sat up and swung his feet over the side of his cot. 'She has taken cover in Gupshill Manor near Tewkesbury Abbey. She and the Princess Anne.' He looked sideways at Richard, whose face suddenly flushed red. 'Poor Anne Neville, being married by her father to that monster, eh Gloucester?'

Richard was about to deliver an angry retort, but Edward stepped in, keen to keep the peace this night before battle. 'My brother owes a debt of gratitude to Governor Beauchamp of Gloucester, do you not Richard? He kept the town gates barred to the Lancastrians and forbade them to enter there to cross into Wales. Your city stayed true to you, my Lord Duke!' Richard glared at Hastings but nodded to the king. 'That city remains loyal to us both, brother. As to the battle, the cannon are prepared and we have our commands. We will be ready to march before dawn.'

Edward stood up and stretched his long frame, turning his neck from side to side to ease the tension. 'Will, go and get some sleep. Anthony, see that George is behaving himself then get to bed yourself. I need you all alert tomorrow.' He nodded to their bows, and sat down next to Richard when they were alone again. 'It will be bloody tomorrow, brother. It will be a bloody battle, but we must scotch these damned Lancastrians once and for all.'

'I know, Edward, I know. Cousin Warwick taught me well, but didn't know enough to save himself from death in the field. Tomorrow must be our final fight.'

'We will do it for our father, Richard. For love our of father and our blessed mother.'

Little Malvern Priory, Worcestershire, 7ᵗʰ May 1471
Mother Prioress flattened herself against the cold stone wall as the great gates swung open and troops wearing murrey and blue swarmed into the courtyard. The old lady had been shocked beyond her soul when Queen Marguerite and her party had

slunk in two nights before, tired and dishevelled, begging for lodgings after their army was smashed at Tewkesbury. They had been put up in the guest cottage in the grounds and given a meagre meal of fish and stew, all that the poor nuns could afford. Now with the arrival of soldiers wearing York colours, the old nun was not sure her heart could stand the thrill.

'Mother, where is the woman calling herself queen?' Sir William Stanley, a man loyal to Edward, swung his leg over his horse and jumped down beside her. 'We know she is hiding here, we have had men out scouting for several days.'

'She is not hidden, my Lord, she's over there in the cottage, that one with the three windows on the upper floor and the green door.' The nun was almost hopping in her frenzy; this was the most excitement she had known in her seventy years. She pointed with her old gnarly hand. 'That one there.'

'Thank you Mother. You have been most helpful and I will tell our king so.' Sir William strutted across the cobbles, a detachment of his affinity following. Nobody noticed the Duke of Gloucester slip off his destrier and follow behind.

Marguerite of Anjou had finally stopped cursing at the soldiers and was brokenly weeping at the news of her son's death as she was strapped to her horse. Her hopes, her dreams and her ambitions were shattered in one blow; it was all over for her now. Her stalwart Duke of Somerset lay among the dead too. She had dreamt of victory in battle and of her and her beautiful son riding in glory to London and releasing her husband from the Tower. All she could look forward to now was a life of poverty and degradation, she who had once been Queen of England. Sir William nodded to his captain to take her reins and lead her out of the convent, into obscurity.

As the party moved out, a small figure stood in the doorway, hesitant and unsure of what she should do. Anne Neville, once Princess of Wales and now a widow, watched as the troop trotted away. As the dust settled, the light was blocked and a shadow appeared to her right. She turned to the figure, momentarily scared until she heard Richard's familiar voice.

'My Lady Anne. Welcome back to England. Would you be so kind as to accompany me to London?'

The Tower of London, 21st May 1471

Dirty, dusty and still armoured, the tall man and his great friend stood outside the heavy oak door. Inside the chamber rested a sleeping king and his priest. Their voices were low, and the dark haired man looked up to his liege lord.

'It will be done by my hand,' the leader said, 'but it *must* be done.'

'An annointed king. And mad.'

'Still.' He put his hand on the door. 'It must be done, and done now.'

The shorter man bowed his head. 'May God forgive us.'

Baynard's Castle, London, 22nd May 1471

The cleaning of Gloucester's armour was finished and his men directed the pages to lay out fresh clothes for their master, ready for him when he had bathed. Francis Lovell picked at a tray of pastries that had been provided and spoke with his mouth full.

'Edward did honour our Richard before all others! To give him the vanguard in the battle at Tewkesbury was to show how much trust he places in a brother only eighteen years old. No surprise that the king has made him Great Chamberlain of England! Glorious Gloucester!'

'Francis, stop spraying us with crumbs!' Rob Percy wiped his shoulder clean while Tommy Parr snickered and lowered his voice to whisper,'

'And not to give Clarence a command at all! Made him stay by his side like a child all through the battle! Clarence was beyond angry, but what could he do, I suppose? He had knelt before Edward to beg his forgiveness and swear him fealty, *again*, but I doubt Edward will ever be able to trust him fully.'

'We will pray to God that with the death of Edouard of Westminster and that bastard Duke of Somerset, we will never have the need to look for Clarence's support on the battlefield again.' Rob crossed himself and Francis nodded.

'Richard's second battle, and hopefully his last. He did confide to me his secret fear that the pain in his back and shoulder would hinder his ability on the field, but that fear was unfounded. He has proved himself a most able commander and Edward's man heart and soul. The king must surely reward him beyond all others.' Francis sounded more like a proud father than a friend, and none could doubt his love for Gloucester.

'Speaking of rewards, I hear Anne Neville has been brought to London with honour,' Tommy added innocently. 'Now that she is a widow, and presumably a rich widow with prospects, I wonder if the king will seek another marriage for her?' The friends exchanged knowing glances and smirks.

They all turned as they heard Gloucester's voice coming

towards their chambers, and before the door could open, Rob silenced the rest with a look and a smile.

Duchess Cecily sat with the spring sunshine streaming though the oriel window. London was quiet now, thank God. A rebel force led by her brother William's illegitimate son, the Bastard of Fauconberg, had demanded the release of King Henry and a force of seventeen thousand fired upon the Tower of London. Thankfully Anthony Woodville, now Earl Rivers, had control of the City of London and drove back the rebels until they fled, and Cecily was grateful that the man she had no good opinion of had kept them safe. Time to confess her sins again, she thought, and ask Our Lord for a more charitable nature perhaps. So, peace had finally descended on them and her boys Edward and Richard, sprawled on settles, were home and exhausted after their punishing march from London to Tewksbury, chasing Marguerite of Anjou before she could reach Wales. Richard had a minor wound on his arm from the battle that saw the restoration of the House of York, but she had still sent for her physician and apothecary to tend him. Her sons, realising that there would be no peace until she was satisfied, had let their mother fuss until she was content. Now she sat back in her chair, apparently at peace, but still with worries on her mind.

'So, now the dust of battle is settled, we will discuss the future. You have won two great battles in less than a month that have destroyed the Lancastrian threat and restored the House of York. I know your father's heart would be bursting with pride. The three sons of York are reunited and Richard has proven himself to be a worthy leader of men. King Henry suddenly died in his chambers in the Tower, of melancholy you tell me, and

Edouard was killed on the battlefield. They were our enemies, but they must be treated with respect and honour, I will not have it otherwise.' She looked severely at Edward.

'Do not fear, Lady mother. Abbot Streynsham will bury Edouard in the sanctuary at Tewkesbury under his name. Henry was an anointed King of England, albeit mad at the end, and so I have arranged for his body to be respectfully conveyed to Chertsey Abbey for his interment.'

'Speaking of sanctuary,' Gloucester swung around to face Cecily, 'Bishop Stillington came to me with some reassurance. After the battle, Lady mother, many of our Lancastrian enemies hid themselves in the Abbey Church of St Mary The Virgin at Tewkesbury, and Edward gave orders for those men to be brought out by force and face justice for their treason. People were claiming that Edward broke the laws of sanctuary by these orders, but Stillington tells me that the Abbey does not hold a Papal Bull or a Royal Charter to issue such sanctuary, so Edward's conscience can be at ease.'

'Thank you brother. Good man, that Stillington. Very reliable in a crisis.' Edward clasped Richard on the knee and stood up. 'Marguerite is confined at Wallingford Castle, and her claws cannot reach from Oxfordshire to here. She is out of our way. Maybe I'll ransom her back to France one day. Anne Neville will live with her sister Isabel and George for now; she was forced into that marriage against her wishes and I bear her no ill-will. Jasper Tudor has fled, probably to France, and has taken his young nephew Henry, Margaret Beaufort's son, with him. I have a son and heir in the cradle and our line is secure.' His good humour faded. 'But I do want to talk about King Henry's death, Lady mother.' He looked down at his boots for a moment.

'No Edward. I do not wish to discuss it further. You have won these battles for our House, and they must be the last. The Lancastrians are either dead or gone now, except perhaps for that Henry Tudor and he is just a boy in exile. York must reign in peace from this day. This cousins' war will end now.' Cecily looked at her boys; men now, battle hardened and blooded. 'I will accept that Henry died from his heaviness of heart, and the people must believe it too, whatever the truth of the matter. I wish to know no more. You cannot govern this country with any blemish upon your character.' For a moment, Cecily believed she saw Edward colour in shame, but could not guess the reason. But she had not finished her speech.

'I want to speak of Warwick. He was the son of my brother and for that reason I will see him honoured.'

'Our cousin of Warwick is to be buried in his family tomb at Bisham, I have already given the order. We did love him too, Lady mother, and if I could have prevented his death I would have. But he took his own path at the end.' Edward looked to Richard for support.

'Warwick died a traitor to York, but in death he will be honoured as a Neville.' Richard clasped Edward on the shoulder. 'Come brother, let us find George and celebrate both our victories and your new baby son. Our mother needs peace now.'

The door clanged behind them, but Cecily could find no peace. Warwick was once her husband's man, her sons' protector and guardian. In her secret heart Cecily did blame Edward and his queen for Warwick's discontent, but he had chosen his own road to treason. Still, he was of her House. They were both Nevilles, Cecily and Warwick. She opened her Book of Hours and dipped the quill into the ink. She owed him this much.

CHAPTER 3

Nolite confidere in principibus: in filiis hominum, in
quibus non est salus.
Put not confidence in Princes: in the children of men,
in whom there is no salvation.

Fairleigh Hungerford Castle, Somerset, 5ᵗʰ August 1471

George of Clarence looked down at the dead body of the old dog, his expression blank. It lay in front of the door to the gardens as though it had just fallen asleep. He was not sure how to feel about it; he remembered Merry as a pup his father had brought home, remembered how he took it when he and Richard were sent to the Low Countries after their father died. He felt he should have some good memories of his time with the hound, but he could not recall them. The only emotion he was capable of feeling now was discontent; nothing pleased George anymore. Not too long ago he had aspirations of being King of England, a dream he had harboured for years. To realise this dream he had slandered his mother, betrayed his brother and made his bed with Warwick, even marrying his daughter to secure the deal. Then he had been forced to turn his coat again and rejoin the fold of the three sons of York. He snorted at this thought; for a while he had been able to forget the humiliation of kneeling before Edward and Richard and begging their forgiveness, hoping for a place at Edward's side and on his Council. It seemed, though, that Edward could mouth the words of reconciliation but did not truly mean them. George knew he was treated badly and was neglected; it was his younger brother Richard who got all the awards and accolades, so George had taken himself to the country to lick his wounds.

Lick his wounds! He remembered how Merry used to lick his face in excitement when George entered the room, so pleased he was to see his master. Did he enjoy that? He wasn't sure, but he knew that he had savoured the attention the hound gave him. All the death of the dog meant to him now was another disappointment, someone else who had let him down.

He called for his man. 'Burdett. Burdett!' The servant entered the sunny room and stared at the body lying on the floor. George pointed, 'Get rid of him.' The man scooped up the large hairy form in his arms and turned away.

'Thomas.' George called after his man. 'Thomas, see he is buried under the oak tree near the park.' His voice dropped. 'I would talk to my old friend again soon.'

Coldharbour House, London, 10ᵗʰ August 1471

This time Richard had brought her some new ribbons of brown velvet that he said matched her eyes. Anne tucked them in her pocket out of sight, not wanting to share her excitement with Izzy just yet. Her sister was still melancholy although she made an effort to be joyful when they were together. Anne knew her sister would be happy for her, but perhaps not right now. She and Richard had been clever at hiding their feelings so far; he would come and spend time in the solar with Isabel at their London house, then ask Anne to show him the gardens before he left. They always walked down to the edge touching the River Thames and lost themselves behind trees and bushes. It was pleasant to live here with Isabel, even more so when George was not at home. He had never been overtly discourteous to her, but the atmosphere was certainly more amenable when he was not here. Richard clearly felt this too, and came when his brother was away. Out of sight of the house, they talked of their time at Middleham and of the good times that they had had there with Francis and Rob. They talked of Richard's work for Edward and how he was kept busy as Constable of England and Lord High Admiral. There were things they had spoken of only once, and tacitly agreed never to mention again; the betrayal and death of her father, her marriage to Edouard and the seclusion of her mother in Beaulieu Abbey. These were subjects they would not discuss again; the air between them was clear and they were at peace. Now, Anne found herself daily looking out for Richard's men, wearing his White Boar badge, to come riding into the courtyard at Coldharbour announcing his arrival.

Their most recent meetings had become even more exciting. He kissed her for the first time when she was telling him about the plums in the orchard, and he had said he wanted to see if he could taste them on her lips. She had been astounded, then thrilled. When he did not attempt to kiss her again on his next visit, she tried talking about the apple dumplings they had had for dinner but he laughed at her, and kissed her anyway. Being with him made her feel fresh and innocent, like the past had never happened, like they were the innocents they had been in Yorkshire. He had told her about his two children living in the north, but she accepted that as the way of things for men; even her father and King Edward had illegitimate children. It made no difference to her, or to their future. But aside from arranging his next visit, Richard never mentioned the future to Anne. Despite the butterflies she felt in her stomach whenever he was near, her joy was overshadowed by the fear that Richard did not mean for them to have a future together.

Sheen Palace, Surrey, 11th November 1471

Edward looked down at his wife with distaste. Queen Elizabeth was leaning over a bowl, vomiting noisily while Jacquetta held her daughter's long silver hair clear of the mess. He guessed she must be breeding again and he was hoping for another boy. One son in the nursery was not enough, he knew that from the death of Edmund. Three princesses they had, Eliza, Mary and Cecily, and while he loved them as a father should, it was more boys he wanted. Elizabeth had two sons by her first marriage, and Edward was pleased that Thomas and Richard Grey were not his own; they seemed to have inherited their mother's avarice and arrogance but he showed them their duty as a good stepfather must do.

The king moved away from the smell and noise and reached for another glass of wine. Even the fine Venetian goblet annoyed him; the price of one alone would keep twenty soldiers in the field for a month, and Elizabeth had ordered dozens of them. He knew he should curb her spending and greed, but in truth he could not resist her. It was a strange combination of feelings he had towards his wife; he disliked the personality she had revealed after their hasty marriage but he could not resist her beauty or allure. He bedded her, regularly and with pleasure, but was more than happy to leave her bed when he was done. He would not admit to himself that Warwick had been right all those years ago. He should have made a dynastic marriage to a French princess instead of filling his court and country with the upstart Woodvilles, but he would kill any man who said so. He had married her to bed her, plain and simple, a trick that was not unfamiliar to him and this was something that he never even admitted to himself. She had ensnared him and kept him happy for several years while he was blind to her faults; try as he might, though, he could not love her as he once so passionately did. But she was his wife now for good and all, and the expression made him reach for another glass.

'Your Grace.' Squire Ralph entered the chamber unobtrusively. 'His Grace of Gloucester has arrived and seeks an audience.' Edward jumped up, relieved to have an excuse to leave his wife to her misery and left the room almost at a run.

'Richard, I am more pleased to see you than you know!' Gloucester knelt to the king then rose and embraced him. 'Brother, I am glad to bring you joy. All is well with you?'

'Do not even ask, I feel that marriage is a grindstone around my neck.' Edward pulled two chairs together and gestured for Richard to sit.

'Ah, well. It is marriage I wish to discuss. Do you have any wine?'

Coldharbour House, London, 18th January 1472

'You will not! Over my dead body!' Clarence squared up to his brother of Gloucester and drew back his shoulders.

'Whether I will or not is not in your gift George.' Richard fought down his temper and outwardly appeared calm and nonchalant. 'The king has given his permission for me to marry Anne Neville and I will do so, whatever you say.' He sat back and stared up at his blonde goodlooking brother; he looked so much like their mother that he found it disconcerting that he disliked him so much.

'I am Anne's guardian and I refuse to consider it.' George could not back down or speak in modulated tones like Richard.

'You are not Anne's guardian. She needs no guardian; she is a widow and therefore free to choose for herself. She lives with you and her sister at Edward's command, and Edward has no objection to our marriage.'

'Well *I* object! I refuse to allow it!' George was as much riled by Richard's calmness as he was at his words.

'What you object to, *brother*, is not Anne's marriage to me but to the fact that she will bring half the Despenser and Beauchamp lands from her mother when we wed. You thought to keep them all to yourself through Isabel and you cannot countenance me having them in her name.'

George blustered and stuttered. He had known for weeks that Richard was paying court to his sister-by-law, often behind his back, but had not believed that the king would so favour Richard and rob George of what was his by right. The lands in question, held by Countess Anne of Warwick, were vast and valuable. The property owned by Warwick himself had already been shared out amongst Edward's favourites, but his wife's inheritance was still up for negotiation. Technically the Countess still owned these lands but as she was in seclusion at Beaulieu, and the wife of a traitor, the king felt he could distribute them as he wished. 'I will take this through the courts, Richard. I will take this to the king himself. I will not permit it! Those lands will come to me, and me alone.'

'I have already told you George. You have no say in this matter, the king has blessed my marriage to Anne.' Richard rose and turned to leave when he saw a slight figure in the doorway. He hesitated, embarrassed and speechless for the first time that day.

'Your marriage? To me?' Anne Neville came forward and Richard heard her raised voice for the first time. 'Were you planning on asking my opinion, my Lord of Gloucester?'

They were in their usual seat in the arbour by the riverside. Richard had followed Anne when she had turned on her heel in George's chamber and made her escape before she allowed him another word. She flew down the stairs and through the garden, and they both heard George laughing as they left. She would not say a word to him, had ignored him when he tried to explain that the lands meant nothing to him and turned her head away when he said he loved her for herself. Richard was on the point of giving up, thinking he had misjudged the whole situation and wondering what George would say when told Anne had refused him, when he heard her little whisper.

'Would you love me if I were poor? If I were a maid who churned the milk in the dairy?'

Richard supressed a smile and knelt before her and took her tiny hand. 'My Lady, I think I have loved you since I first saw you at Middleham. I have loved you through all these years and I will love you 'til the day I die. Will you marry me Anne?'

He could not hear her answer through her tears, but took the nodding of her head as assent.

Baynard's Castle, London, 20ᵗʰ March 1472
Duchess Cecily held up one of the blue velvet cloaks with pleasure. 'Very fine, Kat, very fine indeed.' Her chief lady-in-

waiting was smiling broadly; her mistress had ordered five of the cloaks for her ladies to wear when they accompanied the duchess outside the castle, and all the women were delighted at the richness of the material and the fur trim around the hoods, very suitable for this hard winter. 'Come ladies, don your finery and let us show ourselves to London! Well, at least to my son of Clarence.'

'Her Grace the Duchess of York, King's Mother.' Burdett was deferential to Cecily when he bowed her into Clarence's presence chamber at Coldharbour. Isabel came forward immediately, dropped a little curtsey and kissed her on both cheeks. George rose slowly and briefly knelt for his mother's blessing. Cecily could see he was surly and anger was simmering just below the surface of his politeness. She turned to Isabel. 'Perhaps you would be good enough to show my ladies the fine altar cloth you commissioned, I know they would be so pleased to see it.' Isabel cast a grateful look at Cecily and ushered Kat, Madge and the rest of the ladies, all wearing the fine blue cloaks, from the chamber, eager to get away from her husband's temper.

Duchess Cecily settled herself in one of the silk upholstered chairs and indicated to George to sit beside her. 'Well, my son? What is the cause of your sourness?'

'You cannot guess mother? I am sure you know all about it, indeed you know everything that goes on in London.' George stood up and stalked to the window. 'You know what it is! Edward has agreed that Richard can marry Anne Neville, who is under my protection. I refuse to let it happen!'

'You refuse to share her mother's inheritance I believe? Well, as to that I cannot say. It is for Edward to decide, and the woman is not dead yet anyway. But surely, other than the lands, you can have no objection? It is right that they should marry; they have known each other for years and I say it is all very tidy.' The duchess rested her hands complacently in her lap and stared at the back of George's head.

'He cannot have Anne and he cannot have the lands! I will not allow it!' George turned and raised his voice.

'I will forgive the manner in which you are addressing me George, but do not let it happen again.' Her satisfaction at the thought of Richard finally marrying was replaced by a rare surge of temper. 'But what do you think you can possibly do to prevent it? You cannot lock the girl away, she is free to decide herself and they have the king's blessing!'

'You will find, Lady mother, that I can prevent it.' George made for the door, 'When Richard returns to London from his northern excursions, you will all find that I can prevent it. The one thing you will not be able to find is Anne!'

As the litter trundled towards her London home, Kat turned to her mistress. 'Are you quite well Madam? You look out of sorts.'

Cecily turned to the lady who had become her closest friend. 'I am well, my dear. Just tired. Were you impressed by the altar cloth at Coldharbour?'

'It is beautiful, but the Duchess of Clarence fears the duke her husband means to give it away.'

'Is that true? It seems unlikely, Isabel is so proud of it.' Cecily raised her eyebrows in surprise.

Kat lowered her voice confidentially. 'Indeed, it appears the duke has made several visits to the Abbess of the Minoresses of St Clare at Aldgate. The duchess told us that he said the cloth was to be used as payment, but I am sure I don't know what for. Madam, are you sure you are well, you have gone very pale.'

'Good God Kat. Good God!'

Winchester Castle, Hampshire, 10th April 1472

'Another girl, Will. Another damned girl when I need princes!' Edward was drunk and belligerent. He had sloshed the wine over his clothes and was having difficulty focusing his eyes, but Hastings was his great friend and his partner in their drinking and whoring, so he passed the king another flagon. 'Was it all worth it? Useless bitch.'

'Any healthy babe is to be celebrated, Your Grace. A new child is a gift from God.'

'Yes but it means it was all for nothing!' Edward slurred his speech and spilt the wine from his cup. 'I married them but no one was happy, and I have only one son.'

'Please, speak with care Your Grace. You may say too much.' Hastings tried to pry the cup from the king's hand but he wouldn't release his grip on it. 'Perhaps that is enough to drink now, shall you go and give the new princess your blessing?'

Before Hastings could haul his master out of the chair, the squire Ralph burst in. 'Your Grace…' He saw his king hanging out of the chair with wine tipped down his doublet.

'Give the message to me Ralph. The king is indisposed and I *am* his Lord Chamberlain.'

Ralph stepped forward with the leather roll. 'A message from the Duke of Clarence, my Lord.'

'Christ, what does he want now?' Edward managed to catch that last part of the conversation.

'It seems the Lady Anne Neville has disappeared, Your Grace. He says she's gone missing!'

Baynard's Castle, London, 17th April 1472

Anne had been here a week but was still afraid to look out of the window in case she was seen. Her fear of George, and possibly Izzy, had not subsided even though Duchess Cecily assured her of her safety. She had recovered from the shock of finding out that Clarence had intended to put her in a nunnery, a closed order from which she would not have been able to escape but she was still surprised at the cleverness of Cecily's plan to rescue her without Clarence knowing. When the duchess had explained it to her, explained that to keep her from marrying Gloucester, George had been prepared to secrete her away in a convent where none would find her, she was relieved that he had not thought to murder her and try and explain her death away. She would put nothing past the wickedness Clarence would carry out to prevent the wedding.

Duchess Cecily had explained it all to Anne when she brought her back from Coldharbour to the safety of Baynard's. Anne thought it was a brilliant plan, although she had not known what was happening at the time. It had appeared that the duchess was paying a regular call to Clarence, with her ladies in tow, when a blue velvet cloak had been thrown around her shoulders and she was hustled out of the courtyard with four of the duchess's ladies surrounding and concealing her. Kat had hushed her when she tried to cry out in shock, and even clasped her hand over Anne's mouth, but the whisper of 'Gloucester awaits you' had seen her quieten and go along with the ruse.

Except that Gloucester was not waiting for her. Richard had gone to Wales as their Chief Justice and was not expected back for some time. George had obviously waited until his brother had left London before he tried to carry out his wicked scheme, but thank God in Heaven that Cecily had saved her. But she wanted Richard. She wanted to feel his arms around her and to put her head on his shoulder; that was the only thing that could take away her fear, knowing that Richard would keep her safe her whole life.

Church of St Martin Le Grand, London, 22nd April 1472
The priest's eyes were alight with pride as he announced the Duke of Gloucester and ushered him into the warm chamber. Anne Neville rose and politely curtsied, 'Your Grace.' Richard bowed and responded.

'My Lady. Thank you father.' He turned to the old man in the black robe. 'I believe my men downstairs would appreciate hearing Mass before we leave.' The priest nodded and hurried away to get his vestments, and didn't see Anne rush into Richard's embrace as the door closed behind him.

'That should keep him busy for a while. Come here, my sweet Lady and kiss me.' Anne giggled and did as he bid, before returning to her seat by the fire. The showers had turned the air damp, and she was grateful for the heat. She had been grateful for so many things recently, and the cosy room was just one of them.

Richard had returned from Wales, dusty, weary and with much pain in his back. He had thought to have a joyful reunion with Anne at Coldharbour, only to find her ensconced at his mother's home. He had been truly shocked to learn that Clarence had intended to put Anne in a nunnery so she could not marry him, and was even more stunned to learn that Cecily had disguised Anne as one of her ladies to remove her from the house right under George's nose; something about the duchess arriving with four ladies-in-waiting but leaving with five and how she was lucky no one had noticed. How she had learned of the evil plan Richard was not clear; something to do with an altar cloth, but he didn't care. He was so angry with his brother that the duchess had had to physically restrain him from storming over to Coldharbour House and begged him to be calm for Anne's sake. She had held onto his arm until he was still, and Cecily had made Richard promise he would take no action or harm George in any way, saying she would deal with Clarence. Only when she had exacted such assurances that satisfied her would she send for Anne so they could be reunited. They all agreed that for Anne's protection she would be removed to a place of sanctuary for a time to ensure her safety and the priests at St Martin's had provided her with the best of care, for which Richard had ensured they were amply rewarded.

Now they sat close to each other by the fire and Anne laid her arm on his sleeve as though she could not bear to let him go.

'Are you well, my Lady? Are you well cared for?' Richard visited Anne daily, but asked these questions every time.

'Yes Richard, I have everything I need. Well, everything except for one thing.' She leant over and kissed him again, blushing at her own forwardness. Richard smiled; he knew she did not like to appear too bold, but her desire for him was plain as day. He considered taking her into his arms properly and thought of the priest downstairs with his men and wondered how long they would be. But no; Anne's honour and trust were paramount to him, so instead he contented himself with holding her hand.

'I have sent my man William Catesby to Rome. He's a good lawyer and trustworthy. When he has the dispensation we can be married, beloved. Then you shall be safe and none shall come between us ever again. Not George, not Edouard, no one. Can you wait for me, my Lady Anne?'

She leaned over and whispered, 'Richard, need you ask?'

Coldharbour House, London, 30th May 1472

'And what are you celebrating my son?' Duchess Cecily noted that George did not ask for her blessing when she arrived but made no comment. He looked to have been drinking since dawn, so cloudy were his eyes. She seated herself across the table from him, with Isabel hovering nervously by the window.

'What have I to celebrate Lady mother? He drained another cup of ale and banged the pewter mug on the table. 'I hear the crossed keys of Rome have delivered good news to my brother of Gloucester. He thinks he is to marry my sister-by-law.'

'Only thinks it?' Cecily looked across to Isabel. 'Why should he only *think* it?' Isabel didn't reply, only looked down at her wringing hands. George answered for them both.

'Because I still refuse! I will take this through the courts of England, Richard be damned. *Edward* be damned too! I will drag this matter on for so long that they will both grow old and die before it's over.' George started to laugh and Isabel nervously put her hand on his shoulder.

'My son, what has happened to you? You were not raised in jealously or resentment. Where does this spite for your brother come from?' The duchess's voice almost broke, but her determination saw her clear her throat and touch George on the arm.

'I have been overlooked and bypassed mother. I shared grief and sorrow with Richard as a child; the death of father and Edmund, *you* sending us away.' That made Cecily withdraw her hand as though it were burnt. 'I did share these things with Richard, but I will not share my fortune and what is mine by right.' Clarence's voice was growing steadily louder and Isabel had backed away again in fright. 'And then, *then*, you steal the girl from under my very nose! You took Anne away from my house, without my authority and without my permission. Perhaps this is where my *spite* comes from.'

'Very well.' Cecily straightened her shoulders. Geroge had said many cruel things about his mother's honour when he was allied with Warwick, and she feared she was becoming accustomed to his spiteful nature. 'Let us be blunt. What will make you agree to Richard's marriage to Anne. What is your price my son?'

George finally smiled and sat back contentedly. 'At last. A woman who asks a sensible question. I want the Earldoms of Warwick and Salisbury. Then I might consider it.'

'Is that all? What about you Isabel? What do you want?' Cecily's voice was hard and cold and Isabel burst into tears and fled.

'My wife wants the love of her sister back, but I am not sure if that is possible. So, that is my price mother. You may tell Edward so.' George rose and stretched his neck, the drunkenness seemingly disappeared.

'Edward is comforting his wife; Jacquetta has died and I doubt he has room for anything other than his wife's misery today. Good day my son.'

'Oh mother, there is one more small thing I want.' George smiled, his face so handsome in his pleasure. 'I want the Earldoms from Richard but I also want the office of the Great Chamberlain of England. Richard has enough titles already. I am sure he won't miss that one.'

Westminster Palace, London, 12ᵗʰ July 1472

Squire Ralph opened the double doors of the Painted Chamber and bowed to his king and queen. It was a small gathering with some wine and pastries, and a trio of musicians were quietly playing at one end of the room. He straightened up and announced the guests in an unnaturally loud voice.

'The Duke and Duchess of Gloucester.' He bowed again and heard voices rising in cheer as he closed the door behind him.

'Richard, Anne! Welcome! Let us raise our glasses to the happy couple!' King Edward stood and lifted his goblet and the court followed suit. The people gathered in the beautiful room were Edward's nearest and dearest; his sisters and mother had wide smiles on their faces and even the queen, gathered with her princesses, managed a small smirk. Thomas and Richard Grey muttered to each other and Will Hastings was speaking to Francis Lovell. Rob Percy was engaged in conversation with Jane Shore, the red-haired beauty rumoured to be Edward's latest mistress, while Tommy Parr was making eyes at Cecily's youngest lady-in-waiting. Standing to one side of the windows was Thomas Lord Stanley, stroking his long black beard. While nobody really liked him, he had been made Edward's Steward despite his previous support of Warwick's uprising; he had a tendency to turn his coat to suit his mood but his wealth and influence made him a hard man to ignore. Next to him, wearing a red velvet gown, was his new wife Lady Margaret Beaufort, she who had been married to Edmund Tudor then Sir Henry Stafford. As mother to Henry Tudor, the heir to the House of Lancaster who was now in exile with his uncle Jasper, the court were not sure if she had truly turned her face to York or whether she was biding her time along with her new spouse. She cast a knowing look at Bishop John Morton who was stood to her left. Morton was a long-time supporter of Margaret Beaufort, or Lady Stanley as she was called now. He was another who had been pardoned by King Edward after Tewkesbury; he had been a staunch Lancastrian until then, even drawing up the Attainders against Edward's father and brother in the Coventry Parliament, but the king was forgiving of his enemies and had made the lanky cleric his Master of Rolls. Near to the dais, Stanley's brother, Sir William, was politely examining Princess Eliza's embroidery. Bishop Stillington, stout and jolly, was eyeing the table laden with food but was too shy to help himself before anyone else. Noticeably absent from the gathering was George, but nobody would have suggested that the presence of Clarence would have added enjoyment to the celebration.

Richard and Anne both knelt before the throne, before Edward hugged them heartily and led them around the guests so all could share in his joy. The wine was flowing as usual at the king's court and he was determined to celebrate with the newly-wedded couple.

'So Richard, you bring me another daughter, who I welcome heartily to the family.' Duchess Cecily kissed Anne on the cheek and smiled warmly at the pair. 'I wish you joy and happiness for all the years of your life, and I will ask God to bless you with many children.' Anne blushed and looked down, while Richard grinned at his mother and reached for Anne's hand. 'It is my wish that you have this Anne.' Cecily unwrapped a green velvet pouch and withdrew the contents. She placed into Anne's hand a lozenge-sized gold pendant with intricate engravings. It was mounted with a large blue sapphire that glowed in the sun pouring through the windows.

'It is beautiful, my Lady, I thank you.' Anne raised the pendant so she could see the engravings of the Holy Spirit on the front and marvelled at the delicacy of the work.

'If you turn it over my dear, you will see the Virgin Mary kneeling before the Baby Jesus and this will bless your union and fertility.' The Duchess spoke briskly, trying not to catch Richard's eye as he was caught between blushing and laughing. She glanced over at the thrones on the dais where Queen Elizabeth was glaring at her husband who was sharing a cup with Mistress Shore. She drew a breath.

'I have made a decision which seems appropriate to announce today Richard. I am intending to withdraw from court and will live at Berkhamsted in peace; I really do not enjoy being in London anymore and I do not relish the company over much.'

'Why not Fotheringhay, Lady mother? Surely that is more comfortable and familiar? It was where I was born, after all?' Richard looked down on his mother and caught her rueful smile. 'Ah, did I hear that the queen enjoys the comfort of it also?'

'Well, whatever the case, Fotheringhay has too many memories of your father. I will be happy at Berkhamsted. I will take a vow to devote my life to God, as Edward has no need of my advice and my position as King's Mother is truly worthless.' She threw a look over her shoulder at her enormous son, wearing the crown of England and talking to Jane, a woman of most dubious morals, and continued; 'I will live a life of prayer and I trust that I will not be too troubled by the promise of chastity that I will take!' She giggled like a girl, her good humour suddenly returning. 'And what of you two? Shall you live at Crosby Place, I know you like it there?'

'No mother. We shan't live in London.' Richard took Anne's hand and raised it to his lips. 'We are going to Middleham. We are going home.'

Berkhamsted Castle, Hertfordshire, 20th August 1473
Duchess Cecily watched as Kat and Madge wrapped the silver cups in cloth of gold and packed them securely in the wooden boxes. They were gifts ready to send to her new grandchildren; little Margaret born to George and Isabel, and Prince Richard, a second son for Edward and Elizabeth. She thanked God for the safe delivery of two more babies into the House of York, and hoped that these births would send some contentment to her sons. Edward could finally be at peace knowing he had two sons for the throne of England and she prayed that George may find some harmony in his life with the birth of a healthy girl. Cecily had been touched that Clarence named his daughter for Edward's baby, Margaret, who had died just before Christmas, but she had been told privately that this was Isabel's idea. She found that she worried about George more than anyone else and made more entreaties to God on his behalf than she did for any other. She rarely saw him and Isabel now; they divided their time between Farleigh Hungerford in Somerset and Warwick

Castle, but she was kept abreast of their news by Isabel's lady, Ankarette, who was good to send her intelligence letting her know how the Clarences fared. Anne, in Middleham, was a regular correspondent and Cecily had been pleased to learn recently that Richard had persuaded Countess Anne of Warwick to leave sanctuary at Beaulieu and was now living under their protection in Yorkshire. She had hoped to hear of a baby born to her youngest son but it seemed that God had not blessed them yet. Still, they were both young and with the help of the Holy Spirit would have long lives ahead of them to have children together.

'Thank you ladies. Please give the boxes to Colyngbourne and ask him to have them sent immediately.' The Duchess nodded and smiled and sent them from the room. As she turned back to her table, she caught sight of her reflection in the looking-glass, and for a moment did not recognise the old lady staring back at her. She was not yet sixty but thought that the fading golden hair escaping from her wimple and her sombre dark gown made her look nearer a hundred. She gave a quick laugh and shook her head. What had she to be doleful about? She had three sons and three daughters, all healthy with families of their own; what matter if she looked old? She felt the future was secure and she could look forward to an old age knowing that the House of York was safe in the hands of her offspring. She was just like her father in that.

Middleham Castle, Yorkshire, 28th June 1475

'Thank you Your Grace.' Seamstress Kate packed the tools of her trade back into her cedar chest and straightened up. 'I will have the new coats made up in the blue velvet, the buckram and the red damask.'

'I am grateful Mistress.' Richard shrugged on his old surcoat, feeling how tight it was across his back now. As his spine twisted more over time, his right shoulder got a little higher every year and the padded garments the talented Kate made ensured that it was not noticeable when he was dressed. He was self-conscious of how he looked naked, but all those he trusted never mentioned it. His faithful men did not comment on it all, and his beloved Anne would offer massages with lavender oil which helped ease the pain. To keep the secret, he paid for the seamstress's skills privately, never recording the details in his accounts. He often felt now that the pain and movement of his spine was a minor inconvenience in his charmed life. He had married Anne and their marriage was everything was he had hoped for; he lived at beautiful Middleham, he was surrounded by dependable knights and the steadfast people of the area. King Edward had made him Lord of the North, and he rewarded the trustworthy folk of Yorkshire with good lordship and fairness.

As Mistress Kate was ushered out, Countess Anne of Warwick stormed into his private chamber brandishing a rolled parchment.

'Gloucester, have you seen this? Did you know?' She was near hysterical and Richard was too surprised to give her his customary bow.

'Did I know what, my Lady? Why are you so distressed?' He tried to take her hand but the Countess snatched it away as her voice rose to a shriek.

'That I am dead! Dead! Your damn brother's Parliament has declared me dead!' She was almost dancing on the spot in her rage.

'My brother *the king* did inform me some time ago,' Richard could not let any slight to Edward go unchecked, 'that he thought that such a legal declaration would settle the matter of your lands. It is no reflection on you madam, it is merely a legal device for fairness.'

They both turned as the door opened again. At once, Richard's face softened at the sight of his wife. 'My Lady, your mother has had upsetting tidings. Please, sit down Anne.' He guided his wife to a seat and stroked her face. Always precious to him, her recent news had made him want to wrap her in cloth of gold and protect every hair on her head.

'Upsetting! I am more than upset, I am dead!' The Countess sank onto a stool as though the wind was taken from her sails. Her daughter reached for her hand.

'Lady mother, it is only a legal provision to ensure that Isabel and I will share the inheritance, that is all.'

The Countess raised her head to look at them both. 'You are talking to a dead woman. I cannot hear and I cannot answer because I am *dead*. You are carrying a child now Anne. I pray that you will never know the pain of losing a child as I have lost you. I have all eternity to pray for that, now I am dead.'

Eltham Palace, London, 24ᵗʰ December 1475

Duchess Cecily was not happy about returning to her son's court, but she desperately wanted to see her new grandchildren. Queen Elizabeth had had another girl, and Isabel had given George a son! She was so thankful and hoped that Clarence could finally find some peace in his life. He seemed to live in a constant state of anger and disappointment and she had asked

God to bestow peace and tranquillity on her troubled son now. She did chuckle at the thought of the cost the new christening cups would have on her household accounts, but knew it was not an extravagance for her own personal vanity. The lure of seeing the new additions to her House outweighed her dislike of the increasingly debauched and drunken court she felt Edward kept now; it was a never-ending scene of feasts, celebrations and wine and this did not suit the duchess' more spartan lifestyle. She also did not want to hear the court gloat over what they were calling a victory at Edward's planned invasion of France to reclaim lands historically belonging to England; instead of restoring the lost inheritance and bringing battle to France, Edward had capitulated to King Louis' oily charm and skill and had accepted vast quantities of bribes and rewards to leave the regions untouched. By all accounts only Gloucester had refused the monetary gifts, instead withdrawing from the negotiations in protest at Edward's stance and not signing the treaty they had agreed at Picquigny. His personal motto may be '*Loyaulté me Lie*' but it was the first instance she could remember that Richard did not support his brother and on this occasion he had felt his loyalty to his conscience overrode his loyalty binding him to the king. She hoped that this would not lead to further divisions between her sons.

'Her Grace the Duchess of York, King's Mother.' Thomas Lord Stanley announced Cecily and guided her into the presence chamber. The king and queen were surprised to hear her name called as neither really expected her to attend the Christmas Feast as she so rarely left Hertfordshire now. Edward lumbered down from his throne on the dais and approached her. 'Lady mother, I am so pleased to see you. Please, give me your blessing.' He was half drunk already, and William Hastings had to grasp his elbow to raise his bulk off the floor. Cecily bobbed a curtsey in reply and kissed him on the cheek. 'Edward, season's greetings to you. And to the queen.' She turned and curtsied to Queen Elizabeth.

'Thank you Duchess. What a joy to see you here.' Elizabeth's smile did not reach her eyes. 'I suppose you wish to hear all about Edward's success in France this past summer? And about the drowning of Henry Holland of Exeter on the journey home? Wasn't he once husband to your daughter Anne?'

'Thank you, no. I believe the military campaign that was funded by Parliament's money was not a military campaign at all, just an excuse to reap rewards from Louis of France in the form of pensions and plate. Or so I have heard; what should I, a mere woman, know of these things?' Cecily matched the queen's unfriendly grin and turned away from the throne. 'And the sea is welcome to the Duke of Exeter. I have not travelled these miles in winter to discuss politics or policy, or a convenient death. I am here to see my new grandchildren.

The gathering was glittering and opulent and the guests made merry throughout the day. The Princess Eliza, Edward's oldest girl, had become betrothed to the Dauphin of France as part of the terrible treaty the king had made, and was parading around the room telling all who would listen that she would one day be Queen of France. Her younger sister Princess Cecily was looking sour and refusing to dance. Thanks to a peace treaty agreed with Scotland, she had been promised in marriage to the Scottish heir, James, Duke of Rothesay but was jealous of her sister's better fortune. Duchess Cecily smiled at her kindly and turned her attention to the Clarences.

'So the queen has had another little princess for England, and your wife has had a son, George!' Isabel and Clarence sat close to the duchess with a little bundle wrapped in red velvet, and she kissed the baby's tiny head. 'Another Edward! How wonderful. God bless you child.'

'We did name him for the king, of course, but we call him Teddy.' Isabel passed the baby back to her lady Ankarette hovering behind her, and drew her little daughter forward. 'Maggie, greet your Lady grandmother.' The two-year-old girl looked at her shyly and Cecily laughed. 'Ah, this truly is a blessing. Everyone gathered for the birth of Christ and we are welcoming new babies into the House of York.'

King Edward approached his mother with a fine glass goblet in one hand and a golden platter of sweetmeats in the other. 'Can I tempt you Lady mother. I assure you *this* plate is English!'

Middleham Castle, Yorkshire, 12th February 1476

Gloucester and Francis Lovell were dealing with the accounts for Richard's household at nearby Sheriff Hutton Castle. Francis was not only a great friend to Richard but had also proved himself to be an able and clever man, capable of good administration and fair dealings. Under his guidance, a tutor and nurses had been appointed to live at Sheriff Hutton to care for Richard's children born out of wedlock, little John and baby Katherine. Not only had Anne agreed to this arrangement, she was instrumental in organising the household there, knowing that all the children of a duke needed a good upbringing.

It had been Francis' suggestion to open the heavy ledgers

for inspection this late afternoon; he knew Richard needed some diversion from the activity going on in Anne's rooms. Her labour had started last night, and he had spent every hour since pacing the corridor outside her chambers, denied entry by the strict midwives. As her screams grew louder and closer together Richard had become despairing, and finally Francis was able to lead him away, convincing him that he needed his strength to visit his new family later.

Richard had shown Francis a gift he had had commissioned from the jeweller merchants in York; a tiny gold book fashioned with its pages opened to show engravings of St Margaret and St Leonard, the patron saints of childbirth. He thought that perhaps he should have given Anne the jewel before her travail started but it was too late now. He had faced death, exile and battle and he knew now that he would rather meet them again than have to listen to the distress and cries of his wife. Never had he felt more hopeless or helpless and Francis' attempts to discuss the cost of furnishing a nursery were making him more agitated by the moment. Just as he felt he must punch Francis or push him out the window, the door opened quietly and Tommy Parr showed in Anne's lady, Tess.

'My Lord of Gloucester. You have a son.'

Berkhamsted Castle, Hertfordshire, 17th February 1476

The journey back from Windsor Castle had been exhausting for Duchess Cecily. She was sixty years old and wondered for how much longer she could sit in a litter for an uncomfortable trip. She felt drained, both in her body and her mind. The funeral for her daughter Anne had been well attended; her second husband

Thomas St Ledger had commissioned a place in his family chantry and both the king and queen were present to honour her. Cecily could find a place in her heart for this son-by-law, he was a far better husband to Anne than the Duke of Exeter had been. But childbirth was a game of chance for women, poor Anne had lost her life delivering a daughter and Cecily had shed bitter tears for her own loss and that of the poor little girl, never to know her mother. It had brought to her mind all her own losses; not just her husband and Edmund, but all the little ones returned to God before they were out of short clothes.

Kat and Madge had been pillars of strength to their mistress and had tried to provide every comfort they could think of, from warming pans and furs for the journey to a hot meal and soft bed on their return. The one thing that did lift her spirits was the news from Richard in Yorkshire and it seemed to be God's plan that they must make room on this earth for all the new children born to the House of York; what He gives, He also takes away. She had added another entreaty to her daily prayers now; that this be the last death she would witness in her family.

'Ladies, please send for my silversmith; two more christening cups are required thanks be to God.'

Church of St Mary and All Saints, Fotheringhay, Northamptonshire, 29th July 1476

Duchess Cecily rose from the pew as the funeral cortege approached the altar. Her son of Gloucester led the procession clad in a black hooded robe, preceding the Lords and priests who had been on this long journey with him. Eight days ago the bodies of her husband and son were taken from their humble graves at the chapel of the Mendicant Friars in Pontefract and had begun their final journey, back to Fotheringhay and the church of their fine castle where they had spent so many happy times in their younger days. This vault under the choir was a much more fitting resting place, and they would now lie alongside Richard of York's uncle Edward, the duke who had died at Agincourt. She swore to herself that all her family would be buried with such honour.

The funeral procession had stopped in towns such as Doncaster, Newark and Grantham and each night Vespers for the Dead were said over the biers and a vigil kept lighted candles around the sacred remains of Cecily's loved ones. King Edward had entrusted his brother of Gloucester to see all respect was given at every stage of the sombre journey, and had paid for a fine feast to be held this very night for all who had come to honour them; Cecily had overseen the housing and feeding of the fifteen thousand people who were expected to raise a glass to the fallen of the House of York after the committal service.

As the litters bearing the bodies approached the altar, the priest ascended the fine pulpit donated by the king and opened his breviary. Cecily knew now where her old bones would rest when she was called to God; here alongside her Lord and husband. She bowed her head and her blue veil covered her face and tears as the priest began. *'In nomine Patris et Filii et Spiritus Sancti.'* Her tears were of sorrow for her loss, but of joy also. Richard and Edmund were home at last.

Middleham Castle, Yorkshire, 26th December 1476

The wetnurse was getting annoyed with the Duke of Gloucester, but it was far from her place to say so. She had just got the little lad settled after his feed, and in he came, trying hard to be silent and stealthy and managed to kick over a stool and nearly toppled a candle. He had leant over the crib, and when he saw his baby son's eyes open, he scooped him up and sat himself down in the rocking chair. Every time little Edward's eyes started to close, the duke kissed his forehead and whispered his name; 'Ned, Ned, how shall I tell your mother?'

'My Lord, shall I take the little Earl now?' Bessie, mistress of the nursery, shooed the wetnurse away with a frown, and stood respectfully with her back against the wall. 'Shall I put him in his crib?'

'No Nurse. You shall not. I will hold my son until his mother arrives back from the church.' He looked up from his seat by the fire and softened his voice. 'Thank you, but I will stay here with him until the Duchess comes.'

'Very good, my Lord.' She hesitated briefly. 'You know the physicians say they think he may be growing stronger now. I am sure there is no need for you to worry over his health.'

'It is not my son I fear for today Nurse. Please, leave us now.'

She bobbed a curtsey and turned to the door as Anne came in, bringing a gust of cold air. Her cheeks were flushed from her walk back from St Alkelda's where she had been giving alms to the poor on this St Stephen's Day. Anne had endured much during the birth of their son and the midwife was worried the injuries she had suffered may cause difficulties for her in future childbearing. She had been confined to her bed for months afterwards and had only recently begun to venture from the castle and go into the village, but today she seemed well and happy. Richard knew, however, the news he had to bring her would reduce her to despair again. Anne nodded as the nurse left, then turned to her husband with bright eyes and a laugh in her voice.

'I look all over the castle for you, and here you are, tucked up warm in the nursery with your heir. I should have guessed!' She took little Ned from his father and put her cold cheek against his warm head. She kissed him and laid him gently in his cradle.

'Richard? What ails you?' She took his hand to lead him from the cosy chamber, but he caught her arm and stopped her. 'Richard?'

'My Lady.' He cupped her face in his hand and stoked her hair. 'Anne. I have had a message from Warwick Castle. It is about your sister.' Anne gripped his arm and pulled it away.

'From Izzy?' Her sister had given birth to a second son a few weeks ago. 'Is her new baby well? Richard, you are frightening me, what is it?' He put his arms around her and pulled her to his chest and spoke into her soft flaming hair.

'Isabel is dead, my love. I am so sorry, but your sister is dead.'

Berkhamsted Castle, Hertfordshire, 16th April 1477

'So you have named him George, for your brother.' Duchess Cecily gestured for her page to pour the king another glass of ale. 'How wonderful, another baby! Three sons of York to follow you, Edward. You must be so content.'

'Yes, Lady mother, I am. Three boys and the future looks secure. Prince Richard is a strong lad and now I have Prince George. Prince Edward is happy at Ludlow, learning the business of a Prince of Wales. It sours me to know that his guardian is my wife's brother, Anthony Woodville, but that was her price

173

for allowing him to set up his household so far from London.'
Cecily rolled her eyes at the mention of the queen's brother; she
thought him to be gallant and dashing, but generally perfectly
useless unless he was writing poetry or jousting.

Edward was paying a brief visit to his mother's castle as
he was on a short progress of the southern counties. He had
thought to visit his brother in Warwick Castle, but George had
refused to answer his letters in his grief. He had lost his wife
then the new baby they had named Richard followed soon after;
the king had sent Bishop Stillington to offer comfort and solace
to Clarence and he had reported back that the new widower
seemed mad with grief and anger. Naming the boy the queen
gave birth to last month for George was intended to be a gesture
of kindness and kinship, but it appeared that he had found no
consolation in the token at all.

Still, his mother's hospitality was liberal and Edward was glad
he had come. Her cook made the finest lamb and herb pies and
her cellarer was generous. He was aware she held no love for the
queen and she had withdrawn to Hertfordshire to be away from his
court. Better to keep the two women apart, he thought, and he did
not regret his mother's absence in London as she was too fond of
giving advice and frowning on the excesses which were a daily part
of his life now. Added to the cost of the feasts and barrels of wine
that came in at an enormous sum, Edward found that the expense
of new clothing to cover his increasing girth was becoming quite
a burden on his accounts. But, he thought, a king needs pleasures
and pastimes or what was the point of being king at all!

Duchess Cecily watched her eldest boy as his eyes drooped
and he nodded off into sleep. He had once been such a fine
figure; a man of muscle, strength and vitality; now instead of
her battle-hardened son, he was becoming lazy, gluttonous and

vice-ridden if her sources at court told truth. But the room was warm and the chairs comfortable, and soon Cecily found that her eyes too were heavy with sleep.

The afternoon sun had slid past the solar windows when Will Hastings opened the door in a rush. Cecily sat up straight and was instantly awake, but Edward carried on snoring. Hastings bowed to her; 'Your pardon, my Lady, but I must see the king.' Cecily gestured toward the padded chair in which Edward was slumped, and watched as the Lord Chamberlain began to shake him. Edward wakened with a start, some remnants of his vigor bringing him alert in seconds.

'What is it Will? What ails you?'

Hastings glanced at Cecily and hesitated before answering. 'It is the Duke of Clarence, sire. Your brother George?'

'Christ, what now?' Edward took the leather messenger roll from his friend, but did not open it. 'What does he say?'

'The message is not from Clarence but from the Sheriff at Warwick. He tells a shocking tale. George has convinced himself that his wife was poisoned, and has arrested, tried and hanged Isabel's maid, Ankarette, for her murder!'

'What?' Cecily reached for the leather roll but Edward was clinging on to it. 'Ankarette is dead?'

'Yes my Lady. The Sheriff says that George bribed or bullied the jury into returning a guilty verdict on her, despite there being no evidence.'

Edward's mouth was hanging open in shock. 'The stupid fool! He takes the law into his own hands and thinks I will do nothing? Is he insane?'

'I fear sorrow and despair have made him run mad! Isabel surely died of childbed fever and the poor babe was never

175

strong.' Cecily read the letter from the Sheriff which she took from Edward, who had stood up and was pacing the room in anger.

'Mad or not, I cannot let this go, no matter what relation this fool is to me. Will, send men to Warwick Castle, speak to Clarence's people there. Dig deep and bring me the truth.'

Hastings nodded and bowed, turned and left the room. Cecily laid a calming hand on the king's arm. 'Edward, remember he is your father's son and he has witnessed the death of his wife and child.'

Edward shook off her arm and said scathingly, 'Lady mother, I am King of England and ruler of this land. If my laws have been broken, the guilty man will face the consequences. No matter who he be.'

Berkhamsted Castle, Hertfordshire, 22ⁿᵈ May 1477

Duchess Cecily was weeping bitter tears as Kat and Madge stood behind her chair. Colyngbourne perched on a small stool close to his mistress, distressed at having brought her such news but knowing he had had no choice.

George of Clarence had indeed run mad, he thought. It must have been madness, or perhaps it was just his true nature coming to the fore. After years of disappointment and what he saw as being overlooked, he had truly gone too far now, the duchess' servant reasoned. Clarence's man, Thomas Burdett, had been investigated after the events at Warwick and was discovered to have been predicting the date of the king's death by sorcery and circulating this news amongst the people, to hasten Edward's demise as a prophecy that must fulfil itself.

Colyngbourne, who had no great opinion of King Edward himself, supposed that George had been behind this whole plan, and it was rumoured that he had a letter signed by old King Henry stating that it was George who was to inherit the throne of England. George had also planned to marry the daughter of Charles of Burgundy, as she had inherited the fortune and the duchy on her father's recent death. King Edward had forbidden this, which Colyngbourne thought sensible, as who knew what Clarence would do with a foreign army at his disposal. George must have thought this was another obstacle to his success and thought to bring the king to account for his actions; he had begun to spread sedition and rumours across the land yet again, saying Edward was no true king. For his use of necromancy, Burdett had been executed at Tyburn and had made a speech from the scaffold declaring his innocence. George had shouted these words to the Royal Council after breaking into their meeting at Westminster Palace, and Edward's patience had finally snapped.

'How could he?' Duchess Cecily had composed herself enough to speak, and her plaintive wail rang around her chamber. 'How could Edward arrest his own brother?'

'The charge was for contempt of the laws of the land, my Lady.' Colyngbourne knew his mistress well enough to know she needed to hear the truth. She had never been one for shying from accuracy and demanded plain speaking from those around her. Nevertheless, his words brought fresh tears to the duchess, and her ladies laid comforting hands on her shoulders, while casting disapproving glances to the older man. He ignored them, and steeled himself to tell the rest. 'There is more, Your Grace, I am afraid. After his arrest, my Lord of Clarence has been confined to the Tower of London.'

As Colyngbourne rose from his stool and headed for the door at Kat's insistent wave, the duchess' shrieks were ringing in his ears.

Berkhamsted Castle, Hertfordshire, 6th January 1478

The Feast of the birth of Christ had been celebrated quietly by the duchess' household. There could be no true joy or merriment when Cecily was so distraught at events happening in London. She had not forgotten to give her ladies and servants their usual gifts of bolts of cloth and coin, but it was obvious her enjoyment of the celebration had been muted. The gifts from Richard and Anne at Middleham had included a fine sable throw and miniatures of all the children, which she had kissed and placed on a side table next to those of her husband, Edmund and Anne. Cecily had been pleased that the Clarence children, Maggie and Teddy, had been taken into their household in Yorkshire, and in her secret heart she wondered if their upbringing there would indeed be better than if they had been left at Warwick with nurses and servants. Isabel and the baby were cold in the ground at Tewkesbury Abbey and the feckless George was in the Tower, but well housed with all his whims and requirements met. When Gloucester's man, Sir Richard Ratcliffe, had arrived with the parcels from her son, she sent him on to see Clarence in confinement, and he had reported back to her that George was well fed and housed, but was clearly still beyond anger and rage at his brother the king. Ratcliffe, on further probing, disclosed that George was drunk for most of the day on his favourite sweet malmsey wine, and would have no conversation with anyone except Bishop

Stillington. He had even returned Cecily's gift of new leather boots and her own mother's paternoster beads.

After a quiet Twelfth Night feast Cecily retired to her private chapel, knowing full well that her household would now celebrate the holy season with mummers, music and laughter. She almost begrudged them their ability to set aside their worries for an evening, but realised that her concerns were not shared by everybody. She was aware that most thought it safer for the country if George was locked away and none really missed his presence, and perhaps she could agree with them. What drove Cecily to her knees five times a day was not George's current circumstances, but what would happen in the future. He had been incarcerated, albeit in relative luxury, for months, but if King Edward pardoned and released him, who could believe Clarence would take himself off to live quietly in the Midlands for the rest of his life? And if Edward would not forgive him, what was the alternative?

Westminster Palace, London, 15th January 1478

'You stupid bastard! You fool! Do you know what you have done?' King Edward swept his arm across the table so goblets, papers and ink flew to the floor. He was moving fast for a man his size, pacing between the table and the windows while Bishop Stillington remained on his knees with his head still bowed. Will Hastings flattened himself against the silk covered wall and said not a word.

'Forgive me sire, I did not intend to tell him but I thought he knew! He was ranting and shouting that you were not the rightful king and that your sons should never follow you on the throne, so I thought you had taken him into your confidence. I thought you had told him!' The stout bishop was past tears; now he was fearing for his life. He wrung his hands together and gibbered in his distress. 'Please, Your Grace, please…'

'What?' Edward stopped his frantic pacing and towered over the bishop whose head was nearly bowed down to the floor. 'Please what? We were the only ones that knew. Now George knows and God knows who he will tell! I sent you to him in the Tower to comfort him and see if he is willing to retract his nonsense about his wife being poisoned, and now this! I have trusted you all these years to keep the secret, I have rewarded you and given you positions of honour, and you cannot keep your mouth shut!'

Edward drew himself up to his full height and grasped Stillington by the elbow to haul him to his feet.

'Well that fat stupid mouth has bought you your own cell in the Tower. Guards!'

Hastings and Edward faced each other across the table. The older man poured the wine and pushed the cup across to his king. The fight had gone out of him now; he was ashen faced and staring down at his boots. Hastings had to crane forward to hear him speak.

'If George knows I was betrothed to Lady Eleanor Butler all those years ago, he will never keep that to himself. It's more powder in his gun, isn't it?' Hastings put his elbow on the table, turned his head and scratched his ear.

'You're right, Your Grace. Clarence will never keep that quiet. He is like a loose cannon already; with what he knows now from that idiot Stillington, well, I fear for your throne.'

'That's not all I fear Will. Ask the queen to come to me will you?'

Elizabeth Woodville had finished throwing the golden plates at Edward's head, but he still had the red marks on his face where she had slapped him. He had taken the hits from her silently, allowing her to release her mighty anger on him as he would never allow a man to do. He waited until she had stopped panting and spitting and was finally sitting in a chair.

'So. If I hear right, Edward, you married this Eleanor Butler before we were wed, and she was still living when I became queen. I assume you married her to bed her, then got tired of her. You tell me that the bitch is dead now, which I must say is a blessing, but our marriage is not legal! Do tell me if I have any details wrong.' Her sarcasm made her spit her words at her once-handsome husband but she had no fear that he would retaliate. 'Bishop Stillington performed this love match between you two, and for years only you plus Hastings, *of course*, knew. Now, for some reason that I still do not understand, the reverend bishop has told George of Clarence! For the love of God Edward…' The queen fell to sobbing again, and they were tears of anger and near despair.

'Elizabeth I have said I am sorry, which is not a word I use often. But now we must deal with this.'

'Deal with it? Christ, Edward! Deal with it? You do realise what this means? The raving Clarence knows your dirty secret; but worse, this is to disinherit our sons! You were not free to marry me, you are a bigamist and our children are bastards! Don't you see? George *is* the rightful next King of England after all!'

Edward slumped into a chair, but still taking care not to be within striking distance of the woman who once so entranced him.

'Fear will keep Stillington's mouth shut and Hastings is loyal to me. They will not speak a word of this. But what shall I do about George?' He finally looked at his wife and reached for her hand.

The queen took a deep breath to calm the raging storm inside her. 'What do *you* think Edward? How many ways can you think of to keep Clarence quiet for the rest of his life?'

Middleham Castle, Yorkshire, 21st January 1478

'His Grace approaches, open the gates!' The new Master of Horse, Dominic Franke, shouted ahead of the small cavalcade in his deepest voice. He secretly feared that he could not fill his old father's boots as keeper of the duke's stables, so often resorted to these subtle tricks to prove he was as good as the old man. The small group clattered into the castle's courtyard after a hunting trip in the hills. 'Quick lad,' he called to a groom. 'Take the duke's horse, walk him 'til he's cool and then give him a good rub down.' Franke looked back at Richard of Gloucester to reassure himself his master was pleased, and lightly touched the White Boar symbol he wore proudly over his breast.

The duke dismounted and was laughing with Rob and Tommy about the stag that was too quick for them. He clasped the Master of Horse on his shoulder in thanks, and the trio were walking under the gateway towards the private chambers when Francis Lovell intercepted them.

'Your Grace! Richard!' The duke felt his heart flutter briefly in fear; although he would not admit it to even his closest friends, he hated being away from the castle when Anne and little Ned still seemed so weak. He thought by the look on

Francis' face that he brought bad news from the physicians about his precious family, but Lovell held out a parchment.

'It's from the king, Richard. It is not good news.'

'Of course I understand Richard, you must go at once. Your Lady mother needs you, and God knows what the king is thinking.' Anne was seated by the fire in her cosy solar, her sewing fallen to the floor when her husband came bursting in.

'He cannot execute George! In God's name, what has got into Edward?' Richard was pacing the floor. 'He writes and tells me as though it were an invitation to a banquet!' He picked up the message again and waved it in his hand. 'High treason! He accuses George of rebellion, sedition and plotting against the queen and their children and he is to be executed for high treason! Has Edward run mad, do you think? Is it the wine?' Anne had never seen her husband so distressed. She flew out of her chair and clasped his hands, her face pale and her limbs weak.

'Richard, you must leave today. You have to see the king and speak with him, you cannot allow this to happen.' The duke took a deep breath and exhaled slowly. He raised Anne's slim hand to his lips.

'My Lady, my Anne. I hate to leave you but what if I cannot stop him? How shall my mother bear it?'

Windsor Castle, 17th February 1478

'I have no choice brother. George will die tomorrow.' The king was wearing his crown this day, as if to reinforce his position and status so none could dispute with him. He had withdrawn to Windsor so not to see the reaction of the people in London when his command was carried out, but said publicly it was for the fresh air of the castle near the river.

'Edward, I do not understand.' Richard of Gloucester, sleek in his dark long coat and boots, was trying to catch the king's eye. They were alone but for the queen, and both were ignoring her. Edward refused to look at Richard and kept his eyes fixed on the window looking down the sloping grassy hill to the Thames. 'What has George done? In the past you found it in yourself to forgive him when he turned traitor, can you not do that again? His mad ramblings can surely be attributed to the loss of Isabel and the baby; I do not understand why now you are proposing to execute him. Just listen to the words! Execute George? Edward, you know in your heart you cannot do this.'

'Richard, I have no need to explain myself. I have brought a charge of high treason against him for his crimes. The Act of Attainder has been passed and the sentence will be carried out at noon tomorrow.' Edward finally met Gloucester's eyes, and his face was as hard as stone.

'Edward, you are the King of England and I am your man, heart and soul. You know this. You know I would do everything in my power to protect and serve you, but for the last time, I ask you not to do this. I ask you to spare George's life.'

'No. It cannot be.' Edward stood up and went to approach his brother but Richard took a step back. He bowed his head formally but the king did not respond.

'My Liege.' Gloucester turned to the door. 'I will show in our mother.'

Duchess Cecily, King's Mother, stood outside the door of the presence chamber and wondered how she had the strength to stand. She was weak in her knees and her arms felt as heavy as logs. She was wearing her habitual blue gown with trailing sleeves, and her hair was in a jewelled net. It felt like an omen, wearing these mourning clothes, but today it was her words, not her appearance, that mattered.

The double doors opened and Gloucester approached her, his face like marble.

'Lady mother, I cannot move him. You must try.' He turned to his left and stared out of the paned glass with his back turned.

Duchess Cecily walked slowly into the vast chamber where the king and queen were seated on their thrones. She could hear her heels echoing through the room and thought it was the sound of her pounding heart. Cecily stopped before the dais and forced herself into a deep curtsey, then waited for Edward to come forward to receive her customary blessing. When he did not move she took a step closer to her son and stared at him.

'Edward,' Cecily started to speak then realised she had no words. 'Edward, please.'

'We agreed to see you, Lady mother, as a courtesy.' Cecily noted that he was including Elizabeth Woodville when he addressed her. 'We have brought a charge of high treason against George Duke of Clarence and his crimes are punishable by death. The matter is now closed.'

'Closed? Edward, you cannot sentence George to die, he is your brother! He is your father's son! What of Maggie and Teddy? Edward please!'

The king stood up suddenly and began to shout. 'I have forgiven him all these years for his wrongs against me and I have shown him mercy for every treasonous act he committed, but not anymore! Now his sins cannot be forgiven, he accuses me of using black arts, and he says I am illegitimate and not rightly king, and this is a slur on your honour also! He tries to rally men against me. How shall I forgive him this time, mother?'

Cecily shrank back in the face of Edward's outburst, then watched as he slumped back into his gilded chair. She turned to the queen, sitting silently beautiful in a gown of silver thread that shimmered in the light.

'Is this your doing?' She addressed Queen Elizabeth directly. 'You have never forgiven George for the death of your father and brother, you have always blamed him. Have you finally persuaded Edward to kill him so you can get your revenge?' Cecily's voice had risen to a shriek and her move to approach the throne was stopped by the king.

'Be silent Duchess!' His voice, always so powerful, made her draw back and bow her head. 'I am King of England and it is my word that condemns Clarence, not the queen's.' He stared down at her and was not moved by the tears that started to run down her face. 'However, I am mindful that he is the king's brother so I will spare him the disgrace of a public execution and have given instruction that he is to be executed in his cell, in private. That is all.'

'Edward please…' Duchess Cecily brought her clasped hands together in front of her breast and looked up at her oldest son. 'Edward, you cannot kill your own brother! He is my son! He is only twenty-eight years old! My son, please, I beg you. I cannot lose another child!'

She was met with no response. The king stared at a point over her shoulder and would not look at her.

Duchess Cecily slowly sank to her knees. She raised her hand and tugged at the net on her head until it came away and her long hair, once golden and shiny, fell about her shoulders. She bowed her head so the greying strands fell either side of her face, then lowered herself to the ground and spread her arms out wide, in supplication, in appeal, and begged for the life of her son. She remained there, her face amongst the rushes, until she heard the footsteps of the King and Queen of England leave the chamber and she was alone with her anguish.

Tower of London, 18ᵗʰ February 1478

Richard Duke of Gloucester stood outside Bowyer Tower in the shadow of the imposing fortress of the White Tower, and looked up at the south turret on the first storey. His ever-faithful Francis Lovell was at his side, not knowing how to comfort his friend and master, especially this day when the sun would set on a son of York. George had refused to see Richard, telling the guards to send him away but to tell him that he would have a glass of wine in his final hour, in memory of him. Richard was not sure if this was George mocking him or saluting their years together, and now he would never know. He was Constable of England, he could force them to let him into George's rooms, but he knew that Clarence must want his final moments to be shielded behind the grey stone walls and his last minutes to be witnessed only by his priest and his executioner. He would stay, though. He would stay outside the doors in case he was sent for, in case his brother changed his mind and wanted a familiar face with him when the time came.

Richard turned to Francis and clasped his hand on his shoulder. 'I hope George had a friend as good as you, Francis.' Lovell smiled down at the shorter man, sympathy and sorrow in his eyes. 'I hope he will soon be at peace.' He looked up again at the window. 'I hope he will forgive us.'

Duchess Cecily sat in her privy chamber in the comfort of Baynard's Castle straining her ears for the chapel clock to strike the midday hour. She realised that her chair was soft and padded and the room warm and inviting, and suddenly she hated all these luxuries. How could she be surrounded by pleasant furnishings and log braziers when she wanted the cold darkness of a tomb? How could she live in this world knowing that her eldest son took the life of his own brother? George had many faults and flaws but he did not deserve to die, and she wondered how Edward could live with that on his conscience.

Cecily already had her Book of Hours open, and as the chimes rang out for noon she looked down at the list of names. Her family had been taken from her by war and battle, never by a cold-blooded execution by one of her own. But she was an old hand at death now and she knew she could live without George, as she lived without Edmund and her husband. What she was not sure of was, could she live with Edward?

CHAPTER 4

Amplius lava me ab iniquitate mea:
et a peccato meo munda me.
Wash me more from my iniquity:
and cleanse me from my sin.

St George's Chapel, Windsor Castle, 22ⁿᵈ March 1479

Duchess Cecily stood in the second row of mourners and watched as the tiny coffin was placed in the tomb. She stared at the back of the king's head and looked on as his shoulders drooped and shook with sobs. Queen Elizabeth was not present; apparently her grief was too much to bear and she had not left her rooms since their two-year-old Prince George had died of an infection the previous week. The little princesses surrounded their father and young Prince Richard was holding his grandmother's hand staring at the floor, bereft at the loss of his baby brother.

King Edward led the procession out of the great double doors into the spring sunshine as the priests intoned the final words of the service: '*In paradisum deducant angeli, chorus angelorum te suscipat,*' and Cecily led the translation, 'May the angels lead you into paradise, may the chorus of angels receive you.' This was the first time in a year since she had seen her oldest son, having determined never to return to the court she could no longer abide. She had even missed Prince Richard's marriage to the wealthy five-year-old Anne Mowbray, whose red hair she could see streaming in the breeze outside the chapel.

Edward approached her now and with some grunting, knelt for her blessing. Cecily's hand was like ice as she laid it on his head, then she gave her own reluctant curtsey to him.

'Lady mother, I am most pleased to see you.' The king wiped his blue velvet sleeve across his face and it came away covered in snot and tears. 'This is a day of great sadness and sorrow to us, but to know you share our grief makes the pain more bearable.'

Duchess Cecily looked up at the man who had once been her pride and her comfort but who now bore no resemblance to the fine athletic figure he had been. His heavy, bulky body was clothed in the finest of materials but they could not disguise his corpulent form.

'Indeed, Edward. The anguish of losing a child compares to no other heartbreak.' Cecily's heart was as hard as the marble that covered the little prince's tomb. 'The loss of a son named George is a bond we both now share.'

Eltham Palace, London, 21ˢᵗ April 1479

The queen had moved to the beautiful house at Eltham further down the Thames to rest after her loss. She could not bear to hear the chatter and prattle of the princesses so she had left them in the care of their nurses and retreated to find peace with just her brothers and her Grey sons for company.

Anthony had come from Ludlow at the news of the little prince's passing to comfort his sister and found the queen in the newly built Great Hall, alone except for Lionel their brother who was Dean of Exeter and headed for a bishopric, and Edward the youngest but fearless Woodville up from his castle at Porchester. Elizabeth had always preferred the company of men; whether it was because she could shine without comparison to others of her sex or if she found their conversation more stimulating, Anthony was not sure. But here he found her, almost distraught with her brothers holding her hands and her cries echoing around the empty vast chamber.

'The fault is mine, don't you see?' She shook her head and the tears spattered across the table. 'I am to blame for the death of my precious boy.'

'The physicians said the illness came on so fast, sister, there was nothing to be done.' Edward Woodville stroked her face and wiped her eyes with his thumb.

'Indeed, and he is in the hands of God and our parents now. He is at peace.' Lionel was trying to use his holy office to bring solace to the queen, speaking in the deeper voice he employed during his sermons.

'No, I don't mean that!' Elizabeth took a shuddering breath. 'I don't mean I could have saved him, I mean that his death was foretold! It is God's punishment that my Prince George was taken.'

The men hushed their comforting tones and a stillness descended amongst them.

'Clarence. You mean George of Clarence, don't you?' Anthony, although based with the Prince of Wales at Ludlow, knew very well what had happened with the king's brother. 'You insisted that Clarence should die because he knew that the king was already married when he met you, and now you think your baby George was taken in retribution for his death.'

'Yes!' She screamed and broke away from her brother's restraining grasp. 'I told my husband that George had to die, and now God has taken *my* George as well!'

'Elizabeth,' Anthony lowered his voice and looked around the hall to ensure they were alone. 'You had no choice. If Clarence told anyone that your marriage was not legally binding, it would have been the end for you.'

'The end for all of us.' Edward Woodville nodded at the others. 'If it came out that the princes are *not* princes, but bastards, well Christ knows what would have happened.'

'He is right Elizabeth. You are Queen of England and your son will follow Edward on the throne at his death. You had no option. George had to die to let Prince Edward inherit.' Anthony was firm, he felt coddling his sister now was not the way forward. 'We present here now, along with the king and your Grey sons, are the only ones who know. You had no choice.'

'You are not alone sister.' Edward stood up and bowed to her. 'We are the family of Earl Rivers. The rivers run deep. We are with you in this and we share your grief, but it was the right thing to do. We take this secret to the grave with us.'

Berkhamsted Castle, Hertfordshire, 22nd February 1480
On the top of the pile was a bill from the town merchants that Duchess Cecily was ignoring. The price of almonds and pepper was extortionate at twenty-two shillings and she was determined to speak to Cook before she paid it. Steward Godfrey must really come to a better agreement with the merchants, she decided, or they would find only plain mutton

broth on the table for weeks to come. She sniffed at the idea that these traders thought to inflate their prices when dealing with her servants, and reached for the next letter in the jumble of papers.

'Ah, it's from the Princess Cecily, how lovely of her to write.' Kat smiled up from her stool where she was mending the lace on her mistress' nightgown, and Madge was near her, reading *The Sayings of the Philosophers* that had been translated by Anthony Woodville. She preferred tales of French knights but all the other ladies secretly gushed over the queen's brother, so she thought she should read it too. 'I hope she is well, Madam?'

'She is quite distressed I believe. Would you move the candle closer my dear, my eyes are straining in this light.' Kat moved the silver holder while Madge lit another candle and the scent of beeswax filled the air. 'Poor child, she fears her betrothal to Scotland's heir is in jeopardy. The Scots are making raids on our borders, rebelling against King Edward and breaking our peace treaty, so he is losing patience with them it seems.'

'I heard that Alexander of Albany, the brother of King James III of Scotland, is after his throne and has gone to France.' Kat got most of her information from the traders who passed through their town and was proud that as a woman she could have news of the realm.

'Indeed, causing trouble no doubt, and desperate to be the next king. To keep the alliance, Edward has demanded Scotland return Berwick to English hands and wants Princess Cecily's betrothed, the *real* heir to the throne, Prince James Duke of Rothesay, to live in London, but they have declined. I fear she is more concerned about not becoming a queen like her sister Eliza than she is about not marrying the spotty duke!' The duchess shook her head and scanned the rest of the letter. 'She says she has received a gown from my daughter Margaret in Burgundy in the new style, decorated with gold brocade, with a high neckline and fur lining! Gracious me, that child is worldly.'

Kat nodded and carried on with her work, giving a little smile when she heard the duchess mutter, 'Just like her mother.'

Westminster Palace, London, 10th March 1480

The meeting of the Council had been in session for over an hour, and the king was getting tired. They were there to discuss only one topic; Scotland. Bloody Scotland, Edward thought. He had thought his warring days were over but King James was breaking the old alliance of peace and spitting in England's face. Despite his weariness of war, Edward thought that he was being pushed right to very edge of it once again. James' brother, Albany, was almost certainly behind the killing of English officials on the border and the pillaging raids and had sought the help of spidery Louis of France to overthrow his brother James. It appeared that Louis would not help though, and Edward's Council breathed a sigh of relief at this. Will Hastings had pointed out that Louis might want to see war between England and Scotland, he just didn't want Edward getting the idea of invading France again.

'It's all a bloody mess!' Edward reached for his cup, only to discover it was empty. He threw a baleful glaze at Squire Ralph, who rushed forward to refill the golden goblet with haste. 'Does James want war? He's crossing my borders and begging me to retaliate! And what's Albany up to? He wants his brother's throne and he's begging Louis for support! Are we to be attacked on two fronts? You're my Council, tell me what's happening!' Edward was belligerent and getting angry, and his Council sought to find the answers he wanted.

'Your Grace,' Thomas Lord Stanley stood up and stroked his beard. 'Because of King James' raids, you rightly stopped the dowry payments for Princess Cecily's future marriage. King James has refused your demands to give us Berwick and his heir. I believe that war is now inevitable.'

'I agree with my brother.' Sir William Stanley, far shorter and uglier than his brother, rose also. 'War with Scotland cannot be avoided, but I believe that an invasion by France will not happen. Not yet anyway. As for the Duke of Albany, in time I think he will come to us, begging for a deal to support his claim for the Scottish throne.'

Bishop Morton, as usual, spoke last. 'Your Grace, let us leave France and Albany aside. We can deal with them at a time that suits us. Now we must prepare to attack Scotland. I propose you command Jack Howard to sail up there and frighten them into behaving.'

'Thank you, my Lords. I will go further though. I propose making my brother of Gloucester Lieutenant-General of the North and he will issue commissions for the border defences, and raise men should we need them. The benevolences I have raised from among the wealthy Lords of this land means I have no need to ask the old women of Parliament for the funds to bring war to the Scottish bastards.'

As the lords bowed and left the Council Chamber, Edward sighed and turned to Hastings.

'War again. I'm getting too old for this Will. Let us hope Gloucester is ready for the challenge.'

Eltham Palace, London, 9th November 1480

'My ladies, *please*! Is this seemly behaviour for Princesses of England?' Lady Margaret Stanley stood with her hands on her hips and frowned at the girls who were squabbling and snatching scarves and belts from each other. Princess Eliza was willowy and beautiful like her mother while Princess Cecily was darker in colour, and both could be catty and spiteful when their parents were not present. Lady Margaret began gathering up the discarded luxuries and placed them back in their wooden boxes. 'And what is the cause of *this* disagreement, Your Graces?'

'Eliza said that when she's Queen of France I will be her lady-in-waiting so I should give her my new dress from Aunt Margaret! It's not fair!' The eleven-year-old girl angrily wiped the tears from her face and looked away from her smiling sister.

'My Ladies, there are dresses enough in Burgundy for you both. And a future Queen of France should conduct herself more fittingly.' Lady Margaret stared at the older girl who dropped her smirk and turned her shoulder.

Queen Elizabeth Woodville appeared at the chamber door and looked enquiringly at Lady Margaret, who dropped a curtsey and began to explain.

'No need, I heard everything. Eliza, Cecily, go and practise your music.' As the girls left, the queen sat in the chair by the fire and smiled. She had not really liked Lady Margaret when she first came into her service but had been forced to offer her a place in her rooms to appease Lord Stanley upon his marriage to her. Lady Margaret was the mother of Henry Tudor, the last Lancastrian heir and cousin to Henry VI; the queen had wondered where her loyalties truly lay when she married the

King of York's Steward, but after several years of service, the queen believed that she had turned her coat and was loyal to their House. She was perhaps a trifle too holy for the queen's taste, but excessive piety was a trait Queen Elizabeth was prepared to overlook in a woman who offered her good service and kept her children well behaved.

'Edward's new treaty with Burgundy will undoubtedly mean more dresses in the new fashion and that will perhaps keep the girls quiet.' The queen scrutinised Lady Margaret, who had never seemed troubled by vanity. She always wore a dark gown and white wimple which made the queen shine by comparison.

'Is the Council meeting over, Your Grace?' Lady Margaret nodded at the queen's gesture she should sit on a stool near her. 'Will the king be returning soon? My husband Stanley tells me that war has been declared on Scotland now.'

'He should be back soon, he is overseeing the funds to be sent to his brother Richard to pay the wages of the soldiers. No doubt he will be wanting his dinner as soon as he comes.' The women smiled at each other; the king's appetite was legendary and the cooks were hard pressed to keep up with the constant flow of platters and bowls that he demanded. 'Edward says that we will be safe here in London though. Scotland won't get far over the border, not with Gloucester and his men up north to protect us.' The queen's voice took on a sour note; she did not like Edward's brother over much. She thought he was too righteous and looked down on her, and she did not enjoy anyone having more influence over Edward than she did. Since Edward's devastating revelations about Eleanor Butler, she found he was more eager than ever to give her what she demanded to keep the truce between them. Peace with Scotland was breaking down, but Richard was a good commander and at his base in Penrith was well-placed to defend English lands.

'King James has asked Louis of France for money for guns, I am told. Bishop Morton says that the Scots will not return Berwick to us and we will have to take it by force.'

The queen noted that Lady Margaret seemed to be cosy with the stern bishop and wondered again at her loyalties. Both Margaret and Morton had supported old King Henry years ago, as had Lord Stanley. She hoped that Edward was right in accepting their fealty and putting his trust in them.

'And how is your son, Lady Margaret?' Queen Elizabeth narrowed her eyes, suddenly wanting to deliver a barb. 'He must be more than twenty years old now. Do you hear from him.'

Lady Margaret bowed her head. 'Henry has lived in exile with his uncle Jasper in Brittany these ten years, Your Grace. His title, Earl of Richmond, was taken from him and I believe they live quietly there under the protection of Duke Francis.'

The queen gestured that Lady Margaret could leave her. As she left the room after curtseying, the queen realised that Margaret had artfully managed to avoid answering the question.

Fountains Abbey, Yorkshire, 1st July 1481

They had met at Ripon the previous evening, and at dawn travelled together in a comfortable litter, following the River Skell for three miles towards the Cistercian Fountains Abbey. The two women had chatted of inconsequential matters; the weather, the spring flowers and how pleased they were it was dry this day. They felt the litter lean forward as the road sloped down the enclosed valley and the vast Abbey gates came into view. The keeper of the gate was present to greet them, and they stepped out into the sunshine and were shown across the courtyard to the Abbot's lodgings.

'Her Grace the Duchess of York and Her Grace the Duchess of Gloucester.' The keeper of the gate was used to introducing important personages to his Abbot, but preferred it when they were men. He bowed and closed the heavy oak door silently behind him.

Abbot John Darnton made the sign of the cross over Cecily and Anne's heads. 'My Ladies, you are both heartily welcome to Fountains Abbey. The Duke of Gloucester is a regular visitor here, in all his benevolence, and we are pleased to welcome his Lady wife and mother.'

'Thank you Abbot.' Anne stepped back, she was happy to let Duchess Cecily take the lead. 'We are grateful you have made allowances for us to visit you on our pilgrimage of peace, and we look forward to praying before the High Altar.' Cecily stretched out her hand and discreetly passed the Abbot a small sack of gold half-angels. The Abbot quickly made the bag disappear up the wide sleeve of his white robe and bowed the distinguished visitors out of the room in the direction of the guest lodgings.

Tess and Kat unpacked their mistress' gear and stoked the fire. The ladies had agreed to bring just one woman each to assist them, knowing how the male dominated environment of an Abbey made it difficult for women to be amongst them.

'Do they fear we may corrupt them?' Tess giggled as Kat, glancing out of the window towards the springs that gave the Abbey its name, replied flatly, 'This place was founded by rebel monks. I think it more likely they will corrupt us.'

Duchesses Cecily and Anne attended the service of Sext at noon and had retired to the Guest Hall for the midday meal. They were not permitted to eat with the twenty-two monks of the Abbey in their refectory, nor were they allowed in the Chapter House for their regular meetings. But the Hall, next to the lodgings on the west side of the cloister, was comfortable and they felt at home with just their two ladies to attend them. From the kitchens they were served fine bread, a dish of baked eggs as well as trout from the lake. Cecily suspected they were eating better than the monks and lay brothers of the Abbey but made no objection, particularly when a stone cask of wine was laid on the table.

'I noted that a prayer for peace in Scotland was said in the church; I hope it will be answered and war can be avoided.' Cecily touched her napkin to her lips and looked at Anne. 'Have you had news from Richard lately?'

'Yes, Lady mother, I have.' Duchess Anne pushed her plate away; she was not a hearty eater and had left much of the fish on her plate. 'King James' soldiers continue to make raids across our border so he has commanded our ships forward to frighten the Scots. I believe King Edward will be headed north this summer to take command.'

'It does sound like a land invasion is inevitable then. If that damned Marguerite of Anjou had not given Berwick to Scotland I am sure none of this would have happened.' Cecily pursed her lips at swearing in a holy place, but she was sure that the king would fight, and risk more English lives, to take back what was rightfully his. 'Well, Edward no longer asks my advice, so I am pleased Richard takes you into his confidence.'

'He travels regularly between Middleham and Penrith, so I have not had to do without his company for too long. Lady mother, shall we walk in the gardens before afternoon prayers?'

Cecily was seated by her fire wrapped in the fur-lined robe that Kat had draped across her. She had listened as the monks went about their work and had seen them after Vespers, trailing to their dormitory above the Chapter House. Their lives revolved around sacred reading, manual labour and attending services; Saint Benedict had ruled that idleness was the enemy of the soul, and these holy men were busy every hour of the day in the service of God, or at least made it appear that way. She was still waiting for Anne of Gloucester to return to their lodgings and could not understand why she was taking longer at her prayers than the monks did.

Her reverie was broken when the outer door opened and she heard Anne tiptoe into her chamber. Cecily rose, went along the passage and knocked on her door.

'Anne, my dear. I was starting to fear for you! How long you have been.'

'I am sorry, Lady mother, I was at prayer.' Anne started to take off her headdress but could not wipe away her tears in time.

'Oh my dear, what troubles you? Do you fear for Richard's safety?' Duchess Cecily was all sympathy and took the hands of her beloved daughter-by-law.

'No, Richard is a fine soldier, he assures me he will be safe. No, it's not that. Oh Cecily, I have been on my knees to God praying for another child!' The younger woman sat abruptly on a wooden chair, forcing Cecily to bend her old knees to get down closer to her. 'We had little Ned five years ago, and since then I cannot conceive another.' The tears came harder to Anne now. 'Richard is so good and never rebukes me, but I so want to give him another baby. We have his John and Katherine with the Clarence children all thriving and growing strong, but our little boy is so fragile and I fear I will lose him and never have another!'

Duchess Cecily sat back on her heels, ignoring the pain in her legs, and wiped away her own tears.

'My poor child.' She was at a loss for words of comfort and resorted to what she had relied on all her life to sustain her through her own troubles. 'My poor child, my heart bleeds for you.' She was suddenly brisk again. 'Come, this Abbey is not going to help us now. My faith is strong enough for us both and I have a better plan!'

Anne looked up and smiled at the stalwart duchess. 'Yes?'

'Yes. The monks are no use to us, we need the Virgin Mary! We shall go to the shrine of Our Lady of Walsingham; we need the power of the Queen of Heaven and I believe I am in good credit with Her.'

Berkhamsted Castle, Hertfordshire, 2nd October 1481

The small service in the Chapel had ended, but the duchess stayed on her knees while the candles burnt down and the priest tidied up his vestments and put away the chalice. Cecily had much to say to God this day and while the wind whipped up outside and the cold air blew under the doors, she continued her prayers as the damp crept up her bones and brought a chill to her whole body. But she never noticed her discomfort, not while she had so much to say to God, and surely His Son Jesus Christ knew more of pain that she could ever imagine.

Her thoughts and appeals ranged far this day. She had given thanks to the Lord for her family and called for His blessings on her people, but she begged for more. She asked God to give her husband and sons in heaven eternal rest and to keep death from her door now, as she had suffered more than enough. Cecily also wanted peace in England and pleaded for the safety of the soldiers on the border; she begged for another child to be given to the Gloucesters and she prayed that the Lord, in His mercy, would allow her to forgive her son Edward for taking George away.

'Long life, really. That's all I ask for.' She clasped her hands and whispered, 'Long life for my family.' Her Book of Hours had too many names written in it, she thought. Too many names for a woman of sixty-six. Two sons and a husband in the grave was enough. Today was the anniversary of the birth of Richard of Gloucester, so she said an extra prayer for him too; twenty-nine years on this earth, and only one legitimate son to follow him. Surely her pilgrimages and supplications would send him another child, please God that it would. Cecily thought Richard suffered enough, what with the constant pain in his back and the twisting of his spine; filling the nursery at Middleham did not seem too much to ask.

Cecily heard the priest shut the door quietly on his way out of the Chapel, and saw Kat slide in to wait to help her mistress back to her room. She raised herself to her seat with a grunt of pain, then used the prie-dieu to haul herself upright. She curtsied to the altar and turned away. 'Long life and if it please you, Lord, relief from my aching bones.'

Woking Palace, Surrey, 28ᵗʰ October 1481

Woking Palace, Surrey, 28th October 1481

Thomas Stanley wiped his lips on the fine linen napkin and signalled to his steward to pour him another glass. He was not one for large meals but he did enjoy the fine cellars of this house. It was another perk of marrying the well-connected Lady Margaret, he thought. His first wife was Warwick's sister Eleanor and she had died the year after Warwick himself went down in flames at Barnet. She had been a mild-mannered woman who had never troubled him much and she had given him many children, some of whom he even liked. He had his heir, Lord Strange, so his line was secure. He had been married soon after Eleanor's death to the Lancaster stalwart Lady Margaret Beaufort. She had been widowed while still a child, then married again to Sir Henry Stafford who was uncle to the duke and had been granted this great house and filled it with the best of everything that his Buckingham money could buy. Soon after both Stafford and Eleanor went to their reward, Thomas and Margaret had married quietly, and for mutual profit. Stanley was aware that he had taken a great risk marrying the mother of Henry Tudor and bringing her to the Yorkist court, but if he was anything, he was a man who would risk everything for power and influence.

Stanley had a reputation for delaying his actions until he knew where his best interests lay. He was not a man of conviction for a cause, unless the cause was beneficial to him. He had promised to support Marguerite of Anjou then failed her, he supported King Edward until he turned his coat again and joined Warwick in his rebellion, then finally declared his fealty to the House of York and had risen though its ranks. Since Tewkesbury, he had been outwardly steadfast in his loyalty to Edward, but never lost his taste for double-dealing and intrigue, and it was this that had prompted his marriage to Lady Margaret. She was the mother of the heir of Lancaster, and he delighted in the prospect that this could be to his advantage should any mishap befall the White Rose. From his wife's point of view, this marriage would give her status and may help promote the cause of her son, so they both knew they had wed for mutual benefit only.

The outer door from the north quadrant opened, bringing

a gust of chilly air which flickered the candles. Lady Margaret, as cold as the wind itself, nodded briefly at her husband as she passed by the table.

'You have missed dinner, wife, but I am sure they will find something in the kitchens for you.' Stanely tossed the comment over his shoulder as she headed for the inner chambers. 'Or are you fasting again?'

'I have been in the Chapel, on my knees begging for God's help, while you have been gorging yourself and drinking. I have no mind to join you.'

'Ah, praying to the saints again? Asking them to bring your son home from exile?' He sniggered at his own words, determined to provoke an argument.

'It was you who promised to help my Henry return to England and you have done nothing so far. Asking Saint Jude for help on his feast day is my only hope now.' Lady Margaret returned to the table and towered over her husband.

'Sit down wife, sit next to me.' His mood changed to conciliatory. 'Edward has two sons to follow him on the throne, he is softening in his regard to your own boy. He may well, with my advice, allow Henry to return to England soon.'

'Do you really think so?' Margaret sat in the carved chair next to Stanley. 'Do you think he will be allowed to return?'

'Of course, one day, why not?' Stanely raised his cup to his lips again. 'It's not as if he could ever take the crown now, is it?'

Nottingham Castle, 1st December 1481
Richard Duke of Gloucester crossed the dry moat and entered through the gateway on horseback; Tommy Parr and Rob Percy

led his household troop and Francis Lovell had gone on ahead to warn the Chamberlain that his Lord was arriving.

The flag of the White Rose gusted mightily in the wind over the battlements and Richard could see the new tower commissioned by King Edward had reached at least three storeys. The House of York held a special place in their hearts for Nottingham Castle which had always been loyal to them, and Edward had taken much care with the new construction and added expansion of the building.

'Richard! Brother, I am glad to see you!' The king came forward to embrace the slighter man, and Richard was shocked at Edward's appearance. He seemed bloated and red in the face; he could hardly believe this was the slim, athletic giant who had won at Towton. He knelt before his king, then rose and hugged him. Relations between the two men had soured for a time after George's execution but Richard had taken the pragmatic view that he had to live in Edward's world and he had sworn loyalty to him, no matter what. He regarded himself as the king's man through and through, although he was grateful to live in the north and not in London.

'Brother, I am pleased to be here. It's been a hard ride down from Yorkshire, the weather has been against us all the way and I am frozen to the bone.' Richard stretched his back in front of the large fire in the chamber, and tried not to wince at the pain it gave him. The cold air seemed to make his discomfort worse, but he knew that an hour or two on the training ground in the morning with Tommy would ease the agony he felt at the moment.

'And how are things up on the border?' Edward sat back on his padded chair and pulled another forward. 'Are those bastard Scots beaten yet?' he said with a laugh. Richard smiled as he lowered himself on the seat.

'Not quite, My Liege.' He stretched out his legs and noted the mud on his boots; he would have to make sure he was wearing clean clothes before he went to evening prayers. 'No, you are aware of my latest report to your Council. King James becomes more unpopular with his lords each day it seems. His brother Albany has a good following, and he is desperate to be king. It is my belief that to beat James back to heel and stop his border raids, we could come to some agreement with his brother.'

'Hmm. Just like George of Clarence, wanting his brother's throne; James should have Albany's head sooner rather than later!' Edward laughed heartily, but Richard did not join in. He could live in peace with Edward and serve him as his subject, but did not find jibes about George's death amusing.

'Well, anyway.' Edward noted his brother's stern face and changed the subject. 'I did want to discuss our invasion of Scotland, which I fear is now inevitable. I need Will, wait a moment. Hastings! Will Hastings!' The king shouted at the closed door until his squire came in. 'Where is my Lord Chamberlain? Send for him, will you?'

Squire Ralph bowed. 'He told me he was gone on pilgrimage Your Grace. I will fetch him immediately.'

As the lad left the room, Richard spoke up. 'Pilgrimage, Edward? Will Hastings is making a pilgrimage?'

Edward laughed at his brother's surprised face. 'No, brother, not really! That's what they call the brew house cut in the rocks below the castle. They say old Richard The Lionheart stopped there on his way to Jerusalem or something. Stopped for ale. So the men say that now when they want wine and women outside the castle walls.' He carried on chuckling and Richard smiled at the joke.

'Anne and our mother returned from their own pilgrimage before the bad weather set in. They went to Walsingham.'

Edward laughed again, 'No ale or whores there I imagine! Just nuns, priests and women praying for a child…' He broke off from his jest and looked Richard, his face immediately full of sympathy. 'I am sorry brother. I was not thinking, I meant no disrespect to you or Anne.'

'I know Edward, I know you did not mean harm. But we have both hoped for it for so long, and Anne felt an offering at the shrine may help us.'

'Richard, I will keep you both in my prayers and I will beg Our Lord to send you another child. I am an anointed King of England, He may listen to me!'

As they entered the Great Hall the assembled men banged the tables in applause for their king and for the Duke of Gloucester. Edward nodded and smiled and allowed Richard the honour of washing his hands in the scented water before he did. Hastings, Lovell, Parr and Rob Percy were seated at the high table with them, ready with their spoons and all looking forward to the meal after their journey.

When the boards were cleared, just Will remained with the king and Richard and the serious discussions began.

'Your Grace,' Will Hastings as Lord Chamberlain began formally. Richard was surprised at the change in tone; until this moment the men had been laughing and enjoying the company and now he felt something had changed. 'Richard, the King's Council have been much occupied with the business of Scotland, as you know.'

'As have I, Will, having been protecting the borders these many months.' Perhaps Richard spoke more harshly than he intended, but he worried for a moment that the king was unhappy with his governance.

'Yes, of course. So you know better than anyone, as Lord Lieutenant, that a land invasion of Scotland is planned for the spring.' Will looked at his king who nodded, then turned back to Gloucester. Richard looked from one man to the other in puzzlement and replied:

'Yes, Edward will lead the offensive when we have the weather on our side. We may even have Albany on our side then too.'

'Well, that's the issue Richard. The king will not lead the invasion. *You* will.' Gloucester stared at Hastings in surprise, then looked to Edward for confirmation, which came in the form of a nod.

'Edward? Is this true? The army of England will cross into Scotland and you will not be leading them?'

The king nodded again and looked down, embarrassed. Hastings took over for his old friend and explained: 'The king and his Council do not believe his health is strong enough to go to war again Richard. He trusts you as his brother, and as Lord of the North, to lead his armies to victory in his name.'

'I cannot do it, Richard.' Edward spoke softly, still not meeting anyone's eyes. 'I am not the man I was ten years ago. I am too weary and fat for war anymore. It pains me more to tell you this than anything else, but I cannot go.'

'Edward, I can't imagine going into battle without you. We have always stood shoulder to shoulder when facing our enemies. Are you sure?'

'I won't stand at the back with the pack horses and the wagons, Richard. If I can't lead my men, I will not go at all. But *you* can. You can lead them into battle and you can lead them to victory.'

Richard got out of his chair and knelt before his king. 'Your honour me with your trust, Your Grace. Of course I will lead your army.'

Edward rose and looked at his younger brother; his clear complexion, his hard body and whip-like strength made the king feel more cumbersome than ever. 'I know you for my most loyal subject, brother, just as you promised you would be all those years ago. I trust you with my life, the lives of my children and the lives of my soldiers, my most honourable Lord of Gloucester, commander of my army.'

St George's Chapel, Windsor Castle, 28ᵗʰ May 1482

The great procession made its way into the Chapel, followed by bishops, priests and nobility. The king and queen were not present at the burial of their fourteen-year-old daughter Princess Mary, but Duchess Cecily was honoured to represent the House of York and be chief mourner along with the queen's sister, Anne. Together they had seen that the child was dressed in a glorious gown for the interment, fit for a young woman who had the beauty of her mother and the grace of her grandmother. Her death had been a terrible blow to them all, particularly the queen who was reported to have screamed until she fainted away.

Cecily had looked into her heart to see if this death could make her feel more sympathetic to Elizabeth Woodville, and to her shame found that it did not. She did not like what this said about her, and had felt compelled to go to her priest for forgiveness and absolution for what she saw as her callousness.

She saw Thomas Grey, Marquess of Dorset, standing aloof and proud. He really was his mother's son, she thought, then immediately rebuked herself for this uncharitable thought. He was twenty-seven now, and grown into his self-confidence as the stepson of the King of England. He was certainly like Edward in that he had an eye for the ladies. He gave a brief nod to the Duchess, then carried on examining the fine ceiling of the Chapel. She thought he had never been particularly fond of the princesses, preferring to align himself with the great lords of the court and on the Privy Council. His brother, Sir Richard Grey, was at Ludlow with young Prince Edward and his uncle Anthony Woodville. Cecily did not have much of an opinion of the other son of the queen and her first husband, except to be naturally suspicious of him as she was of all the queen's affinity.

As Princess Mary's coffin was laid alongside her little brother's tomb, Duchess Cecily shook her head and made the sign of the cross. Another death in the family, she thought, another soul in heaven at God's right hand. The princess had been the most pleasant of all the girls, she thought, then knew it was time for another visit to the confessional to absolve herself and pray for a more compassionate nature when it came to the Woodvilles.

Fotheringhay Castle, Northamptonshire, 11th June 1482

The sun shone brightly on the imposing castle, casting shadows from the huge keep onto the orchards. Duchess Cecily looked out of her chamber window to the bailey and watched as the procession crossed over the lake bridge then under the ramparts and headed towards the Great Hall. The heralds carried the white saltire on blue of Scotland. She had claimed her visit to Fotheringhay was to see the new stone tomb that she had commissioned for her late husband in the nearby church, but she knew her sons would be meeting at the Castle with Alexander Duke of Albany, King James' brother. Although Edward never asked for her advice now, Cecily wanted to be present to see them come to an agreement; for once she wanted to be part of something of importance rather than just running her estates in Hertfordshire. Her beloved husband had always included her in his discussions and meetings, and she secretly hoped that the king would feel she could contribute some value to their meeting with the Scottish king's brother. She hoped for this, but doubted it would happen. Still, it would give her chance to meet up with some members of her family that she had not seen for a long while.

Duchess Cecily led the ladies into the banqueting hall in the absence of the queen. She had been right, she thought. Edward did not ask her opinion or seek her thoughts on the treaty that had just been signed. Fortunate really, she thought; it was nonsense in her opinion. Just because the Duke of Albany wanted to become king instead of his brother, it did not give Edward the right to proclaim him 'Alexander IV' of Scotland in return for his fealty and promise to unite their two kingdoms. Still, they had signed a treaty to that effect and all the men seemed overjoyed at the outcome. Her son of Gloucester would lead an invasion against King James very soon, and would have 'King Alexander' in his train along with the other great lords of the realm. Still, perhaps it was worth it if it resulted in an unbreakable peace between England and Scotland.

'Duchess, how pleasant to see you!' Cecily leaned forward to see Harry Stafford nodding at her across the table. The Duke of Buckingham was nearing thirty but looked much younger in his gold coat and silk shirt.

'Harry! I did not know you were here! I didn't see you at the signing ceremony this morning.' Cecily remembered him as a spoiled boy years ago during her confinement at Maxstoke, but hoped he had matured over time. She knew the king was not keen on his company and did not include him in his Council, and wondered if his presence here now was a sign he was rising in favour.

'Well, no, I wasn't part of it.' There was the pout she remembered. 'However, I thought to come and offer my services if Edward has need of them.'

'And does he?' Cecily's grandson, John de la Pole, leant over from her left to enquire. She cast him a stern look but had to purse her lips to keep the smile from her face.

'Well, not yet, but I am sure that the men I command may be of some interest to him.' Harry tried to be nonchalant and sat back to sip his wine.

'Of course, and you are married to the queen's sister are you not? For many years now, I believe?' John was relentless in his taunting, which Cecily wondered at. She was not aware they were close, but most of her family did not have much praise for Buckingham.

'Yes we were both children when we were wed.' The sulky tone was back in his voice. 'The daughter of a nobody like Earl Rivers would not have been my choice, but she has given me two fine sons, so it does place me near the throne.'

'Not near enough to be invited this morning though.' John rose from the table, bowed to them both, and went to speak with his uncle of Gloucester.

'Young pup!' Buckingham stared at his back as John approached Richard, seated next to the king. 'How dare he! I am a duke and he is just an earl.'

'Yes, Earl of Lincoln. Son of my daughter Elizabeth.' Cecily looked reprovingly at him, and in an instant a sunny look came over his face.

'Of course, my Lady. The King's Mother, related to everyone!' He raised his glass in a toast to her. 'Shall we speak of more pleasant things? Peace in Scotland or Burgundian fashion perhaps?'

Duchess Cecily smiled at the irrepressible man and raised her own glass in return.

Windsor Castle, 6th September 1482

The heat was stifling in the banqueting hall and all the ladies were discreetly wiping their brows of sweat. The warmth did not seem to bother the men, however, they were all in a fever of excitement at the news from Scotland and were determined to enjoy the celebratory feast despite their discomfort.

The noise was clanging and jarring, and Duchess Cecily wondered if she would give offence if she made an early departure. She had kissed and congratulated her son of Gloucester on his victory at retaking Berwick after all these years, and was surprised when he appeared to be almost drunk; whether on his success or on wine she was not sure. The men were raising glasses and cheers to each other, celebrating King James being taken prisoner by his own Lords and the English taking the town of Edinburgh while their king was in the castle. There were some doubts that Albany would have enough support to take the throne for himself now, but nobody celebrating in London really cared. They were joyful at the news that Richard had led the king's army to victory and nothing could stop the flow of wine and the shouts of exuberance.

'Richard of Gloucester, a prince of chivalry!' Cecily heard the toast called for him. Lord Jack Howard raised a jug in his honour and was heard explaining that Gloucester had forbidden his troops to sack the city of Edinburgh as he showed pity on the unarmed common people and saved their women and children from the brutality of war. 'A noble victory for a brave and knightly leader.' Cecily smiled wryly; it was perhaps true that Richard's hours of poring over books on courage and virtue, those mirrors for princes, had certainly rubbed off on him.

King Edward was slouched over the top table, his head on the cloth and a puddle of wine at his elbow. Cecily thought he was drunk even before the feast had begun, and she had made her curtsey to his throne without him even noticing. Queen Elizabeth had long left his side; she was sitting with her brothers Anthony and Edward, their heads close together in whispered conference. Princess Eliza was flitting about the room, a beauty in her sixteenth year, gathering compliments wherever she went. She did not seem too troubled that her betrothal to the Dauphin had been called off. France and Burgundy had come to an alliance that excluded England, and King Louis' retaliation was to cancel the marriage plans. From the joy on her face, Eliza was relieved not to be forced to leave her mother for a foreign husband and none could doubt she could have her pick of eligible English noblemen. Prince Edward, brought back for the celebration from his castle at Ludlow, was in deep and serious conversation with Lord Stanley and Will Hastings, no doubt discussing weighty matters from his Principality. Only Princess Cecily and young Prince Richard looked sober. Cecily was still not promised in marriage, and seemingly could not take to the single state as well as her older sister, and poor Richard's child-bride, Ann Mowbray was dead at the age of eight. However, Duchess Cecily noted that nobody in the Great Hall had eyes for these miserable children, so intent were they on their own pleasure. She smiled at them both, then signalled to Kat to help her pull back her chair.

'I must go, my dear. My bones cannot take these hard seats anymore and my ears are ringing from this noise. Help me to my rooms now.'

'Yes Madam.' Kat offered a supporting elbow to help her mistress up. 'Shall you take leave of the king, my Lady?'

Cecily looked up at the table on the dais to see her son falling sideways out of his chair, his squire endeavouring to haul him back upright. 'I shall see him another time Kat. Edward is dead to the world.'

Middleham Castle, Yorkshire, 25th December 1482

The dark blue sky was lit by hundreds of stars that seemed a good omen for the day ahead. It promised to be fine and if so, the gentlemen of the household were intending to lead a hunt up into the hills before the first feast of the yuletide season. They had all been fasting during advent but the cooks had long been preparing for this day, and the villagers would benefit from the bread and meat they would be receiving as part of the local tradition.

The midnight Mass had finished and the smell of candles and incense hung around the opened chapel door as Richard and Anne led their people out and headed towards their private chambers in the South Courtyard. He helped his duchess on the steps, an arm around her back to support her as they climbed the stone stairs. Their room was warm and Tess was ready with a cosy fur-lined robe for her mistress. Richard's man, Thomas Brayne, stoked the fire before serving hot mulled ale.

When they were finally alone and seated before the burning logs, Richard looked out of the window towards the corner tower. 'I think I will just go and see Ned, make sure he is fast asleep.'

'Richard, I am sure he is fine. Have you ever known Nursey Bessie to leave him?' Anne took his hand and the duke smiled at his wife.

'My Lady, if you knew how George and I behaved around our nursey all those years ago, you would set armed guards around our boy.' Anne coughed slightly and moved her head away from the smoke.

'The king sent some fine gifts for us this season, my Lady. A beautiful collar of gold for you and a fine white destrier for me. And little Ned got his first sword!'

'Well, that will match the bow and arrows your mother gave him. Really, what was Duchess Cecily thinking? Surely a book would have been a better choice for him.' She smiled and shook her head. 'She is preparing him to be as fine a soldier as his father.' Richard took Anne's hand in his and kissed it.

'My Anne.'

'Richard, you know there is one gift that I want more than anything to give you. I am so sorry husband, I am so sorry.'

'Anne, you have no need to be sorry. Another child would be a gift from God, but if it does not happen, you must not distress yourself.' He wiped away the tears that streaked down her face. 'I love Ned with all my heart. When he is strong, I am sure he will keep the whole castle in uproar with his antics, just as you did as a child!'

Anne pushed her chair back, headed towards the table and opened the box of parchment and quills.

'What are you doing now, my Lady?'

'I am writing to Cecily,' she said determinedly. 'It is time we took another pilgrimage!'

As the Twelfth Night feast came to a close, Duke Richard pushed back his chair and walked through the Great Hall, mingling with his friends and the people of his household. He raised a glass with Francis and Rob, then suggested they carry Tommy to bed as he had fallen asleep with his head on his arms across the table. He embraced Lovell once more and clasped him on the back as he moved on. Finally he came to Harry Stafford's table and nodded at him and the Duke of Buckingham's men.

'Season's greetings to you all, I hope you are enjoying your time at Middleham. It is not often we see you up in Yorkshire; my wife and I hope you have been made welcome.'

'Right welcome, thank you Richard.' Harry stood up and toasted the Duke of Gloucester. 'I had the pleasure of dining with your honoured Lady mother recently, and the Duchess Cecily told me of the hospitality of your great castle. I should visit more, it is beautiful here and I have lands not too far away. Baron Scrope tells me the hunting here is beyond comparison and has invited me out with him at Bolton Castle.' Harry pulled out the chair next to him and politely bowed to Richard as they sat.

'John Scrope is a good friend to us, and a valuable advisor. You will certainly enjoy the hunt with him, he is an excellent host.' Duke Richard smiled at Harry. 'If it's wild boar you are after, the hills are full of them!' The men laughed together and Harry poured more wine for them both.

'Speaking of boars and advisors, Richard, there is something I would say.' Gloucester nodded and looked more serious at the change in the tone of the conversation. 'Well, it's just this really,' Harry continued. 'We have known each other for many years, since you stayed with my grandmother at Maxstoke Castle when you were banished there by old King Henry.'

'Yes Harry, I remember those days well. My father was under attainder in Ireland and Edward and Warwick were running around Calais together. My mother never had a peaceful night's sleep for worrying about them all.'

'Exactly Richard, exactly. We have been friends for a long time, and well, I wish to offer my services to you.' Harry looked slightly abashed and glanced at Richard to see if he would mock him. 'I know your brother the king does not require my advice or counsel, but I want to make clear that should you ever need me, or the support of my affinity, well, you only need ask.' Stafford finished in a rush and took a breath. He wanted to be close to the throne, and supporting Richard was the next best thing if he could not be at Edward's side.

Duke Richard stood up and bowed. 'Thank you, my Lord of Buckingham. Your friendship is valuable to me, and I would be foolish to refuse the fealty of such a noble House. Loyalty is the most important quality I value in a man and I will be pleased to count you as my ally.'

Berkhamsted Castle, Hertfordshire, 7th January 1483
The pageboy bowed as he announced the visitor. 'Lady Margaret Stanley, Your Grace.' He had taken an almost instant dislike to

the stern woman, although he could not say for sure why. She held herself erect and bobbed a polite curtsey.

Duchess Cecily rose and welcomed Lady Margaret. She gestured for her to sit near the fire, but did not trouble herself to offer her refreshment. She had some sympathy for the daughter of John Beaufort, dead by his own hand, but no liking. She knew Margaret had been forced to marry King Henry's half-brother Edmund Tudor at the age of twelve and had given birth to her son Henry the following year, and God knows what kind of damage that did to a girl. She was not fond of the woman, now on her third marriage, and was surprised that she had paid her a visit.

'Lady Margaret, how pleasant to see you.' Cecily sat and smoothed down her dark blue dress. It perhaps was not the height of fashion, she was too old for that sort of thing, but it looked much more stylish than Margaret's. Cecily had a sudden flashback to her brother Richard of Salisbury, talking out of the side of his mouth and wearing clothes that looked like they came from the last century. This made her warm to her visitor, and she injected some friendliness into her voice. 'What a delightful surprise to see you here.' She smiled. 'Are you well?'

Lady Margaret turned nervously on her seat. 'Thank you, Your Grace, for seeing me.' She clasped her hands together. 'I am come to ask for your influence and support.'

Cecily had suspected as much, although with her husband Thomas being so close to the king, she did wonder what Margaret thought she could do that Stanley could not. 'Really? How may I help?'

'It is about my son, Henry.'

'Of course it is.' Did Margaret have any other interests apart from her only child?

'Well, King Edward was considering the notion that he may be allowed to return from exile and swear fealty to your House.'

'Yes. I am sure you will be pleased to have him home again.' Cecily cocked an eyebrow.

'I am here to ask you to if you would use your influence to support this.' Lady Margaret took a breath. 'I know how the king favours your advice in such matters.' Cecily nearly snorted at this; was Margaret so unaware that she did not know that it was Queen Elizabeth who had more political sway than she, or had she approached the queen and been refused?

'Lady Margaret, I believe that sons should be close to their mothers. I am told that Duke Francis of Brittany, in whose dominion your son lives, has agreed that he can return to England if we give him our support against the French.' Margaret nodded eagerly. 'However, if Maximillian of Burgundy marries his daughter to the French heir, who knows what will happen. Alliances will shift.' She watched as Margaret sagged in her seat. 'Do not despair though. When I see the king at Easter, I will ask him to take Lord Stanley's advice on the matter. Perhaps in a few months the situation will have been resolved and they might find a way home for young Henry.'

Margaret arose. 'Thank you, Your Grace.' She nodded her head, 'I knew this would not be a wasted journey.'

Westminster Palace, London, 9ᵗʰ April 1483

'I would see my son now, Lord Hastings. I have travelled near on sixty miles in great haste and I will not be forced to remain in his presence chamber any longer.' Duchess Cecily drew herself up to her full height but still did not reach Hastings' shoulder. 'Announce me now.' Just as she was about to push past him, the doors to the private rooms opened and Queen Elizabeth approached her mother-by-law and saw the older woman drop into a curtsey.

'Your Grace, thank you for your letter. I came as soon as I could and I am much grieved to hear the news.'

'Edward insisted I sent for you, Duchess. He is failing fast and his physicians fear he will not last the night.' The queen looked haggard. 'At first we thought it was just a chill, but his fever has worsened since Easter Sunday and now his pain and sickness are consuming him.' She broke off and glanced down at her wringing hands as if she were surprised by them.

'Please follow me Duchess.' Hastings took Cecily's arm; her legs felt weak and she was grateful for the support. 'The king has sent for all his advisors and lawyers, I believe he is to make adjustments to his will.' Hastings' composure seemed to be held together by a thread, Cecily thought, and she was glad they were grasping onto each other.

'You are his friend and Lord Chamberlain. I know you will do whatever he requires of you.' They reached the threshold of his bedchamber. 'Thank you. I will see my son alone now.'

Cecily had been seated by the great bed for nearly half an hour before the king opened his eyes. His breathing was laboured and his fever made his body wet and sour smelling.

'Lady mother? Oh mother.' His voice was rasping and weak.

'Yes Edward, I am here. Oh my poor boy, my poor son.'

'Do not weep mother, please. There are some things I must say to you.'

'Say them later Edward. Tell me them when you are well and strong again.' She reached for his hand, and forced herself to smile at the ruined body.

'I won't be well again mother. The doctors tell me I am at the gates of heaven.' He glanced at the black-robed men huddled around a table in the corner of the chamber. 'Old crows, look at them!' He smiled at Cecily and forced himself to keep his eyes open. 'I have sent for my Council, I have to put the kingdom in order. I will make them clasp their hands in unity, those who dispute amongst themselves, and I will force them to keep the peace this country has known since Towton.'

'Yes Edward. They love you and will honour your wishes I am sure.' Cecily brushed back the blonde hair from his damp forehead and reached for a cooling sponge.

'My brother of Gloucester, my beloved Richard, will be Lord Protector and he will guard my son and heir. He will see him to his majority.'

'Richard will shield him, Edward, you know he will. Do not worry.'

'He must make sure my son becomes king, mother, he must not let rumour and gossip stand in his way.' The king turned his head from side to side on the pillow in agitation and she feared he was rambling.

'Be calm Edward, try and lie still now.' She gently wiped his brow then took both his hands in hers.

'Lady mother, soon I will stand in judgement before God, and I do not know how I will do that. I feel my life is mired in lies and death. I will see my honoured father and brother Edmund at God's right hand, but I will have to answer for George. Mother, I am so sorry about George!' Edward began to weep in his distress. 'I had no choice, I had to protect my sons and my throne, but I should not have had him killed!' He took a shuddering breath and his voice dropped to a whisper. 'Will I be forgiven?'

Duchess Cecily took a moment to answer. She was not sure that God would forgive the sin of killing a brother, but how could she tell Edward that on his deathbed? Surely it was her duty as a loving mother to reassure him, or would it be better to tell him the truth? She thought for a moment, and hoped she found the right words.

'Edward, Jesus is our Lord and Saviour. He knows what is in our hearts, He will know if you are truly sorry and repent of your sins.' It seemed the best she could do; now the tears were pouring down her face and dripping on to the king's fine linen sheets.

'Do you forgive me mother? Do you forgive me for taking George's life?' Cecily bowed her head and tried to get her sobs under control. This would be her third son who had reached his maturity to die, but the first one she had been able to speak to when he was *in extremis*. She knew that whatever she said, it would be the last thing Edward would hear. She took a deep breath and looked at him to answer.

'My son, I will write your name in my holy Book of Hours alongside those of your father and brothers. I will honour all those names until the day I join you all in heaven. Be at peace now Edward.'

CHAPTER 5

Circumdederunt me dolores mortis:
pericula inferni invenerunt me.
Tribulationem, et dolorem inveni:
et nomen Domini invocavi.
The sorrows of death have compassed me:
and the pains of hell have found me.
I have found tribulation, and sorrow:
and I called on the name of our Lord.

Middleham Castle, Yorkshire, 13ᵗʰ April 1483

The click of Anne's heels on the stone flags rang loudly through the corridors. She had waylaid the king's squire, Ralph, in the stables to ask what brought him this far north then grabbed her skirts and ran when she heard the news. She flew across the courtyard and up the steps, her chest burning with the exertion, and through their private chambers until she reached her husband's study. The door crashed open, then the duchess stood still on the threshold, hesitating before she entered.

'Richard.' She took a tentative step forward and called his name again. 'Richard, my love.' He was in his great carved chair, the letter in his hand and his head bowed. 'I have heard, Richard. I am so sorry, I am so sorry for you.'

He looked up at her, his face haggard and drawn. 'My brother is dead. He is dead.' Anne rushed forward and knelt beside him. She rested one hand on his knee and with the other, reached up to stroke his face. 'I cannot imagine a world without Edward in it.'

'Oh my poor dear.' Anne raised herself up until she could embrace her husband. She cradled his head against her and gently rocked him as she would have if little Ned had taken a tumble. 'I am so sorry Richard. I know you loved Edward above all other men, and I know he took great comfort in that.'

Richard kissed Anne's cheek and gently untangled her arms. He stood up and walked to the window, and gazed at the view over the Wensleydale hills. He kept his back turned to her until his tears had passed and he wiped his face on his sleeve.

'The letter is from Will Hastings. The queen could not trouble herself to write to me of the death of my own brother, the Lord Chamberlain had to do it.' He turned to face his wife. 'He says that Edward made me Lord Protector to my nephew, the new king, until he reaches his majority.'

'Well I am not surprised at that. Edward truly valued your loyalty and knew you would be diligent in carrying out your duties.' Anne coughed, then walked towards him and took his hand once again. 'Will you go to London?'

'No, my Lady. Hastings bids me to go and meet young Edward on the road as he comes from Ludlow and escort him to the capital.' Richard glanced down at the letter again, not sure of how much he should reveal.

'Why? Should you not go straight to London and greet him as he enters the city?' Anne's face was puzzled.

The duke knew he had to tell her everything. They had never had any secrets from each other, and this was not a good time to start keeping things from her. 'I don't believe the situation is that simple, my Lady. Hastings says that Queen Elizabeth will oppose my protectorate; she thinks the new king should be guarded and advised only by the Woodville family. He is of the opinion that her brother Anthony will refuse to allow me to take up the office as my brother ordered.'

'How dare she?' Anne was indignant at the slight to Richard. 'She cannot countermand her husband the king!'

'She dares because she is a Woodville, and the mother of the new king.' Richard smiled wryly. 'I will head to Northampton and intercept their train. I'll send a message to Harry Stafford too. It's only right that the new King of England be greeted by the Dukes of Gloucester and Buckingham.' They shared a sad smile. 'But first, I will go to York and order a requiem service. The North will affirm their loyalty to King Edward V and swear fealty to him, and I will lead them.'

'That is right and proper Richard. A good plan.' Anne reached up to kiss her husband's cheek.

'Thank you, my Lady.' He kissed her back. 'I must write to my mother though, before anything else.'

'Oh poor Duchess Cecily.' Anne turned to the table and sat. 'I shall write too. She must be devastated at the loss of another son.'

St George's Chapel, Windsor Castle, 19th April 1483

It had all been done properly, Cecily thought. He had been honoured in death as a king should be. Edward's body had lain in St Stephen's Chapel in Westminster Palace for eight days whilst Masses were said and vigil was held. As chief mourner,

John de la Pole Earl of Lincoln and the king's nephew, had led the procession to Westminster Abbey in ceremony to prepare for another great service where all the nobles of the land paid their final respects. The funeral cortege left Westminster headed for Syon Abbey, and John had ensured the six horses and the carriage were draped in black velvet to reflect the country's sorrow. John had given his sister Anne, a nun at Syon, a large payment of gold for the sisters to pray for the king's soul. After another night of Masses, the fourth King Edward began his final journey to Windsor, and the tomb that held his children when they were called to God. Four archbishops said the holy words over the body, which was finally entombed in its elaborate resting place.

Duchess Cecily, no longer called King's Mother, sat in the pew long after the mourners and bishops had gone. The royal family had shuffled out sniffing and crying, all the children unmarried and now without a father. Cecily stared at the ornate tomb and watched as the soldiers laid her son's sword, armour and banner in front of the marble, knelt briefly in reverence, then departed. Three sons in the grave now, she thought. Edmund, George now Edward, dead at only forty. Edward the king, once a magnificent soldier, now a rotting corpulent figure ruined by the excesses of his life.

'What of my life?' She looked up at the altar, still glowing with candles and illuminating the magnificent crucifix behind it. 'What shall I do with my life?' Her faithful Kat and Madge slipped into seats behind the duchess and bowed their heads in prayer. 'Lord Jesus, send your blessing down on me, and give me a purpose for my remaining years, I beg you.' Cecily's whisper did not reach her ladies, but they knew what she would be praying for; a life free of more sorrow and heartbreak, wanting only to watch her family grow and thrive. She would play no part in the reign of her grandson, the new King Edward; Elizabeth Woodville would make sure of that. She just wanted peace now, peace in her old age and a life dedicated to the cause of God.

The ladies-in-waiting settled their duchess into her rooms in the castle at Windsor where she would rest before returning to Berkhamsted. It was a cold and draughty room that she had been assigned, but they had pulled the tapestries across the window shutters for her, and lit a great fire in the hearth.

'Wine, Madam?' Madge held out the silver jug and poured some hot mulled wine into Cecily's cup.

'Thank you, my dear.' She took a sip gratefully, and it seemed to warm her old bones at once. 'Has Kat found a new page to serve us yet? I will miss the last lad, but he has gone to his knights' training now he reached a good age. You have better things to do than pour my wine.'

'She has, Madam. I will ask her to show him in.' Madge slipped out of the door and it was only a moment before both her ladies came in with a young lad, dark haired and clean looking, between them.

'Here is your new pageboy, madam. This is Owen Thomas.'

Duchess Cecily looked at the youth; dark hair, sallow skin but no sign of grubby nails or boils on the back of his neck. He stood up straight and was not afraid to meet her eye.

'Owen, you say? Not Welsh are you?' Cecily knew she could look fearsome when she wanted to, and it was hard to keep a straight face when Kat sniggered from the corner.

'Welsh? God no, Your Grace. I'm a true Englishman, thank the Lord.'

'Well, that's a relief.' Cecily smiled and held out her hand for him to kiss. 'Welcome to my service, Owen. We will stay in London for the coronation of the new king, but you will find us a quiet household when we return to my home. We will live peacefully in Hertfordshire from now on, away from the court of my grandson. It will be a life of solitude and reflection for us all.'

'Yes Your Grace. More wine?'

Northampton, 29th April 1483

They made a solemn sight, the Dukes of Gloucester and Buckingham and their five hundred men. They wore mourning cloaks of black to reflect their sorrow at the death of the king, and they were covered in a fine layer of dust from their journey from York. All the nobles and Lords had proclaimed their loyalty to the new boy-king at the Minster in that city then travelled down to meet the king's party as they made their way from Ludlow to London.

'Are you well, cousin?' Harry Stafford glanced to his left where Richard rode his fine grey stallion. He thought he looked in pain, and Buckingham was not sure if it was at the death of his brother or the impending meeting with the Woodville party coming from the Welsh Marches, but Gloucester looked slumped and twisted in his saddle with the high back cantle.

'I am very well Harry, I thank you.' Richard straightened his back and tried to ignore the spears of pain that shot up his shoulder. 'Our scouts say the king's party is not too far ahead now.' He smiled at his cousin. 'In all truth, though, I am looking forward to a good meal tonight with my nephew and a soft bed after.'

'When we meet the king's troop, I will find billets in the town for our men. We are quite near Grafton, this is Woodville country, is it not? The king's men should be made welcome!' Harry sniffed at the thought; he had no liking for his wife's family at all, and he believed that Gloucester disliked the vast Rivers tribe too, although he had not made that much plain. Buckingham wanted to make himself useful to Richard though, partly in gratitude for having been asked to accompany the north-men on their journey to escort the new king to his capital, and also because he finally had hope of a position on the new Lord Protector's Council. After a lifetime of being overlooked, Harry Stafford felt he was finally coming into his own. After all, he was descended from the fifth son of Edward III.

'Your Grace!' The scouts in their murrey and blue tabards of York galloped towards them, kicking up more dust and sand from the rough road. 'The party is just ahead.' Buckingham made a great show of coughing and clearing his throat while Richard trotted forward.

'I suppose Earl Rivers heads the column?' He glanced back at Harry and frowned at his noise.

'Yes My Lord, it is Anthony Woodville for sure, but it's not a column he leads.' The scouts looked at one another, and the lead man wearing the White Boar insignia of Gloucester kicked his horse a pace forward.

'Not a column? What then?' Richard enquired in a low voice. The dark canopy of trees overhanging the road seemed to close in on him at this news.

'It is an army, Your Grace. Two thousand is my guess, and the king's banner is not among them.' The scout raised his eyebrows; as a loyal man from Middleham he heard the gossip from the south and knew about the Rivers' ambition. 'And many wagons, My Lord, heavily guarded and covered.'

'Jesus Christ!' Buckingham came alongside Richard and heard the words. 'Two thousand men! And the new king not with them? Christ, Richard, that's an army, not an escort!'

'Indeed.' Gloucester dropped his head in thought, but it may have been sorrow. 'It seems the dowager queen has told her brother that Edward's will proclaims me Lord Protector and she realises that the Rivers' will not have control of their boy now.' He shook his head, and raised his voice so that his captains could hear him. 'We will go forward and meet the Earl, maybe he has a good explanation for this.'

A camp of tents had been hastily erected and the cooks were rustling up a meal of chicken and bread for their Lords. The two thousand men from Ludlow were scattered about, under wagons and cloaks, claiming the inns were full and they were happy to be on hand.

'So, Anthony, you say my nephew the king has gone on ahead?' Richard poured Woodville a cup of wine and smiled at him. His dark hair flopped in front of his face and he brushed it back to meet the handsome Earl's eyes. He took a quick glance at the tent door as he got his reply.

'Yes Your Grace. King Edward, fifth of his name, is not many miles south of here. I thought it best the lad had decent shelter for the night; he is young and distraught at the death of his father.' Woodville, all blonde charm, nodded and returned the smile. 'My sister's son, Sir Richard Grey, is with him to ensure his safety.'

'Of course.' Gloucester stood up and flexed his neck. 'But surely it is *my* job to ensure his safety?' Richard now towered over him. 'You were his guardian when he was Prince of Wales in Ludlow. Now I am Lord Protector, I will see my brother's wishes carried out.'

Anthony Woodville glanced up and shrugged his shoulders. 'I have my orders from the queen, Your Grace. To bring him to London.'

'Ah yes.' Richard moved away from the seats to stand by the candles. 'And did the *dowager* queen order you to hide my nephew from me and bring an army into the capital?' His voice was soft and pleasant, and he threw several glances to the tent flap, as if awaiting a visitor.

'Richard.' Anthony Woodville stood up and strolled around the narrow space. 'We want the same thing. To see the boy crowned King of England and take up the throne. What matters who escorts him?' He smiled, turning on his winning Woodville charm, and was about to continue when Harry Stafford threw the tent door back and strode in. 'Ah, my Lord of Buckingham. How wonderful to see you. And how is my sister Katherine, your beloved wife?'

For once, Harry ignored the spite of the Woodvilles and held back his angry retort, instead switching to geniality.

'My dear Earl Rivers, have you been explaining to the Lord Protector why you needed an army of two thousand men to accompany you?' He smile was broad and gleeful. 'And why your troops are concealing wagon loads of arms and weapons from us?'

Richard nodded at Buckingham. 'Thank you Harry. So, Anthony, what say you?'

The dawn broke clear and it promised to be a fine sunny day. As the Duke of Gloucester nodded to a detachment of his troops

233

to depart north, Buckingham came to his side, straightening his fine gold velvet coat and swinging his cape about his shoulders. The five hundred who travelled from York were getting ready to depart with the dukes, and there was no sign now of the huge army from Ludlow.

'So, Richard, let us go and greet our king. I have sent the scouts on to find out where he is.'

'I know where he is Harry. Sir Richard Grey and his Chamberlain have him at an inn in Stony Stratford. No doubt waiting for his dear uncle Anthony to arrive.' Richard tightened his mouth and shook his head.

'Ha!' Buckingham clicked his fingers for the grooms to come forward with their horses. 'He'll have a long wait then!'

The sun was fully up, bright and blazing, as the horses clattered over the cobblestones towards the stable yard of the inn. The inn's sign swung in the breeze, the rose and crown newly painted in glittering colours, and several Welshmen milled about outside. Richard and Harry, with only their small household guard, dismounted and strode to the door. The main body of their men formed a loose ring around the coaching house, seemingly casual but nonetheless wary and aware.

Richard pushed open the old oak door and found his way blocked by Sir Thomas Vaughn, Chamberlain to young Edward. The old man was grey and gaunt looking, but still powerful in his stance. Once in the service of old King Henry, he had used his skill and clever tongue to worm his way into the affections of Edward of York and had been appointed to his position at Ludlow as his reward.

'Sir Thomas, announce me to the king.' Richard of Gloucester was shorter than Vaughn but did not let that cower him.

'His Grace is not to be disturbed, my Lord Duke.' Vaughan's

voice was hard and held no apology. 'He is at rest now. I am sure he will see you when he is ready.'

Harry Stafford stepped forward. 'Perhaps your old ears did not hear correctly. The *Lord Protector* has given you a command.' His chin jutted out and he inched back his shoulders.

'I take my orders from Earl Rivers, and the king.' Low voiced and not matching Stafford's aggression, Sir Thomas had no intention of letting the dukes pass.

'You old bastard! Get out of our way!'

'Harry.' Richard laid his hand on Buckingham's shoulder. 'I am sure that when the Chamberlain here realises that Earl Rivers, and the two thousand from Ludlow, are nowhere to be seen, he will open that door. Or face the consequences.'

Sir Thomas Vaughan cast around, glancing behind the dukes and saw only unfamiliar faces. He nodded in resignation and put his hand on the iron knob and heaved open the door to the inner chamber to let the visitors enter. He then tried then to push past them and make his way outside, but felt his arm grabbed by Buckingham and he almost fell into the room as the men from York strode in.

King Edward, twelve years old and with the blonde good looks that came from his parents, sat at a small table which held a book and a half-eaten apple. By his side was Sir Richard Grey, son of Elizabeth Woodville from her first marriage, who had for years been a companion to the lad, making their court on the Welsh Marches together and revelling in chivalry and poetry.

Richard and Harry Stafford knelt before the boy and bowed their heads.

'My Liege. My cousin of Buckingham and I are honoured to see you. We swear to you our fealty and loyalty, in the name of God.' Richard looked up at King Edward; his resemblance to his father was strong, and Richard felt his heart tremble for a moment as the grief for the brother he had not yet mourned threatened to overtake him. He cleared his throat and met the lad's eyes. 'We have not seen each other much these past years, but I do know that you will be a fine king, just like your father.'

The new king glanced to his right at his half-brother, nervousness written plain on his face.

'Thank you, uncle. Thank you my Lord of Buckingham.' He ran out of words so dropped his eyes to his lap.

'My Lord of Gloucester.' Sir Richard Grey put his hand on the king's shoulder and was about to continue.

'Lord Protector, please Sir Richard.' Gloucester rose and gestured Harry to stand up. 'My Liege, your father placed you into my care until you come of age and can rule alone.' He looked at the Grey son of the dowager queen. 'In *my* care. And I am come to take you to London.'

'We are on our way to the capital now, Lord Protector.' Sir Richard took a step forward. 'We have our own escort but I daresay you can fall in behind us.' He smiled scathingly, then noticed Vaughan shaking his head from the doorway. 'What is it Thomas?'

'What the old Chamberlain means, Sir Richard, is that your men are gone.' Buckingham smiled cruelly. 'It is *our* men who will escort the king to London.' Sir Richard took a step back in shock as Sir Thomas nodded confirmation.

'Your Grace.' Gloucester knelt again before the king. 'It seems that your uncle Anthony Woodville had evil planned. He brought an army and many weapons with your train.' He looked at Sir Richard. 'Rest assured that I will seek out those who mean to deny my position as your guardian. I am the Lord

Protector; any acts against me or my office are treason; loyalty binds me and I have a dark place in my heart for treachery.'

Baynard's Castle, London, 4ᵗʰ May 1483

'I can hardly believe it Richard.' Duchess Cecily sat back in her padded chair in the sunny solar, her favourite room in the vast building on the Thames where she had come to from her home in Hertfordshire. The pageboy, Owen, stood near the door, keeping watch on the cups in case they needed refilling.

'Can't you mother?' Gloucester smiled thinly at her. 'You can't believe that the Woodvilles would plot to undermine my position, overthrow me and rule the boy-king themselves?' He was rewarded with a giggle.

'Well, I am not surprised they thought about it, but to actually carry out their plans? I am astonished. So what happens now?'

'I had Anthony Woodville, Richard Grey and Thomas Vaughan arrested and sent north to Pontefract; the size of the army they brought with them and all the weapons showed that they did not mean to honour Edward's will and intended to overthrow me as Lord Protector.' He stood and strolled to the window where he looked out on the river. 'They came ready for a fight, Lady mother.'

'And how did the new king take the news? I saw him today, riding into London resplendent on his fine horse and wearing a suit of blue. He looked just like his father!' Cecily's eyes momentarily clouded with sadness. She took a sip of her drink. 'He is the image of him, just as you are like *your* father.' Owen took a step towards the table that held the wine, ready for his moment.

'I explained the whole plot to him but I am not sure he

believed me. I fear he has been under Anthony's influence too long.' Richard smiled sadly. 'He could be a fine king one day, but I had to get young Edward out of their clutches.' He nodded as his cup was refilled. 'Thank you lad.'

'And he is residing at the Bishop of London's palace?' The new Lord Protector nodded in answer. 'Good. You can care for him there while you plan the coronation.'

'It will be next month.' Richard sat down again and faced Cecily. 'Another York king, Lady mother!'

'Do you really think so?' They both turned in surprise at Owen's comment, and he went red under their scrutiny.

'Who gave you permission to speak, boy?' Cecily raised her voice at the page, who put his hands behind his back and bowed his head. 'You should be seen but not heard!'

'Wait, mother, please. What do you mean lad?' Gloucester leant forward and raised his eyebrows in friendly enquiry. 'What do they call you?'

'He is named Owen and he will be looking for another place if he speaks out of turn again!' Cecily was embarrassed that someone in her service had stepped so far out of line to join in a conversation of his betters, and she resorted to anger to cover her chagrin.

'What did you mean Owen. You can answer me.' Richard glanced at his mother and widened his eyes. 'Her Grace will not mind.'

'Sorry, sire, I only meant that, well, do you really think that the new King Edward will be a York? Or even a Plantagenet, like yourselves?' Cecily and her son swapped an astonished look.

'And why do you think he is *not* a York? Speak up boy!'

'Your Graces, I meant no offence to anyone! I just mean that this King Edward is a Woodville! He has been raised only by the queen's family. He belongs to them, not to York.' Silence filled the chamber at his words and no one spoke for a moment.

At Cecily's nod, Owen bowed and left the room, closing the door softly behind him.

'Well.' Richard sat back and laughed. 'He's not wrong, is he mother? We need to keep Edward away from Elizabeth Woodville and that whole family, it's as clear as day. Clever lad, that Owen. He should be a lawyer!'

Crosby Place, London, 18ᵗʰ May 1483

'Thank you, My Lords, for coming here for our meeting today.' The Lord Protector smiled at the men arranged around the large table in the London house that Richard preferred to Baynard's Castle; it was smaller, with pleasant gardens and fewer prying ears and eyes to interfere with his business. He knew that the dowager queen was being fed information that came from his Council meetings, and he trusted the servants at Crosby Place to keep all the discussions private. 'Our only order of business today is King Edward's coronation plans.'

Bishop Morton and Thomas Lord Stanley glanced at each other and the former coughed politely.

'My Lord, may I interrupt?' John Morton, full of his own self-importance, stood up and addressed the assembled men. Richard nodded and gestured with his hand, allowing him to speak. Francis Lovell glanced at Rob Percy and gave him a secret smile; neither were fond of the former Lancastrian. Sir William Stanley and William Catesby, one of Richard's principal advisors, glanced up at the tall priest while Richard sat down. He did not much like Morton either but the man knew about the running of the country and was well connected; like the wealthy Lord Stanley, he was more tolerated than admired.

'I believe the Council should address the issue of the men you have sent to Pontefract Castle; Earl Rivers, and Sirs Richard Grey and Thomas Vaughn.' He looked serious and lowered his voice. 'May we ask what your intentions are, Your Grace?'

Richard turned his head to look at the tapestry on the panelled wall, and answered slowly.

'What would this esteemed Council think my intentions should be to men who were prepared to overthrow me? They had an army and weapons, their purpose was to refuse me my right, my *obligation*, to take up my office as Protector and deny me access to the king.'

Sir Robert Brackenbury, treasurer to Richard in the north, spoke up. 'It is treason, Bishop, treason. Those men were arrested for treason, and must face trial!' Brackenbury, a giant of a man with a grey beard down to his chest, glared at Morton, then nodded his head to Richard. He was a loyal friend from Yorkshire, he would not stand for anyone threatening his liege lord.

'Thank you Robert.' The Lord Protector stood, and gestured for the bishop to take his seat. Another man loyal to Richard was Sir James Tyrell, who sat on a chair under the window. Not a Council member, but a supporter, he came forward and poured his master more wine while Richard continued. 'You all know me, you know I believe loyalty to be the most important virtue a man has; without it, he is nothing. Those men were arrested for treason, and I will send Sir Robert Ratcliffe to Pontefract to set a date for their trial.' His voice was firm and he would brook no argument or take advice on the matter.

Harry Stafford, who had been surprisingly quiet during the meeting, now spoke for the first time.

'Well, that is settled. The Lord Protector has spoken.' He gave his winning smile and shuffled some papers around in front of him. 'Now, back to the matter in hand; the coronation. It is set for the twenty-second of next month, and I already have given orders for Westminster Abbey to be scrubbed from top to bottom to make ready. As is tradition, the king always stays in the royal apartments at the Tower of London before the coronation, so I propose we make arrangements to put that in hand.' He gave them a sunny look. 'Any objections?'

Palace of Westminster, London, 10th June 1483

Sir William Catesby bowed as Duchess Cecily entered the Lord Protector's chambers in the palace. He had just been given orders by Richard, who trusted him as an old friend and good lawyer, and his face was grave and solemn.

'Bid you good day, Your Grace.' He nodded towards the huge oak desk where his master was seated. 'Your son will be pleased to see you, I dare say. I must not tarry though, I have my orders.' He disappeared and softly closed the door behind him.

'Gracious Richard, what a rush William was in!' She touched his head in blessing as he knelt briefly before her, then he pulled out a chair opposite his own for her. 'What is going on? I have come to talk to you about my man Colyngbourne, but I feel I have come at a bad time.'

'No indeed, Lady mother, you are always welcome, but it is true that matters are turning grave here.' He moved some papers around on the table, then rested his hands on top of them. 'I have known for some time that details of our Council meetings are being passed to Elizabeth Woodville and I have many to choose from as suspects!' He smiled grimly. 'Bishop Morton was a faithful Lancastrian and probably no true friend to my late brother, and Will Hastings has been acting strangely too. I thought he was my supporter as he wrote to me with the details of Edward's will. And of course, Thomas Stanley is stepfather to Henry Tudor, so he could want to see things go wrong for me as well.'

'Richard, you have inherited all these men. You should have your own Council members now.'

'Yes, I know mother, but they are influential, wealthy and well-connected. I need them for the time being, until I know which way the wind blows. Except Hastings.' He glanced over at her. 'I will not give him a position on my protectorate Council much longer. I cannot have a man who led my brother the king in his excesses and debauchery being a responsible advisor to the new young king.'

'And does he know this? If he does, it explains why he has changed is character towards you.' Cecily's mind was sharp and her son appreciated this.

'I told Harry Stafford of my plans, and I believe he was not able to keep such important news to himself.' He looked exasperated, then continued. 'But Catesby has just told me that the one passing messages to the dowager queen is Jane Shore.'

'Jane Shore? What, Edward's old mistress? But who is she getting the information from?' Duchess Cecily was astonished. 'I know she is now in the bed of Thomas Grey but who is feeding him your secrets?'

Richard smiled. 'Your intelligence network does you credit, mother.'

'It is hardly a network, my son. I had a visit from the Princess Eliza recently. She told me.'

'Well, the question remains; who is telling Jane Shore, and

why?' The Lord Protector sat back and looked at the ceiling. 'I have sent Catesby to have the Shore woman arrested, then maybe we will know more.'

Mother and son had enjoyed a quiet dinner, just the two of them with Rob Percy and Tommy serving the dishes. The Lord Protector insisted they join them, and it turned into an enjoyable time with the four talking about life in the north and how the Duchess Anne had her hands full, looking after the Clarence children, as well as Gloucester's illegitimate children John and Katherine, plus their own little Ned. God had not blessed the Gloucesters with another child yet, but Richard hid his pain at this and said he was pleased that Anne's mother, the Countess of Warwick, was lending a hand in the nursery.

'Shall Anne be coming to London for the coronation?' Cecily passed the decanter to Rob.

'I hope so, Lady mother, but she writes that her cough has returned and she is feeling weak at the moment.' Richard poured wine for Tommy. 'We really should have a page doing this. How is your lad, Owen?'

'Keeping his head down for the moment, for which I give thanks.' They all laughed. 'I am not happy with Colyngbourne though. I wanted to talk to you about that. He is making enquiries into my son Edward's past financial matters! He was a good friend to me once, or so I thought.'

Richard was about to speak when the door was flung open and Francis Lovell stepped in.

'Francis! You've missed the pies but we might have a crust of bread for you!' Tommy Parr raised a glass in salute to their old friend, but froze when he saw Lovell's serious face.

'Richard, I am sorry to burst in, but you must hear this

news.' He came to the head of the table and rested his hands upon it. 'Two things; the first is that Elizabeth Woodville has taken the princesses and young Prince Richard, as well as Thomas Grey, and fled to Westminster Abbey where she is claiming sanctuary!'

'Again?' Cecily spoke up as Richard seemed lost for words. 'Who is she claiming sanctuary from this time?'

Francis looked abashed. 'I am not clear, but I believe she has heard of the arrest of her brother Anthony and her younger Grey son, and now says she fears that our Lord Protector is her enemy.'

'Christ!' Uncharacteristically Richard swore. 'My apologies Lady mother, but this makes me look like an adversary to the whole Woodville clan, including the new king!'

'She not only took the children, Richard. She took as much of the treasury as she could carry too.' Lovell pulled up a chair next to Cecily. 'God knows what mischief she will get up to with that.'

'What was the other news, Francis.' Rob leant round Richard to ask. 'You said there were two things.'

'Yes, Catesby was in the stable yard when I arrived. He has found out who is passing information to Jane Shore.' He paused. 'It is Will Hastings. Hastings has made Jane the conduit to get messages to the Woodvilles, and Margaret Stanley's doctor is involved too. Will has turned his coat, it seems. Catesby was told that the Woodvilles would give Hastings a position on the king's Council if he will act against you now, Richard. He knows that his time in power is finished otherwise.'

All sat in silence, digesting the news and its implications. Duchess Cecily was the first to speak, and she took Richard's hand as she did so.

'My son, I will give you one piece of advice. Do not act

in haste. Take time to discuss these events with your *trusted* friends, then proceed. I doubt Hastings is alone in this plot to seize control of the boy king; you must find out who else he has been speaking with. Thomas Grey is untouchable in sanctuary, for the moment, but I would not be surprised if there were others involved.'

Richard smiled at her, strained and pale. 'My father relied on your valuable guidance, Lady mother. I shall do so too.'

Baynard's Castle, London, 13th June 1483

'Lady mother, how lovely to see you.' Duchess Cecily's daughter Elizabeth kissed her on both cheeks and made a little curtsey. She had made the journey from her home at Wingfield to be in London for the coronation of King Edward. As his aunt, she was counting on a good seat and fine robes being provided for her. Elizabeth was Duchess of Suffolk and mother to John de la Pole, and had always been a favourite with her late brother. John followed her into the chamber and knelt for Cecily's blessing. 'You remember Mary, don't you mother?' Elizabeth gestured towards the old crone behind her, the nurse she had many years ago who never left her service.

'Ah, Mistress Digberry, won't you take a seat?' Duchess Cecily had always had a fondness for the bent old woman, and was touched at her loyalty to the family. She apparently had a way with herbs and potions and was rumoured to be something of an alchemist. 'Please, take some wine.' She nodded to the page Owen to pour a cup for them all.

Elizabeth and John sat on padded seats ranged around the window overlooking the Thames, while Mary Digberry took a stool near the door. Cecily placed a bowl of early strawberries, prettily arranged on a silver platter, on the table for them to share, and the conversation flowed along as smoothly as the river outside.

'So Prince Richard will be joining his brother in the Tower apartments?' Duchess Elizabeth reached for more fruit and washed it down with a swallow of wine. 'Well, he will be company for his brother the king while they await the coronation.' Mary Digberry approached silently and tried to remove the cup from Elizabeth's hand. She knew her mistress' stomach was weak; too much wine and she would spend the evening on the close-stool and they would all be sorry then. Elizabeth kept a tight grip on the pewter cup though and refused to relinquish it.

Cecily raised an eyebrow and exchanged a smile with John. She knew about the weak stomach, and the loose tongue her daughter had after too much wine, and was grateful for the old nurse's ministrations. She started to talk about the procession the new king would make from the royal apartments in the Tower westwards to the great Abbey when the door was pushed open with such force that Owen fell sprawling to the rushes.

'Good God!' Cecily jumped up as quick as her old bones would allow, then relaxed when she saw it was the Lord Protector striding into the room.

'Sorry, lad. My apologies, mother, but I need to talk to you!' Richard saw his sister, mouth hanging open in surprise. 'Elizabeth, John! Well, I am glad you're all here, it will save me more explanations.'

'Richard, what on earth has happened?' Cecily tried to take his hands and draw him to sit, but he broke away from her and strode around the room.

'I have had Hastings arrested! Him and others!'

'William Hastings?' Duchess Elizabeth managed to close her mouth. 'What has he done?'

'I will tell you! Hastings has been conspiring with the queen to overthrow me as Lord Protector and have me murdered, and he wasn't alone! It turns out that Bishop Morton and Archbishop Rotherham were in on the plan too. Rotherham has even given Elizabeth Woodville the Great Seal of England!'

'I thought she was in sanctuary?' John de la Pole, speaking calmly as usual, poured some wine for Richard and guided him to a seat.

'Thank you, nephew.' He took a sip. 'She is, but she can now issue commands in the name of the king.' Richard sighed. 'What a holy mess.'

'You have arrested all three?' John looked to the Lord Protector. 'Morton, Rotherham and Hastings?'

'Yes. Rotherham will spend a few months in the Tower, where he can think over his loyalties. I have put Morton into Buckingham's care; he can take him to his house at Brecknock in Wales, Jane Shore will do penance for her harlotry and Hastings must face a trial for his treason.' Richard's face was dark.

'You have given Harry Stafford Wales to command, I hear.' Cecily was not sure she was happy with Buckingham being given so much power but knew her son wanted to reward his loyalty.

'I have, mother.' He nodded to John. 'You and your mother, and of course Mistress Digberry, have the news first, before it goes out among the people. I have arrested my brother's greatest friend and God knows what they will think of me now. As the guards dragged him away, he swore he had kept a secret for love of Edward, but I am past listening to his lies.' His head drooped and he closed his eyes.

'What of Lord Stanley, was he arrested too?' John was aware of the rumours regarding Stanley's loyalties. He was a shrewd young man, not yet twenty-five but with the bearing of an older and wiser man.

'Ah, Stanley. No, I could prove nothing against him or his wife, so I've ordered he be put under confinement at his house for now.' Richard stood and faced them all. 'My brother the king is dead only two months, and nothing is going right under my charge. His wife is in sanctuary claiming she fears me, my nephew the new king hates me for arresting his uncle Anthony and his half-brother, half my bloody Council are traitors to me and I face threats of death wherever I look.' He looked to his mother. 'I fear Edward was mistaken making me Lord Protector.'

'Not so, Richard.' Elizabeth his sister jumped out of her seat, spilling wine down her red brocade dress. 'Edward knew you were the only man who could unite this country.' Mary Digberry nodded to her mistress and took her elbow to guide her back to her chair. She produced a scrap of linen from her sleeve to wipe the gown and moved her cup out of her reach.

'Your sister is right Richard,' Duchess Cecily took command of the room, 'even if it is the wine that makes her speak sense.' She smiled. 'You have done the right thing, putting these disloyal men under arrest. Let them think on their sins for a while, but you must protect yourself now. Send a man back to Middleham, send for a force to guard and support you while the king is in his minority. And send for Anne.' She took his hand. 'Have your wife brought to London too; her love and support will see you through these difficult times.'

The Tower of London, 20ᵗʰ June 1483

As the dawn broke purple and red over the white stone walls, William Hastings, once Lord Chamberlain of England, was brought through the small door onto the green. He looked up at the sky as he walked, whispering under his breath. Mounting the four steps, he stared defiantly at the Lord Protector and his men ranged around the green, but spoke no words to them. Hastings nodded to the priest who had preceded him to continue reading from his holy book, then handed a small bag of coins to the executioner. 'Make it swift, sirrah. I would join my master soon.'

'Baron Hastings you have been found guilty of treason against the Lord Protector of England by the Court of Chivalry.' The sheriff's voice boomed out in the quiet dawn. He was standing just in front of the priest but there was no need for his loud tone; Richard had decreed this would be a private execution and would not have the whole court present to gawp. 'Found guilty, and sentenced to death.' The sheriff stepped back as Hastings knelt on the rough boards and waved away the blindfold the executioner's apprentice went to tie around his head.

'I'll go to my death with my eyes open, boy, looking at my murderer.' He glared at Richard in front of the platform. Richard did not drop his gaze but remained blank faced with his hands clasped in front of him. He watched as the hooded executioner swung his axe back slowly then brought it down with huge force. Only when it had fallen and the great gouts of blood had finished spilling over the sawdust did he drop his head and take a deep breath.

'Jesus Christ Francis.' The Lord Protector's voice shuddered. 'Jesus Christ, I have had Edward's greatest friend executed.'

'It was treason Richard. You know it was, and so did Will.' Francis put his hand on Richard's shoulder. 'He knew what he was doing.'

'He loved Edward to the last, maybe that was his undoing.' He turned away as the priest and the executioner trampled through the blood towards the body. 'I will have him buried with Edward at Windsor. They can be together in death, as they were so much in life.'

Francis chuckled. 'I hope there is wine enough in heaven for them both.' Richard smiled for the first time that day.

'Aye, they can make a toast to the House of York for evermore.' He looked at his old friend. 'I will not have him attainted though; his wife and sons will inherit his lands. No need for them to suffer for his sins.'

Francis was about to reply when he saw Richard's face turn into a mask of horror. He was looking up at the King's Lodgings, the window of which overlooked the green. Francis turned to stare up at the window, where, framed by a stone lintel, the boy King Edward and his brother Prince Richard watched as the body of their father's oldest friend was being stuffed into a box.

Westminster Palace, London, 21ˢᵗ June 1483
Francis Lovell and Harry Stafford stood either side of Richard's chair, where he sat with his mouth open listening to Bishop Stillington. Francis put his hand on the carved oak to steady himself and Harry had almost forgotten to breathe.

'I did not come forward before, Your Grace, well, because of fear.' The stout cleric had tears running down his face. 'Your brother King Edward swore me to secrecy and had already imprisoned me once.' He took a shuddering gasp. 'But it is all true. The king was already married to Lady Eleanor Butler when he wed Elizabeth Woodville. The marriage was not valid, and therefore the young princes, well, all his children, are illegitimate.' He looked down past his stomach to the floor.

'Who else knew?' Richard seemed incapable of speaking, so Lovell asked the question. 'Who else knew of this?'

'William Hastings knew, and probably the queen.' Stillington faltered. 'I mean, Dame Grey I suppose, as she is not really queen is she? And your brother George, he knew. I told him, I'm afraid.'

'Bishop, wait outside.' Francis gestured towards the door. 'But don't go far away.' Stillington nodded, fearing another stint in the Tower cells but powerless to resist. He shuffled out and softly closed the door behind him.

The Lord Protector rubbed his face with his hands. 'God Almighty. This is unbelievable.'

'Well at least we know what Hastings' secret was.' Harry Stafford paced in small circles. 'Would he have used it to bring you down or support you though, that's the question.'

'Support me?' Richard looked at his cousin. 'What do you mean?'

'Well it's obvious, isn't it?' Stafford stopped before Richard's chair. 'Edward's children are illegitimate, Clarence is dead and attainted therefore his son is ineligible, so who is next in line to the throne?' His face shone with excitement. 'You, Richard, you! You must be the next King of England!'

Duchess Cecily and Richard's wife Anne sat with him around the shiny oak table. Francis had sent for them both to come to him after Harry's shocking pronouncement. He needed his family with him to discuss the earth-shattering news and to plan the way forward. Harry and Francis sat at the far end, away from the others, where the women were holding Richard's hands.

'I don't want it.' His voice was flat but determined. 'For so many reasons, I do not want to be king.'

'But who else is there?' Cecily was over her shock and anger at Edward's foolish lustfulness, marrying Elizabeth when he was already wed, and was gripping Richard's hand so tight it was hurting them both. 'Those boys are illegitimate, they cannot inherit the throne. Nor can George's son. You are the only one.'

'Why, my love? Why do you say no to it?' Anne's quiet voice was soothing amidst the turmoil.

'I want to live in the north, I want to live with you and Ned at Middleham, my Lady.' Richard's voice got stronger. 'I hate the court, I hate the intrigues of it and the factions and the treachery. I was Edward's man heart and soul, but I do not want his position and throne.' He dropped his head and looked at Anne's hand clutching his. 'I have seen what kingship does to a man, and I will not have that happen to me.'

'You are not Edward.' Anne was becoming determined. 'You will not live or rule as he did.' She leant over to whisper so only he could hear. 'You have me to help you and always will.'

'Anne is right, my son.' Cecily sat back and straightened her shoulders. 'Now we know why Edward had George killed, because he knew his secret. And it explains why Stillington was put in the Tower for months. God forgive me, but you will be a better king than your brother. There is no other; it must be you.'

'And it will solve the problem of the Woodvilles having the boy king in their clutches!' Stafford piped up with excitement. 'I say it works out well!' Francis silenced him with a frown. His exuberance was annoying at the best of times, and now it was completely wrong. Francis agreed with Cecily that Richard must take the throne but he knew his old friend well; he believed that Richard's sense of duty would win in the end but he would not meet it with joy or acclaim. He would have to come to the idea slowly and overcome his reluctance.

Anne and Richard had been alone for an hour. Now Francis held the door for Stafford and Cecily to rejoin them and they saw that Richard had lost his look of dejection.

'We have decided that I will accept the crown, but on condition that it is offered to me freely by the Lords Temporal and Spiritual of England and by the Commons. I will not take it without their petitioning me to do so.' He looked determined. 'I will not take it by force or without legality, I will not be seen as an usurper.'

'Richard, you know this is the right thing to do.' Francis knelt beside his chair. 'But now we have to plan; the coronation was supposed to be held tomorrow, everything is ready for it and we've even had new coins minted with young Edward's likeness. We need to prepare the people for such a change.'

'We will not make a proclamation that I am to be king, not without Parliament ratifying it.' Richard was determined on this.

'I'll get a preacher.' Harry Stafford stepped forward. 'Old Ralph Shaa, the king's chaplain, he'll do it.'

'Do what?' Anne looked up at Buckingham. 'What will he do?'

'We'll get him to stand outside St Paul's and tell the people what Bishop Stillington has said; that Edward was married before and so his children are illegitimate.' Buckingham's excitement was mounting at his plan. 'The people will believe him, he's a priest and brother to the Lord Mayor. They'll believe him when he says that Richard here is the next rightful king.'

'They'll believe it, Harry, because it's true.' Duchess Cecily nodded her head. 'Francis, send for the Speaker of the House, John Wode. We need to talk to him too.'

Richard stood, walked to the window and gazed out over the bustling streets. He neither smiled nor spoke, instead just nodded his head.

Crosby Place, London, 26th June 1483

Sir Robert Ratcliffe laid the papers on Richard's desk and shuffled them into a neat pile. He was conscientious and meticulous and Richard knew that he had a good man in Robert; he valued his cautious advice.

'He named you as executor in his will, Your Grace.' Ratcliffe cleared his throat as he leant over the table. 'The Earl of Northumberland presided over the trials of all three and the executions were carried out yesterday. Anthony Woodville requested that he be buried under an image of The Virgin Mary and nominated you to carry out his wishes.'

'All beheaded? Woodville, Richard Grey and Thomas Vaughan?' Richard did not raise his head.

'Yes, Your Grace.'

'So I have killed Elizabeth Woodville's brother, one of her sons and disinherited the rest.' He put his head in his hands. 'Jesus Christ. Will I be forgiven?'

'It was a proper trial for treason, Your Grace, and by

naming you executor, Anthony Woodville showed that he accepted his fate for his actions.' Ratcliffe straightened up. 'He was a pragmatic man, he rolled the dice and he lost.'

As his master was about to reply, Tommy Parr tapped on the door and entered.

'The Mayor is here Richard, with a committee from Parliament. They have asked for an audience.'

'Oh God.' Richard stood. 'I have no choice now, do I?

Tower of London, 6th July 1483

Anne Neville smoothed down the scarlet velvet gown and stared at her reflection in the silver mirror. Duchess Cecily bent down slowly and arranged the train of the dress so it would flow behind her as she walked. Neither spoke until Richard entered, wearing the purple robes trimmed with ermine that he would wear at his coronation. All three stared at each other, and it was Cecily who broke the silence.

'It is all legal, my son. You were offered the crown by the Lords and Commons of England. They have drawn up a Royal Title confirming your right to the throne which will be ratified when Parliament assembles.'

'Your Lady mother is right. There is no one but you.' Anne took his hand and kissed it. 'I know you do not want it, but it is your responsibility to unite the country as its rightful king.'

'This country cannot be united until Elizabeth Woodville comes out of sanctuary and shows the world she does not fear me. Until then, there will be those that still think I have taken my nephew's place.' Richard sat on the padded oak seat by Anne's mirror. 'I will keep the boys in their apartments here for a while longer, until things are quiet. Then perhaps the Woodvilles can be reunited somewhere in the country.'

'Your Grace.' Francis Lovell poked his head round the chamber door. 'The coronation procession to the Abbey is ready to begin.'

'Thank you Francis.' Richard waved him away, then turned to the women. 'It's odd, isn't it? You, mother, were to be queen when my father was heir to Henry's throne, and Anne was to be queen alongside Edouard of Westminster. You have both been so close to the throne, but I have never wanted it.' He took their hands and kissed their fingers. 'I will swear my oath to serve my country, and I will need the support of you both to be a just and fair king.'

Anne and Cecily dropped into deep curtsies and said in unison, 'My Liege.'

Richard, third of his name and King of England, bowed in return.

York Minster, 8ᵗʰ September 1483

Little Ned began to cough as he walked down the steps of the vast sand-coloured church. The air was warm and there was no breeze that day but stepping out into the northern air brought on the wheezing that had plagued him for most of his seven years. He raised one hand to steady the princes' coronet balanced precariously on his head, and waved delightedly at the crowds with the other. His mother and father followed behind, smiling as they saw the people crammed together to catch a glimpse of the King and Queen of England and their only son. King Richard had been heartened to see the joyous response of the commoners as he had made his progress from London up to

York, stopping in the cities of Reading, Oxford, Tewkesbury and Warwick amongst others to receive their fealty. He had decided to have Ned meet them at Pontefract and rewarded York for its loyalty by investing him as Prince of Wales in the city that held him and his wife in such high regard.

'My Lady?' He turned to Anne.

'My King.' His wife smiled in return, using the title that gave her such pleasure to say.

'Our prince looks tired. Do you think we should delay the banquet?'

'No, Nursey Bessie will make sure he rests well tonight.' She nodded to the older woman who came forward and began to guide the prince towards the coach that had been made ready for him.

King Richard's smile, which had been unceasing throughout the feast, faded fast as Lord Stanley approached. He always looked like he was the bearer of bad news, whether or not it was true, but Richard had begun to trust him as a loyal servant. Both he and his wife Lady Margaret had offered their services to the new monarch and Margaret had even been given the honour of carrying Anne's train at her coronation.

'I have news, Your Grace.' Thomas Lord Stanley stroked his long beard. A revolt had begun in the south of England led by Elizabeth Woodville's son Thomas Grey and her brother Lionel, and Harry Stafford Duke of Buckingham had been sent to quell it. 'It seems that the rebels are no longer calling for the illegitimate Lord Edward to be made king.' Richard knew he was referring to his own nephew, still safe in The Tower of London with his brother and their doctor to look after them. He had absolutely refused Harry's suggestion the boys should be called

The Lords Bastard; they could not be referred to as princes now, so he had decreed their title to be simply, Lord. 'They are now calling for someone else to take your throne.'

'Who?' Richard pushed away his cup and gestured for Stanley to sit. 'Who are they calling for?'

Lord Stanley flushed red and coughed. 'It appears that the rebels are supporting Henry Tudor now.'

'Henry Tudor? Son of your wife and *your* stepson?' Richard's voice dropped and turned angry.

'Yes him, Your Grace.' Stanley rushed to explain. 'I believe the rumour is that the boys in the Tower are dead, so they want Henry Tudor to be king.'

'Dead? The boys are in the Tower! What does your wife say about this, she who proclaimed herself loyal to me and my queen?' Richard was furious. 'Does she even remember that her Beaufort family were barred from making any claim to the throne by Henry IV? By what right does that bastard Tudor have to claim *my* crown? And who says the boys are dead?'

'Your Grace, I cannot believe my wife is involved!' Stanley felt he could be fighting for his life here. 'She would not turn her face against you, I am sure!'

'Are you?' Richard stood and watched as Nurse Bessie led Ned from the chamber amidst huge applause. He raised his glass to his son in farewell. He turned back to Stanley. 'You had better be damned sure, because I will have no treachery in my household.' As Stanley bowed his way back from Richard's chair, the king waved over Francis Lovell, now his Lord Chamberlain.

'Francis, how fast can you ride back to the Tower? I have a mission for you.'

Angel Inn, Grantham, Lincolnshire, 19ᵗʰ October 1483

The King's Chamber on the upper floor of the inn was crowded and smoky. The hearth had been hastily lit by Richard's man Thomas Brayne but the wood must have still been green as the smoke belched forth and caused the men to wipe their eyes. Tommy Parr and Rob Percy sat close to the king, watching as Thomas Stanley looked down from the window though the rain onto the street.

'He comes, Your Grace, he is here!' Stanley opened the door and waited at the top of the stairs for the Clerk of the Chancery to lumber upwards. Robert Blackwall had to duck to enter the chamber to avoid banging his head on the low beams, and he approached the king carrying a bag made of red velvet. He knelt; always conscious of his height, he was aware King Richard was a shorter man and had no wish to tower over him.

'The Great Seal of England, My Liege.' He proffered the small sack. 'Sent with all haste by your Lord Chancellor Russell.'

'I give you my thanks.' King Richard nodded for Rob to open it and withdraw the Seal. 'Find yourself a meal and rest now.' He reached for the only piece of paper on the desk and drew it towards himself. It was a warrant for the arrest of his cousin Harry Stafford Duke of Buckingham for treason and it was awaiting the imprint of the Great Seal to grant it authority. He was grateful the Seal had been wrested out of the hands of Elizabeth Woodville in sanctuary, and was pleased to have it in his own hands now. He watched as Rob pushed the Seal into hot wax and pressed it on the document. Another man he thought true to him would die at his command.

The court had been at Leicester when they had learnt of Harry Stafford's treachery. He had been sent to put down the rebellion against the king but Richard had put his trust in the wrong man. Stafford had conspired with Bishop Morton, his own prisoner, to rise up and join forces with Henry Tudor and support his invasion. As violent storm rose as Buckingham was to gather his men from Wales and meet Tudor at Plymouth. Brittany had given Tudor nearly four thousand men and ships to transport them and claim Richard's throne as his own, but they had been defeated by the weather. The king sent Jack Howard, now Duke of Norfolk, south to block the rebels, but the wind and rain caused Tudor's ships to sink or return to Brittany and turned the roads into impassable mud trenches. The waters of the Severn rose too high to let Buckingham cross into England and Richard put a bounty of one thousand pounds on his head. The warrant served to authorise his arrest and eventual trial, if he was ever found.

As they had travelled to Grantham, the king found himself questioning his own judgement and wisdom. He had trusted Hastings, Morton and Rotherham, yet they all turned against him. He had put more faith in Harry Stafford, and rewarded him better than any other, and again he had been betrayed. Stafford was indeed the most untrue man who ever lived, Richard thought, and wondered who else he had judged wrongly. Who among his advisors showed one face of loyalty to him but was planning treason behind his back?

As the warrant was rolled and dispatched by his couriers, another visitor arrived at the inn. The man was covered in mud kicked up from the horses' hooves and was tired and sore. He had ridden hard these last few days and was glad to finally get out of the rain into the warm. King Richard was the first to see him, leapt out of his chair and, unheeding of the mud, embraced him.

'Francis, thank God you have come.' He drew him towards the fog around the fire and pushed him into a seat. 'I feared for you on the treacherous roads, the rivers have broken their banks and I know some bridges are washed away.' He took a cup of mulled ale from Brayne and handed it to Francis. The king waved away the men who had come forward to hear the news so he and Lovell were alone.

'Francis, did you do as I asked? Was Brackenbury helpful to you?' Richard lowered his voice. He would trust no other with this secret.

'Giving Robert Brackenbury the Tower to command was a wise move, Your Grace. He has cared for your treasures there, and kept them safe when others tried to take them away.' Lovell sipped the hot ale and felt it warming a path down to his wet boots. 'I escorted the treasures all the way to the castle at Sherriff Hutton and by the grace of God, did it in total secrecy. Not one person we met knew what I was carrying in the wagon so now all the children are under one roof. We will keep them safe, and we will keep them together.'

Francis looked too tired to say much more, and Richard was about to call over Tommy and Rob and get them to escort him to a comfortable room, but Francis had one more thing to say. He stood and made sure his back was to the rest of the room when he spoke a few words which drained the blood from Richard's face. He nodded, then bowed and turned away. As he went to find a bed, he heard the king's voice.

'Lord Stanley! You will come before me now and answer for your wife.'

Baynard's Castle, London, 27ᵗʰ December 1483

They had spent a quiet Christmas in London, with the king's closest family and friends around him. Ned had returned north for his health under the trusted protection of Sir James Tyrell and the king and queen had sent him a new pony to celebrate the feast of the birth of Jesus. King Richard had spent many hours on his knees in his mother's private chapel, examining his thoughts and praying for the strength to overcome the weaknesses he saw in his character. He prayed for wisdom to judge his faithful friends and he begged for the strength to be a just king. He had not wanted this, but he swore on his soul that he would do everything in his power to defend his kingdom against treason and disloyalty. His mother had given him at the Christmas feast a ruby ring that had once belonged to his father, and as he gazed up at the golden crucifix over the altar he turned the ring over on his finger and prayed to be made worthy of his high position.

The king walked in the cold gardens with Duchess Cecily and spoke of the weather and the fine food her cooks had produced. Neither had wanted to spoil the blessed atmosphere of the season with talk of treachery, so they spoke of the Lords Edward and Richard, as the former princes were now called, safe in the north with Teddy and Margaret Clarence and the king's own children. John of Gloucester, Richard's illegitimate son was a man now and recently knighted. He was destined to be Captain of Calais and his father could not have been more proud of him. Katherine Plantagenet had grown into a beauty and marriage for her was not too far in the future. George's son Teddy was a bright boy, the image of his sire without his anger or disaffection and Maggie was a mother to him in every way. Cecily and her son talked of such pleasantries until Richard found he could no longer avoid the subject.

'I doubt Margaret Stanley enjoyed roasted pheasant and suckling pig at her Christmas table,' the king said wryly. 'But perhaps her husband allows her that much. I do not know.'

'Or care.' Cecily was completely unsympathetic to Lady Margaret's comfort now. It was found that she had been conspiring with Elizabeth Woodville and Harry Stafford to aid her son Henry Tudor's invasion and overthrow of Richard. Margaret's great friend Bishop Morton had escaped abroad where he was supporting Tudor. Her treachery had been discovered and she was now under house arrest and under the control of her husband, who had been granted all her property and possessions. It was certain Margaret wanted her son to be the next King of England, and had colluded with both Elizabeth Woodville and Buckingham to achieve this. 'What made Harry turn against you, do you think? Would he really have supported Tudor as king?' Cecily pulled her fur collar tighter around her neck.

'I think Harry wanted to be king in his own right; he had seen that Edward's death made me king, and he wanted the same for himself. He had royal blood himself after all. I believe he would have aided Tudor's invasion so I had to meet him in battle, then Harry would have fought the victor to take the throne himself.' He smiled grimly. 'Neither were as clever as they thought.' The Duke of Buckingham had been defeated by the rain and was captured and handed over to the king's men; he was beheaded at Salisbury marketplace the previous month after Richard had refused to speak to him. Richard's hatred of Harry did not extend to his widow Katherine, Elizabeth Woodville's sister; he had granted an annuity and brought her to London to live under his care.

'So Margaret is confined and Stafford is dead. But I do not think that is the last we will hear of Henry Tudor.' Cecily took Richard's arm to ascend the steps back into the castle. She was so cold that her legs were becoming numb and she was hoping that Kat and Madge would have a warming drink and a blanket ready for her. The chill in the air made the king's back and shoulder ache but he was used to ignoring his pain.

'You are right, Lady mother.' He put his hand on her back to guide her though the doors into the stone corridor to her apartments. 'He has sworn an oath at Rennes Cathedral to marry Edward's daughter Eliza. To get the Woodville supporters on his side I suppose.'

'You should have attainted Margaret, she is clearly guilty of treason Richard.' Cecily was grateful to finally arrive in her own solar and seated herself before the fire.

'Perhaps. But I need the support of her husband.'

Cecily grabbed Richard's hand and dug her nails into his skin. 'Do not put your trust in Lord Stanley, my son.' She looked at her husband's ring on his finger and stroked it with her thumb. 'He stands to gain more from Henry Tudor being on the throne than he does if you keep it.'

'If I keep it?' He smiled as he bent down to kiss her cheek. 'I have prayed for guidance Lady mother. With the help of God, I will know who my true friends are and I will keep the crown that should have gone to my father.'

Westminster Palace, London, 1ˢᵗ March 1484

Thomas Brayne was not sure how to announce her to the king. The woman who was once a queen strode regally through the familiar hallways towards the presence chamber that used to belong to her husband, striding though the rooms as though they were still hers. Was she Dame Woodville, Lady Grey or should he say Dowager Queen? She was keeping her head held high, not acknowledging the stares of servants who not so long ago had bowed to her.

'Dame Grey, Your Grace.' Thomas stepped to the side and allowed Elizabeth Woodville to come forward. King Richard was seated on his throne, but came forward to take her hand and kiss it.

'Lady Elizabeth, you are most welcome.'

She was thrown for a moment at his pleasant greeting and managed to nod her head. She studiously ignored Duchess Cecily, seated off to the side, and looked Richard in the eye.

'I thank you.' Elizabeth found it hard to form the words; she was in a state of nervousness and did not trust her voice to betray her feelings. Near on a year she had been in sanctuary since the death of Edward, and being in the vast palace of Westminster gave her a heady sense of freedom and she was almost cowed at the size of it.

'Please.' King Richard guided her towards some comfortable chairs grouped around his mother and the threesome were forced into close contact. 'We are more pleased than we can say that you have joined us, are we not, Lady mother?' Richard raised an eyebrow to Cecily, who forced herself to smile thinly and nod. 'Now that you have left the confines of the Abbey, we wish to speak of the future.'

Elizabeth Woodville smoothed her dark blue dress over her slim hips, glancing at Cecily's more old-fashioned robe that covered her widening girth. She sat demurely and waited.

'We want to assure you of our good faith and reward your return to the world.' Richard reached for some papers.

'Despite your treason with Margaret Stanley and the Duke of Buckingham.' Cecily cut in and her voice was hard. 'You know the former is her husband's prisoner and the latter is dead? You are lucky that my son shows forgiveness to you.'

'Thank you mother.' Cecily took the rebuke in silence. 'Lady Elizabeth, I will publicly swear that you and your girls will not be harmed by me and you have no reason to fear us. I will find good husbands for your daughters and will provide them with generous dowries. I do not forget they are the children of my brother.'

'And where is your son, Thomas Grey?' Cecily could not keep silent. 'Joined Henry Tudor in Brittany with your brother Edward Woodville, I hear.'

'Unlike my son Richard Grey, dead and buried in Pontefract with Anthony.' Elizabeth shot back. 'Dead at your son's hand.'

'Elizabeth, your son and brother were guilty of treason. Whether it was at your command I prefer not to speculate.' The king sat forward in his seat and turned his shoulder so Cecily was blocked from the conversation. She had insisted on being present and he knew he should have refused; she was unhelpful and he regretted allowing her to attend. 'Parliament has ratified my Royal Title, and declared your children by Edward illegitimate and unable to inherit the crown.' He proffered the papers but she refused to touch them. 'However, you know my brother's sons are safe in my keeping; you will not be permitted to see them as I think it better they are kept out sight until matters are settled. I have heard rumours from abroad, no doubt started by Bishop Morton, that the lads are dead, but you know well enough that this is just to slander me.'

'Indeed.' Elizabeth gave a brief nod. 'Will it work, I wonder?'

'My right to the throne is not contested, Elizabeth.' The king fixed her with a stare. 'The Three Estates of the realm petitioned me to accept the throne as your sons are not now permitted to, and the Lords and Commons have willingly accepted that. The boys are safe, out of the reach of any supporters you may still have, but they will not inherit.' He softened his voice now. 'But you and your daughters are free and will be treated with respect. All this I have promised.'

'And my Eliza?'

'Ah yes. Henry Tudor has promised to marry her, presumably with your agreement.' Richard twirled the ring on his finger. 'Eliza will be taken under my personal protection and will live in comfort with my wife the queen. Better not let her anywhere near Tudor, eh?' He tried to lighten the mood but failed. 'I have granted you a house and seven hundred marks per year to live in comfort; in return I ask that you be faithful to my crown and do not conspire against me again.'

Elizabeth stood without answering. She dropped a deep curtsey, turned her back and walked away.

Nottingham Castle, 10ᵗʰ April 1484

Queen Anne giggled as her husband reached down for a swift kiss. It was a fine spring morning with just a touch of frost in the air, but the sun was shining through the trees and it promised to hold fair for the rest of the day. The king was in good spirits although had some pain in his spine from the journey up from Cambridge, and he resolved to speak to his Master of Horse about getting a new saddle to support his back. Anne had travelled in a litter for most of the way; she was tired after their visit to Queen's College in the university town, but was pleased at their reception of her endowments. Together, king and queen and had resolved to grant funding to many charitable causes, and the college's promise of Masses for Richard and Anne pleased them well.

Despite the rebellion of last year, Queen Anne felt that this first year of her husband's kingship was progressing well. Richard's first Parliament was successful and they hoped that the benefits of it would soon be felt by the people. In addition to recognising his title and inheritance of the crown, Chancellor Russell had pushed through Richard's determination to bring fairness and justice to the Commons. Laws regarding the granting of bail and having proper juries were coming into effect in courtrooms around the country and he had commanded his judges to dispense justice promptly and fairly. The Parliament had also dealt with the hated benevolences or royal demands for money and ensured that the people would no longer be burdened with these payments, and it improved trade rights and stronger rules to avoid corruption. Perhaps above all, the king had decreed that laws were from now on to be written in English and not Latin or French, so the law of his land was clear and accessible. Matters were going well for them, and this early morning walk through the crisp gardens gave them a moment of privacy and some time to be alone.

'I do so love Nottingham, the people here are good to us and the castle is most comfortable.' Anne glanced up at the huge tower and the arms of England that fluttered above it.

'My brother Edward spent much money on improvements here, he did so like his luxuries.' Richard smiled as he remembered the good times they had shared here. 'It was in this very castle that he commanded me to lead our forces into Scotland.'

'You miss him, don't you?' Anne took his arm and gave it a gentle squeeze. 'You never speak of him, but you feel an emptiness now he's gone.'

Richard looked down on his pretty wife and smiled sadly. 'My Lady, I miss him like the sun misses the moon.' He looked up and took a deep breath. 'For all his faults, and he had many as it turns out, I miss Edward every day.' They shared another smile. 'I hope he forgives me for taking his son's throne, although I had no choice.'

They reached the garden steps and Anne was keen to go indoors and change her damp and dirty shoes. They would share bread and meat together before their duties of the day began, and both were grateful for these precious moments alone.

'My Lady.' Richard held the door for his wife.

'My King.' Anne lifted her skirts over the last step and headed towards their private solar. She did not see the man rush forward from the passageway until Richard jumped in astonishment.

'James! Good God man, where did you come from.' The king smiled in his surprise, then halted. Sir James Tyrell was supposed to be at Middleham with Ned. His face went white and he unthinkingly grabbed Anne's shoulder and gripped it. 'What is it? What brings you here?'

Sir James did not speak, or could not. His eyes filled with tears and he dropped to his knees in front of them both. Anne thought she had stopped breathing, that she would never breathe again, and through the rushing sound in her head, she heard Richard's whisper. 'What is it?'

Before Sir James could tell them that their son was dead of

a fever, Anne had fallen to the floor amid the damp rushes and mud, and never wanted to rise again.

Middleham Castle, Yorkshire, 10th June 1484

As the litter rumbled over the drawbridge the pains shot up Duchess Cecily's legs and she was desperate to finally get out and ease the soreness. Francis Lovell had provided every comfort he could think of for the long and arduous journey, but Cecily had insisted he bring her north to see her son. As she was handed down and her feet finally touched the lush grass of Yorkshire, Kat provided a steady hand for her mistress until she was sure of her footing. Both Lovell and Kat had thought that at nearly seventy years old, the duchess should have settled on just writing to Richard but she had been determined to make this trip that she saw as a pilgrimage.

As she watched her bags being unloaded, the lithe figure of her granddaughter Eliza flew through the door leading from the Great Hall and into her arms.

'Lady grandmother!' Eliza kissed Cecily's cheeks and embraced her. 'We never thought to see you in Yorkshire! How lovely of you to come at this terrible time.' Lovell bowed and turned away to let the women talk.

'My dear girl, you look well. The fresh air here must feel wonderful after all those months cooped up in Westminster.' The duchess stepped back and looked at the eighteen-year-old beauty. She had the elegance and refinement of her mother but the charm and charisma of her father. Cecily could not fail to think of Edward when she gazed at her. 'How are the king and queen?'

'It is so terrible for them! That poor little boy!' Eliza took Cecily's arm and they began to stroll towards the apartments. 'My uncle the king haunts the battlements and corridors as if searching for Ned, and the queen has shut herself up in her rooms. She will see no-one and I am sure she is not eating or drinking a thing.' Eliza's voice faltered. 'She won't even speak to Uncle Richard and I think his heart is breaking.' They stopped at the entrance to the private quarters, and Cecily kissed her granddaughter.

'You go along with Francis, my dear. I will see them both now.' Eliza bobbed a curtsey and flittered off with Lovell, headed in the direction of the chapel.

The castle Steward appeared from the stone arch, bowed low and guided Duchess Cecily towards the private apartments, pretending he could not hear her deep sigh as she saw the steps she would have to climb.

As she reached the top and stopped briefly to catch her breath, the outer door opened as King Richard came out to meet her. He said not a word but went down on one knee before her and put his arms around her waist. She cradled his head against her and leant down to kiss his dark hair. They stayed like this until the steward took himself away and went to see about refreshments.

'I did not mean for you to make this journey mother. When I wrote to you, I just wanted your prayers and your blessing.' They were seated in Richard's private chamber, all alone except for one of the castle hounds who was sleeping under the open window.

'My son, you always have those.' Cecily reached out and patted his arm. 'My heart broke for you when I heard the news

271

of Ned. I have had Mass said for him every day and I have been down on these old knees begging Our Lord to take him into His care and to be carried to heaven on angels' wings.'

'Was Francis good to you on the journey? Didn't bore you with tales of our childhood did he?' Richard wiped his face on his velvet sleeve and changed the subject; he felt as if any words of kindness now could make him weep and he could not speak of his son and keep his composure.

'I love hearing about your days together when you were boys, I feel I missed so much of them.' Cecily saw that her son wanted to speak of practical matters to hide his agony. 'I agree with your suggestion to replace William Colyngbourne with Francis in my service. William has become most odd these last months, since he lost his offices and lands in Wiltshire; I fear he blames you for that. I will value Francis' guidance in all matters. He is a practical lad, and a good choice should I need advice.'

'Thank you mother.' Despair overcame him again. 'I do not know how to bear this loss.' He put his face into his hands; he had tried to be brave and kingly and not show his all-encompassing grief to the world, but now he was in Cecily's presence, he became a little boy again and felt no shame when the tears came. 'My precious son, mother, my little Ned!'

Cecily rose and went to his chair. She stretched her arms around him and stood rocking him until the sun moved past the window and shadows fell onto the floor.

She had knocked twice on the oak door but received no reply. Cecily reached for the iron handle and turned it, and was surprised to find it unlocked. She peeped around the door of the queen's chamber and saw Anne sitting in her chair under the window. Her feet were up on the seat and her arms were around her knees, rocking and staring into nothing.

'My dear Anne.' Cecily went forward and kissed her forehead. 'My poor child.' She cupped the back of the queen's head and under her hand the hair felt dry and brittle. It seemed she had shrunk in her grief; she looked tiny and frail and Cecily wondered if she had all her wits still.

'My boy is dead.' Anne's voice was flat and there was no sign of emotion apart from the constant rocking. 'My baby is dead.'

'Oh my dear. He is with God now, that is the only comfort you can take.'

Anne's feet suddenly dropped to the floor and she looked at Cecily's face. 'Why did God take him? Why would He take my only son?'

'We cannot question Him.' Despite her faith, the duchess could find few words that seemed fitting now. 'He took my husband and sons too, perhaps to test our strength. We just have to find a way forward now, and to learn to live with our losses.'

'I am not sure I want to live with this loss.' Anne took a shuddering breath. 'Look.' She opened her hand to reveal the gold and sapphire pendant Cecily had given her on her marriage. 'This promised fertility and blessings.' She gave a strangled laugh. 'I am not blessed and I am not fertile; I will never have another child and Richard will not have a son to follow him.' She gripped the jewel more tightly and welcomed the pain in her hand. 'I have failed him as a wife, a mother and a queen. What is left for me now?' Anne rose, went to the window and pushed open the casement so the fresh northern breeze ruffled her hair. She opened her grip and stared briefly at the pendant before she threw it far out towards the fields surrounding the castle and watched as it fell amongst the stones and grass.

St George's Chapel, Windsor Castle, 12th August 1484

'That was done well, I think.' Duchess Cecily and Francis Lovell watched as the priests and choristers lifted the hems of their robes and climbed the steps beside the High Altar. The mourners were filing out and the workmen would bring their tools later to fix the marble but the new tomb reflected the status of the old king.

'It has long been in Richard's mind to reinter King Henry here. It was where he was born, and to be buried here is fitting I believe.' Francis had supervised the transfer of Henry's body from the Lady Chapel at Chertsey Abbey and accompanied it upriver to Windsor to watch the reburial with all the ceremony Richard had demanded.

'How is my son?' Cecily took Lovell's proffered arm as they descended the shallow steps and strolled in the warm sunshine up the hill back towards the castle.

'I think the grief will never leave him, Your Grace.' Francis gazed up at the huge stone turrets. 'He and the queen seem far from each other now, and he cannot reach past her sorrow to comfort her.'

Cecily stifled the tears she felt welling up.

'I have lost sons too, Francis. I feel his anguish.'

'But he has no-one to follow him and that pains him too. I believe he intends to make Clarence's son Teddy his heir, but the attainder against George will have to be lifted first. That will take time.'

Cecily had to stop for a moment to catch her breath. As the people milled about them, the duchess had to lean against a wall halfway up the hill. She knew it was not elegant but at her age, she really felt she had no choice.

'Well, Teddy is a bright boy and very studious. I hear from his tutors at Sheriff Hutton that he and Edward's sons apply themselves well to their lessons.'

'That is true, Your Grace.' Francis led the duchess to a stone seat at the edge of the grass. 'The Lords Edward and Richard found it hard at first, being taken up north in secrecy and with such a change in their circumstances. They miss their mother but their sister Eliza sees them regularly and is helping them adjust. Although with Ned's death, I suspect that Lord Edward hoped for another chance at his father's throne, but of course he cannot.'

'No, he cannot!' Cecily was momentarily horrified. 'He is illegitimate!'

'Indeed, but the boys find that hard to accept. But until the king can confirm the new title on Teddy, I believe he will make his nephew John de la Pole, Earl of Lincoln, his heir.'

'A good choice, John is prudent and loyal to Richard. And above all, he is a *man*. I do not believe this country wants another boy-king, should anything happen to my son of course.'

'Ah, you are thinking of Henry Tudor.' Francis tipped his head back for a moment. 'He and Jasper have sworn an oath to invade again and claim the throne for Lancaster. He is perpetuating the rumour that the boys were murdered in the Tower and he will avenge them.'

'Richard should show the boys in London to disprove that gossip!'

'But who really believes it?' Francis turned to her. 'The people know that Richard accepted the throne as Lord Edward could not inherit, they welcomed his coronation. He had no need to have them killed; Tudor and his supporters are trying to slander Richard to justify his own illegal attempt to take the crown.'

'But does Tudor have much support?' Cecily questioned her son's oldest friend.

'He has some outcasts and villains.' Francis was dismissive. 'But either France or Brittany will have to give him support if he wants to try and invade again.' He stood and offered Cecily his arm. 'The Tudors have no claim to England's throne, the Beaufort line was barred from it. But if he can get the ships and the men, he will try again.'

Berkhamsted Castle, Hertfordshire, 24th December 1484

Duchess Cecily gazed up at the crucified Christ, her eyes watering from the incense swirling around the chapel. The Mass had long since finished but she remained in her seat, her paternoster beads twisting around her swollen knuckles as the candles guttered down and went out one by one. The Christmas feast was an ordeal for Cecily; it had been ever since she had lost her beloved husband at this time of year. She could put on a show of gaiety and conviviality, hand out gifts and join in with the merrymaking, but since she had become a widow, her heart was not truly in it.

As she sat, alone and lonely, she reflected on the years of her marriage and the richness she had shared with her Lord husband. It was the act of a traitor that had lured him and Edmund from Sandal Castle to their deaths and she shared her son Richard's loathing of turncoats now. She thought of other battles that had been lost by betrayals and remembered how she had prayed for loyalty amongst their people but she had been snared again. William Colyngbourne, her loyal man who once protected her young sons, had been executed. He was found to have been involved in Buckingham's rebellion last year and had since corresponded with Henry Tudor in his attempt to overthrow Richard. He had even been responsible for writing a disparaging rhyme about the king and pinning it to the door of St Pauls. For all his crimes he had been tried and faced the ultimate penalty.

Cecily slid from her seat onto her knees and begged the Almighty to protect her only living son from faithless and corrupt men who were the curse of England. It was here Kat found her; Kat who had grown grey and bowed in her mistress' service but who swore only death would part them.

'Madam.' She touched her shoulder gently. 'Come Madam. It is time you and I were abed.'

Westminster Palace, London, 25ᵗʰ December 1484

Queen Anne sat back on her padded seat and gazed out over the room. The Painted Chamber was full and bustling, the guests revelling in the fine food and wine of the feast and enjoying the lively music. The lutes and shawms were joyous and people were eager for the dancing to begin. Anne watched as her husband walked amongst the company, smiling and nodding and clasping the odd shoulder as his friends and supporters bowed to him. She felt detached from the proceedings, as if she was a statue in the corner. There was no delight in her at all; she was a cipher in these rooms, alone and separate from them all. Her only thoughts were of a cold little tomb at Sheriff Hutton where she had buried her heart. She had done all that was expected of her this Christmas season, joining in with the traditions and customs and presenting favours to the nobles and servants alike, but it meant nothing to her. She had even gifted Eliza a dress as fine as her own, made from the same cloth of gold and silver embroidery but took no pleasure in the girl's gratitude. She cared for nothing and could feel little except her ever-present grief and the constant burning in her chest.

Anne saw the king speaking with Rob Percy and Lord Stanley and knew they would be talking of Henry Tudor and the alliances he was making with the French. Old Louis had died, leaving his young son as the next king, and the Regent, his sister the Duchess of Bourbon, were playing host to Tudor's court in exile and promising him help. Anne found she did not even care about an invasion, so deep was she in her sorrow. She knew that Richard was hoping Brittany and Burgundy would deliver Tudor into English hands and was sending envoys flying over the Narrow Sea to persuade them to hand him over.

She was coughing again as she watched as Eliza tried to pull Richard into the circle of dancers that were forming and saw his smile and shake of the head as he bowed and declined. He looked handsome in his dark red velvet with the White Boar emblem on his collar. He mounted the small dais where his queen was seated and smiled as he lowered himself into his own chair.

'My Lady.' He reached for her hand and found it cold and stiff. He raised it to his lips but she did not respond. 'The ambassador from Portugal has asked to be presented to you. He is here to discuss Eliza's betrothal to their king's son.' She said nothing, as she had hardly spoken for the last eight months. 'Anne?'

She turned towards him. 'I am sure she will make the Duke of Beja very happy. She makes everyone very happy.'

'And you, my Lady? Can I do anything to make you happy?'

The queen rose and stood frail and weak before her husband. 'I will never be happy again Richard.' She coughed. 'I care no longer for this life.' She curtsied to him and he watched as her lady Tess came forward and helped her mistress down the shallow steps, too weak to take them unaided.

Baynard's Castle, London, 16th March 1485

'Richard, do eat some more.' Duchess Cecily pushed the plate of pastries towards him. The page, Owen, stood ready with the wine but neither had touched their cups. 'You look very pale, are you quite well?'

'No, Lady mother, not really.' He moved his neck from side to side to ease the pain in his back. The king was weary and disheartened; he had hoped a visit to his mother would bring him some comfort but he found that his problems followed him no matter where he went. 'Anne is abed with the inflammation of the lungs and the doctors fear for her. They even had the audacity to forbid me from being with her.' Cecily knew that the queen was more ill than Richard would admit to and that the advice was to prevent the king falling sick too.

'Have they bled her?'

'They have, but nothing helps.' He shook his head. 'I fear I will lose her as I lost Ned.' He picked up his silver cup and drained it before gesturing for Owen to refill it. 'Is this my punishment, do you think? I took my brother's throne, so God takes away my wife and son in revenge?'

'God is not vengeful, Richard.' She scrutinised his face. 'Do you really believe these things have been sent to you in retribution?'

'What else could it be?' He fiddled with his father's ruby ring. 'Why would I be so cursed?'

'You are a good man, Richard, and a good king.' Cecily's voice was determined. 'You took the throne because you had to. You have made good and just laws and have been fair and benevolent. You are not cursed.'

'Am I not? Why has God sent Henry Tudor to hound me then?' He rubbed his face in his hands. 'In France they are calling him King of England! The French have given him a fleet so he can invade England, and he calls me a tyrant!' He took another swallow of his drink. 'You know he has sworn to marry Eliza? If he weds her, he will have to make her legitimate, and so the boys Edward and Richard would be legitimate too! And therefore rightful kings! Does he even think of these things?' Owen coughed politely from his position by the door. 'What say you, lad?'

'I say this, sire.' Owen nodded his dark head. ''If he declares them all to be legitimate, he cannot allow those boys to live.' There was a stunned silence.

'He would kill the boys if he marries their sister?' Richard stared at the duchess and her page. 'God in heaven. I have them in the north to keep them away from the Woodvilles, now they are in danger from Tudor's agents too.'

The king arrived back at the palace of Westminster, his guard riding ahead of him in their finery. It was a bright morning and near to noon as they clattered through the gates and the grooms came forward to take the king's reins and lead the horses back to the stables. As Richard threw his leg over the saddle to dismount, he was aware of a change in the sky. It suddenly felt darker, more like dusk, and he shielded his eyes as he looked up at the sun. A shape like a coin or plate was moving in front of the sun's bright rays, like it was about to be swallowed up. The soldiers milling in the yard stopped their chattering and looked fearfully at each other, then at the king. Richard stared back at them as the light from the sky became dimmer. He turned on his heel and sprinted through the main door, down the stone corridor until he got to the stairs. He took them two at a time, up towards Anne's chamber, where the maids and an apothecary were mixing some potion outside the opened door.

'Your Grace!' The physician lifted his arm to stop Richard approaching the bed but was pushed aside as the king grasped the velvet cover and knelt beside his wife. She looked like she was made of wax, he thought, pale white but a spot of blood on her blue lips. He could see the veins in her eyelids and he reached for her icy hand. Tess came forward to light a candle branch as the room was plunged into black as if it was midnight. He could hear the nervous chattering of the servants behind him, scared of the sudden shadows filling the room.

'Anne.' He rose and sat on the edge of her bed, careful not to crush her tiny body. Her eyes remained closed but he thought he saw the trace of a smile form on her mouth. 'My Lady?'

Her voice when it came was like a whispering sigh, the fluttering of a leaf.

'My King.'

Richard bent down and gently kissed her lips and when he raised his head, he knew that he was alone in the darkness.

Priory of St John of Jerusalem,
Clerkenwell, London, 30th March 1485

Duchess Cecily stumbled slightly on the cobbled ground as she approached the Priory gate. Sir Robert Brackenbury, the burly northerner and old friend to her son, proffered his arm which she accepted gratefully. She was feeling weak and tired but had insisted she would attend this meeting that Richard had called with the Mayor of London and aldermen. Sir Robert had come from the Tower where he was Constable to bring her to the assembly being held in the home of the Knights Hospitallers of Jerusalem, an ancient order dedicated to easing the suffering of the poor. Very fitting, she thought as they walked under the pointed Great South Gate archway emblazoned with their emblem, the eight-pointed white cross on a black background. Her heart was breaking from the loss of Anne and the terrible rumours that had started since.

As the duchess was shown to a bench at the side of the hall, she could see Richard on the dais, surrounded by Prior Douglas, the Lord Mayor, and his closest friends. He had already begun his speech and she heard his voice raised in determination and anger.

'And to those who spread these rumours and lies, I say on my honour as King of England and son of my noble father, they are in all respects untrue.' Cecily watched as Richard lifted up his chin and continued. 'My cherished queen was taken from us by God, not by my hand, and I deny these false accusations that I hastened her death to marry the daughter of my brother Edward; they are baseless and without foundation. Who among you could believe that I would think to marry my own niece Eliza, for whom even now I am arranging a foreign wedding to a most noble lord, befitting her status?' He took a breath and his voice dropped. 'The death of my wife lies heavily on my heart, she was most beloved and full of goodness, and I say that her loss will be felt by all good English people.' There were several cheers of agreement to his words, which gave the king the heart to continue. 'I command the Lord Mayor to punish any who speak these falsehoods; Queen Anne of England was called to God and her name will be immortal. *Requiescat in pace.*'

'May she rest in peace.' The assembled monks bowed their heads and prayed.

The king could not settle and was pacing between the fireplace and the window in his agitation. Duchess Cecily, with Francis, Sir Robert and William Catesby, watched as he strode back and forth and continued to vent his anger.

'Marry Eliza? How could any sane man believe that?'

'It is just spiteful gossip, my son. You should pay it no heed.'

'But it doesn't stop mother! Rumours that I killed my nephews, that I poisoned Anne and now that I want to marry my niece! God in heaven but I am cursed.'

'The death of the queen and your son is God testing you Richard. You must find the strength inside yourself to fight on, as you fought at Barnet and Tewkesbury alongside your brother.' Cecily reached for his hand as he went past her. 'I too have been slandered over the years, remember, both by Warwick and George.' She rubbed her thumb over his ring. 'I found the courage to face down those scandals; they will go away in time.' Richard stopped his pacing and took a stool next to her.

'I must fight on, I know.' He looked around at his friends. 'I must fight these falsehoods, but my poor Anne, not even cold in her grave at Westminster!' His friends and mother looked away as the tears came to him, and Cecily turned the talk to more general topics until he recovered himself.

'And were the Lords Edward and Richard pleased with their new clothes, Francis?'

'Yes, my Lady. I had Master Davy and Sir James Tyrell deliver them doublets and coats in silk and some shirts. I understand that they were pleased at their uncle's generosity and send their thanks. Lord Edward even gave a gold chain to Tyrell to thank him for his care.' He nodded and grinned. ' Now I hear that Teddy wants a new coat too!' They all smiled, and waited until the king rejoined the conversation.

'I have knighted Teddy and made him a member of my Council. I am sure we can find the funds for a new coat.' Richard stood and warmed his hands at the fire. 'He is a fine boy, and the nearest heir I have.'

Francis and William shared a glance. 'Richard.' His oldest friend knew the king would hate to hear this, but it had to be said. 'The Portuguese ambassador tells me that his king's daughter, Joanna, could be approached as a possible wife for you.' Francis did not shrink back at the angry look Richard fired at him. 'We loved Anne and we all miss her, but a new wife and son would make your throne secure.' The king looked out of the window and refused to answer.

'We could make it a double wedding; you to Princess Joanna and Eliza to the Duke of Beja.' Catesby couldn't keep the excitement from his voice. 'That would make Tudor think twice about invading!'

The king turned and faced them all. 'So I have to fight rumours that I murdered my wife and nephews, I have to fight rumours that I want to wed my niece and, once and for all, I will have to fight Henry Tudor.'

284

Duchess Elizabeth of Suffolk pushed away her plate and eyed the pewter jug of wine. Her servant Mary Digberry moved it further out of her reach and instead offered her mistress a bowl of grapes. She hoped that the fruit would satisfy the duchess for now, until she could drink of its juice later in the morning. Elizabeth had been staying with her mother Cecily for some days, having been in London for dress fittings; her frame seemed to be expanding with age but she did like fine gowns and ordered them in her favourite colours of red and blue.

Duchess Cecily smiled at her daughter, and at the efforts of Mistress Digberry to keep the wine away from her.

'Your son is with Richard now, I believe?'

'Yes mother. John and the king are at Kenilworth Castle. Warwickshire love him for his wife, poor Anne Neville. What a tragedy, wife and son in the grave.'

'Indeed, although it puts John in a good position, possibly Richard's heir?'

'You know I would never have wished harm to come to little Ned, even though John may take his place now.' Elizabeth was indignant. 'But he does wear the White Boar with pride.'

'I know, of course.' Cecily sat back, enjoying the conversation with her daughter. Margaret was far away in Burgundy so she relished Elizabeth's visits as a chance for friendly conversation about family. 'How is your husband?'

'He is well, I thank you. Trying and failing at writing poetry when I left.' Elizabeth's husband was a descendant of the great writer Geoffrey Chaucer, but had unfortunately inherited none of his talent. 'He generally occupies himself by arguing with his neighbours and trying to make himself a force in the county.'

Cecily sniffed at this. Elizabeth's husband the Duke of

Suffolk was not held in particularly high esteem by King Richard, or his brother Edward before him, and was not in their confidence. Unlike the reliable son John de la Pole, his willingness to commit to Richard's cause was in doubt.

'Can we count on the duke to support Richard when Tudor invades, do you think?'

'*When*?' Elizabeth was shocked, and Mistress Digberry deftly saved the plate that went toppling from the table. '*When* he invades? Will that truly happen, do you think?'

'Yes Elizabeth, it is almost a certainty.' Cecily fixed her daughter with a steely glare. 'Henry Tudor has the support of the French who will supply him with ships and men and there is no doubt he will try to invade again.' She nodded for Owen the page to come forward and pour wine; maybe a drink will better enable Elizabeth to focus, and she needed her support. 'The king, your brother, can raise militia from his own lands but he will need the support of the nobles to form an army. Troops must be raised to defend England, and they must come from the lords of this land calling a muster of their tenants. Richard will be depending on them.'

Elizabeth took a deep swallow of wine. 'Well I know that Jack Howard of Norfolk can raise thousands for him and is loyal to his boots, but I am not sure he should trust the Stanleys.' Cecily smiled; Elizabeth really was better after she had had a drink. 'I know the brothers are wealthy and influential, but will they truly support the king? Lord Stanley will become stepfather to the next King of England if Tudor succeeds and God knows what riches will come to Sir William then.'

'That is exactly the case, Elizabeth. Richard must have the support of the nobles, including your husband, if he is to hold the crown.' Cecily looked at Mistress Digberry and Owen, but they both had their eyes diverted and seemed to be paying no attention. 'I also have doubts about the Earl of Northumberland. I fear Henry Percy is jealous of your son John, whom Richard favours to rule the north now.'

'My poor brother.' She pointedly coughed until Owen stepped forward to pour more wine. 'Surrounded by rebellious Yorkists and Lancastrians who pin their hopes on a bastard Welshman.' She drained that cup too and pushed back her chair. 'I will pray for him, mother, and I will pester my husband to declare himself.'

She curtsied and left the room, tossing a coin to the pageboy on her way out. Owen opened his hand to reveal a gold half angel. He rubbed his thumb over the image of Archangel Michael slaying a dragon and turned it over. He saw the words and repeated them softly. 'Richard by the Grace of God King of England.'

Beskwood Lodge, Nottingham, 1ˢᵗ August 1485

King Richard closed the book and carefully laid it next to his psalter. His back was aching after the morning's sword practice and he had been grateful for a chance to rest before his lords assembled. He laid his hand on the copy of the book written by Giles of Rome and thought of the words he had read a hundred times. A Christian ruler should be a moral leader above all things and righteous in his dealings; only this way could he guide his people in faith and morality. Richard had strived to be principled and ethical in his life and prayed daily for integrity and courage, and to be worthy of the name king. He shook his head in wry amusement; Anne had often laughed at his seriousness and dedication and he sometimes wished he could have been as carefree and joyful as she was. Now here he sat, in the hunting lodge just north of the castle, alone and facing danger once again.

'Ah, here you are.' Francis Lovell poked his head around the door, the Duke of Norfolk close on his heels, and saw Richard sitting in the half darkness. The oak trees had spread their branches until almost all the windows were shrouded in shadows despite the fine weather and bright sunshine outside. Francis bowed to his king and waited until he was waved into one of the chairs gathered around the shiny long table. ' "On the Government of Rulers",' he read, peering at the book's title. 'Did you find any good advice in that?'

'Yes.' Richard responded by pushing the book towards him. 'Be prepared for an invasion, it says, and meet Henry Tudor in battle and crush him.' The three men were smiling at each other when Sir Richard Ratcliffe and William Catesby joined them. It wasn't until Robert Brackenbury and John de la Pole arrived that the serious talk began.

'If he's waiting for a fair wind, he won't have to wait much longer.' William spoke in his usual precise tone. 'My agents report that Tudor has got thirty ships and about two thousand Frenchmen, although I suspect he will gather more when he lands.'

'Will he find much support though?' John clasped his hands on the table as he spoke. 'Apart from a few thick Welshmen, I mean?'

'The name Tudor will bring more to their side, I think.' Brackenbury shifted his bulk on the chair. 'Those who love his uncle Jasper will come too.'

'What say you Sir Richard?' The king had long trusted the advice of his old steward. 'Will many join him?'

'Yes, Your Grace, I think some will.' He silenced John's interruption. 'Apart from the bloody Welsh, there are Woodville supporters who will flock to him and the old Lancastrians we never managed to weed out.' He looked at the king directly. 'I fear other nobles will cleave to Tudor as they do not approve of your plans to curb the powers they had before your parliament began to eradicate the corruption that plagued this country.' He lowered his eyes. 'They may declare their support for you, but I fear their hearts are false.' Jack Howard shook his head when Richard glanced enquiringly at him; he did not see the point in talking just to hear his own voice.

There was silence in the room, and the men watched as their king tipped his head back to stare at the carved oak ceiling.

'Well, at least we won't be caught unawares. We will remove to Nottingham Castle and warn our loyal lords to prepare.' The king stood up and nodded to his trusted friends. 'We will be ready to muster when we hear Tudor has landed. Thank you, gentlemen.'

As the men bowed and headed for the door, the king called one of them back.

'Jack.' The Duke of Norfolk turned and waited. 'Write to Lord Stanley and his brother will you? Tell them I command they join me now.'

'Yes, Your Grace.' Norfolk hesitated. 'Shall I fetch Stanley's son, Lord Strange, Your Grace?' He smiled wolfishly. 'Might be worth having him close by, you know, just to help Stanley remember where his loyalties should lie.'

'Well I won't!' Duchess Cecily folded her arms across her chest and jutted out her chin.

'This king commands it, my Lady.' Francis Lovell had repeated himself several times, but the old woman was stubborn. 'He asks you to go to Berkhamsted for your safety. Tudor has landed near Milford Haven and is marching inland, gathering men as he goes.' Francis took the liberty of taking Cecily's hand in his. 'The Lieutenant of Wales, Rhys ap Thomas, has deserted his post and joined Tudor and Richard fears more will follow. Should his army reach London, you would be in danger.'

Kat and Owen exchanged glances. Fear was in Kat's eyes but the young lad looked determined and fierce, making Cecily wonder what he was thinking. The duchess let out a long breath.

'I thought he only had traitorous Welshmen, stinking convicts and the French on his side?'

'We fear it is more than that, duchess, and he has now crossed into England.' Francis was impatient but trying to speak persuasively to her. He had a long ride this day and wanted to be gone.

'Surely my son has more men on his side? Have all his nobles called their musters?' Cecily was not to be rushed.

'Many have answered his call, including Henry Percy who is marching down from Northumberland. We expect to raise about ten thousand.' Lovell was forced into honesty. 'But Lord Stanley and his brother Sir William have not yet joined the king and we suspect they have already met up with Tudor in secret. Other lords have openly joined him too.'

'God in heaven.' Cecily slumped down into a chair, the defiance finally leaving her. 'What are Richard's plans?'

'His Grace will shortly leave Nottingham and head to

Leicester. Tudor is marching that way and we expect battle to be met shortly. All lords loyal to him are expected to meet there.' Francis knelt at her feet. 'Please, Duchess, for your son's peace of mind, leave now and head to the countryside. It would be one less worry on his mind.'

'Of course I will, I will leave today.' She nodded to Kat. 'Pack my things please, and tell the stables to be ready.' She lowered her head and whispered to Francis. 'How is Richard? Is he confident of victory?'

'He is determined to hold the throne that should have been his father's, Your Grace.'

'I mean, well I mean is his heart in it, truly?' Cecily swallowed a lump in her throat. 'Now that Anne and Ned are gone, will he fight?'

'Richard will fight to the very end. Tudor is a usurper and has no place in England, and the king is determined to keep his throne.'

'Francis,' Cecily put her hand on Lovell's head. 'Send my son my blessing and my love. Tell him I will pray for him, tell him that I think of him all the time.'

'I will, Duchess.' Francis stood and bowed. 'Now, I have a long ride to Leicester so you must forgive me.' As he turned for the door, Cecily saw Owen straighten his shoulders and try to follow him out.

'Don't even think of it, lad.' The duchess called after him. 'Your place is with me here.' She smiled at his disappointment. 'I have need of your protection, so do not desert me now.'

'Jesus.' Sir Robert Brackenbury eased his bulk on the narrow bed and clung on to the side as it threatened to tip over. 'I would be more comfortable on the floor.'

'Not as nice as the White Boar, I admit.' Tommy Parr tied down the tent flap as Rob Percy was polishing the king's sword. 'We should have asked Thomas the landlord if we could bring some of that roasted venison with us.'

'What about His Grace's mace, Tommy, is that ready?'

'Yes, it's with his armour.' Rob nodded and rubbed his hands together. The nerves were beginning to show and they were trying to keep busy to take their minds off what tomorrow would bring.

'Here he comes, up you get lads.' Robert heaved himself upright as the king entered with Jack Howard, followed by Catesby and Ratcliffe.

'So, we fight at dawn.' The king was all business, and briskly settled at the makeshift table. 'Jack, you have the van at Ambion Hill, and you'll likely face the Earl of Oxford.' He nodded to the Duke of Norfolk. 'You outrank him, so make sure he takes the brunt of the attack.' The men smiled at the joke; the battle plans had been discussed at length in Leicester but Richard wanted to go over them again. 'Henry Percy of Northumberland will have our rearguard and I'll take the centre and hopefully have Tudor in my sights.' All the men nodded agreement. Francis Lovell appeared at the entrance to the tent and bowed.

'Lord Strange has written to his father Lord Stanley at your command, Your Grace, but neither of the Stanleys have arrived yet.'

'He said he will see you on the battlefield, sire.' William Catesby raised his eyebrows.

'Aye, but from which side?' They forced a laugh at Rob's

comment, but all knew that if Stanley supported Tudor tomorrow it could put their cause in doubt.

'You have your orders Robert.' The king looked up. 'I have said I will execute Stanley's son if the father betrays me.' The mood turned sombre. 'We have, what, about twelve thousand men?' Ratcliffe nodded agreement. 'Tudor has half that, but if the Stanleys take their five thousand over to his side, that makes it about equal.'

'Well, hopefully he values his true son over his stepson.' Tommy poured wine but the king did not touch his.

'Gentlemen, before I hear Mass, I would say this to you.' Richard rose and stood at the head of the table. 'You are my most loyal friends and comrades, and I thank you for your faith and allegiance. You are my brothers, and I could not be more proud to have you fight at my side. Never have better men accompanied a king into battle and with God's help, we will have victory tomorrow.'

'King Richard! God save King Richard!' His friends raised their cups in a toast to him, and Rob found that he had tears in his eyes. They knelt as the king bowed to them, and they crossed their right arms over their hearts in salute.

'Francis.' The king called to Lovell as he left the tent. 'I will inspect our troops before I say my prayers. Ride with me?'

As the two men rode around the camp, letting the soldiers see their king the night before battle, Richard turned to Francis. 'What would Anne say, do you think?'

'She would raise her hand in blessing over you, sire.'

'And what would my brother Edward say?'

'Ah, Edward would say "kill the bastards".' They shared a laugh before the king turned serious again. 'And what do you say, Francis? What does my oldest friend say?'

'I say victory is yours, Your Grace.' Francis was startled when the king swung round to stare at him.

'Do you? I have no wife or son, my heart died with them. Does God truly want me to be king?'

For a moment, Francis was lost for words. He thought then spoke slowly.

'Richard, you are rightful King of England. Tudor has no claim to your crown and you know that.' The king reached over and clasped him on the shoulder. 'All these men, Richard, all these soldiers know you for their liege lord, and they will fight for you. As will I, my friend, I will stand with you to the very end.'

Richard dismounted before the tent that the priests had turned into a temporary chapel. He threw his reins to a groom and held Lovell's horse as he jumped down next to him.

'No, Francis, you won't.'

'What?'

'You won't fight with me tomorrow.'

'I don't understand.' He stared at the king. 'I don't understand what you mean!'

'I sent you to London to ensure my mother's safety, now I send you north to protect the children.'

'The children? At Sheriff Hutton?'

'If the battle goes against us, Tudor will find Eliza and marry her to secure Yorkist support. That puts the Lords Edward and Richard in danger as they will be made legitimate again, and Teddy is my nearest male heir and he could fall into their clutches.'

'But if you win?'

'If I win, then they are safe. But I make plans now, just in case. You must take Edward and Richard to safety. Take them to Burgundy, to my sister Margaret. If I lose, they must fight their way back to England's throne.'

'Jesus, Richard, don't ask this of me.' Francis pleaded and grabbed Richard's elbow. 'Don't send me away now.'

'I trust you above all men, you are the only one I can ask.' Richard stepped back, out of his reach. 'Will you do this for your king?'

Francis knelt in the mud, tears on his face, and bowed his head.

Church of the Greyfriars Priory, Leicester, 25ᵗʰ August 1485
Kat threw a cloak around the duchess' shoulders as she alighted the litter, and pulled the hood up over her hennin. Owen glanced around to ensure they had not been seen and took a firm grasp on the wooden cudgel in his hand. The moon lit the iron gateway on St Francis Lane and Cecily flinched at the creaking noise as it was pushed open.

'In here, my Lady, this way.' Brother Lawrence held the gate open with one hand while he waved the small party through with the other. He peered up and down the street before pulling the door closed and reached for a sconce on the wall and withdrew the torch to light the dim passageway. He held it aloft to see the three pale faces huddled together.

'Father Wallace sent his message, said you were coming.' His voice was low and hurried. 'You really shouldn't have, it is too dangerous.'

'Brother, save your breath. We are here now, and we will do what we must.' Kat snapped her reply while the Duchess Cecily said not a word but leant on Owen for support; her old legs were weak and she could barely stand straight. Many hours in the litter had passed since she had received word from the battlefield, but she had been determined to come. Surprisingly, Kat had agreed that they should undertake the dangerous journey without hesitation and Owen had been more than willing to accompany them. It was Owen who, upon asking around at the inns in Leicester, had discovered that the king's body had been laid out for all to see in the Church of the Annunciation of Our Lady but was being moved that night for a hasty and secret burial.

The streets had been full of rowdy Lancastrian soldiers, drunk and wild in their victory, but none knew where the triumphant Henry Tudor was now. 'Good,' Owen had muttered to himself. 'Don't want to bump into him tonight.' It was perilous to come to the Greyfriars Priory after dark but the roads seemed quieter now and the hordes of men had thinned out and were dispersing.

Brother Lawrence's grey habit seemed black in the poor light, but he was confident of his steps as he lead the way though the nave to the buttressed choir building. He hurried them past the oak stalls until they reached the end, muttering all the while. 'Always supported York we have, so we told Father Wallace from the Annunciation, we'll take him, we'll bury the king. Terrible it was, seeing him laid out like that, naked and shamed with everyone gawping at him.' The friar stopped his monologue only when Owen thumped him in the back with his club and told him to hush.

Duchess Cecily was panting at the fast pace they had taken but held her breath as Brother Lawrence placed the torch on the wall, and they saw four candles lit around the bier. There was no coffin, no casket, just a sack dumped on the wooden stand. Kat and Owen stepped back as the duchess approached the canvas bag that held the mortal remains of her last son. Her beloved Richard, betrayed and killed on the battlefield. Treason had led to this destruction of his body, on the orders of a usurper. Those the king had trusted, those that had proclaimed loyalty to him, were the cause of his death by treachery. King Richard had died under a hail of savage blows, just a fingertip away from Tudor himself. It was Sir William Stanley who had picked up Richard's crown and offered it on bended knee to the Welshman who had lived most of his life abroad.

She touched the canvas, ran her hands over it, stroking her son's head. Carefully, she peeled away the material until she could see his dark hair, matted and filthy, and reached down to place a tender kiss on his cheek. She saw his arms, tied at the wrist, and his father's ring glinting on his finger. She drew it off slowly and clasped it in her fist. She stepped back and nodded at the friar.

'He'll be buried here, right in the choir, my Lady.' He came forward and covered up the ruined body. 'We'll not let them despoil him further, we'll look after him.' Kat handed Brother Lawrence a small bag of gold coins with a whisper.

'Mind you do, Brother, this is a King of England you are burying.' She put her arms around Cecily who had said not one word, and followed Owen through the dark corridors back to the street. She was the Dowager Duchess, mother to no sons, broken and finally beaten.

EPILOGUE

Ego sum resurrectio et vita: qui credit in me, etiam si mortuus fuerit, vivet, et omnis qui vivit, et credit in me, non morietur in aeternum.
I am the resurrection and the life: he which believeth in me, although he were dead, yet shall he live: and everyone which liveth, and believeth in me, shall not die forever.

Berkhamsted Castle, Hertfordshire, 31st May 1495

Cecily's hair streamed out behind her as she galloped over the fields behind Raby Castle, laughing as Richard Plantagenet, the young Duke of York, struggled to keep up. Her father waved from the battlements and shouted encouragement to his beautiful young daughter, his Rose, proud of the fine woman she was becoming. As they rode through the main gate into the stable yard, she pulled up her sweating horse and reached out her hand to her new husband. He took it and raised it to his mouth for a kiss. She could see the sun catch the ruby on his finger and for a moment it looked as if his hand was bleeding.

Owen Thomas heard the duchess moan quietly, and gestured to the maid to wipe his mistress' brow. He missed Kat almost as much as Cecily did, but he made sure the new girl was as tender with the old lady as she deserved. He was a fine, strapping man now, but saw no shame in his duties of caring for the duchess and making her life comfortable. She was eighty and soon to meet God, and he had promised her that all the rites and rituals would be carried out as she had wished. Her bones would soon be decaying at Fotheringhay but he thought she had lived a long life dedicated to Christ and her family and he was determined she would be honoured in death.

The noise of the cannon firing from Ambion Hill near the town of Market Bosworth was deafening, and Cecily covered her ears with her hands. She was high above the green grass but could spot her son shouting orders from the back of his fine grey warhorse. Two forces stood unmoving; those of the Earl of Northumberland and the Stanley brothers. Duchess Cecily called to them to advance, to join battle as they had promised her son the king, but her voice floated to the sky and was lost amid the screams and cries of the men on the field. Mist seemed to rise up from the marshy ground where the Welshman, Tudor, was hiding with his bodyguards and from her position near the rising sun, Cecily saw King Richard skirt the main force of the battle with his mounted guard and gallop towards him. She watched as her son killed a standard bearer and an enormous soldier protecting Tudor, then in horror saw the Stanley forces come to the aid of the man beneath the flag of the Welsh dragon. Mother watched as son took a blow from a halberd to the back of his head and crumple in the mud as the wolves finally beat the boar. Cecily reached down her hand to her youngest child and pulled him up towards her, leading him towards the heavens where his wife and son were waiting for him, leading him to peace at last.

As her breathing grew more shallow, Owen held a wet cloth to the old lady's lips to moisten her dry mouth. He gently moved the maid aside to sit by the duchess and take her hand. He could feel the dry skin and the loose ruby ring on her thumb and thought he felt her squeeze his fingers in recognition of his presence. The pressure grew more intense and Owen knew the end was near and that she would soon pass to her reward.

Duchess Cecily clasped her hands together as she watched the priest hold high the crown, then gently place it on to the head of the blonde-haired lad. She smiled in delight as the Dublin crowd cheered and called out blessings on the young new king who they said looked just like his father, his namesake. It was the Feast of the Ascension and it was fitting that this coronation took place on the day they remembered Jesus rising up to heaven just as she rose now, high above the people, looking down on them all. Cecily laughed and cheered too, believing the throne of England was back in rightful hands at last.

As the priest moved forward at Owen's gesture, he placed her paternoster beads into her hands and bowed his head as the cleric spoke the words from the Holy Office of the Dead. Mother of two kings, grandmother to a queen; her last years had been lived in obscurity and privacy by her own choice and her faithful servants rallied round the old lady so she would not be alone in her final moments. None of her family were present, most were in the grave already and she would soon be back amongst her own.

The double doors to the great chamber at Westminster were flung open as the Tudor King and Queen of England came forward, followed by their children on to the dais. Awaiting them stood Margaret Stanley, her husband and Bishop Morton, victorious and triumphant. Behind the thrones, Cecily could see the red dragon roaring from the banner next to the rose pennant. It was not the flower that she knew and loved, it had been adulterated until it was a mix of the Red of Lancaster and the White of York; it was fitting for this union of Henry and Eliza. As she floated above them all, unwelcome and uninvited at this court, she watched as her granddaughter smiled at the murderer of her son and placed her hand on his. They had two boys of their own now and thought their line was secure, and none but Cecily could see the handsome fair-haired second son and Prince of York sailing across the sea, ready to take back his crown.

The Penance and the Anointing were done and the priest stepped forward for the Viaticum. He held the Body of Christ before the duchess and touched it to her lips. It was the last part of her journey, the final step before she would rejoin her family, and be together with them eternally in God's loving arms. On the table rested Cecily's Book of Hours, her precious link to those she had loved in life, and Owen knew it would be laid to rest with her so she could find her way back to her people.

Cecily took her husband's arm as they strolled about the gardens at Fotheringhay, the fresh breeze catching her veil and fluttering the murrey and blue pennant above the castle towers. They walked through the bailey and up the stairs into the Great Hall where they were awaited. Edmund and George, blonde like their mother, bowed as they entered. Elizabeth, Anne and Margaret turned from the fireplace to smile, all fine women now with husbands of their own. Seated at each end of the table were Edward and Richard, their crowns bright and lustrous, and they raised their glasses in a toast to their parents. Mother and father beamed proudly at their beautiful children and opened their arms to gather them close, and hold them forever.

Duchess Cecily, wife of the right noble Prince Richard Duke of York, opened her eyes and felt weightless. She was as light as feather, not old or crippled and wasted. Her body was ethereal, made of clouds and air, and her spirit rose upwards as her old bones sank into the soft mattress.

Social Services Car Park, Leicester, 25th August 2012

The blond woman in wellies stood at the edge of the trench close to the heavy machinery, just before the rain started to fall. She was breathless, exhilarated and vindicated. Years of struggle and effort had led her to this; she had been right all along and she had brought him home.

The remains of King Richard III, the last English king to be killed in battle, had been found and would be reinterred with all the honour and ceremony that he had been denied in life. His bones, like the bones of his mother, would finally rest in peace.

In manus tuas, Domine, commendo spiritum meum.
Into your hands, O Lord, I commend my spirit.

NOTES

Gloria Patri, et Filio, et Spiritui Sancto, sicut erat in principio, et nunc, et semper, et in saecula saeculorum.
Amen.
Glory be to the Father, and to the Son, and to the Holy Spirit, as it was in the beginning, is now, and ever shall be, world without end.
Amen.

Sir Robert Brackenbury – killed at Bosworth, 22nd August 1485

John (Jack) Howard, Duke of Norfolk – killed at Bosworth, 22nd August 1485

Sir Richard Ratcliffe – killed at Bosworth, 22nd August 1485

Sir Robert Percy – killed at Bosworth, 22nd August 1485

Sir William Catesby – executed, 25th August 1485 by Henry VII

John de la Pole, Earl of Lincoln – killed at East Stoke fighting Henry VII, 16th June 1487

Elizabeth Woodville – died in seclusion at Bermondsey Abbey, 8th June 1492

Sir William Stanley – executed, 16th February 1495 by Henry VII

Edward (Teddy), 17th Earl of Warwick – executed, 28th November 1499 by Henry VII

John of Gloucester – possibly executed in 1499 by Henry VII

Sir James Tyrell – executed, 6th May 1502 by Henry VII

Margaret (Maggie), Countess of Salisbury – executed, 27th May 1541 by Henry VIII

Sir Francis Lovell, 1st Viscount Lovell – fate unknown

Edward V – fate unknown

Prince Richard of Shrewsbury, Duke of York – fate unknown,

INTERESTING READING

The Wars of The Roses, Hugh Bicheno

Richard III The Maligned King, Annette Carson

Battles of the Wars of the Roses, David Cohen

The Women of The Cousins' War, Philippa Gregory, David Baldwin and Michael Jones

Dark History of The Tudors, Judith John

The Betrayal of Richard III, VB Lamb, Revised by Peter Hammond

The Search For Richard III, Philippa Langley and Michael Jones

The Princes In The Tower, Philippa Langley

The Survival of the Princes In The Tower, Matthew Lewis

Richard III Loyalty Binds Me, Matthew Lewis

Edward IV and Elizabeth Woodville, Amy Licence

Richard III His Life and Character, Clements Markham

The Time Traveller's Guide to Medieval England, Ian Mortimer

The Castle In The Wars of the Roses, Dan Spencer

Historic Doubts of The Life and Reign of King Richard III, Horace Walpole

This book is printed on paper from sustainable sources managed under the Forest Stewardship Council (FSC) scheme.

It has been printed in the UK to reduce transportation miles and their impact upon the environment.

For every new title that Troubador publishes, we plant a tree to offset CO_2, partnering with the More Trees scheme.

For more about how Troubador offsets its environmental impact, see www.troubador.co.uk/sustainability-and-community